In Ame

VII

is "THE VOICE OF TODAY'S POSTMODERN THRILLER
GENERATION" (*The Providence Journal*) . . .
His explosive Mitch Rapp novels are

"FANTASTIC" (Glenn Beck) "JUST FABULOUS" (Rush Limbaugh)
"COMPLEX, CHILLING, AND SATISFYING" (*The Plain Dealer*)
"AN EXCITING, LUDLUM-LIKE SERIES" (*Booklist*)

The acclaimed #1 *New York Times* bestseller

"Nail-biting. . . . Nothin
cornered Mitch Rapp."

"Vince Flynn is a must r

"Flynn is a master—may
pages seem to turn them

Catch all
(*The Flor*

THE LAST MAN •

PURSUIT OF H(

PROTECT AND

CONSENT T

EXECUTIVE POW

THE THIRD OP

Also by Vince Flynn

KILL
SHOT

AN AMERICAN ASSASSIN THRILLER

VINCE FLYNN

POCKET BOOKS

New York   London   Toronto   Sydney   New Delhi

 Pocket Books
A Division of Simon & Schuster, Inc.
1230 Avenue of the Americas
New York, NY 10020

First Pocket Books trade paperback edition January 2013

For information about special discounts for bulk purchases, please contact
Simon & Schuster Special Sales at 1-866-506-1949
or business@simonandschuster.com.

The Simon & Schuster Speakers Bureau can bring authors
to your live event. For more information or to book an event,
contact the Simon & Schuster Speakers Bureau at 1-866-248-3049
or visit our website at www.simonspeakers.com.

Designed by Dana Sloan

Manufactured in the United States of America

10   9   8   7   6   5   4

ISBN 978-1-4767-1566-7
ISBN 978-1-4391-0052-3 (ebook)

To
Dr. Eugene Kwon and Dr. Bill Utz
and
Dr. Mike Nanne

ACKNOWLEDGMENTS

ACKNOWLEDGMENTS

FOR some time now, I've been fond of saying I want to make it through life with one agent, one editor, one publisher, and one wife. I like working with people I admire and trust, and I like stability. When you find out you have cancer, this philosophy takes on a much deeper meaning. Instead of facing the scariest moment of your life alone you find yourself surrounded by people you care about and who genuinely care for you. To my agent, Sloan Harris, who is no stranger to this fight, you have brought the same laser-like focus to my health issues that you have used to successfully manage the Rapp franchise. Your opinions and insights continue to give me great comfort. To Kristyn Keene at ICM, your levity is always welcome, and to Chris Silbermann, thank you for continuing to navigate the Hollywood minefield.

To my editor and publisher, Emily Bestler, thank you for your usual grace and calm during a trying year; you make it all much easier than it should be. To Kate Cetrulo and Caroline Porter at Emily Bestler Books for making the trains run on time. To Jeanne Lee for another great cover. To Al Madocs, sorry for putting you through the wringer yet again. To David Brown for your professionalism, unbelievable work ethic, and great sense of humor. To Ariele Fredman for keeping

Mr. Brown out of trouble and your much-needed wit. To Judith Curr and Louise Burke for your divergent and successful styles of publishing. To Anthony Ziccardi, Michael Selleck, and the great sales force at Simon & Schuster, and to Carolyn Reidy, one of the smartest people in publishing. You all make me feel like I am part of the S&S family, and for that I am extremely grateful.

On the medical front I have a long list of people to thank. To Dr. Jason Reed for your concern and diligence. To Dr. Bill Utz who made the diagnosis and has continued to quarterback my care for the last year. Your professionalism, faith, and intensity help me sleep better each and every night. And to the rest of the staff at Urology Associates, especially Jim and Adriane. To Dr. Badrinath Konety at the University of Minnesota Center for Prostate Cancer, for being the first person to give me hope. I'm not sure I will ever be able to fully express my gratitude for the gift you gave my wife and me when we needed it most. To Dr. Eugene Kwon at the Mayo Clinic: you are a rock star. In addition to being possibly the smartest person I have ever met, you might also be one of the funniest. Knowing you are down in Rochester on the front lines looking for a way to kill this cancer allows me to do things like write this book. To Dr. Douglas Olson at the Fairview Southdale Radiation Therapy Center and Dr. Richard Diaz and your phenomenal staff, for making eight weeks of radiation a breeze.

I have received countless prayers and well wishes from fans and friends, and they have meant a great deal to my family and me. This fight can be pretty lonely at times, and knowing that you are all out there makes it a little less scary. I am blessed to have grown up in a big family and in a town where people really care about each other. To Tom Tracy, who I think may have taken the news harder than me, I am lucky to still call you my best friend after thirty-one years. Thank you for starting Mitch Rapp & the Killer Moustaches for Movember and raising a nice chunk of change for prostate cancer research. To Mike Dougherty, who was told he was going to die from prostate cancer more than a decade and a half ago. Thank you for showing me what can happen when a stubborn Irishman refuses to quit. To Gary Petrucci, who is a one-man research machine. Thank you for keeping me abreast of all the latest and greatest in the fight to find a cure for prostate cancer. To Eric and Kathy Schneeman for all the great times at the Pub. You have been a godsend to my family this past year. To Jodi Bakkegard and Dennis Gudim for keeping me as healthy as possible. And to Dr. Mike Nanne for showing me how to deal with cancer with faith and courage.

To Ed Kocourek, my unofficial spiritual mentor. Thank you for pushing me when I needed it. The Adoration Chapel at St. Joseph's has become a place of great beauty and serenity in my life. To Father John Malone, Father Peter Laird, and Archbishop Emeritus Harry Flynn for your prayers and guidance. I am a God-fearing soul and always have been. I choose to believe, and to all of you who have sent your prayers and well wishes, thank you.

Last, but definitely not least, to my wife, Lysa. I don't know how people go through this alone. I am blessed in many ways but none more so than having you as my wife. Thank you for being there every step of the way with your grace, perspective, and love. You are the best.

KILL SHOT

PRELUDE

THE man flew through the air, propelled by one of the other recruits. CIA handler Irene Kennedy watched from inside the house with casual interest as he failed to tuck and roll. He hit the ground flat and hard—the kind of impact that more than likely knocked the wind out of him, maybe even bruised a rib. Kennedy pursed her lips and calculated his odds of making it through the remaining eight weeks of the training program. She'd seen so many men roll through here that she could handicap them like a Vegas bookie. This one she gave a less than 10 percent chance.

Kennedy's thoughts, however, were not really with this batch of recruits. She was more concerned with a certain man who had waltzed through the rigorous training program a little more than a year ago. Mitch Rapp had been her rookie, and in the year since they had unleashed him on the purveyors of terrorism, he had left a steady trail of bodies from Geneva to Istanbul to Beirut and beyond. His record to date was perfect, and that in its own way added to Kennedy's tension. No one was perfect. Sooner or later, no matter how much talent they had, the mighty got tripped up. To complicate the odds, Kennedy had pushed to allow him to operate on his own. No backup. Just an advance team to scout things out and then he moved in all by his lonesome to do the dirty work up close and personal. No team members to bail his ass out if things went south. Rapp had argued that a small footprint would mean less chance of being caught.

Instinctively, Kennedy liked the simplicity. She'd seen more than her fair share of operations that had become so cumbersome in personnel and scope that they never got off the ground. Rapp had successfully argued that if he failed he was just one man with a foreign passport who could never be traced back to Langley. Hurley, the hard-assed spook and trainer, had pointed out that his little game worked only if he was dead. If they took him alive, he'd talk, just like everyone did, and then their exposure would be horrible. Theirs was not a risk-free business, however, and in the end Thomas Stansfield was willing to roll the dice on Rapp. The young operative had proven himself very resourceful and Stansfield needed to cross more names off his list of most wanted terrorists.

This mission was different, though. The stakes were considerably higher. It was one thing when Rapp was lurking about some Third World country practicing his craft, but at this very moment, he was about to do something very illegal, and unsanctioned in a country where he could not afford to make even the slightest mistake.

So intense was Kennedy's concentration that she hadn't heard the question from the man sitting behind the desk. She brushed a strand of her shoulder-length auburn hair behind her ear and said, "Excuse me?"

Dr. Lewis had been studying her for the last few minutes. Kennedy was a complex, confident, and extremely guarded professional. It had become an occupational obsession for Lewis to find out what made her tick. "You're worried about him."

Irene Kennedy's face remained neutral despite the fact that she was irritated by her colleague's ability to read her thoughts. "Who?"

"You know who," Dr. Lewis said, his soft blue eyes coaxing her along.

Kennedy shrugged as if it was a small thing. "I worry about every operation I'm in charge of."

"It seems you worry more about the ones he's involved in."

Kennedy considered the unique individual whom she had found in Upstate New York. As much as she'd like to deny it, Lewis's assessment of her concern over Rapp was accurate. Kennedy couldn't decide if it was the man, or the increasingly dangerous nature of the operations they'd been giving him, but in either case, she did not want to discuss the matter with Lewis.

"I've found," Lewis said in a carefree tone, "that I worry about him less than most. Always have, I think."

Kennedy flipped the comment around in her head. She could easily take it two ways—maybe more. "It's a lot easier when you're sitting on that side of the desk." Kennedy flashed him a rare smile. "I'm his handler. I put him in these situations, and I'm his only lifeline should something go wrong. I would think that clinically"—she raised an eyebrow, mimicking one of Lewis's overused facial expressions—"even you would understand that."

The shrink stroked his bottom lip with his forefinger and said, "Worrying about someone, or something, can be normal . . . and even healthy, but if taken too far . . ." Lewis shook his head and made a sour face. "Definitely not good."

Here we go, Kennedy thought to herself. This was not an accidental conversation. Lewis had been thinking about this for some time, plotting his line of questioning. Kennedy knew from experience that to try to run from the tête-à-tête would only make it worse. Lewis was patient and tenacious, and his reports were given serious weight by the deputy director of operations. The doctor would zero in on a problem and pepper you with questions until he was satisfied. Kennedy decided to lob the ball back onto his side of the net. "So you think I worry too much."

"I didn't say that," the doctor said with an easy tone and a soft shake of his head.

"But you implied it," Kennedy said.

"It was merely a question."

"A question that you asked because you think you've noticed something and you're worried about me. And since you initiated it, I would appreciate it if you would explain yourself rather than treat this like one of your therapy sessions."

Lewis sighed. He'd seen Kennedy get this way, but never with him. Usually it was with Stan Hurley, who was exceedingly adept at getting under people's skin. She was always calm and analytical in her dealings with Lewis, so the fact that she was so quick to anger now was proof that his concerns were valid. "I think when it comes to a certain operative . . . you worry too much."

"Rapp?" Kennedy asked.

"Correct."

"Please don't give me some psychobabble that you think I'm in love with him." Kennedy shook her head as if anything so humdrum was beneath her. "You know that's not how I work."

Lewis dismissed the idea with the back of his hand. "I agree. That is not my concern."

"Then what is?"

"That you do not give the man his credit."

"Credit? Credit for what?"

"Let's start with the fact that he came down here a little more than a year ago, without any military experience, and bested every man we put in front of him, including your Uncle Stan. His ability to learn, and do so at an incredibly rapid pace, is unlike anything I have ever seen." Lewis's voice grew in intensity. "And he does it in every field of discipline."

"Not every field of discipline. His marks in geopolitics and diplomatic affairs are dismal."

"That's because he sees those fields as an utter waste of his time, and I don't necessarily disagree with him."

"I thought we wanted well-rounded people to come out of this place."

Lewis shrugged his shoulders. "Mental stability matters more to me than well-rounded. After all, we're not asking him to negotiate a treaty."

"No, but we need him to be aware of the big picture."

"Big picture." Lewis frowned. "I think Mitch would argue that he's the only one around here who keeps his focus on the big picture."

Kennedy was a woman in the ultimate man's world, and she deeply disliked it when her colleagues treated her as if everything needed to be explained to her. "Really," she said with chaste insincerity.

"Your man has a certain aptitude. A certain ability that is heightened by the fact that he doesn't allow extraneous facts to get in the way."

Kennedy sighed. Normally she would never let her frustration show, but she was tired. "I know you think I can read minds, but today that skill seems to have left me. Could you please get to the point?"

"You do look more tired than normal."

"Why, thank you. And you look like you've put on a few pounds."

Lewis smiled. "No need to hurt my feelings, just because you're worried about him."

"You are a master at deflection."

"It is my job to observe." He swiveled his chair and looked at the eight men and the two instructors who were putting them through the basics of hand-to-hand combat. "Observe all of you. Make sure no one has a mental breakdown and runs off the reservation."

"And who watches you?"

Lewis smiled. "I'm not under the same stress," the doctor said as he spun back to face Kennedy. "As you said, he is your responsibility."

Kennedy mulled that one over for a second. She couldn't disagree, so she kept her mouth shut. Plus the good doctor excelled at compartmentalizing the rigors of their clandestine operation.

"I'm looking out for you," Lewis said in his understanding therapist tone. "This double life that you've been living is not healthy. The mental strain is something that you think you can manage, and I thought you could as well, but recently, I've begun to have some doubts."

Kennedy felt a twist in her gut. "And have you shared these doubts with anyone?" Specifically she was thinking of Thomas Stansfield.

"Not yet, but at some point I am bound to pass along my concerns."

Kennedy felt a sense of relief, even if it was just a brief reprieve. She knew the only way to avoid a bad personnel report was to allay Lewis's concerns. And the only way to do that was to talk about them. "This aptitude that you say he has, would you care to share it with me?"

Lewis hesitated as if he was trying to find the most delicate way to say something that was brutally indelicate. With a roll of his head he said, "I have tried to get inside Rapp's mind, and there are days where I swear he's so refreshingly honest that I think I know what makes him tick, and then . . ." Lewis's voice trailed off.

"And then, what?"

"There are other days where I can't get past those damn dark eyes of his and that lopsided grin that he uses to defuse anyone who goes poking around in his business."

"That's the aptitude that puts you at ease? His lopsided grin?"

"No," Lewis scoffed. "It's far more serious than his ability to be open one moment and then impenetrable the next, although that may have a hand in how he deals with everything. I'm talking about the very core of all of this. Why are we here? Why have we secretly funneled over fifty million dollars into this operation? I'm talking about the fact that he is a one-man wrecking ball. That he has methodically, in a little over a year, accomplished more than we have accomplished in the last decade. And let's be brutally honest with each other." Lewis held up a finger. "The 'what' that we are talking about is the stone-cold fact that he is exceedingly good at hunting down and killing men."

Kennedy did not look at Lewis, but she nodded. They had all come to the same realization months ago. That was why they had turned him loose and allowed him to work on his own.

"I'm here," Lewis continued, "to observe and make sure we have the right people and that their minds can handle the unique stress of this job. I have stress, you have stress, but I doubt ours compares to the stress of operating alone, often behind enemy lines, and hunting down a man and killing him."

"So you're worried that he's going to snap on us."

"Not at the moment. In fact, I think he has coped extraordinarily well with the rigors of his new job. I've kept a close eye on him. When he's back here, he sleeps like a baby. His head hits the pillow, sixty seconds later he's out and he sleeps straight through the night."

Kennedy had wondered about this same thing. Not every operative handled the taking of another human being's life with such ease. "So how does he deal with it . . . the blood on his hands?" she asked.

"He is a linear creature, which means he doesn't allow a lot of ancillary issues to muddy the waters of his conscience. These men . . . the ones we target . . . they all decided of their own volition to get involved in plots to kill innocent civilians. In Rapp's mind—and this isn't me guessing, he's expressed this very clearly—these men need to be punished."

Kennedy shifted in her chair. "Simple revenge."

"He says retribution. The distinction is slight, but I see his point."

"Given the loss of his girlfriend, I don't find that particularly troubling. After all, this is a job that requires a unique motivation."

"Yes it does, but his runs deep. He thinks if these men go unpunished, it will only embolden them to kill more people. To screw up more people's lives," Lewis answered.

"You'll get no argument from me. Nor from our boss, for that matter."

Lewis smiled. "There's one more thing, something that adds a unique twist."

"What's that?"

"He wants them to know he's coming after them."

"Theory or fact?"

"A bit of both. He knows that he can make them jumpy. Keep them up at night worrying when he's going to show up. He wants them to fear his existence."

"He told you this?" Kennedy asked, more than a bit surprised.

"Parts of it. The rest I pieced together," Lewis said with a nod.

"And why didn't you tell me?"

"I'm telling you right now."

Kennedy moved to the edge of her chair. "I mean, why didn't you tell me when you first learned about it?"

"I told Thomas," Lewis said, covering his bases.

"And what did he say?"

"He thought about it for a long moment and then said making these guys lose a little sleep might not be the worst thing."

"For Christ's sake." Kennedy pressed her palm against her forehead. "As his handler, don't you think you should let me in on stuff like this?"

"I'm not sure I understand your concern. I think he's fine, and Thomas does as well."

Kennedy pinched the bridge of her nose in an effort to stifle the headache she felt coming. "This isn't the NFL. We don't trash-talk. We don't taunt the other team in order to throw them off their game. My men need to be ghosts. They need to sneak into a country, quietly do their job, and then disappear."

"Irene, I think you are exaggerating your concerns. The enemy knows something is afoot. Bodies are piling up at an unusual clip, and if the fear Rapp is generating causes some of these men to be a bit jumpy"—Lewis shrugged—"well then, so be it."

"So what in the hell are you trying to tell me . . . that you're okay with Rapp, but you're worried about me?" Kennedy asked, the suspicion in her voice obvious.

"I'm okay with both of you, but I do think you worry too much."

"I'm worried about him because he's about to kill a high-ranking official in the capital of one of our closest allies and if he screws up, the blowback could be so bad every single last one of us will end up in front of a committee on Capitol Hill, be indicted, and then end up in jail." Kennedy shook her head. "I don't know what your shrink books have to say about all of this, but I think a fear of going to jail is a healthy thing."

"My point, Irene, is that Rapp is good. Maybe the best I've ever seen, and his target is a lazy, overfed bureaucrat. Tonight will go fine. That's not what I'm worried about."

Kennedy was so focused on Paris that she almost missed the last part. "Then what *are* you worried about?"

"Mr. Rapp is unique. He has already proven his penchant for autonomy. He bristles against control, and so far, Thomas has been willing to ignore all of these little transgressions because the man is so damn good at what he does."

"But?"

"Our country, as well as our beloved employer, has a glorious history of throwing those men who are at the tip of the spear under the proverbial bus when things get difficult. If they do that to a man like Rapp . . ." Lewis winced at the thought.

"Our country and our employer don't even know he exists."

"I know that, Irene. I'm looking down the road, and I'm telling you there is a real danger that at some point we might lose control of him."

Kennedy scoffed at the idea. "I haven't seen a single thing that could lead you to that conclusion."

"Irene," Lewis said in a far more serious tone, "strip it all down and what we have is a man who has been taught to kill. Kill people who have harmed innocent civilians or threatened the national security of this country. Right now, his mission is clearly focused. He's out killing bad guys who live in foreign countries. What happens if he wakes up one day and realizes some of the bad guys are right here? Living in America, working for the CIA, working on Capitol Hill."

"You can't be serious?" Kennedy said, shocked by the theory.

Lewis folded his hands under his chin and leaned back in his chair. "Justice is blind, and if you train a man to become judge, jury, and executioner . . . well, then you shouldn't be surprised if he some-day fails to see the distinction between a terrorist and a corrupt, self-serving bureaucrat."

Kennedy thought about it for a moment and then said, "I'm not sure I'm buying it."

Lewis shrugged. "Only time will tell, but I know one thing for certain. If there comes a time where you need to neutralize him, you'd better not screw up. Because if he survives, he'll kill every last one of us."

CHAPTER 1

PARIS, FRANCE

RAPP secured the gray nylon rope to a cast-iron vent stack and walked to the edge of the roof. He glanced at the balcony two floors below and then looked out across the City of Light. Sunrise was a few hours off and the flow of late-night revelers had faded to a trickle. It was that rare moment of relative inactivity that even a city as vibrant as Paris fell under once each day. Every city had its own unique feel, and Rapp had learned to pay attention to the ebb and flow of their natural rhythms. They had their similarities just like people. For all of the hang-ups about individuality, few understood that for the most part, people's actions were habitual. They slept, woke, ate, worked, ate some more, worked some more, ate again, watched TV, and then went to sleep again. It was the basic drumbeat of humanity the world over. The way people lived their lives and met their basic needs.

All men also had their own unique attributes, and these often manifested themselves in habits—habits that Rapp had learned to exploit. As a rule, the best time to strike was this witching hour, between dusk and dawn, when the overwhelming majority of the human race was asleep, or trying to sleep. The physiological reasons were obvious.

If it took world-class athletes hours to warm up before a major event, how would a man defend himself when yanked from deep sleep? However, Rapp could not always choose the appointed hour, and occasionally a target's habits created an opening that was so painfully obvious, he simply couldn't ignore the opportunity.

Three weeks earlier Rapp had been in Athens. His target walked the same bustling sidewalk every morning from his apartment to his office. Rapp had considered shooting him on the sidewalk, as there was plenty of cover and distraction. It wouldn't have been difficult, but witnesses were always a concern, and a police officer could always stumble by at the wrong moment. As he studied his target, he noticed another habit. After arriving at work, the man had one more cup of coffee and then went down the hall with his newspaper and took a prolonged visit to the men's room.

Other than catching people asleep, the next best thing was catching them with their pants down. On the fourth day, Rapp waited in the middle stall of three and at the appointed hour his target sat down on his right. Rapp stood on the toilet seat, leaned over the divider, called out the man's name, and then after their eyes met, he smiled and sent a single 9mm hollow-tipped round through the top of the man's head. He fired one more kill shot into the man's brainpan for good measure and calmly left the building. Thirty minutes later, he was on a ferry slicing through the warm morning air of the Aegean Sea, headed for the island of Crete.

Most of the kills had been like that. Unsuspecting fools who thought themselves safe after years of the United States doing little or nothing to pursue them for their involvement in various terrorist attacks. Rapp's singular goal was to take the fight to these men. Bleed them until they began to have doubts, until they lay awake at night wondering if they were next. It had become his mission in life. Inaction was what had emboldened these men to continue with their plots to attack innocent civilians. The belief that they were secure to continue to wage their war of terror had given them a smug confidence. Rapp was single-handedly replacing that confidence with fear.

By now, they were aware that something was wrong. Too many men had been shot in the head in the last year for it to be a coincidence. Rapp's handler had reported the rumors. Most suspected that the Israelis had resurrected one of their hit teams, and that was fine with Rapp—the more disinformation the better. He was not looking for credit. In spite of his hot streak, tonight would be it for a while. The powers that be in Virginia were getting nervous. Too many people were talking. Too many foreign intelligence agencies were allocating assets to look into this rash of deaths among the world's most notorious terrorists and their network of financiers and arms dealers. Rapp was to return stateside for some rest and relaxation when he finished this one. At least that's what Rapp's handler had told him. Even after a quick year, however, he knew how things worked. Rest and relaxation meant that they wanted to observe him. Make sure some part of his psyche hadn't wandered down a dark corridor never to return. The thought brought a smile to Rapp's face. Killing these assholes was the most therapeutic thing he'd ever done in his life. It was more effective than a decade of psychotherapy.

He placed his hand over his left ear and focused on the tiny transmitter that was relaying the sounds of the luxury hotel suite two floors below. Just like the night before, and the night before that, he could hear the portly Libyan wheezing and snoring. The man was a three-pack-a-day chain smoker. If Rapp could only chase him up a flight of stairs, he might be able to accomplish his task.

Rapp followed a delivery van as it quietly passed beneath on the Quai Voltaire. Something was bothering him, but he couldn't place it. He scanned the street for the slightest evidence that anything was out of place and then turned his attention to the tree-lined walking paths that bordered the Seine River. They too were empty. All was as it should be, but still something was gnawing at him. Maybe things had been too easy of late, one kill after another, city after city, and not so much as a single close call. The law of averages told him that sooner or later, something would go wrong, and he would end up in a jam that might land him in a foreign jail or possibly cost him his life. Those two thoughts were always in the back of his mind, and depending on what country he was in, he wasn't sure which would be his preference.

There was little room for fear and doubt in what he did. There should be caution and a keen eye to detail, but fear and doubt could incapacitate. He could stand up here all night thinking up excuses not to proceed. Stan Hurley, the tough SOB who had trained him, had warned him about the pitfalls of paralysis by analysis. Rapp thought about the stern warning that Hurley had given him and decided it was more than likely his handler's anxiety. She had warned him that if the slightest thing didn't seem right, he was to abort the mission. An American could not be caught doing this kind of dirty work in Paris. Not ever, and especially not now, given the current political climate.

In the big picture, the target was a link. Another name to cross off his list, but to Rapp it was always more personal than the big picture. He wanted to make every last one of these men pay for what they'd done. Each kill would grow more difficult, more dangerous, and it didn't bother Rapp in the least. He welcomed the challenge. In fact, he took sincere joy in the fact that these assholes were looking over their shoulder each day and going to sleep every night wondering who was hunting them.

Rapp asked himself one more time if he should be concerned that the Libyan was traveling without security. There was a good chance that the man felt safe in his position as his country's oil minister. As an important member of the diplomatic community, he probably thought himself above the dirty games of terrorists and assassins. *Well,* Rapp thought to himself, *once a terrorist, always a terrorist.* Dress him up in a suit and tie and put him up in a thousand-dollar-a-night suite in Paris, and he was still a terrorist.

Rapp scanned the street and listened to the Libyan snoring like a pig. After half a minute, he made up his mind. The man would not see another sunrise. Rapp began to move in an efficient, almost robotic way as he went over his gear one last time. His silenced Beretta was secured in a shoulder holster under his right arm; two extra magazines were safely tucked away under his left arm; a double-edged four-inch combat knife was sheathed at the small of his back; and a smaller 9mm pistol was strapped to his right ankle. These were merely the offensive weapons he'd brought along. There was a small med kit, a radio that was tuned to the hotel's security channel, flex cuffs, and a perfectly forged set of documents that said he was a Palestinian recently immigrated from Amman, Jordan. And then there was the bulletproof vest. Wearing it was one of several things that had been beaten into him during his seemingly never-ending training.

Rapp flipped up the collar on his black jacket and pulled a thin black balaclava over his face. He hefted the coil of climbing rope, looked over the edge of the building, and said to himself, "Two shots to the head." It was a bit redundant, but that was the point, and the essence of what this entire exercise was about.

Rapp gently let the rope play its way out and then swung both legs over the lip of the roof. In one smooth move, he hopped off the ledge and spun 180 degrees. His gloved hands clamped onto the rope and slowed his descent until he had dropped fifteen feet and he could reach out and put one foot on the railing of the balcony. Holding firmly to the rope, he gently stepped down onto the small black iron grating. He was careful to keep himself off to one side despite the fact that the blackout drapes were pulled. Dropping to a knee, he took the rope and brought it around the railing so it would be available should he need to make a quick exit. He had disabled the lock on the balcony door when he'd planted the listening device two days earlier. If there was time, he would retrieve the device, but it was nothing special. Rapp always made sure to use devices that couldn't be traced back to one of the high-end manufacturers that Langley used.

He had the layout of the suite memorized. It was one big room with a sitting area on the left and king-sized platform bed on the other. Rapp listened to the noises on the other side of the doors. The prostitute was more than likely there, but Rapp couldn't hear her over the obnoxious snoring and wheezing of the Libyan. Everything was as it should be. Rapp drew his Beretta and slowly began to place pressure on the brass door handle with his gloved hand. He moved it from the three o'clock position down to five, and then it released without so much as a click.

Rapp pulled the door toward him and swung it flat against the side of the building. He placed his free hand on the seam of the blackout curtains and pushed through in a low crouch, his pistol up and sweeping from left to right. It was six steps from the balcony to where his target was sleeping. The bed was up so high that the platform had a step that wrapped around three sides. A massive, gaudy mirror served as the headboard. The elevation put the target at waist height for the six-foot-one Rapp. With the tip of the silencer only four feet from the Libyan's head, Rapp stole a quick glance in hopes that he could locate the prostitute. The best he could do was get a sense that she was somewhere on the other side, buried under a jumble of pillows and blankets. He would never shoot her, but he might have to pistol-whip her in the event she woke up and started screaming.

Rapp moved a half step closer and leveled his weapon. He placed the orange dot of his front sight on the bridge of the man's nose and then brought the two rear dots into position. The pressure was already on the trigger, and without so much as the tiniest flash of hesitation, Rapp squeezed and sent a bullet into the man's head. The suppressor jumped one inch, fell back in line, and Rapp fired the second shot.

He looked down at the Libyan. The second shot had enlarged the dime-sized hole by half. Death was instantaneous, which meant that the snoring had stopped. In the new silence of the room, Rapp's eyes darted to the jumbled pile on the far side of the bed, and after three seconds of no movement he dropped to his knee and reached around the back of the nightstand. The fingertips of his right hand had just found what he was looking for when he felt the floor beneath him tremble.

The vibration was intense enough that Rapp knew it could be caused only by one thing. He withdrew his hand, leaving the listening device where it was, and rose enough so that he could look over the bed to the hotel room's door.

There, in the thin strip of light under the door, Rapp saw one shadow pass and then another. He cursed to himself, and was about to make a break toward the balcony, when the door crashed open, flooding the suite with a band of light. As Rapp began to drop, he saw the distinct black barrel of a submachine gun, and then a bright muzzle flash.

CHAPTER 2

THE room smelled. It was a brew of sweat and other odors given off by men stuffed for too long in close quarters. It was also tinged with a hint of fear. That troubled Samir Fadi deeply even though he understood the cause. They were hunting a ghost—someone who had silently and steadily begun killing their brethren nearly a year ago. Samir could not change their situation, nor could he change the facts. The longer the men waited the more bored they became, and the more bored they became, the more their minds wandered. It was not difficult to see it in their young faces as the gung-ho nature of their operation dissipated under the strain of monotony. They were each recalculating their chances for success, and the odds were moving in the wrong direction.

Samir did not fall prey to this weakness. They would meet this ghost with overwhelming firepower and they would rid their cause of a major problem, and he would be celebrated as a hero. That was no small thing for Samir. He had felt for a very long time that Allah had magnificent plans for him, and when he returned from this operation with the head of the assassin, he would bask in the glory he so rightly deserved.

Samir had been the lucky one to stumble upon the beginnings of a solution. They had all been shocked to hear that this was the work of one man. Samir had asked the most basic question, "How do you find and kill an assassin whom no one knows?" They had worked their sources across Europe and in Moscow and come up with nothing. Some on the council continued to argue that it couldn't be one man. It had to be multiple teams operating simultaneously. The Spaniard, however, held his ground. His source was above reproach. In addition to the source, the Spaniard had gotten his hands on some of the official police reports that were filed after the various murders. The reports all pointed to the fact that it was the work of one man. A support network and funding, to be sure, but it was one man doing the killing.

The answer to Samir's question was every bit as simple. The Spaniard told the council that they needed to set a trap. Samir had been cut out of the following sessions. Only the Executive Council was allowed to weigh in on that decision, but Samir got the gist of it. They needed a plump target to lure the assassin out into the open. That plump target was now sleeping across the hall and three doors down. Samir was not told the identity of the bait until seven days earlier, when he and his men arrived in Vienna. For four days, they had sat stuffed in a hotel room, slightly smaller than this one, and then on that fourth morning, they pulled out and left for France. They all traveled alone, dressed in suits, but on the same train. When they'd arrived in Paris they were met by the Spaniard and a trusted brother who had prepped the hotel room with weapons and surveillance equipment.

The bait had arrived by plane later that day, and after a brief lunch at the hotel, he left to do some shopping. One by one, at random intervals, Samir's men entered the hotel and checked into different rooms on different floors. By nightfall, when the bait was out having dinner with a prostitute, they had all converged on the single room down the hall. Silenced submachine guns were waiting for them. The Spaniard and Samir both agreed that the assassin would strike at night. Most likely in the predawn hours, and it would be in the hotel suite, where he could control the situation. Samir saw the wisdom but felt the window of opportunity was too small. From sundown to sunup, he had his men on high alert. During the day, two men were always on alert, just in case. The other three men would head back to their rooms, order room service, and sleep.

After four nights in Vienna and now three in Paris, Samir could tell that the men were beginning to doubt the wisdom of the operation. The idea that they would dare question his authority upset him a great deal. He had chosen each man for his discipline and skills and above all else absolute obedience to his orders. They were told up front that this mission would require a great deal of patience. That it was likely to take several trips before the assassin showed up, but Samir and the Spaniard were adamant. The assassin would show up, and when he did, they would be ready to pounce.

Over the course of the last two months, Samir felt that he had gotten to know this assassin. He was a man of unknown nationality who had penetrated their organization and begun methodically killing off the financiers, arms dealers, foot soldiers, and facilitators who allowed their organization and sister organizations to move about Europe, the Middle East, and North Africa. Thanks to the Spaniard, Samir had studied five of the kills in detail and was sure he understood how the assassin thought. He was ready to face him; he just wished it would be sooner rather than later.

Samir checked his watch, looked around the room, and shook his head in disgust. There were two twin beds, and two of his men were lying on them in their street clothes, their heads propped up against the headboards. Both had dozed off, their silenced weapons resting on their laps. A third man was on a chair by the door, leaned over, with his face buried in his hands. Samir couldn't tell, but he wouldn't be surprised if his eyes were closed as well. The fourth man at least was sitting attentively in front of the two monitors. They provided two angles of the room down the hall. He was also wearing headphones. The first few nights they had all eagerly taken turns listening and watching while the lumpy Libyan had sex with a prostitute. Seven nights into it, the novelty had worn off. Even so, Samir did note that despite the Libyan's apparent bad health he was extremely virile.

It caused Samir to wonder if he could do the same, and he was still not thirty. Samir was not a pious man when it came to his faith. He was a Muslim, but he left the holy prostrations to those who were more devout. He saw himself as a soldier tasked with taking Islam's fight to the dirty Jews and the rest of the decadent West. To blend in, he needed to act like them, and if that meant drinking their liquor and sleeping with their women, then so be it. As long as insinuating himself into their culture would allow him to kill more of them, he was sure Allah would reward him.

Samir stood and stretched his neck to one side and then the other. He was somewhere in the neighborhood of five feet ten inches tall and extremely proud of his physique. There wasn't an ounce of fat on his perfectly sculpted frame. He wore his raven-black hair midway between his ears and his neck in the fashion that was so popular with the French youth. There was a mirror over the bed and he paused to study his reflection before brushing his hair back behind each ear. He looked down at his chest under the tight white T-shirt and nodded his approval. He'd done thousands of pushups to maintain his rock-hard muscles. It made him think that it would be a good idea to have the men get up and do some pushups to get their blood flowing. By chance, he glanced at the surveillance monitors and something caught his eye. He moved quickly to the screens and shook the man who was tasked with watching them.

"Muhammad," Samir hissed, "did you see that?"

There on the black-and-white screen a shadowy figure moved across the suite. Samir felt his throat tighten. The assassin was here. Samir turned and slapped the feet of the men on the beds. Restraining himself from yelling, he said, "He's here. Get up, you fools." Samir grabbed his silenced submachine gun and lined his men up, slapping and shoving them into place. Within seconds, they were in position at the door.

Samir's heart was racing, and he could tell by the wide-eyed expressions of his men that they were going through the same thing. He placed his hand on the door handle and nodded once before yanking it open. The men rushed past him exactly as they'd practiced, into the hallway, running toward the suite on the right. Samir fell in behind the last man. Up ahead he heard someone stumble and watched as Jamir caught himself before he fell. Samir cursed himself for not waking them sooner and getting them ready. He knew the assassin would strike in the predawn hours. He should have had the men ready. At least two of them had just been yanked from their dreams. He hoped they remembered to flip their safeties off before they went in. Samir took a wobbly step and realized he'd forgotten to take his own weapon off safety.

Abdul was first in line and had practiced the next move. Samir had told him not to hesitate. "Do not worry about the rest of us. Kick the door in and start firing. We will be right behind you."

Samir was crouched near the wall, the thick black muzzle of his silencer pointed up. His finger was on the trigger, and as he watched Abdul step back to kick the door he felt a dry lump in his throat. He swallowed hard, and then the lock busted through the frame and the door flew open. Samir waited a second and then pushed his brother to join the fight. Still in the hallway, he heard the steady spit of the guns in front of him unleashing their deadly volley on the assassin, and a wolfish grin spread across his face. There was no way the killer would survive this onslaught. After tonight, Samir would become a legend among his peers.

CHAPTER 3

RAPP took cover behind the bed and its heavy platform. The distinctive spit of bullets leaving the end of a suppressor at a high rate was followed by the mirror above the bed shattering with a crash. After that, bullets began thudding into the walls, furniture, and mattress. Rapp pressed himself into the floor as he tried to count the shots. The steady thumping of one gun being fired was quickly joined by at least two more. Rapp stole a quick look at the balcony a mere six steps away and fought the urge to bolt. With this much lead flying, he would never make it. Plaster was raining down on him and he could hear bullets impacting the mattress just a few inches above his head.

Rapp pressed himself to the floor, taking cover behind the carpeted platform that elevated the bed, and told himself not to panic. His only avenue of escape was cut off, and he was cornered and outgunned. As the hail of bullets continued around him, he was reminded of something his trainer, Stan Hurley, had once said. It took Rapp a half second before he realized it was his only chance. Grabbing a spare magazine from under his left arm, he focused on the area past the foot of the bed and waited for his chance.

Even with the suppressors there was a great deal of noise, as there was a near continuous spit of bullets flying and the metallic clank of slides blowing back and slamming forward. It was considerably quieter than normal gunshots, but by no means silent. Rapp guessed they were using MP5s, or a close cousin. His mind jumped through the possibilities in a split second. MP5s almost certainly meant thirty-round magazines, and with the weapon's rate of fire on full automatic a man could burn through all his rounds in a matter of seconds.

One of Rapp's assets was the ability to slow things down in his mind's eye. He'd honed it on the lacrosse pitch in high school and college. He could calculate what the other players were going to do and react. When things were tense like this, he could block out the fear and extraneous information, focus on what was important, and slow things down. Panic-induced decisions had a nasty way of leading to bad, or in this case, fatal outcomes. Rapp's angle and concealment were as good as he could hope for, considering the fact that he'd been caught so off guard, and he used these few seconds to look at the tactical situation from 360 degrees.

The natural mistake was to get so caught up in your situation that you failed to analyze the motives, maneuvers, and talent of your opponent. The motive of this group was clear. They wanted to kill him. As to how they knew he'd be here and how they had avoided detection from the advance team, Rapp would have to search for those answers later. His mind now seized on a critical detail in the blink of an eye. They were not a trained SWAT team. Tactical teams practiced disciplined fire. They didn't simply enter a room and begin hosing it down with bullets. From that, Rapp discerned a very comforting fact—he could kill them.

Police were off limits. He could maim or physically subdue, but he was forbidden to kill a law enforcement officer. Such were the rules of restraint that were placed on him, and he did not argue. Governments could look the other way when certain unsavory individuals were killed on their soil, but kill an innocent bystander, or worse, a law enforcement officer, and you could create an international incident that would bring the kind of attention that they could not afford.

Rapp realized quickly that these guys were making a big mistake. They assumed their overwhelming firepower would win this battle in the opening salvo, but as Hurley had told Rapp repeatedly, "You never want to blow your wad in the first few seconds of a gunfight. Better to take cover and let the other guy empty his gun." Taking this several steps further, Hurley and the other instructors forced him to learn how to classify different guns by sound alone, and more important, to keep track of rounds fired.

The latter was hopeless in this situation. Three or more submachine guns firing on full automatic were impossible to count with any accuracy, but at this rate of fire it was pretty much a foregone conclusion that they would all be reloading in the next few seconds. Rapp anticipated what would happen next. He was on the verge of losing his cover. Rather than wait for the first shooter to move far enough into the room and get the angle on him, Rapp would broaden the angle first. He stayed low and crawled forward two feet. With his head near the edge of the foot of the platform, he could now see close to three-quarters of the room. Standing no more than fifteen feet away, he saw his first target.

The man was dressed in jeans and a T-shirt and was in the midst of ejecting a long, curved magazine. Rapp swung his left arm around and shot him once in the face. He kept moving his pistol and found two more targets. One was still firing wildly and the other was reloading. Rapp shot the second man in the nose and the third man in the throat, and then before he could find the next target, bullets began thudding into the carpeting near his face. Rapp yanked his arm back and scurried in reverse for cover. He'd fired five rounds, which meant he had fourteen left in the magazine and two full magazines of eighteen rounds plus his backup gun.

Now was not the time to stay pressed against the floor. If the man or men who were left standing decided to rush him, he'd be toast.

Rapp popped up onto one knee and raised the pistol above the bed. Again, firing from left to right he squeezed off six quick shots. On the fifth one, he heard a grunt and knew he'd hit someone in the torso. He moved his muzzle back a few degrees to the left and fired four more shots, and then all was quiet. Rapp paused and then squeezed off his last four shots at the door. He quickly switched out magazines, hit the slide release with his thumb, and seated a fresh round in the chamber. He brought up his gun and took a quick peek over the top of the mattress. There, silhouetted in the doorway, was a stunned man, clutching his belly with both hands. It was time to move.

Rapp stood, and as he took his first step to his left, he saw more movement in the hallway. Staying in a crouch with his gun leveled, he squeezed off one round. He buried it in the man's chest rather than his head, sending him stumbling over the threshold. A gun appeared in the gap between the door frame and the dying man. Rapp kept moving and squeezing off shots that were splintering the edge of the door frame. When he reached the heavy curtains, he fired one more volley and then pushed through, out onto the balcony. The rope was right in front of him and he dove for it with his right hand while still holding on to his Beretta with his left.

As his gloved hand closed around the rope, he launched himself over the railing. His upper body was clear when he felt a solid punch hit him from behind. Rapp knew at that exact moment that he'd been shot, and his brain became overly focused on the fact that a piece of lead had just blasted its way into his body. The shock drew his attention away from the rope to the pain in his left shoulder, and he began to fall. Desperately, his right hand reached out in search of the black rope as he stared up at the night sky, the hard pavement rushing up to meet him from below.

CHAPTER 4

ABDUL continued straight into the room, sweeping his suppressed rifle from left to right, laying down a steady stream of bullets. Right on his heels, Jamir joined the fight, spraying his bullets in a zigzag pattern. Muhammad was next and then Samir's brother Habib.

Samir's feet felt heavy, as if he was suddenly wading through sand. He forced himself to move forward as the gap grew between him and his brother. For all of his bravado and threats of violence, there'd been a sliver of his ego that feared facing this assassin. He did a good job keeping it in check and made sure the men never got a whiff of it, but it weighed on him. As the line of men pressed into the suite, Samir was steadily falling behind. He listened as the hail of bullets reached a fevered pitch—objects crashing and shattering under the fusillade of metal.

Samir suddenly felt woozy. His chest tightened and his vision grew fuzzy at the edges. "Breathe," he rebuked himself. He was almost to the door now, and he took two deep breaths as he watched his brother enter the room. Samir stopped at the door frame and listened to the barrage of bullets shredding the room. With fresh air in his lungs, he allowed a nervous smile to spread across his face. There was no way the assassin could escape this. "The hunter will become the hunted." It was a mantra Samir had repeated for months.

The man I have been sent to kill will finally die, and I will be rewarded handsomely, Samir thought. Samir had played this out in his mind evening after evening, and the end result was always the assassin lying dead in a pool of his own blood. Four men with submachine guns against a single man with a pistol, and he was in reserve just in case—hundreds of bullets against a handful. This would surely end in his favor.

Samir was just about to enter the room when the clamor came to an abrupt stop. In the silence that followed he heard a sound he couldn't quite place. Cocking his head to one side in thought, he tried to figure out what was the cause of the strange gurgling noise. At the precise moment he figured it out, he heard his brother grunt in agony. Samir froze where he was. A second later his brother began to stumble back through the doorway without his weapon, his hands clutching his stomach. No more than a foot or two in front of him, Samir saw a bullet hit his brother in the chest, exiting out his back and spraying blood all over the wall across the hall. Horrified, Samir reached out to grab him and the door frame suddenly exploded, sending splinters of wood flying. Samir jerked back, feeling the sting in his cheek.

His right eye began blinking frantically as he watched his brother fall, and then fear seized his every muscle as it occurred to him that the assassin might be coming for him. Without really thinking, Samir moved his submachine gun to his left hand and swung it around the door frame, closed his eyes, and unleashed a volley on full automatic.

Samir stayed in the hallway and fired two more quick bursts into the room. In the quiet that suddenly fell over the scene he looked down at his brother, who was staring up at him with vacant eyes. The guilt hit him like a knife in the chest and his anger took over. Samir swung the black suppressor into the room and held down the trigger. He moved forward, wildly sweeping the weapon back and forth until he was out of bullets.

Stopping in the half light of the hallway, he took in the mess. Three of his men lay dead at his feet, but there was no sign of the assassin. Samir ejected the spent magazine and inserted a new one while his eyes settled on the drapes that blocked the balcony doors. His feet were moving before he'd made a conscious decision. He fired a quick burst through the curtain and then threw the fabric back to the side. The first thing he saw when he stepped onto the balcony was the rope. He followed it to the ground, where he saw a man in black running across the street.

Samir shouldered his weapon and put the gun's hoop sight over the moving target. He squeezed off a quick three-round burst, but had no way of knowing if he'd hit low, high, right, or left. The assassin changed course and Samir adjusted, this time holding the trigger down and sending a steady stream of bullets after the man. After a few seconds the bolt suddenly slammed into the open position, telling him he was out of rounds. Samir watched the assassin disappear into the shadows and fought back the urge to scream.

He moved back into the room and looked at the carnage. He'd lost three of his men and his own brother was dead in the hallway. He had failed miserably. He began to shake with a mix of fear and white-hot rage. What would he tell their mother? What would he tell the Spaniard and Rafique? Where had he gone wrong? Samir shook his head in disgust but somewhere deep in his brain he knew he was lucky to be alive. He could never say that to the others, though. He could never look so frail in front of them, or they might kill him.

Samir's mind was shocked back to his current predicament by a sound in the hallway. He needed to get the hell out of there, and quickly, before the police showed up. He slid a fresh magazine into his gun and hit the slide release. At the doorway his eyes were drawn to his brother, but he couldn't handle the grief. Fighting back the tears, he moved down the hallway toward the stairs. A door on his left opened, revealing a skinny woman in a white bathrobe. Samir raised his weapon and without breaking stride, pumped five rounds into her chest. Two doors later a man stepped into the hallway on his right. Samir squeezed off another burst. He rushed down the stairs, through a short hallway, and into the back alley where he came face to face with a hotel worker. The young man saw the gun and raised his hands. Samir didn't hesitate. He pulled the trigger back as far as it would go and sent the man sprawling backward into a pile of garbage bags.

CHAPTER 5

Rapp had never been shot, but it wasn't the type of thing one had to experience to recognize. Bullets had been flying at a rapid pace and one of them had found its mark. The impact had caused him to drop his gun to the street below, but he had held on to the rope. The zip of bullets cracked above his head as Rapp fell over the railing and then dropped. He clamped down with his right hand, the maneuver causing him to spin 180 degrees and come crashing back to the building. He got his feet out in front of him just in time to stop himself from slamming face-first into the stone facade.

Dangling with a bullet wound from a rope and with his gun forty-odd feet below him on the street gave Rapp a sense of vulnerability he did not like. The thought of grabbing his backup gun occurred to him, but his legs were already bending at the knees and kicking him away from the wall. He needed to get away from this place as fast as possible. He loosened his grip on the rope and dropped ten feet before clamping down again. His feet found the wall once more and he used them to push himself away from the building.

When he reached the pavement he looked down to find his gun

just a few feet away. He grabbed the weapon and quickly looked left and right. No headlights were visible, but the police would be here shortly. Rapp was already moving across the street and toward the river. He was halfway clear when bullets started snapping in the air around him. He jerked left, crouched a bit, and then broke into a full sprint. The bullets followed him and he jerked right and then his feet found the grass and shadows of the trees. The bullets stopped, but Rapp continued to the right for another fifty feet to make sure he was fully concealed before he committed to his true course.

The bench and walking path were exactly where Rapp expected them to be. He crossed the path and turned left, his feet barely making a noise as they moved lightly along the asphalt. His lungs and legs were working fine, carrying him at a quick clip toward a spot he had scouted out a few days earlier. Just before he reached the bridge the first wave of pain hit him. It came rolling in, building in intensity until it hit, throbbed, and then diminished. Rapp resisted the urge to touch his shoulder and assess the damage. He could feel the slick wetness under his shirt and that told him enough. The wound was somewhere in his left shoulder, which meant he should be able to handle it unless it had hit his axillary artery. If that were the case, he would most likely lose consciousness and bleed out in the next few minutes.

Up ahead he sighted the low-slung bridge with its curved stone arches. Rapp suddenly couldn't remember its name, which made him wonder if his brain wasn't getting enough blood. He slowed his pace and left the path. The crunch of dirt and gravel under his feet told him he had found the foot-worn trail. He followed it slowly to the south embankment of the river and the base of the bridge. The ledge was no more than three feet wide. Rapp paused and peered down the length of it. There was just enough light from the city bouncing off the water to see that he was alone. He ducked under the curved arch and crouched his way to the middle. He sat down on the ledge, his feet dangling a few feet above the water of the Seine.

Out of habit, Rapp moved to switch his silenced Beretta from his right hand to his left so he could holster it, but his left hand did not respond in the way he would have liked. He managed to move it a few inches and then a stabbing pain told him it was a bad idea. Rapp cursed under his breath and then set the gun down on the ledge next to him. Using his teeth, Rapp tugged off the glove on his right hand, finger by finger, and dropped the glove next to the gun. He opened his jacket and then undid the next two buttons on his shirt. His hand slid over the rough fabric of his bulletproof vest and found his bare shoulder soaked in blood. A wave of pain peaked and he bit down hard. As the surge passed, his index finger found what he was looking for—the exit wound. Rapp breathed a sigh of relief. The bullet had gone all the way through and the hole was no bigger than the tip of his finger. If it had been a hollow-tipped round the exit wound would have been much bigger and the damage far worse.

Reaching around his back, he found the entry wound and sensed there was less blood, but it was hard to tell. He unfastened the small pack around his waist and opened the med kit. His fingers found a small pen flashlight. Rapp placed it against his thigh and turned it on. Satisfied that the red filter was affixed, he placed the small flashlight in his teeth and found the first of four syringes. He popped the cap, letting it fall into the river, and then, pressing the plunger, he soaked his shoulder in iodine.

Rapp looked at the next syringe for a second and hesitated. He had gone over this in theory, but now, sitting here bleeding, he began to realize just how much it was going to hurt. Before he did that, though, he had to plug the hole. He tore open a package of gauze and started feeding it into the entry wound on the back of his shoulder. The pain was more manageable than he'd expected, but this would be the easy part. When he was done, he picked up the next syringe and dropped that cap into the river as well. Grabbing his left wrist, Rapp brought it up and hooked the hand's fingers around his jacket and shirt, exposing the exit wound, and then let the limp arm hang there. Not wanting to think about the next move any longer than he needed to, he placed the tip of the plastic syringe into the exit hole, took a deep breath and then shoved the needle in as far as it would go. It took every ounce of control not to scream. Rapp's entire body went rigid with pain, his eyes rolled back in his head, and for a good five seconds he feared he might pass out.

The shock of the initial pain began to recede and Rapp took several deep breaths. When he was ready, he placed his thumb on the plunger. Then he pressed down and the first few cc's of the powdered blood coagulant flowed into the wound. Rapp pulled the syringe out an inch and pumped more of the powder into the wound. He repeated the process two more times until the syringe was empty. After discarding it, he grabbed the next-to-last syringe, popped the cap, and jabbed it into the wound. A muffled curse escaped his lips this time, and he grunted while he hit the plunger, sending super glue into the wound to help stop the bleeding.

Police sirens could now be heard coming from every direction. Rapp tossed the syringe out into the current and leaned back. He had to get moving. He fished out the last syringe. It contained a broadspectrum antibiotic. He sat up straight and found a patch of skin under his bulletproof vest. He jabbed the needle through the fabric of his dress shirt and didn't so much as feel a pinch. Not knowing how he would secure the med kit and thinking that he had pretty much done all he could, he dropped the entire thing into the murky river. He stared down at his gun for a second and was about to dump it as well, but decided against it. Where he was going he would have plenty of opportunities to dispose of it. Rapp grabbed the weapon with his good hand, reversed it, and nudged the tip of the suppressor into the holster. As he snapped it into place, he heard voices off to his right. He knew the temperature of the water, the speed of the current, and roughly how long he would last until hypothermia took his life.

As the voices grew louder, Rapp scooted his butt to the edge, gripped the stone with his right hand, and slid himself quietly off the ledge and into the water. He sank beneath the surface smoothly, the suction of his clothes pulling him down. He knew not to panic. As soon as his clothes were soaked, they would be neutral. Rapp bobbed to the surface five seconds later, the current already pushing him to the west. He took in an easy breath and ignored the chill of the dark water, telling himself it would help slow his blood flow. He was going to take a casual swim through the heart of Paris, and in a few hours, he would find the right place to make ground.

Rapp rolled onto his back and gently scissor-kicked his legs under the surface. As he cleared the relative darkness of the bridge he looked up at the night sky and for the briefest of moments wondered how many people had died in this river—if his would be just another body to add to the count. The thought made him smile. Always up for a challenge, Rapp felt his survival mode kick in, and he told himself that he would live through this night as surely as the sun would rise in the east in the morning. And then he would go searching for answers. Something had gone horribly wrong tonight, and Rapp needed to know how the enemy was on to him. No matter what Kennedy and the others ordered, he would not be going back to the States for some time on the couch with Langley's resident shrink.

CHAPTER 6

COMMANDANT Francine Neville of the French Judicial Police stood amidst the carnage holding a cup of coffee in one hand and desperately wishing she had a cigarette in the other. Her people were picking through the slaughter with gloved hands and various tools. A photographer stood in the doorway clicking away. Neville was momentarily conscious of the fact that she wasn't wearing any makeup and her hair, which she wore in a swooping bob midway between her ears and shoulders, was probably sticking out in a way that made her look slightly deranged. She'd been to enough crime scenes over the years, though, to know it was a waste of time to worry. If this crime was ever solved, and brought to court, she would have to endure the less-than-flattering photos with the rest of her team, who had all been yanked from their beds before sunrise.

Neville was good at her job. She had risen quickly through the ranks of the National Police, both in spite of the fact that she was a woman and because she was a woman. Political pressures had ushered in the brave new age of women in positions of command and Neville knew there were still plenty of misogynists around who thought the only reason she'd made commandant at the relatively young age of thirty-seven was that the bosses had to reach their quota. She ignored all of the whispers, focused on her job, and took comfort in the fact that the men she worked with knew she was qualified and had earned her position. On nights like this, however, she questioned why she had chosen police work.

Neville's face was a pinched scowl as she surveyed the chaos. This one would be a real circus. She had a fat naked man in the bed with a skinny woman half his age lying next to him. Both were dead—riddled with bullets. Four more men, paramilitary types by the look of them, were also strewn about the floor. These bodies were relatively intact, with only one or two slugs in them. Down the hall, two more bodies were sprawled out in separate doorways. Neville figured they were hotel guests who had heard the commotion, and when they'd gone to investigate, had been killed by the crazy bastards who had done all of this. Also, an unfortunate young employee of the hotel who did the overnight laundry was now prostrate in the alley with five bullet holes in his chest. Neville tallied the carnage—nine bodies in total. In her sixteen years on the force, the biggest investigation she'd been involved in was a triple homicide. It was of course a love triangle, murder-suicide. While sensational, the case was not hard for the press and public to figure out. Wife cheats on husband, husband kills wife and her boyfriend, and then kills himself. It wasn't the first such murder, and it wouldn't be the last.

This was an entirely different scenario. The number of victims pushed her mind in two separate but linked directions. They'd had a real problem with the Slav gangs that had flooded into the slums after Yugoslavia fell apart and spiraled into civil war, and now the Russian gangs with their newfound independence were beginning to assert themselves. As always, she would need to keep her mind open, but those two groups were at the top of her list.

Gnawing at the back of her mind were two other entities—

her superiors at the National Police headquarters and the press. Submachine-gun fire at a five-star hotel in the heart of Paris was sensational enough; throw in the nine dead bodies and she was guaranteed a media circus the likes of which the city hadn't seen since the Dreyfus Affair. Her superiors would find it nearly impossible not to interfere and she already knew how they would do it. A few would try to micromanage her investigation and the bulk would spend their lunches leaking to the press.

Anxiety crept up on Neville as she realized this entire mess could end her career. Her attention turned to the dead man lying on the bed. It was something out of one of those American mobster movies. Feathers and tufts of fabric were everywhere, and a good amount of it was clinging to puddles of blood. She looked to the four paramilitary types on the floor. They could easily be Serbs or Croats. They had that swarthy look. Neville had sent one of her officers down to the front desk to find out whose name the room was registered under. She heard a cackle of grating laughter from the hallway, and a moment later a man appeared in the doorway, stopped, and looked down at one of the dead bodies.

If Neville needed any confirmation that she was in the middle of a shit storm, it was now standing in the doorway. She had hoped to get through the rest of her life without ever seeing Paul Fournier again, and she had made it nearly four years, but tonight her luck had run out. Fournier was DGSE—France's General Directorate for External Security. It was the organization tasked with the external security of the country—the key word being *external*. Neville had a sinking feeling that Fournier was here because of the man in the bed. As her gaze shifted between the two men, one dead and the other alive, she knew that this case had just become infinitely more complicated.

"Francine," Fournier called far too loudly from across the room. "A pleasure to see you. It's been far too long."

Neville sighed and said, "Paul, what are you doing here?"

"You know how things work at the Directorate," he said with a broad grin under a salt-and-pepper mustache. "We go wherever the Republic needs us."

"I thought you specialized in subverting the unstable governments to our south."

Fournier laughed heartily and stepped carefully around the dead bodies. When he was a step away from Neville, he held out his arms as if he was ready to embrace an old friend.

Neville shuddered at the thought of touching him. With a frown on her oval face she put out her right hand, signaling him to keep his distance. His audacity had certainly not diminished over the years. "Why are you here?"

Fournier let the wounded look fall from his face and began patting the pockets of his gray trench coat in search of something. A moment later, he fished out a pack of cigarettes and a lighter. He lit one and then extended the cigarette to Neville.

The gall of this man, she thought to herself. When she had first met Fournier, nine years ago, she had been drawn to his confidence, but in the end, she realized that what looked like confidence was actually the facade of a cold, calculating, manipulative, selfish prick. Straining to keep her cool, she shook her head at the offer and said, "Why is everything so difficult with you?"

"I'm sorry?" he asked, pretending to not understand.

She shrugged. "I ask you a simple question, but you refuse to answer."

Fournier suddenly looked offended. "Come now, my dear Francine. I know things did not end well between us, and I am sorry for that, but it was, what . . . ten years ago? Surely we can be professional about this."

She ignored the fact that he was off by six years and instead focused on a thousand things she'd like to say to the jerk. All of them would have felt good, would have been accurate, and they would all have been a mistake. Accuracy and truth had no sanctity to Fournier. For him they were devices to be used to advance his agenda and schemes. He would obfuscate and claim the mantle of victim no matter how egregious his sins. Engaging him was exactly what he wanted. "Paul, I am being completely professional about this. That is why I asked you why you are here. This is my crime scene. Directorate of Security or not, I need to know why you are here."

"Fair enough," Fournier said in an easy tone. He exhaled a cloud of smoke and turned to the bed. "Do you have any idea who that is?"

Neville was suddenly very angry with the officer she had sent down to the front desk to find the answer to this exact question. She straightened a bit and said, "I do not."

The answer brought a smile to Fournier's face. "Well, let's see." He wheeled back toward the dead bodies and said, "Four men with suppressed automatic weapons, all dead." Gesturing to the bed he continued, "An overweight man in his sixties and a skinny young woman less than half his age . . . most likely a prostitute."

Neville acted bored. The conclusions were obvious. She was tempted to say so, but knew the less she said the better. Fournier had his stage, and he needed to play out this little game in order to diminish her in front of her men. "The man's name?" she asked in a dispassionate voice.

"I'm getting there," Fournier said, holding up a cautionary finger. "Six bodies. That's rather a lot."

Neville didn't bother to correct him and tell him about the other three bodies. She would offer as little information as possible in hopes that the spook from Directorate of Security would get what he was looking for and leave.

As Fournier continued to analyze the obvious, his eyes were busy noting the more interesting aspects of the crime scene. There were certain incongruities that Neville and her team would eventually notice, but for now, it was hard to see the proverbial trees through the forest. He placed himself in the room when it all went down. Looked at the shattered glass headboard, the bullet-pocked plaster wall, and the two bodies on the bed, riddled with bullets. Brass shell casings littered the floor. Hundreds of rounds had been fired. That the assassin had escaped was a miracle. Fournier looked at the nearest man on the floor and noted the precise location of the bullet hole in his forehead, and couldn't help but nod in respect for the man whose aim had stayed so steady under a fusillade of bullets.

"The man's name?" Neville asked again.

Fournier approached the bed. He looked down at the heavyset man, noted more than a dozen shallow entry wounds, and then his eyes found the near-perfect dot just above the minister's nose. That would have come from their assassin. Fournier inhaled deeply and waved his cigarette at the bed. "That, my dear, is Tarek al-Magariha."

Neville waited for him to expand. It was a long moment that grew longer, and when she tired of the wait, she asked, "And who is Tarek al-Magariha?"

"He is Libya's oil minister, and these men I presume are, or I should say were, his bodyguards."

Neville closed her eyes for a moment and clenched her fists. Serbian and Russian gangsters killing each other was one thing—it wasn't good, but to a certain extent the good people of Paris didn't care as long as they were killing each other. A foreign diplomat, however, was an entirely different mess. A Libyan diplomat was even worse, and their oil minister the worst of all. Neville didn't know the exact number, but she knew her country received a large portion of its oil imports from the country across the Mediterranean.

"Any idea who killed him?" She found herself asking the question before she could stop herself, and she instantly regretted it, for she knew Fournier was incapable of telling her the truth.

"No idea at the moment, but the usual suspects will be looked at."

"The usual suspects?"

"The Israelis . . . a few others." Fournier knew much more than he was letting on, but he wasn't about to tell someone from the National

Police that al-Magariha had spent most of his career working for Libya's brutal intelligence service, the Mukhabarat el-Jamahiriya.

Neville eyed Fournier with suspicion. All of her instincts told her he was holding back information. "How did you find out so quickly?"

"Quickly?"

"That he'd been murdered."

Fournier flashed her a proud smile. "I have my sources."

Neville wondered if the DGSE had had the Libyan under surveillance. She was about to ask the question but thought better of it. He would never give her an honest answer. She would pass her suspicions on to her bosses, and they could lock horns with the higher-ups at DGSE. "I'm still a bit confused as to why you are here."

"We have a dead foreign diplomat, my dear. I would think you would understand the need for the Directorate to be involved."

Neville gave him nothing.

Fournier shrugged. "Well, my superiors want me to keep a very close eye on your investigation, so we will be seeing quite a bit of each other."

Neville's light brown eyes were fixated on the inch-long piece of ash that was precariously dangling from the end of Fournier's cigarette. "This is a crime scene. I don't care how much clout you think you have, if that ash hits the carpet, I will have you handcuffed and removed."

"Sorry," Fournier said, wide-eyed, as if he'd suddenly realized his mistake. He held a hand under the ash as he made his way to the balcony door. With light breaking in the morning sky, he could see the bullet holes in the curtain. He shouldered his way through the curtains and out onto the small balcony. Fournier flipped the ash over the edge and followed it down to the sidewalk. The police barricades were up and a few members of the press and curious onlookers were beginning to gather. Word would continue to spread and this place would be a circus by midmorning. He turned his head toward the roof and took note of the fact that his man had retrieved the rope before the police had figured out it was there. Fournier wasn't sure how much more he could do to help muddy the waters, but he did know he needed to get out of here before too many cameras showed up.

He walked back into the hotel suite and began stepping around bodies. "Francine, I will be in touch. If you need me, you know where to find me."

Neville turned away from the examination of several shell casings on the near side of the bed. She felt a great sense of relief as she watched him leave the room, but then within a few seconds, asked herself why he was leaving so quickly. Something didn't feel right, and in that moment, Neville had final confirmation that Paul Fournier was going to be a major complication in an already complicated case.

CHAPTER 7

LANGLEY, VIRGINIA

THOMAS Stansfield was accustomed to working Saturdays. The world did not stop for the deputy director of Operations for the CIA to rest so he worked six and a half days a week. He was, however, not accustomed to being rousted by the secretary of state at four in the morning on a Saturday. Even so, he kept his cool as the secretary told him the news of a dead Libyan diplomat in Paris. He also managed to patiently listen as the secretary made some extremely wild and uninformed accusations. Stansfield assured him the CIA had nothing to do with whatever it was that had happened in Paris, and before hanging up, he promised America's top diplomat that he would have some answers by noon.

By 8:00 a.m., Stansfield was ensconced in the Situation Room at the White House with most of the National Security Council. With the president off playing golf in Maryland and the vice president AWOL, Secretary of State Franklin Wilson led the meeting. After two hours of idle conjecture, and a lot of bluster about putting pressure on Israel, Stansfield finally managed to break away from the meeting.

With the morning already half gone, Stansfield was irritated that he didn't have a single salient fact. The questions were piling up, and he knew if he was going to get some answers, he would need to escape this meeting of Washington's power elite and have a much-needed discussion with one of his junior operatives and an old colleague who had better be waiting in his office back at Langley.

Stansfield found Irene Kennedy sitting in his small lobby and signaled for her to follow him into his soundproofed office. In his eternally composed way, Stansfield motioned for Kennedy to sit in one of the chairs opposite his desk and then asked, "Where is Stan?"

Kennedy shrugged. Her shoulder-length hair was pulled back in a simple ponytail. "He wandered off a while ago. Said he needed to talk to someone."

Stansfield unbuttoned his gray suit coat, took it off, and draped it over the back of his leather office chair. He was annoyed that Stan Hurley was loose in the building, but he didn't let it show. They had a long, colorful history together and Stansfield was intimately familiar with the man's abilities as well as his weaknesses. There were some very good reasons why Stansfield had turned him into a private contractor a few years ago. Chief among them was that Hurley was completely tone deaf when it came to the internal politics of Langley. He was like a child who simply couldn't resist touching the paint when the sign clearly said "Wet paint. Do not touch." In the ordered, uptight halls of Langley, he was a disaster waiting to happen.

Stansfield looked at his Timex watch and decided he would give Hurley five minutes before he sent someone looking for him. Turning his thoughts to the matter of most concern, he asked, "Our young friend . . . has he checked in?"

Kennedy knew Stansfield's office was swept for listening devices on a daily basis, but these conversations always made her nervous. "No."

"Any idea why?"

"I would prefer not to jump to any conclusions until we know more."

Stansfield looked at her with his gray eyes, waiting patiently for her to say more. The look on his face was one that was familiar to all who worked for him. He paid his people for their intellect and their opinions, not to play it safe until the answer was obvious. "I know he's still relatively new . . . but I assume you properly impressed on him the need to check in."

"I did, and although he may be new compared to some of the other people around here, in one year's time he's racked up more real field experience than any other ten operatives combined."

Reading between the lines, Stansfield understood that by practical field experience, she meant kills. "Has he ever failed to check in before?"

Kennedy considered the question for a moment, but then the door opened and Stan Hurley walked in. He was wearing a boxy-fitting blue suit, white shirt, and no tie. His mustache was trimmed short but he'd skipped the razor this morning, so he had scruffy stubble that looked like it could be used to sand wood. Stansfield, knowing Hurley's uncouth side better than most, was impressed that he'd actually bothered with the suit at all.

"Sorry I'm late," Hurley announced with a basso voice that he'd developed from years of smoking, drinking, and yelling.

"What have you been up to?" Stansfield asked with sincere curiosity.

"Just checking in on a few old friends."

"Do I want to know who?"

Hurley flashed him a lopsided grin and said, "Boss, you've got more important things to worry about."

Stansfield would find out later. For now they had to figure out what had happened in Paris, and to what extent they might be exposed. Keeping his eyes on Hurley, he asked, "Any word on what happened last night?"

"Nine bodies. Libyan oil minister and a prostitute were gunned down along with his four-person security detail."

The deputy director of Operations gave a slight nod. He'd already confirmed as much.

"There were also three innocent civilians." Hurley leaned forward and rested his elbows on his knees. He stroked his mustache with both hands and folded them under his chin. The man seemed to be in perpetual motion. Even at fifty-three, he had a youthful energy about him.

"Three innocents?" Stansfield asked, betraying his surprise with only an arched brow. He turned to Kennedy. "Did you know about this?"

"No," Kennedy answered honestly.

"Two hotel guests," Hurley added, "just down the hall from Tarek's room, and then a kitchen boy in the back alley."

"Nine bodies," Stansfield repeated, still surprised by the number.

"That's right," Hurley said as if it was no big deal.

"Any chance one of these bodies is the man we're looking for?" Stansfield asked.

"It doesn't sound like it."

Kennedy turned in her chair to face Hurley. "Where'd you get this information?"

"Listen here, Missy," Hurley snarled, "I wasn't the one who planned this half-assed op."

"Let's hear it," Kennedy said with a confrontational edge in her voice.

"Hear what?"

"How the great Stan Hurley would have done it differently."

"For starters I would have never sent him in alone."

"That's pretty much all we've done for the last nine months and he's been pretty successful . . . a hell of a lot more successful than you and your boys have been the last couple years."

"You can bitch all you want, but I warned you. You gave that boy way too long a leash."

Stansfield was not in the mood to referee another argument between these two, so he cleared his throat and asked, "Who's your source?"

"Don't worry about my source. He's impeccable."

"All the same," Stansfield said, "I'd like to know."

Hurley put on an irritated face. He'd known Stansfield for three decades and he knew by the arch of his damn right eyebrow when there was no sense in trying to put him off. "An editor at one of the major dailies over there. She says the press is all over this thing."

Kennedy noted that he'd originally referred to his source as a he. The man was always thinking of ways to throw you off.

"Is this the she I'm thinking of?" Stansfield asked.

Hurley knew how proper his old friend was, and he couldn't pass up the opportunity to say openly what he was really asking. "You mean the editor from *Le Monde* I used to sleep with?"

Stansfield nodded.

"That would be her."

"And how do we know that she has her facts straight? We can assume they have it right on Tarek and the prostitute. What about the other seven bodies?"

"She already has names on all of them. The police have asked her not to release them until they can notify families, but none of the names I was given popped."

"So we can assume he's alive," Kennedy said, with just a hint of relief in her voice.

"And that he fucked up, big-time!" Hurley said, not giving her an inch.

"We don't know that," Kennedy retorted, addressing Stansfield instead of Hurley. She had known both of these men since birth. Her father had worked with them out of this very building. She was perhaps the only person at Langley under the age of thirty who would dare disagree with them. Stansfield admired her for it, while Hurley thought she should keep her mouth shut until she'd served at least a decade.

"What we know," Hurley said, his voice growing in intensity, "is that innocents are off limits. That is the unbreakable rule."

"That means a lot coming from you," Kennedy said with an exaggerated roll of her eyes.

"What in the hell is that supposed to mean?"

"You know exactly what it means."

"No, I don't."

"Uncle Stan," she said in a voice devoid of affection, "you've based your entire career on breaking the rules, and I think the reason he pisses you off is that he's a constant reminder that you are getting old and he's better than you were at your best."

Stansfield knew the words hurt his old friend, and he also knew there was a great deal of truth to them. Most of this was beside the point, however. They needed to focus on the problem at hand. "I want both of you to listen to me. We don't know what happened over there, and as we've all learned before, it's a dangerous thing to rush to conclusions."

"I'll tell you what's dangerous," Hurley snapped, still smarting from Kennedy's comments. "Letting a fucking untrained dog off the leash. Letting him basically run himself without any proper handling. That's what's dangerous." Hurley leaned back, shaking his head. "I've been warning you two about him from day one."

Kennedy turned and gave him an icy stare. "I assume you're referring to the same dog who risked his life to save your ungrateful, stubborn ass in Beirut?"

Stansfield desperately wished these two could work out some truce, but according to Dr. Lewis, there were no signs of things cooling down between them. He listened to them argue back and forth for a half minute and then said, "Are you two done?" He gave them a moment to absorb the fact that he was sick of listening to them and then said, "Does either of you have any useful information that you could give me?"

"I sent some assets over this morning. First flight out. They'll start poking around and see what they can find out."

"Good," Stansfield told Hurley. "I want you to get over there, too, and make sure we keep a tight lid on this thing. Find out what is going on and bring him in."

"That's my job, sir," Kennedy protested. "I'm his handler."

Stansfield shook his head. "You're too official, and you don't have Stan's contacts. I need you here."

Kennedy turned to Hurley, her eyes narrowing in distrust. "Who did you send over this morning?"

"A couple of my guys."

"Who, Stan?"

"Don't worry," Hurley said out of the side of his mouth. "I know how to handle my people."

Kennedy studied him for a moment and asked, "Did you send Victor?"

"What does it matter if I did?"

Kennedy turned her attention back to Stansfield. "If you've read my man's jacket, you know he and Victor have an explosive past."

"This is getting old." Hurley shook his head. "I'm sick of being second-guessed."

Kennedy kept her eyes on Stansfield. "If he gets a whiff of Victor and his thugs things will end badly."

"You're overreacting," Hurley grumbled.

"Ask Tom," Kennedy said, referring to Dr. Lewis. "He'll give you an honest assessment."

Stansfield nodded. "I will, but in the meantime I need you two to find out as much as you can about what happened last night." He motioned with a flick of his hand that they were done.

Kennedy stood. "I understand that this looks bad, sir, but there's a lot we don't know."

"I'll grant you that, but what we do know is not good . . . nine bodies, at least four of them innocent bystanders." The veteran spy shook his head. "This was supposed to be a surgical strike. The target, and as few bodyguards as possible, and that was it. No innocent bystanders. The rules were very clear."

"I know, sir, but there could be an explanation."

The problem, as Stansfield understood it, was that an explanation could be next to worthless at this point, but there was no sense in hammering the handler. He'd knowingly gone along with deploying Rapp despite repeated concerns raised by Stan Hurley. "Anything is possible, but we are in the answer business, and I need some answers."

Hurley stood. "Don't worry, I'll bring him in."

"None of your cowboy bullshit, Stan. I want him back here in one piece."

Hurley left without saying another word. After a few seconds, Kennedy started for the door.

Stansfield, looking at some papers on his desk, ruminated, "There's a chance we misjudged him."

Kennedy stopped abruptly, composed herself, and turned slowly to look back across the sterile office at the man she respected above all others. The disappointment on her face was obvious. "I don't believe I did, sir. The rest of you may have . . . and still are. He has performed beyond anyone's wildest expectations, and at the first sign of trouble you all assume he blew it."

"I haven't jumped to any conclusions. I simply expect my operatives to check in. Especially when their ops end badly." Stansfield picked up a file and said, "I've warned you before . . . don't let your feelings cloud your judgment in these matters. Follow Stan's lead on this and it will all work out." Stansfield opened the file, signaling that the meeting was over.

Kennedy's frustration boiled over. "Maybe you should have this same talk with Stan."

"Excuse me?" he asked, looking over the top of his glasses. Kennedy's father had been a colleague of Stansfield's, and more important, a good friend. He had tragically met his death overseas, and because of that, Stansfield had always felt protective of Kennedy. He understood that he had become a father figure to her, and he welcomed that, but at the same time, he was aware that he was sometimes a bit overprotective of her. Maybe that had led him to think her less capable than some of the others.

"You tell me not to allow my feelings to cloud my judgment . . . what about Stan? He's had it in for Mitch since day one. Mitch even saved his life and the mean old cuss can't say so much as thank you."

Stansfield removed his glasses. "I am well aware of Stan's shortcomings. And trust me when I tell you, he and I have discussed them at length."

"The problem, sir, is that he sees too much of himself in Mitch and it drives him nuts that he can't control him."

Stansfield couldn't disagree. Dr. Lewis had alluded to this very problem in several of his reports. In a soothing voice he said, "Irene, we prepare for the worst on something like this, and the truth is everything will more than likely turn out fine."

She shook her head. "I don't think so."

"I know you don't like the way Stan deals with things, but he does have a very good record of delivering. If he's alive, Stan will bring him in."

"I don't think so," she said in a distant voice. "If you want to bring him in, I'm the one to do it. If you want more bodies, then send Stan and his goons over there to try to collect him. Mark my words, sir, it won't end well."

CHAPTER 8

PARIS, FRANCE

RAPP had floated downriver for nearly two hours. The Seine wound through the heart of Paris like a coiled snake. It was impossible to gauge how far he had traveled, but he guessed it was somewhere around two miles. First light approached at roughly the same time he felt the effects of hypothermia settling in. In a way, the cool water was a blessing. It had helped slow his blood flow and ease whatever internal bleeding he had inside his shoulder. But Rapp did not want to be stuck in the river when the sun came up and he was fearful that he might lose consciousness if he stayed in the water much longer. The river flushed him around a big S turn and he saw an industrial yard with holding tanks for petroleum. This early on a Saturday morning there were likely to be few, if any, workers. He decided it was a good place to make ground.

Rapp swam up to the uneven wood pier and found an oil-slick ladder. He clung to it for a second, ignoring the rats that he heard squeaking under the recesses of the pier. His left arm hung limp, although he found that he could at least move his fingers and make a fist. Using his right hand, he got a grip and then found the first rung with his feet. Muscles stiff, he climbed the ladder until he had a clear view of the area. The yard was probably four to five hundred feet wide. Parked near the end of the shallow pier were a forklift, three oil trucks, and a front-end loader. Beyond the vehicles sat an old brick warehouse that ran the length of the yard. The perimeter was marked by a ten-foot fence topped with barbed wire—all of it covered with vines and ivy.

Rapp searched for motion lights and signs of a night watchman, or worse, a dog. He still had the silenced Beretta. He'd debated deep-sixing it every few minutes while he'd been in the river. It was not the kind of thing you wanted to be caught with, but a silenced weapon was also something he'd learned not to toss away carelessly. The thought of a rabid guard dog lurking somewhere nearby made him glad he'd decided to keep the gun. Rapp turned and looked at the other side of the river. There were more warehouses, and as far as he could tell, there wasn't a light or sound of anyone moving about. Parisians weren't ex-actly known for their work ethic, and he doubted anyone would be showing up too early on a weekend, if at all.

Trying to shake the stiffness from his limbs, he climbed onto the pier and began a slow, water-soaked trudge toward the warehouse. He walked upright and with as much purpose as he could muster. He ig-nored the pulsing pain in his shoulder and focused on his eyes and ears. There was no sense crouching and sneaking around in the open. It would only raise the curiosity of an onlooker who might then call the police.

Rapp made it to the corner of the building and steadied himself. Looking back toward the river, he scanned the opposite shore once more to see if anyone was about. Satisfied, he moved on, acutely aware that if he didn't find some warmth and food, he might lose conscious-ness. The air temperature hovered somewhere in the midfifties. Not harsh, but after a few hours in the cold water his strength was be-ing tested. The first few entrances were nothing more than large bay doors for vehicles. Farther down, though, he found a regular door and checked the frame. There were no signs of security wires and the door looked flimsy enough to kick in, but Rapp didn't want to make that kind of noise, so he pulled out his knife. Wedging the forged blade into the gap of the frame and the door, he found the locking mechanism and worked the knife up and down and then back and forth until he had it in the right spot and then he simply leaned his good shoulder into the door and nudged it open.

Rapp stepped into the building and closed the door. Rather than turn on the lights he pulled out his penlight and inspected the door, checking it for wires. Satisfied that he hadn't tripped an alarm, he turned his attention to the large warehouse space to his right. The entire place reeked of fuel. He kept the light pointed at the floor, its red glow illuminating the first tier of black oil drums. Twenty feet ahead on his left was another door. Rapp moved toward it and found it was unlocked. He entered a hallway and closed the door behind him. There were five doors on the left and only two on the right. The first door he checked was locked, as well as the second, but the first door on the right was unlocked. Rapp nudged it open and found a row of lockers as well as a bathroom and two shower stalls. The thought of a warm shower brought a smile to his face, and he was moving toward them before he stopped himself. Before he could do that, he had to check the rest of the building.

He left the locker room, checking the remaining doors on the left. All were locked, but the last door on the right had no door at all—it was a break room. Rapp scanned the lobby first and then went right back to the dirty break room. He yanked open the refrigerator and found a mess of mold and old food. The thing hadn't been cleaned out in years. He closed the door in disgust and turned to the vending machine. He was about to break the glass when he caught himself—better to leave as few signs as possible that he'd been here. He fished out some wet bills and fed them into the machine. After purchasing several candy bars, he headed back to the locker room and closed and locked the door. Then he walked straight into the shower stall, clothes and all, and let the warm water begin to clean the dirty river from him and restore warmth to his body. He ate the candy bars, and when he was done he began peeling his clothes off one item at a time.

His first look at his shoulder was underwhelming. The exit wound was no bigger than a quarter—the clear glue that he'd pumped into the wound had taken on a rose tinge from his blood. It had formed a hard shell that looked like stretched and burned skin. A bruise was forming around the wound. Considering how bad it could have been, Rapp felt very lucky. If the bullet had hit an artery, he would have been dead long ago. There was likely some internal bleeding but it was probably stemmed by the junk he'd shot into the wound. He was dealing with a soft-tissue wound that, while it wasn't life-threatening, hurt like hell. Pain was something, however, that he had learned to deal with a long time ago.

Rapp continued to wash the smell of the river from his skin and hair, letting the warm water bring his muscles back to life. He rinsed his clothes again, wrung them dry, and laid them out on the bench. He was buck-naked other than his dive watch and the backup pistol strapped to his left ankle. The slow float downriver had given him ample time to ponder just what the hell had gone wrong. He still couldn't figure it out. How did the advance team miss a five-man detail? How did he miss them? Rapp had watched Tarek come and go for two days and not once had he seen a single bodyguard accompany him, let alone five heavily armed men. Rapp had played it by the book and then some. He followed him loose, he followed him close, he watched him from afar and waited patiently to see if there were any trailers or foreign assets connected to the Libyan. There were none. Rapp hadn't seen a single clue, but even so there had been that unshakable feeling that something wasn't right. Slowly, the thought began to occur to him that someone had laid a trap for him, and he had walked right into it. That he'd managed to get out of that room alive with all of those bullets flying sent a shudder down his spine. He was lucky to only have been struck by a single bullet.

Rapp stood under the water for a few more minutes and then felt the urge to move. He needed to find someplace secure where he could rest and try to sort this whole thing out. There was the safe house in the Montparnasse neighborhood and the protocols he was supposed to follow, but all that had changed. How well did he really know his handler and the other people on the team? How many different people did they report to, and could they all be trusted? Until he had some answers his survival instincts told him to do what he was trained to do—operate on his own and under everyone's radar, including the CIA's.

Rapp stepped from the shower and started checking lockers. They were all locked. Rapp retrieved his silenced Beretta and shot the first combination lock through the guts. The lock spilled open and he set it on the bench with his clothes. He was rewarded with a dirty rag and not much else. He shot off two more locks and found a decent towel. Rapp dried off and then set about scrounging for some dry clothes. When he was done raiding the lockers he had a pair of gray coveralls, a pair of work boots, a worn blue canvas jacket, and a black wool hat.

He secured all of his weapons and equipment in his new clothes and then went back to the break room. After some more foraging, he found a paper bag for his wet clothes and a prepackaged serving of ramen noodles. Rapp added water, tossed it in the microwave for ninety seconds, and then devoured the noodles. After putting his clothes in the bag along with the shot-out locks, he started for the front of the building, feeling much better than when he'd arrived.

When he looked out at the yard, he was relieved to see that he didn't need to deal with a guard—just a chain-link fence and barbed wire. In the gray morning light, Rapp spotted the separate gate for employees. He checked the door for security wires and then left the building, closing the door behind him. He walked casually across the yard to the gate and drew his silenced Beretta one more time. Two shots disabled the lock. He stuffed it in the oversized pocket of his jacket, opened and then closed the gate. Rapp crossed the street to the sidewalk and headed away from the rising sun. His mind turned to the operation, and he once again began asking himself how well he knew the people he worked for. The answer was that he didn't and that even at his relatively young age of twenty-five he could spot dysfunction, and there was some major dysfunction in his group. He decided the safe house was out of the question.

Three blocks later, he found himself crossing the river, his mood dark and cautious. Halfway across the bridge he began casually tossing the shot-out locks over the side and into the river. He didn't want to throw away the Beretta, but he knew he had to. He still had his backup pistol, and the silencer would fit it as well, but he would lose the capacity of the Beretta 92F. With his gloves on, he drew the weapon from his holster, unscrewed the silencer, and stuffed it in the oversized jacket pocket. Using his nearly worthless left hand he ejected the magazine, tossed it over the side, and then began stripping the gun, dumping pieces as he went. By the time he reached the other bank, he was focused on Irene Kennedy—his handler. She was by necessity the person who knew the most about him, and the details of this mission. His orders came from her. If anyone were in a position to set him up it would be her.

Rapp thought of his protocols. Missing a check-in was a cardinal sin. They would all flip back in D.C. if he didn't call and do so quickly. Add to that the less than surgical carnage back at the hotel and there would be some very upset people. He could practically hear Stan Hurley cussing at the top of his lungs. Rapp suddenly realized how this would go down. Hurley would blame him for screwing this up. He'd blame him for missing the security detail, and there would be hell to pay. The decision for the moment was easy. Being shot was all the excuse Rapp needed to explain why he didn't check in, at least in terms of D.C., but there was someone else he needed to alert. Rapp did not want to disappoint her, and if he didn't call her, he'd do more than that. She worried about him under normal circumstances, and this was far from normal. She knew something was in the works and needed to be out of France for a while. That was why they were supposed to meet in Brussels at one this afternoon. Their rendezvous was set in stone. If he didn't show up, she might do something stupid like call Stan Hurley.

No one knew they were seeing each other, and if she called Hurley, the man would go berserk. Midstride, a shot of pain seized Rapp's shoulder and ripped down his arm. He stopped walking, stopped breathing, and with his right arm he grabbed a light post to steady himself. Despite the chill, beads of sweat coated his forehead. A wave of nausea hit him and for a second he thought he might throw up. Ten seconds passed and then twenty and thirty, and finally the pain started to pull back like the tide going out. It left his fingers first and then slowly worked its way up his arm. Rapp took a couple of deep breaths and then started to walk again. He needed to find a pharmacy and then a hotel. He had a few in mind, the kind of places where he would blend in with tourists. And he would have to call Greta. Trying to clean the wound on his own would not be easy. She was far from squeamish about what he did. In fact, it turned her on, and the alternative had too many unknowns. If he didn't show, she might cause some serious problems. He would have to find a pay phone and call her. If he was lucky, he might even catch her before she left Geneva. He also missed her, which was something he didn't want to admit to himself. It had only been three weeks since they'd last seen each other, and he'd found himself counting the days until they reunited in Belgium like some love-struck high-schooler.

Rapp laughed to himself as he moved down the empty street. He was walking a very thin line. The list of things he'd kept from his handlers was growing rather lengthy, and he knew they would take it as evidence that he couldn't be trusted. He knew more than they thought, however. He wasn't the only one breaking the rules.

CHAPTER 9

WASHINGTON, D.C.

SECRETARY of State Franklin Wilson was wearing a white oxford shirt under a yellow cardigan sweater. At seventy-one, with thinning gray hair, he looked every part the wise elder statesman. A successful attorney, he'd served in three White Houses; the first as a chief of staff, then as the secretary of defense, and now as secretary of state. The money came from his wife's family—a lucrative auto parts business in Ohio. The reputation was all his. He'd graduated near the top of his class from Harvard Law and joined one of D.C.'s top law firms. In between his stints as a public servant, he would return to the law firm, of which he was now a fully vested partner. It had been a great run. He was one of the titans of the District—a man who was respected by both parties and the press.

Despite all of his accomplishments, he was in a sour mood. The house felt lonely on this fall Saturday afternoon. Wilson had instructed his staff to take a few hours off so he could make this meeting as private as possible. The real reason it felt lonely, though, was that his wife of forty-seven years was gone—not physically but mentally. She'd been diagnosed with Alzheimer's just two years ago, and although they'd all held out hope that the disease would advance slowly, it had instead ravaged her mind at a swift pace. Within a year, she'd forgotten her kids and grandchildren and could barely remember her husband. Six months after that she was dead to the world. One month earlier, Franklin Wilson did what he swore he would never do.

At the urging of friends, his staff, and his children, he checked his wife into a home where she could receive twenty-four-hour care. That was the justification, at any rate, but Wilson couldn't shake the feeling that he'd abandoned her. It haunted him every day. This beautiful Georgetown brownstone where they'd hosted so many parties, with the who's who of D.C., had now become a mausoleum for him. He refused to sell, feeling it would be another betrayal to her and the memory of the great lady she had been before that insidious disease had begun to eat away at the very thing that made her *her*. Wilson knew he'd lost some focus, but the demands of his job kept him busy and provided a welcome distraction from the tragic hand he'd been dealt.

When the doorbell sounded, he felt his mood lift. There was important business that needed to be conducted. Wilson bounded from behind his desk, proceeded across the marble foyer, and opened the door to his five-story Georgetown brownstone. He enthusiastically greeted his guest. "Paul, thank you for coming by on such short notice."

Paul Cooke, the CIA's deputy director, returned the smile and shook the secretary's hand. "My pleasure, Mr. Secretary. I always like an excuse to spend some time in Georgetown on a fall afternoon."

"I know what you mean, and call me Franklin when we're not in our official capacities," Wilson said as he closed the door and led his visitor down the hall. "That's why I bought the place, by the way. No suburbs for me. Too quiet." Wilson opened a door and pointed down the steps. "Do you like to play billiards?"

Cooke hiked his shoulders. "What Harvard man doesn't?"

Wilson slapped him on the back. "Good man. You're class of sixty-five, right?"

"Yes."

Once they were downstairs, Wilson turned on the stereo and flipped a few switches behind the bar. A hearty fire was already burning and a college football game was on the TV. Wilson didn't bother asking his guest what he wanted to drink. He grabbed two lowballs and placed three ice cubes in each glass before filling them halfway with single-malt scotch. He gave Cooke his glass and said, "I hope you don't mind hanging out down here, but I had certain devices installed in this room that make it easier for us to discuss things of a delicate nature."

Working at the CIA, Cooke understood all too well. He wondered who Wilson had used and when the equipment had been installed. Listening devices and countermeasures were constantly changing.

Wilson held up his glass. "To Harvard. The finest institution in the land."

Cooke smiled. "To Harvard."

Wilson made small talk while he racked the balls and continued to keep the conversation light all the way through the first game. After trouncing Cooke, Wilson smashed the second break and moved the conversation in a more serious direction. "Paul, may I ask you something?"

"Of course."

"This is serious, Paul . . . from one Harvard man to another." Wilson looked at the other man from across the table for a moment, allowing the words to sink in. The innuendo was simple. We are both gentlemen. We do not lie to each other.

Cooke inclined his head respectfully, signaling that he understood.

"Do you trust Thomas Stansfield?"

Cooke was in the process of sipping his scotch, which was a good thing because it helped conceal the grin on his face. He quickly put his business expression on and said, "That's an interesting question."

Wilson knew he'd have to lead this one by the nose so he said, "Listen, I've known Thomas for close to thirty years. During the Cold War there was no one better, but the Cold War is over, and I'm afraid he's failing to keep pace."

Cooke had known there was some reason the secretary wanted to see him, but he had not expected it to be about Thomas Stansfield. He gave a noncommittal nod.

"Do you trust him?" Wilson asked again.

Cooke allowed himself to laugh openly. "If you knew him as you say you do, you wouldn't bother asking that question. Thomas Stansfield was born to be a spy and is the most secretive man I have ever met in my life."

Wilson pointed his glass at Cooke and extended his forefinger. "My point exactly."

Treading carefully, Cooke added, "It does kind of go along with the job description."

"To a degree, but he is not a king unto himself. He still has to answer to certain people." Wilson searched the younger man's face for a sign that he could be an ally. So far he was getting nothing. "He's never been very good at handling oversight, and I'm afraid with the director slot open he's gotten even worse."

The previous director had unexpectedly retired for health reasons one month earlier and the president had yet to nominate a replacement, so for the meantime, Cooke was minding the store. "He does tend to run his own turf, and doesn't take too kindly to anyone sticking his nose in his business."

Now we're getting somewhere, Wilson thought to himself. He refilled their drinks and kept the conversation moving in the direction he thought best for his objectives. He would touch on Stansfield and then move on to D.C. gossip or some funny story about him and the president pulling a practical joke on the hapless vice president. But he kept coming back to Stansfield. It was in the middle of the fifth game of pool and third drink that Wilson saw his opening. "Paul, I need to confide in you."

Cooke leaned against his pool cue, understanding that they were finally going to get to the heart of the matter. "All right."

"You're on the president's short list for director."

This came as a surprise to Cooke. His intel had told him that the president was set on bringing in someone who hadn't been tainted by the Agency. "Really?"

"Yes . . . and would you care to know how you ended up on that list?"

Cooke nodded.

"I put you there. I told the president you are a man who we can trust to get the job done."

"Thank you, sir." Cooke's guard was up. He barely knew Wilson. If the man was recommending him to the president for the top spot at Langley, he must want something in return.

"Do you know who else is on that short list?"

"I've heard a few names," Cooke said honestly. The rumor mill in D.C. was churning out a couple of new possibilities every week.

"Thomas Stansfield is on that list," Wilson said, shaking his head. "There's a group of very influential senators who are pushing for him. And I mean pushing hard."

Cooke nodded. Stansfield was connected, and on top of that, he knew where all the bodies were buried. Cooke would never admit it, but he'd always considered the deputy director of Operations a potential adversary and someone not to be taken lightly.

"The last thing we need is a Cold War cowboy running Langley," Wilson said with real vigor. "That's why I'm pushing you. You know the place, you've come up through the ranks, and you already have the respect of the front-line troops. All I need to know is, can you handle Stansfield?"

Cooke definitely knew the place. He'd worked there for almost thirty years. He'd come up on the administration side of things and knew how to run a tight ship. As for the respect of the front-line troops, that was a bit of a stretch, but he definitely had the respect of the majority of the employees working out of the Langley campus. As far as handling Thomas Stansfield, that was a tricky question. He wasn't sure anyone could actually handle the man. His contacts ran deep, and his ability to see three moves ahead of his enemies had always made him a formidable foe. The Russians actually respected him, which spoke volumes. Stansfield saw angles and opportunity where others saw chaos, danger, and a problem not worth tackling. But Cooke had a few surprises of his own.

He took a gulp of scotch and decided to go all in. "I can handle Thomas. It won't be easy, but I can do it."

"Handling and reining him in are two different things. I need you to get the man under control. I need you to promise me you'll get him playing by the rules. I've been warning the president for some time that Stansfield is a ticking bomb. Sooner or later, one of his little operations is going to blow up in our faces and he's going to embarrass the crap out of the president. We'll end up with committee hearings that'll drag on for years. It's hard enough getting elected president, but it's tough as all hell to get reelected and even more so when you're being dogged by a scandal."

Cooke nodded. He'd seen it happen before. "I understand."

"So we can count on you?"

Cooke wasn't sure, but he'd figure something out. "You can count on me."

"Good." Wilson raised his glass and tapped it against Cooke's. "I'll tell the president you're our man."

Cooke took a sip and thought to himself, *Just like that, I'm the next director of the Central Intelligence Agency.* It had been a lifelong dream.

"There's something we want you to look into first," Wilson said.

The glass hadn't left his lips yet and Cooke thought, *Here comes the catch.*

"This crap that went down in Paris last night."

"Yes," Cooke said, hiding his surprise at the new direction of the conversation.

"The president is pissed. He spoke directly to the Israeli prime minister this morning and they are denying any involvement."

"They always do. That's how it works."

"Yeah . . . well, this time it's different. There are certain things I'm not at liberty to discuss, but believe me when I tell you the president believes Mossad didn't have a hand in it."

Cooke's face showed no emotion.

"I wish I could say more, but I can't. You're just going to have to trust me on this. Can you do that?"

Cooke wasn't sure, but he wanted to see where this was headed. "I trust you, Franklin."

"Good." Wilson took his cue and leaned it against the wall. "Here's where things are going to get a little dicey." Not quite sure how to take the next step, he decided to simply spit it out. "I think Thomas Stansfield is involved."

"Do you have any proof?"

"Nothing concrete. Just some things I've picked up. The point is he's been running afoul of congressional oversight for years, and now I think he's really stepped in it."

"Thomas Stansfield is not to be taken lightly. If you want me to get him under control you're going to have to give me more."

"I will, but I need you to do something first," Wilson said, sidestepping the request. "You remember a foul son of a bitch named Stan Hurley?"

Cooke certainly did, but he played it cool. "I know of him."

"I thought you would. The bastard supposedly retired, but guys like Hurley don't retire, they keep screwing with stuff in the shadows until the day they die."

Offering no reaction one way or the other, Cooke simply said, "We have a lot of retired operatives. Not all of them remain as active as Mr. Hurley."

"So you're familiar with what he's been up to?"

"I hear rumors, but they're just rumors."

"Well," Wilson said, nodding his head vigorously, "you can believe at least half of them. The man is a certified paranoid schizophrenic and a sadist."

"He was very effective back in the day. At least that's what they say."

"The operative phrase being 'back in the day.' It's a new world now. No more of this Check Point Charlie, Berlin espionage where we need our own ruthless son of a bitch to go up against the Russians' ruthless son of a bitch. The world is changing, Paul. Satellites and information are tearing down walls. What we need is intelligence and diplomacy. Hearts and minds are the keys. The president wants someone he can trust at Langley. Someone who is not only going to get Stansfield under control but will make sure goons like Stan Hurley are really retired. Can you do that for us?"

Cooke relished the challenge. Mustering up every bit of confidence he had and then some, he said, "I'm your man."

"Good." Wilson slapped him on the back. "Get to the bottom of what in the hell happened in Paris last night, and keep a lid on it. Report only to me. We don't want the CIA airing its dirty laundry and embarrassing the president."

"No FBI?" Cooke asked, feigning surprise.

"If we can avoid getting them involved, great. If we have to bring them in, the president will make that call." Wilson wasn't about to tell him he was making this up as he went. Part of his job was to insulate the president from scandal, and that's what he was doing. "Focus on Stansfield and Hurley. Find out what they've been up to. Bring it to me, and we'll have them dealt with. And then you will enjoy one of the quickest confirmations this town has ever seen."

A broad smile spread across Cooke's face. It wasn't born simply of confidence, or of the thought of occupying the corner office on the seventh floor of the Old Headquarters Building. Cooke had been building a nice thick file on Stansfield and his old friend Stan Hurley.

CHAPTER 10

PARIS, FRANCE

PAUL Fournier looked up at the massive Sacré-Coeur Basilica shining on the hill—a stunning blend of Roman and Byzantine architecture. The church was a thing of genuine beauty that was almost certainly unappreciated by the men he was about to meet. Fournier took a deep drag from his cigarette before flicking it to the curb. Even at this late hour tourists were climbing all over the basilica grounds like ants. Two of Fournier's men were with him. One had already gone ahead to make sure no one was lurking in the shadows and the other was following twenty steps back.

It had been a long day and Fournier wanted some answers, although he thought he had a fairly good idea of what had gone wrong. He walked around the front of the church and continued down a sidewalk, the crowd of tourists thinning as he went. His man flashed him the clear signal and Fournier moved up a short flight of steps, under a stone arch, and tapped on a door three times. A moment passed before the heavy door opened, revealing an old priest with hunched shoulders and cloudy eyes. He gave the intelligence agent a knowing smile but did not speak. With a gnarled hand, he waved for the visitor to enter and then closed and locked the door behind them.

"Thank you, Monsignor," Fournier said in a tender voice. "How have you been?"

The priest answered in a weathered voice. "Life has been good to me, young Paul, but I'm afraid my days here on earth are drawing to an end."

Fournier had been hearing this same line for five years. He did not know the exact age of de Fleury, but he looked to be at least ninety. The monsignor was a legend in the intelligence community. When the Nazis occupied Paris in 1940, de Fleury was a priest at the famous Dome Church in the Invalides Quarter near the Eiffel Tower. The church was the focal point of a grand gesture by Louis XIV, founded in 1670 to honor his wounded and homeless veterans, and of course the Sun King himself. In the subsequent years, the area around the church and veterans' home became an administrative hub for the French military, and most famously in 1840 the final resting place of Emperor Napoleon. Hitler himself came to visit the church and pay homage to the tomb of the man and military tactician he so greatly admired. German troops were billeted in the surrounding buildings during the occupation. Many of them were Catholic, and de Fleury was fortunate to be fluent in German. These German soldiers lined up at his confessional weekly, divulging bits of information, but that was only the start. De Fleury insinuated himself into the company of the high-ranking German officers who were in charge of the occupation. He passed himself off as a Jew-hating Catholic who owed his allegiance to God and the pope. God had not spoken to him, but the pope had made it clear that the Church was neutral in this war. De Fleury passed along crucial information to the French Resistance, and after the war was over, he was privately awarded the Legion of Honor by General Charles de Gaulle.

Fournier had been introduced to him by his old boss years before. The introduction came with the assurance that Father de Fleury could be trusted in all matters involving the security of the Republic.

Fournier placed a gentle hand on the priest's shoulder and said, "But what a great life it has been."

De Fleury gave him a sideways glance. The hint of a grin spread across his lips, and he thought to himself, *If only this young one knew.* "Your guests are here."

"They are early," Fournier responded, not able to hide the surprise in his voice. He himself was thirty minutes early.

"And very nervous." De Fleury kept his eyes on the well-worn stone floor. Shuffling his feet as he moved through the shadows, he added, "And not the most well-mannered men, by the way."

Fournier allowed himself to show some anger. The old man was too blind to see it, and if he did, Fournier didn't see the harm. De Fleury was not long for this world, and his contacts back at the Directorate were all dead. He sighed to release some of the tension that was building in anticipation of the meeting. Dealing with these idiots was testing his resolve. "I'm sorry for their behavior. I will have a word with them."

The old priest stopped at the top of a flight of stairs. He looked down into the dim light of the crypt below. "You will have to excuse me, but my legs will no longer carry me down these stairs, and I will be taking up permanent residence there soon enough."

Fournier laughed lightly at the old man's humor. "I understand, Monsignor." Fournier pressed an envelope into the man's hand. "Your service to the Republic is admired by many."

"We all do our part." De Fleury took the money and slid it into a fold in his vestments. He would count it later when he was alone in his room in the rectory.

Fournier started down the steps. The air grew thick and stale with a mixture of incense and decomposed bodies. When he reached the lower level he looked down the length of the crypt with its vaulted ceiling and alcoves that sprouted to the sides every twenty feet. Fournier moved briskly across the floor, ignoring the various famous people interred in the basement of this celebrated basilica. At the end of the hall, he stepped into a small private chapel and felt the presence of the men off to his left. Fournier put on his mask of calm and approached them. From five paces away, he saw the bandage on Samir Fadi's face.

"Why are you making us meet in such a place?"

"What is the problem now, Samir?" Fournier had known this degenerate for less than a month and he was already tired of this man's caustic attitude.

"This is a fucking Catholic church," Samir snapped. "A shrine built to honor the crusaders who killed my ancestors."

"Actually," the voice came from the far side of the chapel, "this beautiful church is a tribute to France's victory in the Franco-Prussian war of 1870. You should read your history, Samir. The Koran makes you a very narrow-minded person."

Fournier breathed a sigh of relief. It was Max Vega, or at least that was one of his names. Fournier knew of two others. Unlike the two men he was facing, Max was a man of intellect and civility.

"I don't care when it was built," Samir snarled. "It is an offense to my faith."

"The important thing," Max said in an easy voice, "is that this is a safe place for us to meet."

"It is a convenient place for him to meet," Samir said, pointing a finger at the Frenchman. "It reeks of death."

Max wandered over at a casual pace. "Samir, you need to show some respect to our friend, and lest you forget, Christianity predates our faith by some six hundred years." Samir started to complain, but Max shushed him with a wag of his finger. "I have never heard Paul complain when you have asked him to meet you in one of our houses of worship."

"That is different. We don't fill our mosques with dead bodies." Samir spat on the ground.

Fournier was a casual Catholic, but even he couldn't stomach this kind of disrespect. Turning to Max, he said, "I give him protection, and this is how he shows his gratitude."

"He is right," Max announced in a disappointed voice. "Is it possible, Samir, that you are mad at yourself for your own failures?"

The comment stung. "What is that supposed to mean?" Samir asked, his eyes wild with anger.

"I would say it's pretty obvious," Fournier said, folding his arms across his chest and letting his weight settle on one leg.

"You were not there last night, so I would be careful what conclusions you draw."

"Conclusions? What conclusion should I draw from nine murders in the heart of Paris? You came here to kill one man, you failed, and now I have nine bodies to deal with."

Samir stepped forward to within striking distance. "I will only say it one more time. You weren't there, so I think you should be careful what tone you use with me."

Fournier laughed. "I'll use whatever tone I like, you little turd. You are here because of my generosity. I handed you this assassin on a silver platter and you fucked it up so badly I've spent the entire day trying to clean up your mess."

"My mess!" Samir yelled. "I think you set me up! I think you are playing both sides in this. Profiting from them and us with the same information."

"Lower your voice, you idiot," Fournier hissed.

"Why . . . are you afraid the dead people will hear me?"

"No . . . I'm afraid one of the priests will come down here to investigate why they have a screaming terrorist in the basement of their blessed church."

Before Samir could respond, Max stepped forward and motioned for his man to back off. In a sensible voice he ordered, "Samir, tell our friend what went wrong last night."

"I will tell you what went wrong last night." Samir nervously shifted his weight from one foot to the other. "We were set up. The assassin was waiting for us. When we came into the room, he was concealed, and he shot my men before they had a chance to fire their weapons."

Fournier shook his head, not buying a word of it. "You are a liar, Samir."

"How dare you!" Samir snarled.

"I was there, this morning. There were bullet holes everywhere. Shell casings littered the floor, and I saw at least three empty magazines lying next to your men. Your men were not ambushed . . . they were outmatched."

"We were ambushed," Samir said, his eyes wild with rage. "Look at my face. I barely escaped. I have wood splinters in my cheek. I was almost blinded."

"Yes . . . well, you are doing much better than your men, so consider yourself lucky."

The third man finally spoke up. Rafique Aziz looked at Fournier and asked, "How did he know we were coming?"

This one made Fournier nervous. Samir was a zealot, and he was blinded by his own rage, but Aziz was more complex. He had the anger as well, but was more calculating. Fournier had been around killers before, and Aziz had that same look in his eyes. "Who says he knew you were coming?"

"Samir."

"Samir," Fournier said, scoffing at the idea.

"Yes. I believe my brother."

Fournier took a step back and looked to Max. "I know one thing. Samir here was given a golden opportunity last night and he blew it. And then after he blew it, he managed to kill three innocent civilians on his way out of the hotel, and now he wants to blame this on me." Then, looking back at Samir, he said, "I'm not the one who should be explaining myself. In fact, you are lucky I don't have you thrown into the Mediterranean and drowned."

Samir drew his gun and pointed it directly at Fournier's face. "How dare you!"

Aziz drew a knife from his waist. "Maybe we should slit your throat and rid ourselves of a traitor."

"Put your toys away, gentlemen," Max ordered.

Samir did as he was told but Aziz kept his knife out, proving he was less willing to comply. Locking a menacing stare onto Fournier, he said, "Maybe we should start hijacking your planes again and blowing up trains. Maybe our Muslim brothers in Libya will start to divert some of their oil to an ally who appreciates our friendship."

"And maybe I should find this assassin on my own and hand over all of my information on your organization. Give him all the pretty pictures we have of you and your various identities. I'm sure he would be grateful, and based on what happened last night, he would probably move you to the top of his list."

"And maybe we should alert your superiors to your double dealings," Samir shot back.

"Samir, you are not very bright. My superiors know all about this relationship."

"Do they know about the money we have paid you?" Aziz asked.

"I have no idea what you are talking about," Fournier said with a sly grin.

Max cleared his throat. "Enough of this nonsense. What is done is done. Last night was a failure. Now we must decide on our next move."

"Next move?" Fournier asked.

"How do we find this man?"

"We don't do a thing. You two are going to leave France," Fournier said, pointing to Aziz and Samir, "and do so as quickly as possible. You will have to find some other way to trap him."

"Why must they leave?" Max asked.

"Because we have nine dead bodies . . . one of whom happens to be an important diplomat. Every law enforcement and intelligence asset we have will be thrown at this thing, and the press is going to cover every detail."

"But," Max said, "the news reports are saying that it was all the act of a single assassin."

"You can thank me for that, but unfortunately that story isn't going to hold up."

"Why?"

"Because the crime scene investigator is very good at what she does, and sometime in the next forty-eight hours she is going to get the ballistics back on the victims and things aren't going to match. She already noticed some inconsistencies."

"Such as?" Max asked.

"Your four men who were killed were hit with one or two well-placed shots. Tarek, the prostitute, the guests, and the employee were sprayed with a burst of bullets to the chest and then finished off with multiple shots to the head." Fournier shrugged. "I removed certain things from the crime scene to slow them down, but trust me, it will only be a matter of time before the lead investigator figures out that two men walked away from that gunfight."

"How?" Samir asked incredulously.

"Because the assassin is a professional, unlike you. He hit his targets with very few shots while you and your men hit everything except what you were trying to hit. She's going to find a hollow-point slug in Tarek's head that is going to match the slugs that killed your men. She's going to pull a bevy of slugs from the walls that will match the type of ammunition that killed the other two guests and the worker in the alley, and then she's going to find the surveillance equipment we installed and she's going to start sniffing around in places where I don't want her sniffing around."

"Who cares?" Samir said dismissively. "We will kill her."

Fournier was done pleading his case to this idiot. He turned to face Max and said, "If he even suggests this again, I will have him killed."

"I understand." Turning to Samir, Max said, "Do not open your mouth again, or I will kill you myself."

"Last night was a bloody mess," Fournier said. "Libya is raising holy hell, OPEC is furious, and everyone in the French government is enraged that another government might be behind such a bloodbath.

A lot of people are suddenly very interested in finding out the identity of this assassin, and who is behind him."

"So, they will do our work for us."

"That is my hope. This man has proven extremely elusive, but up to this moment, very few people even knew he existed."

"Now everyone will be looking for him."

"Exactly."

"What about this investigator? Are you afraid she will stumble onto what we were up to?"

Fournier had spent much of the day worrying about this, but he wasn't about to tell these fools after they'd suggested she be killed. "I will make sure her focus is on foreign intelligence agencies. For now we need the press to continue to report that it was a single assassin."

"Why?" Aziz asked.

Max finally saw where Fournier was headed. "The assassin has become a liability."

"Correct . . . Up until now the man has been a ghost. Killing only his targets and a few bodyguards. Last night was a mess. Whoever is behind him is not going to be happy that this one was so sloppy."

"You think they will dispose of him?" Max asked.

"We'll see." Fournier thought of what he would do under the same circumstances. If one of his men had created such disarray, he would most certainly have that option on the table. He needed more information. Two avenues had crowded Fournier's thoughts. "For now, we need to sit back and see who pops up."

"Pops up?" Max asked, not understanding.

"Events like this have a way of attracting intelligence assets. The Brits have already called, Libya no doubt has a few men on their way over, and Israel and the Americans have already offered help. It will be interesting to see who shows up over the next few days. We have stepped up surveillance at the airports and the embassies. We will see who comes sniffing around, and with a little luck, they might point us in the right direction."

Max considered this for a moment and then nodded. "That makes sense."

As far as Fournier was concerned, it was their only option. He could not afford to draw any more attention to himself. Fournier had been pulled into this because of his relationship with Max. They had offered him a six-figure retainer and hinted in a not-so-subtle way that his help would go a long way toward ensuring their arrangement that Hezbollah and her sister organizations would stay out of France. Seven weeks ago it had seemed a very straightforward deal. Now it was an absolute mess. Fournier should have asked more questions.

"If you want to catch this man," Fournier said, "it would help to know how Tarek fits in with the other men who were killed by this assassin. Are they linked in some way? Did Tarek do anything while he was working for the Mukhabarat that would cause a country to hunt him down?"

He most certainly had, but Max would have to carefully consider if he would share this information. "I will ask."

Fournier could tell he was holding back. "Max, our relationship has been one of mutual trust. You are going to have to open up if you want my help, and if that means telling me Tarek double-crossed the Russians or stole money from them or some other country, you need to tell me now."

"This has nothing to do with the Russians."

"You're sure?"

"Yes."

"Then who? You must have some idea."

Max did not bother to look at the other two men. "We have some ideas."

"Then please share them, because if you don't, you will never catch this man. As it is, he is probably sunning himself on a beach halfway around the world. After something like this, he will lie low for a long time and the trail will grow cold. If we want to catch him, we have to move fast."

Max was under no illusion that he could trust Fournier, but his points were valid. He could never share everything, but maybe he could give him just enough to help point him in the right direction. "I will pull together what I can and get it to you in the morning."

"Good," Fournier said, turning to leave, "and make sure Samir is on the first flight out tomorrow."

CHAPTER 11

BALTIMORE, MARYLAND

THE bar was decorated in a tacky nautical theme. Thick ropes were wrapped around dry timbers that were meant to look like the pilings of a pier. Fishing nets adorned the walls and were peppered with starfish, crabs, buoys, and nautical flags. A stuffed one-armed pirate with a hook and droopy mustache greeted patrons at the door. Stan Hurley paid the decor a passing glance. As long as they had bourbon and something salty, he didn't care. Hurley liked to drink. He'd done so on six of the seven continents and had imbibed the best brown liquor that money could buy in the world's finest establishments, as well as bellied up to makeshift bars in shacks in Third World shitholes and thrown back counterfeited American bourbon that tasted like paint thinner. The Crab Shack at Baltimore Washington International Airport was tasteless, to be sure, but the booze was real, and at the moment that's all that mattered to the old CIA clandestine service officer.

This Rapp thing had put him in a foul mood—not that he was known for his bubbly personality, but today he was unusually rank. Hurley was a surly bastard, and he'd be the first to admit it. This mess in Paris, though, had him really pissed off. The brown liquid that he swirled around in his glass was helping him focus in the brooding way that so often led him to find the way out of a fucking mess. Hurley blamed himself to a degree, but only because he hadn't screamed louder and more often and bashed in some heads. Hurley would never dream of laying a hand on Kennedy. She was like family to him, and of course, that was part of the problem. He had survived the blast that had killed Kennedy's father and had carried the guilt with him every day since. He knew Stansfield was affected similarly, if not worse, and that only added to the problem. It wasn't that Kennedy didn't have her talents; it was that they had a big blind spot in their hearts when it came to her. It made it all the harder on Hurley. This was her mess, and he had failed her. He should have jumped in and shut this thing down months ago. He sipped his bourbon and thought back to the first time he laid eyes on Rapp. His gut had told him everything he needed to know. He didn't like him, and he didn't trust him. Hurley had tried his best to get him bounced from the program, but Rapp had proven to be tougher to break than he had thought. The little shit had conned them and Kennedy was too naïve to see it. Rapp was all about himself. A one-man wrecking ball, bent on killing every last terrorist son of a bitch he could get his hands on.

A broad grin fell across Hurley's leathery face. Rapp's goals at least were worthy. He had to give him that much, but that wasn't the problem. Hurley wanted to kill the assholes every bit as badly as Rapp did, but it was a bit more complicated than that. This was a delicate business, where patience was every bit the virtue. Yes, you had to have the mind and stomach for killing and getting your hands messy, but you also had to have the patience of a hunter. They called it "clandestine" for a reason. It was important to keep a low profile and keep as many people in the dark as possible. Rapp had blazed a damn trail of bodies around the Mediterranean and had brought way too much attention to their work. They'd argued about it in London only a few months ago. Hurley had tried his best to get Rapp drunk enough to open up.

About all he got out of him was that Rapp didn't care if they knew he was coming after them. He wanted it that way. He wanted his targets sleeping with one eye open. He wanted them to know that he was coming after them.

Hurley had blown his lid. Unleashed a tirade on Rapp, who seemed impervious to everything he told him. When Hurley demanded a response, Rapp calmly explained the psychological toll that he planned on extracting from these men. That it wasn't enough to simply kill them. He wanted them to lie awake at night and wonder who was after them. He wanted them to spend their entire waking day glancing over their shoulders and looking under every car they rode in and every bed they slept in. He wanted to drive them insane. Hurley knew he had his own issues, but he was starting to worry that Rapp had a screw loose. And then Rapp explained his motive. Thousands of people the world over lay awake at night in agonizing pain, lamenting the loss of loved ones at the hands of these cowards. Rapp wanted them to experience genuine fear. He wanted them to be stuck alone with their thoughts, and have to confront what they had done and realize that it was going to lead to their own death.

Hurley remembered the involuntary shudder that had crawled up his back that night. He remembered looking across at Rapp and thinking he was someone to be feared, and Stan Hurley didn't fear anyone. Sipping his bourbon at the bar, he thought back to that night in London and wondered why he hadn't stopped it all then. If he had gone back to the shrink or Stansfield they would have pulled Rapp in, but there was a part of Hurley that savored the idea of unleashing Rapp on these fuck sticks. America had grown too cautious—had turned the other cheek a dozen too many times, as far as Hurley was concerned. There was something basic and satisfying about stepping back and letting Rapp continue on his spree. Hurley knew now it had been a mistake—a horrible one. This quiet little operation had gone public in a very bad way, and it was his responsibility to make sure the mess was cleaned up, before it mushroomed into something worse.

He stared into the amber booze as if it were a fire and allowed his mind to drift down a corridor and consider an option that he was none too fond of using. It wouldn't be the first time he'd had to kill one of his brothers, but the others had been traitors. Three of them in total over all these years, and he hadn't so much as batted an eye at the order. He remembered each kill as if it had been yesterday. The first two he'd shot in the head and the third he'd nearly decapitated with a long combat knife. He wondered if he would have to kill Rapp. The matter had not been discussed, and as far as Hurley was concerned, it didn't need to be. Rapp would either get his shit together and come in like he was told, or Hurley would be left with no other option.

The problem, Hurley knew, was Rapp's maverick streak. The little shit was uncontrollable and clever as hell. He had played Kennedy to perfection. This was her disaster, but Hurley should have been more forceful. It was as if they were two squabbling parents and Rapp was their child. They had argued in front of him, he saw his opening, and he had learned to pit them against each other. He had used it to get what he wanted and now Hurley was being called in to tidy things up. Rapp was cocky, arrogant, and an uncontrollable loose cannon, but one question remained—was he a traitor?

Hurley was of two minds on this one. Part of him hoped Rapp was and part of him desperately wanted them all to walk away from this madness and allow things to cool down. Everything that Hurley had predicted had come true in Paris, and now it was his responsibility to fix it. He'd been warning both Stansfield and Kennedy for months that they were giving Rapp too much latitude. That sooner or later he was going to step in it and create a major incident. They continued to point to Rapp's results as if the ends somehow justified the means. Hurley knew different. Discipline was paramount in this line of work and Rapp was anything but disciplined. He was a cowboy who had a habit of deviating from the operational game plan as a matter of course.

Hurley took a swig and sucked in some air through his lips. He wanted a cigarette something fierce. Unfortunately, while he'd spent the last thirty-some years trotting around the globe killing bad guys, the wussification of America had taken hold. Now if he wanted to smoke he had to travel halfway back down the concourse to some specially designated glass room where all the smokers were on display like zoo animals. He'd visited the room only once, and was so aggravated by all the uptight do-gooders who walked by with their condemning looks that he swore he'd never do it again.

"Fucking sheep," Hurley mumbled to himself. "They don't have a fucking clue."

"Excuse me?" the man sitting to Hurley's right asked.

Hurley didn't feel like it, but he put a smile on his face. "Sorry, just talking to myself." He stared back into his drink and hoped the guy would drop it. He needed to round up his team and get on a flight. Kicking the shit out of some businessman might complicate things. Fortunately, the guy left him alone and Hurley got back to thinking about cigarettes and how he couldn't wait to get to France. *Say what you want about the French, at least they still let you smoke.*

A looming figure approached from the concourse and grabbed the open stool to Hurley's left. He saw Victor in the reflection of the bar mirror. That wasn't his real name, but it was what they all called him. His real name was Chet Bramble, and while he wasn't very soft around the edges, he was someone Hurley could depend on. Victor didn't take a shit without asking for permission, and that was the way Hurley liked it. If it had been Victor and him in France none of this would have happened. Victor knew how to follow orders, and Hurley was too smart to miss four bodyguards. For the hundredth time since hearing about the debacle Hurley asked himself how Rapp could have fucked things up so badly.

"Steve and Todd are here," the big man said.

Hurley looked over at Victor. His appearance was menacing, which was both an asset and a drawback. Big men were nice to have around if you needed heavy lifting, or you wanted to scare the crap out of someone, but they weren't good for clandestine work. They attracted too much attention. In addition to his large stature, Victor scared people. Pending violence hung on him like a neon sign. His size wasn't freakish by any means. He was six-foot-four and weighed a touch more than 250 pounds. It was his block head, thick neck, and broad shoulders that made him stand out. His barrel chest tapered to a relatively narrow waist and a set of powerful legs. And size was not his only problem. His most prominent feature was a hooded brow that hung like a cliff over a pair of cold black eyes. There were plenty of people who didn't like Victor. He'd been run out of the army for punching an officer. Hurley had been in the army himself and could relate to anyone who thought that the big green machine was a little too monolithic. He'd seen his fair share of officers who could use a good smack, so it was easy for him to turn a blind eye to Victor's transgressions.

Besides, Hurley liked having a big rottweiler around to keep people on edge. He held up his glass and shook it for the bartender. The slight man in a puffy pirate shirt hustled over. Hurley ordered another drink and a beer for Victor. That was another thing he liked about Victor. He could handle his booze. He wasn't one of those uptight military academy pussies who had to do everything by the book, or one of those stiff feds. This was not a by-the-book business. Their job was to break laws left and right and not get caught.

"I fuckin' hate traveling without my gun."

Hurley turned to look at Victor. The man was clearly agitated. "Calm down," he snarled. Speaking out of the side of his mouth, Hurley said, "Why the fuck do you think I spend all that time teaching you idiots how to use your hands? A guy as strong as you doesn't need a gun."

"Unless I'm in a gunfight." Victor frowned and crumpled his cocktail napkin.

"When we fly, we all play by the same rules. No guns."

"Why didn't we take one of the Company jets?"

Hurley didn't like having to explain himself to subordinates, but he decided he'd give Victor this one answer. "We're trying to keep a low profile. Don't worry . . . I've made arrangements. Assets will meet us, and they'll have all the guns you want."

Victor took a swig of his beer, chewed on his bottom lip for a second, and then in a quiet voice asked, "Are you finally going to let me kill this little shit?"

Hurley contemplated his fresh drink and the question at the same time. Victor liked to cut to the heart of the matter rather than dance around an issue. "I didn't decide to bring you along for your looks."

Satisfied with the answer, Victor smiled and took a big swig of beer.

Hurley saw how pleased his dog was with the answer and it gave him pause. Those traitors he'd killed—he'd been following orders. There was never any joy in it. Victor seemed downright thrilled over the prospect of killing a fellow team member. Hurley knew there was no love lost between the two, but this seemed to be taking it a little too far. "Let's just hope it doesn't come to that."

"Why?" Victor growled. "You hate the little fuck just as much as I do."

"How I feel about him is none of your business," Hurley snapped. "We're going to give him a chance to come in on his own."

"And if he doesn't?"

Hurley looked into his drink for a long moment and then drained it in two big gulps. He set the glass down on the bar and threw down some bills. As he stood he said, "If he doesn't come in, all bets are off."

Hurley started to walk away, while behind him, Victor took a couple of big swigs and drew his forearm across his mouth to reveal a broad grin. He was clearly happy about the prospect of ending Rapp's life.

CHAPTER 12

PARIS, FRANCE

M ONSIGNOR de Fleury shuffled his feet as fast as they would carry him. He had known what he would do even before Fournier arrived. The three dark-skinned visitors had an ominous presence, or at least two of them did. The tall, well-dressed one was nice enough, but the other two were wicked men. They reeked of menace. The priest had facilitated many such meetings and was used to dealing with bodyguards. These two were not part of a security detail. They did not have that caring, watchful way about them. They were concerned only with themselves.

De Fleury was a faithful man, but that faith was placed in God and not men. He had seen what evil men were capable of, and as a shepherd, it was his job to help protect the flock from the wolves. These men were not sheep, and they most certainly didn't have the best interest of France in their hearts. They were killers. De Fleury had dealt with such men before, and he could see it in their eyes and in the way they moved.

He did not know what the slick-talking Fournier was up to, but the old priest was going to find out. The church was closed and other than the two night watchmen who were patrolling the perimeter, he was by himself. De Fleury moved through the shadows, through the transept, and just before the pulpit he turned right and shuffled down the outer aisle of the nave, past the lesser altars and finally to the wooden confessionals. He carefully opened the third door and stepped in. He left the light off, doing everything by feel. After sitting on the cushioned seat he leaned his head against the wood-paneled back wall, just above an iron grate that circulated air from the chapel below. De Fleury had discovered the acoustic peculiarity many years ago while dutifully listening to confessions. A private mass was being said in the crypt chapel, and the voices floated up from below with such clarity that he found it difficult to concentrate on the penitent sitting on the other side of the screen.

De Fleury had kept his contacts with French Intelligence over the years and a famous church like Sacré-Coeur with throngs of tourists coming and going was the perfect place to meet sources and operatives. This Fournier fellow liked the idea of meeting in the crypt for some reason, and de Fleury made no effort to dissuade the man, or tell him that his conversations could be heard from the confessional above. Secrets were something the priest was accustomed to hearing and not repeating, but he did not eavesdrop for his own indulgence. There was something about this Fournier fellow that was off. It was nothing drastic, but de Fleury had spent a lifetime observing people. In addition to the agent's being rather taken with himself, there was a shiftiness about him that the priest noted from the beginning. The man was an actor and a manipulator, and de Fleury guessed that the underlying drive was the need to feed his narcissistic personality.

It was shocking to him that the Directorate hadn't picked up on these traits earlier in his career. To put someone with his personality in charge of the Special Action Division seemed to be a very dangerous thing. The previous meetings in the crypt had mostly been with double agents who worked for other governments, and while de Fleury had heard some very interesting things over the past few years, there had been nothing that he considered a grievous offense to the Republic.

Tonight, however, he had an ominous feeling that the Republic's best interests were not being guarded.

As the words began to float up from the crypt, his concern only grew. The guests were Muslims and their lack of respect was obscene. Before the priest could get over his initial shock at the slurs against his beautiful basilica, Fournier said something that took his breath away. Surely they weren't talking about the bloody hotel murders that had gripped Paris? Within seconds they answered that question beyond any reasonable doubt. The priest grew increasingly alarmed with each passing moment by what he heard. What in hell was Fournier doing associating with such people? Why would he aid them in any way?

It was money, of course, and some arrangement that the DGSE had made with these animals. A Faustian deal undoubtedly made by careless men with no understanding of history. De Fleury had seen firsthand the horrific results of appeasement. It was a path chosen by feebleminded people who were morally incapable of confronting evil. He saw many parallels between the Nazis, the communists, and these jihadists. They were all sociopaths at heart—obsessed with their own tribal desires and utterly incapable of conferring justice or compassion on those outside the tribe. If you were not one of them, you were a lesser human, and thus deserved to be treated in any way they saw fit. And if that meant blowing up airliners and buses full of innocent civilians, then so be it.

De Fleury did not move when the meeting ended. The normal protocol was for Fournier and his guests to let themselves out at properly spaced intervals from different locations. The doors would lock behind them. The priest sat motionless in the dark confessional for a long time analyzing what he had learned and considering what he would do with the information. His contacts in the government were not what they once were. Almost all of them were either dead or retired. And he couldn't say for sure that he could trust any of the few he had with information of this magnitude. There was always the press, but de Fleury had no fondness for them and no stomach for airing the dirty secrets of the Republic on the front pages of the daily rags. He would have to find another way.

Caution was of the utmost importance. A man like Fournier would do anything to protect his image. The priest knew how it would play out. At his age, it would take nothing to suffocate him while he slept or toss him down a flight of stairs. Either would kill him, and either would be so plausible the police wouldn't even bother with an autopsy. De Fleury stood and stepped from the confessional. As he worked his way quietly toward the rectory a possibility occurred to him—a man whom he had helped a long time ago. He was a foreigner, but a trusted ally. He was still in a position to do something with the information. Maybe he could deal with Fournier and these men without having to go public. The old priest decided he would sleep on it. In the morning he would pray for guidance from the Holy Spirit, and if it were to be, he would make the call.

CHAPTER 13

SUNDAY morning arrived with the sound of church bells clanging in the distance. Rapp slowly opened his eyes and took inventory of his pains and aches. He was surprised that his shoulder didn't feel worse. He clenched his left fist and felt the burn go deep. He took some solace in the fact that it was slightly better than the day before. Raising his right hand from under the sheets he noted the time. It was 9:03. He had slept for nearly twelve hours, and that was after napping for six hours the previous afternoon. He remembered waking once during the night to use the bathroom and take another handful of painkillers. He rolled his head toward the window, looking at the shades framed in white light—his mind already working through the events that had brought him to this hotel, and the one question that he still couldn't answer. Who could he trust?

The desire to flee is not always wise. That was what he'd told himself while riding the Metro in the early morning after the slaughter at the hotel and now he found himself repeating the mantra once more. He had the skills to disappear, but what would he do with the rest of his life? It was one of many things Rapp had learned in his new line of work. He knew he'd changed a great deal in the past year. All of his senses had been sharpened. He could no longer simply walk into a room. Faces, potential threats, and exits all had to be assessed and categorized, and casually so as to not draw any attention. Everything he did was strategic planning on an extremely high level. How do you outthink your opponent when the stakes are life and death? Every move, every variation of each move, has to be analyzed and the risks weighed against options until you can zero in on the path that gives you the best chance for success.

After leaving the warehouse at first light his needs dictated his actions. Shelter, care, and food were at the top of his list, and they all had to be obtained without attracting any attention. That was when the urge to flee was the strongest. To just jump on the closest Metro train and go straight to the Gare de Lyon train station, gather his emergency bag from the locker, and flee the country. He could be across the border into Switzerland in three hours. Run straight into the arms of Greta and there was a good chance Hurley would know within a day. The first order of business was almost always to get out of the country where you had committed the crime, and Rapp had been told specifically on this one that he was to get out of France immediately after killing Tarek.

Getting ambushed and shot had obviously complicated things, but Rapp was disinclined to follow through with those orders for multiple reasons. The police were sure to be on high alert after the shootout at the hotel. They would be monitoring the ports and train stations and the immigration and border control agents would be scrutinizing every detail. While Rapp seriously doubted that they had a description of him, there was enough doubt to make him hesitant. He'd lost blood, and he was in pain. He could chance it, but an alert border agent might have him escorted into a private room for some interrogation and a strip search. Once his shirt was off there would be no denying that he'd been shot.

Fluent in French, Rapp liked the odds of staying put in Paris and blending in with the city's ten million inhabitants. Greta could collect a few things for him and then she could come to him. He did get on the first Metro train he found, however, and after a transfer he was emerging from several hundred feet underground into the grand Gare de Lyon station. Traffic was light, but as he'd guessed the police were unusually alert. Rapp, with his hands shoved deep in the pockets of the stolen jacket, kept his chin tucked in and his eyes uninterested as if he was just another laborer heading off to work. The lockers were located near the bathrooms. He purchased an espresso and a croissant from a vendor and used his wait to casually determine if any of the police had taken notice of him. They hadn't, so he proceeded to the lockers, retrieved his backpack, and stepped into one of the stalls in the men's room.

Four minutes later he emerged in a pair of jeans, hiking boots, blue Roots sweatshirt, and a Montreal Canadiens cap. The Palestinian passport had been torn up and flushed down the toilet and the worker's clothes stuffed into a trashcan. His backup gun was still strapped around his ankle, but other than that he was just another tourist. He left the terminal and stepped onto the first waiting bus, not caring where it would take him as long as it was quickly away from the station. A few minutes later he found himself rolling through central Paris. When the air brakes hissed at the hideous Pompidou Center, Rapp got off. He knew of a Best Western just around the corner—the type of place that catered to tourists eager to be near Paris's great museums.

A half block later he found a pay phone. It was brand new, shiny stainless steel; France Telecom's newest card-operated model to help thwart city degenerates who were fond of breaking into the coin-operated machines. Rapp slid his telecard into the slot, grabbed the receiver, and punched in a number from memory. She answered on the third ring.

"Good morning, Frau Greta," Rapp said in French. "How are you?"

"I am wonderful. Especially after hearing your voice." Her relief was obvious.

"Good. I can't wait to see you, but there has been a change in plans." The chance that Greta's phone was tapped was remote, but nonetheless, Rapp kept things as vague as possible and used their prearranged codes. "I can't leave town. My boss dumped a bunch of work on me. Do you think maybe you could come to me instead?"

"Absolutely," she said without hesitation, concern creeping into her voice.

"Could you drive?" It would be nice to have a car in case they needed to flee. "Maybe we could take a drive into the country tomorrow?"

"Yes, I can drive. Is everything all right?"

Rapp could tell she was worried. "Everything is fine, darling. Well, not perfect, but I'll live." He realized that would not calm her down, so he added, "There's just a few complications, that's all. Once you get here everything will be fine. Can you meet me tomorrow morning?"

"Not today?"

Rapp needed some food and a lot of sleep. And he needed some silence to sort things out. "I'm afraid today won't work. I have to get some things taken care of, but I promise, tomorrow I will have all day to spend with you."

"And the rest of the week?"

"And the rest of the week, too," Rapp lied. He would explain things in person and hoped she would understand. "I have to run, darling. Can you meet me at ten tomorrow morning?"

"Yes. Where . . . the apartment?"

"Not the apartment," Rapp said a little too quickly. Recovering, he said, "I will email you the information." He felt a wave of pain coming down on him and he grabbed the top of the phone booth with his right hand. "I have to go, darling, but I can't wait to see you." Rapp practically bit off his tongue after he spoke the last word.

"I can't wait to see you. I just wish it was today."

Rapp closed his eyes and hung on to the case of the pay phone. The pain kept building and Greta kept talking, asking him if something was wrong. He finally managed to say, "I'll be all right." His voice was tight and clipped. "I have to go now, darling. I'll see you tomorrow." Rapp was pulling the receiver away from his ear when he heard her tell him she loved him. It was a first for the two of them and Rapp wasn't sure if he was unwilling or unable to respond. He hung up the phone, knowing his nonresponse would be an issue. The throbbing pain slowly receded. Rapp retrieved his card, took several deep breaths, and then steadied himself enough to start down the sidewalk.

It was just past 7:00 a.m. when he crossed the hotel's small lobby. He spoke English to the man behind the desk, who assured him that while he did not have a room available at this exact moment, he expected one to free up within the hour. Rapp presented a Canadian passport and a Visa card with the name Bill Johnson. On the advice of a wise Swiss banker, he had obtained the passport and charge card on his own without telling his CIA handlers. He devoured a big breakfast, did his best to ignore the pain in his shoulder, and scanned the papers, even though he knew the killings had happened too late to make the morning editions. The man behind the desk was true to his word and within an hour he was standing at Rapp's table.

"Monsieur Johnson," the man said, "your room is ready."

Within minutes Rapp was in his room sitting on the edge of the bed, transfixed by the TV. The hotel murders were the hot topic on every local channel. The BBC had even picked up the story, but the only thing that Rapp learned with any surprise was the death toll. At first he thought they had their facts wrong. He had killed five people—Tarek and the four bodyguards, and he assumed that the prostitute had also been killed. That accounted for six total deaths. Who were the other three?

His shoulder throbbing, Rapp turned off the TV and headed off in search of some supplies. He kept a wide-spectrum antibiotic in his emergency bag, and a few other essentials, but he needed other supplies to clean and dress the wound, as well as some painkillers and other toiletries. It was now close to ten in the morning and the tourists were out in droves. Rapp hit three different pharmacies in a four-block area, wanting to spread out his purchases so as to not draw too much attention.

Every time he passed a pay phone he had to resist the urge to call Kennedy. He was still trying to figure out if he could trust her. On the face of it he thought he could, but the reality of their curious profession was that he didn't really know any of his coworkers. They were all professional liars. Rapp passed a young couple holding a map and arguing. For some bizarre reason he wondered if he could kill Kennedy. Assuming she had set him up, of course. Hurley would be easy, at least in terms of the decision, but Kennedy was different. He liked her.

The pain from the gunshot wound was getting worse, and was interfering with his ability to focus, so he headed back to the hotel and popped some painkillers. He took another shower before cleaning and dressing the wound. With the pain numbed, he drew the curtains and climbed under the covers. Pain was something he was accustomed to, but this was more acute than the average pull or sprain. It went deep, touching nerves that had never before been touched by an outside object. The discomfort was making sleep nearly impossible, but after thirty minutes the drugs kicked in. Rapp lay there staring up at the ceiling, floating away while trying to understand where the other three bodies had come from. He wondered if he had somehow killed the last man in the hallway. Even then, it meant two more bodies that he couldn't account for.

His dreams were wild and senseless. A jumbled mess of faces known and unknown. When he awoke later in the day, he ordered room service and watched more news on the television. There was little new information other than the announcement that four of the victims were bodyguards for the Libyan oil minister. Rapp scoffed at the information. If the men were bodyguards, why weren't they with Tarek as he moved about the city? The answer was obvious. They weren't bodyguards. They were a team sent to ambush him and Tarek was the bait.

Rapp fell asleep once again, his mind wrestling with all of the implications that flowed from what seemed to be the truth. Had Tarek volunteered for this mission or had he been betrayed by his own brotherhood? Had his value to his organization declined so much that they deemed him expendable? How had they known that he would be next on Rapp's list? That was ultimately the problem that Rapp kept coming back to, for it implied something far more sinister and close to home.

As Rapp looked around the room, he thought of the close circle of people who knew of his existence. The Orion Team was a small clandestine unit, intentionally set up outside Langley with the explicit purpose of hunting terrorists. There was a firewall between the group and Langley for an obvious reason—there were too many bureaucrats in the building, many of them with law degrees, who did not understand the nature of their enemy. Men and women who had never served in the field, men and women who had no grasp of their enemies' lethal designs, and who sincerely thought that everything must be done in the full light of congressional approval and proper legal channels, as if they were conducting a police action.

Rapp sat up and swung his feet from under the covers and to the floor in one motion. He glanced at the bandage on his shoulder and was pleased to see no sign of blood. Kennedy entered his mind. She was his most direct link. He saw her as someone who was genuinely committed to what they were doing, but then again she wasn't exactly an open book. There was Rob Ridley, who ran the advance teams and was there to assist Rapp on the back end if he got in trouble. Stan Hurley, the relentless cuss, knew virtually every detail, as did Thomas Stansfield, the deputy director of Operations at Langley. How many others, Rapp had no idea. Kennedy claimed that there were only a handful of people, but it was no stretch to think that others had been brought into the loop without Rapp's knowledge. A mole in a spy agency was not a novel idea, and the idea caused Rapp's healthy paranoia to kick in.

Rapp hadn't spent much time analyzing the motives of someone who would betray their country. Hatred, jealousy, a martyr complex, or some Dudley Do-Right who saw only black and white and the letter of the law—Rapp didn't really care. He knew as surely as he knew that he had killed Tarek and the others that if he found the person who had set him up, he would strangle that person with his bare hands. The thought that someone back in Washington who was more than likely sitting in a cushy air-conditioned office had sold him out for money or some arrangement enraged him. Who it could be was a big question, and Rapp wondered if he could muster the skills and assets to find out.

He sat there for several minutes, the pain in his shoulder pulsing back to life, analyzing the various paths he could take. Disappearing was still an option and he had the skills to pull it off—at least for a while. Would they bother to look for him? If they knew the whole story, probably not, but the way the press was reporting things they would think he had killed the prostitute and three innocent civilians, and there was no guarantee that they would know anything beyond what the press was reporting. Rapp didn't like that. Intuitively, he knew spending the rest of his life waiting for them to kick in his door was no way to live. More important, he believed in the mission and had no desire to abandon it. He cracked a smile as he briefly thought of staying with the mission, but doing so on his own. Hurley would flip out and hunt him down.

Slowly, Rapp realized there was really only one good avenue open to him. He would have to initiate contact and see how they reacted. He was the one with a bullet hole in his shoulder. They could bitch all they wanted about their protocols, but he was the one getting shot at. He would call Kennedy. It would be a day and a half late, they would be on edge, and if they believed the press reports there was a chance they'd authorized a kill order for him. That possibility gave Rapp an idea. He was a virtual needle in a haystack right now. If they were looking for him, there was just one logical place to start. Rapp considered the dangers involved in going there. Rubbing his eyes, he tried to work the fog of the painkillers from his mind. He was going to need all his wits about him for what was coming next.

CHAPTER 14

WHEN Rapp stood up, his shoulder immediately let him know that it was not happy. He froze between the bed and the bathroom, not sure if he should push on or lie back down. The pain, though, receded more quickly than it had the day before. He was either getting used to it, or it was getting better. He moved into the small bathroom and checked out his shoulder in the mirror. It didn't look good. Bright red and purple bruising was spreading beyond the white bandage in every direction. None of it was migrating down his arm, though, which he took as a positive sign. Then he remembered he'd spent a long time on his back.

Turning to the side, he craned his stiff neck as far as he could and caught the reflection of his back in the mirror. Instead of bright red, the bruising was purple and almost black in a few spots. Rapp cringed and asked himself if it was possible that the bullet had clipped his lateral thoracic artery. He shook his head at his own question. If that big tube was nicked he would have bled out and died a long time ago. Besides, that main highway ran pretty deep. When he'd bandaged the wound the day before he'd done his best to line up the entry and exit wounds. The bullet had punched through close to the middle of his left shoulder and exited closer to the outside. The angle should have carried it clear of the hub of arteries and veins that carried blood to and from his left arm. It was more likely that a good number of capillaries and plenty of tissue had been damaged. The internal bleeding had probably stopped and the blood had pooled while he'd slept. At least that's what he hoped.

He stared at his reflection in the mirror. He made no attempt to deceive himself. The dark black eyes that were staring back at him were the eyes of a killer. Somewhere in the distance he heard more church bells. He briefly considered going to mass and then with a heavy sadness told himself that God would not want him in his house. *Thou shalt not kill* was a pretty big one. Rapp felt himself heading down one of those dark hallways of introspection that led to pity, recrimination, and doubt. After he'd lost his girlfriend and thirty-four fellow Syracuse University students in the Pan Am Lockerbie terrorist attack, there'd been times where he allowed himself to walk down these sunless corridors. After a lot of tears and a lot of time spent feeling sorry for himself, he began to recognize that he could be lost in these hallways for a long time if he didn't practice some mental discipline. The bleak corridors of his mind were full of pain and weakness and no answers.

Rapp flashed himself a devilish grin as he remembered another popular biblical phrase, the one that had pulled him out of his self-pity—*an eye for an eye*. The Ten Commandments were bullet points. A quick reference on how to live your life between the lines. The Bible was the more detailed reference, and it was filled with examples of how the wicked should be punished, especially the Old Testament. *Thou shalt not kill, unless it's a piece-of-shit terrorist . . . or a traitor or a rapist or a pedophile . . .* the list could go on for a long time.

Rapp had bigger and more immediate problems to deal with at the moment. He would have to put off debating his salvation for another day. Right now he was more focused on finding out how Kennedy would react to what he had to say. After that, he would run his colleagues through some tests to see whom he could trust, and if he got the feeling that he was being played he might have to disappear for a few months. Even as he thought it he knew it wasn't an option. Lying low was not how he worked. He would find out who had betrayed him and then he would kill them.

The knock on the door pulled him from his thoughts of retribution. He moved quickly for the silenced pistol on the nightstand and then remembered Greta was supposed to meet him. He kept the pistol as a precaution and started for the door. He stopped dead in his tracks when he saw his reflection in the mirror across the room. He looked like he felt, which was like crap. His dense black hair was shooting out in various directions and he had a thick sheet of stubble, as he had not shaved in two days. That was hardly the worst of it, though. His shoulder was the real problem. He thought about putting on a T-shirt, but it would hurt too much and take too long and Greta was not good at waiting. He knew she'd be mad that he'd put her off for a whole day. He shook his head, sighed, and figured he might as well get it over with. She was going to find out sooner or later.

Rapp stepped softly to the door, stopping a few feet away, and peered through the peephole. There was Greta, all five-foot-six of Nordic perfection. Blue eyes, high cheekbones, and a strong jaw that tapered to a little apple chin. Her blond hair was pulled back in a high ponytail as it almost always was. Rapp preferred it that way. The minimalist look framed her perfect face. In the year he'd known her, Rapp had seen grown men, complete strangers, become so fixated on Greta that they walked into things. She was literally a head-turner. It had irritated Rapp at first, having to deal with all the gawking men when they were in public. After a while he decided to take it as a compliment. If men wanted to stare, then they could go ahead. He soon learned, also, that Greta was more than capable of defending her honor. She did her best to ignore the stares, but occasionally if some man was too forward or too obvious she could go nuclear.

Rapp watched her purse her lips, and then she reached out to knock again. Her patience was wearing thin. Rapp reached down, grabbed the rubber wedge he'd placed under the door, and undid the chain just as Greta started knocking again. He opened the door and turned his left shoulder away so it would not be the first thing she saw. Rapp also kept the gun concealed behind the door. He smiled and said, "Sorry, I was in the bathroom."

Greta's bright blue eyes narrowed with concern. "You don't look very good."

"Why thank you, darling. You look fabulous as always." Rapp motioned for her to come in.

She grabbed the handle of her wheeled suitcase and strode forward. Rapp closed and chained the door while she looked around the small space. She finished her survey at approximately the same time that Rapp finished sticking the wedge under the door. He expected her to act a certain way and she didn't disappoint. Greta was not the type to panic and begin screaming about the obvious. Her eyes zeroed in on the white bandage and her jaw tightened with concern. She stepped closer and slowly reached out. Her soft fingers touched the skin around the bandage, and Rapp felt a small shock of electricity run through his upper body. She'd done it to him the first time they'd met and she could still do it to him. She had the softest, most feminine hands he'd ever encountered. Her touch could make him weak in the knees.

Greta worked her way around his side so she could get a view of his back. Rapp heard her gasp slightly. He winced, not because he was in pain, but because he feared what might come next, more than likely a lot of questions. She surprised him instead by making a statement.

"You've been shot."

Rapp's throat felt suddenly dry. "Yeah," he croaked.

She ran her hand around his shoulder, both front and back. "And it would appear you have not seen a doctor."

Rapp frowned and said, "Not really an option."

Her expression remained neutral. "I don't suppose you are going to tell me how this happened?"

Rapp shrugged and said, "Maybe later."

Greta frowned and shook her head.

If she folded her arms across her chest he was really in trouble, so he said, "I have a few things I still need to figure out." Then he reached out with his good hand, the one with the silenced pistol in it, and drew her in.

She placed her hands on his chest and rested her right cheek just above them.

"I'm just glad you're here," he said, and then kissed the top of her head. The gun was in the way so he tossed it onto the bed.

"I was afraid this would happen," Greta said, her voice filled with gloom.

Rapp waited a long moment and then said, "Yeah . . . I can't say I wasn't aware of the risk but I thought . . ." His voice trailed off.

"You thought that you were indestructible. That you would always be the one doing the killing, and now you have found out that you are human like the rest of us. How does that make you feel?"

Rapp half rolled his eyes and said, "You know me and feelings . . . they don't really go together."

"That may be true with other people, but not with me. I am not judging you. You should know that by now. I don't know everything that you do, but I have a pretty good idea. Have I ever complained?"

"No."

"That's right. I am not here to change you. I respect what you do, but I most definitely would like to see you live."

"That makes two of us."

"Well . . . then you need to be more careful. Learn from your mistakes."

Rapp thought of the hotel room, the five jackasses with the suppressed MP5s, and made his first big mistake of the morning. "You think this shit is easy?"

"Excuse me?" she asked, pushing back.

Rapp realized his mistake. "I'm sorry, it's been a rough few days.

I can't tell you what happened other than to say some other people didn't do their jobs and I ended up with my ass getting shot at."

"Stan?"

Greta's grandfather had close ties with Stan Hurley and Thomas Stansfield. He was a very discreet and successful Swiss banker, which came in handy in Rapp's line of work. He didn't want to get her directly involved in this, though, so he suppressed his theories and said, "I'm not sure, but I don't think so." In an effort to redirect the conversation he said, "You're handling this pretty well."

"What do you mean?"

"I thought you'd be mad."

"I'm not exactly thrilled but I don't see how getting angry would help . . . at least right now. There will be plenty of time for that later, but for now I need to have a look at your wound."

Rapp hesitated. "Have you ever worked on something like this?"

"Not specifically, but I have plenty of first-aid training and I grew up hunting, in case you forgot."

"Of course I didn't forget. I watched you kill an elk at eight hundred meters."

"That's right. And I don't see how I could do a worse job than you." She gestured at his haphazard tape job. "Do you have more supplies?"

"Yeah . . . they're in the bathroom."

"Good . . . get on the bed."

He smiled. "Slow down, princess. I'm not just a piece of meat. Maybe you could buy me breakfast first."

She ignored him and went to grab the supplies.

"Fine, I'll order my own breakfast. Can I get you anything?"

"No, I'm fine." She came back out of the bathroom with a plastic shopping bag and motioned for Rapp to sit on the bed. She set the supplies down and took her jacket off. After pushing the sleeves of her sweater up, she headed back into the bathroom and started scrubbing her hands.

Rapp grabbed the phone and ordered breakfast for two. If Greta didn't eat her food he would. When he was finished ordering she sat down next to him on the bed and began peeling back the tape as carefully as she could manage. Rapp tolerated it fairly well until she pulled the bandage off the back of his shoulder. A semidried scab was stuck to the gauze and came off with it. Greta took a warm washcloth and gently wiped down the entry and exit wounds. After that she started dousing cotton balls with rubbing alcohol and did a more thorough job. Rapp did his best to ignore the burning.

"How does it look?"

"I'm not sure," Greta answered. "There's a lot of swelling. How do you feel?"

"Not bad."

She grabbed him by the chin and turned his face toward her. "Don't lie to me. This has to hurt."

"It doesn't feel good, but it sure as hell beats being dead."

She looked at the front of his shoulder and then the back. "You were shot from behind."

"That's right. How could you tell?"

"The wound on your back is small and the one in front is bigger. You're lucky the bullet didn't hit anything major. What kind of round—nine-millimeter?"

Rapp was surprised. "I think so. How did you know?"

"I told you, I grew up hunting. Almost everyone in my country is taught how to fire rifles and pistols, even the girls. I've seen what a rifle round does to flesh. If you had been shot with a rifle round the exit wound would be much bigger."

"You're right. It was probably a nine-millimeter."

Greta finished cleaning the wound, placed fresh gauze bandages on both holes, and wrapped gauze around the shoulder and under his armpit to make sure everything stayed in place. When she was done she went back into the bathroom and washed her hands. Rapp hadn't missed the fact that she had gotten very quiet over the last five minutes. When she came back out he found out why.

Greta stood directly across from him, leaned against the wall, folded her hands across her chest, and said, "You were involved in that bloodbath at the Hotel La Fleur the night before last."

Rapp was speechless. He should have seen it coming, but the pain pills had made him a little sluggish. "Greta, you know I can't talk about my job."

She looked away from him and starting chewing on her bottom lip. "Innocent people were killed. Several guests and a busboy, not to mention the prostitute, the oil minister, and his entire security detail." She turned her blue eyes on him. "Please tell me you weren't involved."

Rapp was trying to plot the fine line he was going to walk when there was a knock on the door. A male voice announced that it was room service. Greta looked as if she might cry. Rapp grabbed the gun and looked through the peephole. The man was in his early twenties. Rapp pulled the wedge out from under the door to let the waiter in and then walked over to Greta. In a voice barely above a whisper he said, "I will explain everything after he's gone." His words didn't appear to calm her, so he tried again. "Greta, I didn't kill any innocent people. The papers don't have the story right." Rapp kissed her on the forehead and then went into the bathroom and closed the door. He looked into the mirror, took a deep breath, and tried to figure out how much he could tell her.

CHAPTER 15

PARIS, FRANCE

THE unusual pair moved down the narrow sidewalk at a casual pace. One was tall, just under six-four, and fair-skinned, with wispy sandy blond hair. The second man was of medium height and powerfully built. He had thick black hair that looked as if it hadn't been combed in a week. His full beard ran down his neck, where it blended in with tufts of coarse chest hair poking out of the open collar of his royal blue shirt. The tall man was wearing jeans, a brown turtleneck, a rust-colored sweater, and a tweed sport coat with the collar turned up. A tan cashmere scarf knotted around his neck helped fight off the cold. Jones was almost always cold, while his bear of a friend shunned gloves, hats, and scarves even on the rawest of days.

Today, as on most days, though, Bernstein was wearing a field jacket open and flapping as he walked. Bernstein didn't wear the jacket for warmth, he wore it because he tended to carry a lot of stuff. Pockets were a necessity of his job as a freelance photographer. He was never without at least one camera, usually his trusted black Leica M6, which was hanging around his neck. His pockets were always stuffed with extra batteries, film, lenses, and all sorts of tools, including maps and various forms of identification and cash concealed in secret pockets.

The two men stopped at the corner of Rue de Tournon and Rue de Vaugirard. The Palais du Luxembourg loomed across the street. It was an attractive building dating all the way back to the early seventeenth century, but Paris was filled with such buildings and after sixteen years of calling Paris home, the two men scarcely noticed such things anymore. Heavy clouds had settled over the city. Jones regarded the cold gray sky and shivered. He thought the day was supposed to clear up, not get worse. He tucked his chin down, shoved his hands deeper into his pockets, and mumbled to himself.

"Did you wear your long underwear?" Bernstein asked with a sly grin on his face.

"Damn right. It's freezing."

Bernstein slowly turned his broad head toward his friend and said, "It's fifty-six degrees."

"And there's no sun and the wind is picking up. It's freezing."

It never failed to amaze Bernstein that someone who had grown up in Minnesota could be so affected by a drop in temperature. He smiled and shook his head.

"I know what you are thinking. If I put on some weight, maybe I wouldn't be so cold all the time."

"No . . . that's not what I was thinking."

"Then what?"

Rather than argue about something so pointless, Bernstein said, "I was thinking about how excited I am to hear what he wants us to do."

"I'm sick to my stomach over it, actually, but what are our choices?"

"We really don't have any, but that doesn't mean we shouldn't be careful."

"And remember . . . no matter how much he bullies us we don't have to do everything he tells us to do."

Bernstein gave a sarcastic laugh, watched the light turn green, and then began to walk across the street. As Jones fell into step, he said, "He holds all the cards. He recruited us, he helped us get started, and he could easily end our careers . . . or at least yours."

"Don't think he wouldn't ruin yours as well."

"I'm not saying he wouldn't try, I'm just saying nobody gives a shit who I am. If my photos are good or my footage kicks ass, they'll still line up to buy it just like they always have. You, on the other hand, are a whole other story."

They crossed into the park and walked down the east side of the palace. "I've been thinking about that a lot lately," Jones said. "I'm not so sure he would. I don't think Langley would like the exposure any more than we would."

"You're talking Langley. He's not Langley, and he hasn't been Langley in a long time. He hates Langley." Bernstein separated from his friend and allowed an old man with a cane to pass between them. "Your mistake is that you believe he thinks like all of the other government types we deal with." Bernstein shook his big head. "He's nothing like them."

Jones's face soured. "You're right. He'd love to expose us and ruin our careers."

"That book deal you just signed . . . you can kiss that hundred-thousand-dollar advance good-bye."

Jones's face grew angry. It was all so unfair. He had worked hard, more than fulfilled his end of the bargain, but they wouldn't let him go. He hated to admit it but he knew Bernstein was right. Sixteen years as a distinguished journalist, the first ten with the Associated Press, and then the last six as CBS's Middle East correspondent. One whisper that he was a spy for the CIA and he would become the biggest pariah in his field. He'd be fired by his employer and with it his expense account and entire way of life would vanish, and then he would be ostracized by all of his colleagues and hated by almost every friend he'd made over his professional career. *Although, maybe it might help book sales,* he thought. Times had changed, despite what his handler had always said.

The mean old bastard loved to describe to him in detail what would happen to him if he was ever exposed.

"You can't let this shit get to you," Bernstein said, trying to snap his friend out of his funk. "At least hear what he has to say." As they continued down the crushed-gravel path Bernstein wondered about the roles they played. Jones was the on-air talent—the pretty face with the deep voice and sympathetic blue-gray eyes. A nice head of hair, but thinning just enough to give him the seasoning of a man who has seen the world and knows the difference between right and wrong. Insecurity came with the job, unfortunately. There was always someone younger and better looking out there hot on his heels. Bernstein was the hustler—never afraid to go anywhere if it meant getting the shot. They'd both won a mantel full of awards. Where Bernstein was reckless, Jones was cautious. The taller of the two had saved them more than a few times by refusing to enter a particular hot spot. He had an uncanny sense for situations that were about to fall apart, and Bernstein had learned to respect it.

They continued for a good hundred yards without speaking, passing the Octagonal Lake and making their way toward the eclectic corner of the park where the young, old, brilliant, and strange gathered to play chess. As they rounded the lake, Jones decided to make one of his pronouncements.

"I have a bad feeling."

Bernstein was long past giving him shit about these premonitions. He cleared his throat, looked over both shoulders, and asked, "What is it?"

"I think this has something to do with the massacre at the hotel the other night."

Bernstein digested the news, took a few thoughtful strides, and said, "No sense worrying about it until we hear what he has to say."

"I'm not so sure. I'd just as soon tell him to fuck off. I could be in Cairo by nightfall, and they can all kiss my ass. I'll still write my book, and maybe I'll out all these fuckers."

Bernstein knew his friend well enough to know he was prone to theatrics and grandiose statements when he was nervous. "You might want to keep that thought to yourself."

"Oh, trust me . . . I know. I'm the one he yells at, not you."

"That's because I keep my mouth shut." Bernstein shoved his hands into his pockets. "You ask too many questions."

"I'm a reporter. That's what I do for a living. I ask questions. Lots of them."

"Well maybe today you could give it a break. Just sit there and listen for a change."

They found an open table with a little space between them and the guys who were playing chess. Bernstein produced a folding chessboard from his jacket and two Ziploc bags—one filled with white pieces and the other filled with black. Holding the bags under the table, he extracted one piece from each and then held his fists out for Jones to choose.

The Minnesotan tapped the right hand and Bernstein cringed as he opened it to reveal a black bishop.

"Oh, great. You get white. I might as well quit right now."

Bernstein didn't want to hear any more complaining, so he handed the white bag across the table.

"I don't want your charity."

"And I don't want to hear you bitch anymore . . . besides, we both know I don't need the first move to win."

"Oh, fuck you."

"No, thanks," Bernstein responded as he started to set up the black pieces.

The two were so focused on setting up the board that they failed to notice a bald man in a khaki trench coat sit down at the table next to them. He was wearing a pair of sunglasses and thin leather driving gloves. He took a newspaper from under his arm and set it on the table. In a gravelly voice, just above a whisper, he said, "So you'd just as soon tell me to fuck off. Be in Cairo by nightfall and out, my ass."

The color rushed from both of their faces, and Bernstein gave his friend a look that said he would like to shove every last chess piece down his throat. Slowly, they both turned their heads and looked at the man sitting four feet away.

Stan Hurley slid his sunglasses down to the tip of his nose and looked straight at Jones. "How about I put a bullet in the back of your head, and we call it even?"

The tall reporter sat gaping for a moment, as he was too shocked to think of a reply. Slowly his mouth started to move, but no words came out, and then he started to stammer as if he were back in grade school.

"Stop fucking mumbling," Hurley ordered. "How long have I been working with you two?"

Again, Jones began to stutter.

Hurley, as impatient as ever, answered his own question. "Seventeen fucking years and this is how you want to treat me, you selfish prick? I got your ass out of that jam in Turkey. I helped both of you find jobs, and there's been no shortage in cash that has come your way over the years, and you act like you're a fucking victim."

"I was only . . ."

"Shut up. I don't want to hear you speak yet. I'm still trying to figure out if you're worth the risk." Hurley leaned back and crossed his legs. "Turkey, and I'm not talking about Thanksgiving . . . I'm talking Midnight Express. Two stupid college kids deciding they're going to try to bring a bunch of drugs out of the country and then sell them stateside and make a nice profit. I'm talking big hairy Turkish guards gang-raping a couple of East Coast journalism majors. I thought that nice little visual was seared into your brainpans, because it sure did seem like it when you were both bawling like babies for me to save your asses all those years ago."

Bernstein looked solemnly at Hurley and said, "I have not forgotten the fact that you saved us, and I never will."

"You're not the one who worries me, Dick. It's pretty boy here."

Jones had managed to get some saliva in his mouth so he wouldn't have to croak out his words. "I'm . . . I'm sorry. I haven't been feeling all that well and it's put me in a bad mood."

"Mood?" Hurley threw the word back with disgust. "Mood has nothing to do with this. This is serious shit, and while I know you think you made a deal with the devil, you should open your mind to the possibility that all these years you've spent rubbing elbows with all of your fellow bleeding-heart reporters has turned you into a half Commie." Hurley leaned in close. "The U.S. of Fucking A. is not the bad guy in this fight. The CIA is not the bad guy, and if you opened your eyes and fucking looked around at all the nasty shit you've seen, you'd know that. We're not perfect, but we're a hell of a lot better than the opposition. Now . . . I'd like to hear from you, Brian, what in hell has been so difficult about our little relationship?"

Jones looked down at the chessboard and cleared his throat. "It's just that it's unethical for a journalist to work for you and your organization. It puts a lot of stress on me. If word ever got out . . ." His voice trailed off and he began to shake his head.

"Unethical." Hurley laughed. "You mean like trying to transport illegal drugs from one country to another. Would that be unethical or should we just cut through the bullshit and elevate it to a crime punishable by twenty years in a Turkish prison?"

"We were young and stupid."

"And now you're older and still stupid. How about the cash I've given you over the years? I assume you assuaged your ethical burden by giving all the money to the Little Sisters of the Poor?"

Jones lifted his chin and shook his head.

"You know what, Brian, you need to get off your high horse. You're not the only journalist I have in my pocket, and I didn't even invent this game. There's been plenty before you and will be plenty after you. You need to start thinking of me as your godfather. You think you would have won that Murrow Award three years ago if it wasn't for me making sure you didn't get shot?"

"Nope," Bernstein said as if there were doubt in the statement.

"You need to listen to him more," Hurley said, pointing to Bernstein. "Your problem, Brian, is that while you are basically a good guy, you are way too insecure. Stop worrying about what your colleagues think of you. A few of them might be your friends, but most of them would just as soon see you fall flat on your face and take your job. You made a deal with me a long time ago and I saved your ass. That is something you should never forget. If you're willing to step back and take an honest look at this relationship, you'd understand this has been a very beneficial one for all of us. If you're not willing to do that, then let's end this thing right now, and trust me on this, I'll be the one outing your ass and ruining your career, and a month from now they'll find you swinging from the rafters of that cabin you have up in Thunder Lake. You'll be so pumped full of drugs no one will doubt for a second that you committed suicide."

A wide-eyed Jones asked, "How did you know I had a cabin on Thunder Lake?"

Hurley shook his head and said, "Oh, for Christ sake." He turned to Bernstein and said, "I'm putting you in charge of him. You guys have fifteen minutes to get your shit together. A big guy named Victor is going to show up. If you guys aren't here, I'll assume you want to end our relationship, which would be really stupid, because I will assume you are now my enemy and I will be forced to put certain plans in motion . . . the kind of plans that will be nearly impossible to stop once they are started."

"You don't need to worry about that," Bernstein offered quickly.

"Good. I'll dispense with Victor for the moment. I assume you're both familiar with the bloodbath that took place the other night?"

Jones gave his friend a *See, I told you so* look and asked, "At the hotel on the Seine?"

"Yep . . . Are you guys already covering it?"

"The bureau has someone on it."

Hurley thought about that a second. "Maybe you should show some initiative. Start digging a bit. I assume you still have some contacts with the police." Hurley had plenty of contacts of his own all over Paris, but he didn't want to go tipping his hand. At the moment, everything he had was based on gossip and rumor. He needed the hard facts that the police were dealing with.

Bernstein scratched his beard. "We have some pretty decent sources, but this is Paris, so you know what that means."

Hurley did and reached into his pocket. He retrieved a thick envelope. "Ten thousand francs. You need more, let me know."

"Receipts?" Jones asked, regaining a bit of his sense of humor.

"Along with expense reports in triplicate, please." Hurley pulled two relatively small devices from his pocket. He handed one to Jones and the other to Bernstein. "Those, gentlemen, are the newest in cell phone technology . . . the StarTAC by Motorola. My number is already programmed. As soon as you know something I want to know something." Hurley also handed them two chargers. "We don't think the French are up and running on intercepting these things yet, but let's be careful. You've both made enough international calls to know how the game works."

Both men nodded. They had indeed. Countries could get very ugly about foreign reporters wanting to tell the world about certain atrocities that they were committing. Jones and Bernstein often had to work out special codes with their producers back in New York.

"Also . . ." Hurley started, "I might need you to pull some surveillance shifts."

Jones let out a moan that said *You have got to be kidding me.*

"Don't worry," Hurley said. "I'll make sure you're compensated. You get your head back in the game and get me what I need and I'll make sure you both walk away from this with a fist full of cash."

Now that Hurley was calm, Bernstein wasn't going to wait for his friend to inflame him again. "Thank you. We'll get right on it."

"Victor is a big guy . . . impossible to miss. Just do what he says and everything will be fine." Hurley stood and placed his hand on Jones's shoulder. "Brian . . . you're not a bad guy . . . you're just self-righteous. You think you're the only noble man in the game." Hurley shook his head. "Trust me, it's a little more complicated than that."

CHAPTER 16

LITTLE yellow flags littered the grassy area across the street from the hotel. Commandant Neville had received the call shortly after 10:00 a.m. She'd already showered and was lounging with her husband and two kids. She'd given up on going to church with two kids in diapers, so Sunday mornings were spent on the floor of their tiny flat. She and her husband tried to simultaneously read the papers and keep the kids occupied with an endless stream of irritating shows that supposedly were going to make Marc, who was two and a half, and Agatha, who was nine months, the smartest kids of their generation. Neville didn't actually believe it, but she was all for anything that kept them occupied for more than ten minutes. When the call came, she put on a white shirt, black slacks, black pumps, and a gray trench coat. Knowing the cameras would be following her every move, she even put on a dab of makeup and bushed out her short black hair.

A vivid, low fall sun sparkled off the Seine. Neville's eyes were concealed by a stylish pair of oversized Chanel sunglasses that covered nearly a third of her face. She wore them as much to shield her from the bright sun as to shield her from the prying eyes of the reporters.

She had yet to hold a press conference, and she didn't want them reading anything into her expressions until she was ready. She stood in the middle of the area and tried to make sense of it all. The reporters were back, thick as summer flies, shouting questions and snapping photos and in general being their irritating selves. In addition to the press, there were hundreds if not thousands of curious onlookers who couldn't resist the morbid pull of the crime scene.

Neville kept her concern beneath a placid mask. She'd learned over the years that it was best to look serious at murder scenes—even angry could work, but it was never okay to laugh or be caught joking with other officers. The investigation, only in its second day, was becoming something of a mess. These little yellow flags, for instance, had only been placed this morning. The entire area from river to street was now blocked off with bands of crime scene tape and another ten officers to make sure nothing was tampered with. Neville thought it was a waste of manpower, but her superiors had insisted. The problem, she knew, was that this entire space had been crowded with people the day before. They had stepped all over the evidence and if this ever got to court it would be all but useless. She did, however, gain something very important—a new angle.

Neville looked back at the hotel and the balcony outside Tarek's suite. She chided herself for not expanding the perimeter right away, but as her boss had explained, the amount of evidence in the hotel itself was overwhelming. Nine bodies, shell casings and slugs everywhere, and then on top of that they'd found the room with all of the surveillance equipment. They still didn't have that one quite figured out. No one on the hotel staff remembered any security for the Libyan oil minister. They had over fifteen statements from employees saying Tarek had arrived with a single assistant. That assistant was now unavailable for comment, securely locked behind the gates of the Libyan Embassy.

The tough one to stomach for Neville was that she had more than thirty officers assigned to the case, and she had only learned of the spent shell casings that were strewn about the sidewalk and gutter in front of the hotel the previous evening. The press might eat her alive for that one. She went back to the crime scene, examined the casings, and wondered how many had been crushed, kicked, and taken during the course of the long day. They were more or less spread out under the suite's balcony. The logical assumption was that either someone had stood on Tarek's balcony and fired into his room, or someone had stood on his balcony and fired at someone or something down on the street.

She went up to the suite, stood on the balcony, and looked into the room. The wall directly in front of her was untouched, whereas the wall to her right was pocked with bullet holes. Turning toward the river, she looked down at the sidewalk where the shell casings had been found and imagined firing a weapon. After a long moment of reflection she ordered her deputy Martin Simon to rope off the area, bring in the metal detectors, and begin the search for 9mm slugs.

Neville then went home full of self-recrimination for the mishap. She had allowed herself to be sucked into the most plausible theory—that one man, or several men, had killed Tarek, the prostitute, the supposed bodyguards, and then two guests and a hotel worker on his way out the back door. In barely a day's time it was all falling apart. The Libyans were so far refusing to talk, saying only that the four men were there to protect their oil minister. As a police officer, Neville despised being lied to, and like most cops, she had a very well-tuned BS detector. The four dead men were not bodyguards. They might have been sent to keep an eye on Tarek, but they most certainly were not bodyguards. She would have to ask around, but to the best of her knowledge, she'd never heard of bodyguards using silenced weapons.

Neville ignored the reporters who were yelling her name, instead choosing to act as if the pattern of little yellow flags would give her a glimpse into how to solve the crime of the century. Martin Simon approached from behind and called out her name. When Neville turned, she could tell by the open-eyed expression on his face that the case was about to take another turn.

"What's up?"

"Let's take a walk." Simon glanced back toward the hotel. "There's something interesting you should see."

Neville fell into step with the red-haired Simon. Although he was two years older than her, his red hair and freckles made him look as if he were ten years her junior. When they were clear of the throngs of reporters and onlookers, she said, "Please tell me we didn't find another body."

Simon laughed. "No more bodies. I think nine is enough."

"Then you've solved the crime for us?"

Simon shook his head as they entered the lobby. "No, but I think I've found something that is going to upset you."

She pulled off her sunglasses and placed them in her purse. The hotel staff watched them with understandable anxiety. More than half of their guests had checked out and future reservations were being canceled at a quick clip. Neville felt bad for them. They were overworked and stressed and this thing was far from over. Every single one of them, whether they had been on duty or not, would be interviewed at least twice more. It was an avenue that had to be pursued for two reasons. Either one of the employees had seen something without realizing it, or one of them was involved in giving the killer or killers information about Tarek's comings and goings.

They entered the elevator, and when the doors were closed, Simon said, "I couldn't sleep last night."

"That's because you drink too much coffee," Neville said in a matter-of-fact tone.

"Don't start, boss," he said as he watched the brass arrow move from left to right, ticking out their ascent. "While I was lying awake staring at the water marks on my ceiling, I asked myself why someone would stand on the balcony and shoot toward the street and the river."

"And?"

"The nine-millimeter casings we found on the street match the ones that were scattered all around Tarek's suite, and in the hallway, and the ones found by the body at the back door."

The elevator stopped at the top floor and the doors opened. Neville exited first. "So you think they were fired by one of our Libyan bodyguards."

"Maybe . . . but for the moment, I'm more interested in who was being shot at than who was doing the firing."

Neville's thin lips pinched to the left in an expression that told Simon she wasn't following his line of reasoning.

Simon stopped walking in the middle of the hall and acted as if he was holding a gun. "If I'm standing on the balcony and firing at someone below, why am I firing at them, and how did they get there?"

Neville shook her head abruptly as if she was trying to clear her thoughts. "What are you talking about?"

"Somebody, or several people, killed those bodyguards, and then they had to get out of the hotel. We jumped to the conclusion that the same person or persons killed Tarek, the prostitute, the bodyguards, then killed the two guests and the worker."

"Correct."

"Then who was shooting from the balcony down onto the street, and more important, who were they shooting at?"

Neville visualized what he was saying and said, "I see your point."

Simon opened a service door at the end of the hallway, revealing a steep, narrow metal staircase that led to the roof. "Whoever was being shot at was not the man who killed the employee who was in the alley. You wouldn't leave by the back door and then come around to the front of the hotel where there's a greater chance that you'll run into someone." Simon started climbing the stairs. The hatch that led to the roof was already opened.

Neville followed her fellow officer onto the roof and immediately noticed two of her best crime scene technicians.

"So I'm lying in bed," Simon continued, "and I think, the most logical explanation is that someone left that room last night via the balcony, and if they left via the balcony they must have had a rope." Simon stopped next to a black cast-iron vent stack and dropped to a knee. Neville followed suit. "You see where the soot has been rubbed free right here?" He pointed to the general area but did not touch it.

Neville could see a circle that wound itself around the cylindrical vent stack. She nodded.

Simon rose to his feet and walked to the edge where one of the crime scene technicians was taking measurements. "Bernard, tell her what you found."

The man was in his fifties and rail-thin. He pushed his wire-rimmed glasses up on the bridge of his nose and said, "Fibers in this spot right here." He pointed to the ninety-degree stone edge of the cap.

"What kind of fibers?" Simon asked.

"I won't know until I get back to the lab, but they look like the type of fibers used in the construction of climbing ropes."

Neville nodded, looked back at the vent stack, and then at the spot that Bernard had identified. She could see the discoloration in the stone, as if something had rubbed away the grime. She peered over the edge and directly beneath was a balcony. "I assume that's the balcony of Tarek's room?"

"It is," Simon answered.

Neville looked back at the vent stack. "A rope?"

Simon nodded.

"So where is it?"

"That's a very good question. In fact, I began asking our people if anyone removed it. No one did, of course. Our people know better than that. But I did find one officer who was on the scene early, who says he definitely remembered a rope running down the side of the building."

"He's certain of this."

"I had him show me the exact spot where he remembered seeing the rope." Simon pointed down. "He showed me where he parked his car and led me directly to the spot right beneath us."

Neville looked at the buildings to her left and right. The heights didn't match but the buildings abutted each other. "So you're telling me there was an accomplice on the roof when the police arrived who then pulled up the rope and fled."

Simon looked at the sea of yellow flags across the street. "I'm not sure. There's another possibility."

Neville could tell by his expression that he was deeply concerned about something. "What's bothering you?"

"What's not bothering me would be a more accurate question."

She shared the same ominous feeling. "Spit it out."

"I think someone may have tampered with the rope."

"You mean removed it?" Neville asked.

"Yes."

"Shit." This thing just kept getting worse. "We have a list of all the people who've been in and out of here in the last thirty hours?"

"I'm working on it."

"What about the guests?"

"That was the next thing I was going to talk to you about." Simon walked away from the edge of the roof with Neville in tow. "Five guests are unaccounted for."

"What do you mean, 'unaccounted for'?"

"They checked in earlier in the week and didn't bother checking out. Their luggage is still in their rooms."

Neville grabbed him by the arm. "Do we have descriptions of them?"

"Yes," Simon said with a cautious tone.

Neville thought about the dead bodyguards. "Dark hair, dark skin . . . all in their twenties?"

"I'm afraid so."

"Have you talked to the employees who checked them in?"

"Yes."

"Have you had them ID the bodies?"

"Not yet. We're working on getting them to the morgue."

Neville nodded. It was Sunday and they were still trying to wrap their minds around this thing. She was still trying to see how these new bizarre pieces fit into the puzzle when Simon said he had one more piece of information.

"The room with all of the surveillance equipment down the hall from Tarek's . . ."

"Yes."

"The hotel's computer says the room was unoccupied and being remodeled."

"Has anyone on the staff confirmed that it was in fact being remodeled?"

"Not so far, but I haven't talked to everyone."

Neville thought of the missing rope, the missing guests, who were more than likely lying on cold metal tables in the morgue, the strange behavior of the Libyan Embassy, and now this room full of surveillance equipment. "Has the forensic team finished going over the room with the surveillance equipment?"

"Yes."

"Tell them I want them to focus on matching any hair samples with the four bodyguards in the morgue. Nice work, Martin."

"You would have figured it all out," he said, trying to play down the whole thing.

"Maybe . . . maybe not. Let's see if we can punch some holes in it and keep it between us until we know we have it right." Neville headed for the steps.

"Where you off to?"

"Remember the guy from the Directorate who showed up last night?"

"Your ex-boyfriend?"

Neville was about to argue the point, but figured it wasn't worth it. "I have a feeling he and his people know a lot more about what happened here than they're letting on."

"I agree," Simon said, rushing to catch up with her, "and that's why I'm coming with you."

"I can handle it on my own."

"I know you can," Simon said as he started down the steps. "But it's always good to have an extra set of eyes when you're dealing with professional liars from the Directorate."

CHAPTER 17

CHET Bramble sat in the back of the van and watched the monitors come online one by one. The static of the little ten-inch monitors flickered to black and white images of the interior of the apartment. They now had audio and video on the safe house. He could see his two men move from one screen to the next. He adjusted the lip mike on his headset and said, "You two dildos done dicking around?"

"One more minute," the voice crackled. "I need to take a crap."

"Very funny, dickhead." Normally Chet would have laughed at such a juvenile comment, but not today. "I told you two this guy is a sneaky fucker. Get your asses moving and get out of there. If he walks in on you, you'll be dead before I can get in there and save your worthless butts."

The two men began collecting their gear and moving toward the door. Bramble leaned back in the small chair and exhaled, rubbing his right forearm. The temperature was dropping and it was starting to ache. He was a big man—six feet three inches of sculpted muscles and brawn. He had a broad forehead, a thick neck, and a pair of legs that provided a sturdy base to an immovable object. His entire persona exuded violence and he still couldn't figure out how Rapp had beaten him more than a year ago. By rights he should have wiped the mat with the young recruit, but somehow the sneaky little fucker had put him in some move he'd never even heard of and about two seconds later there was a sound like a dry branch snapping in two. There was a moment of nothing and then searing pain, followed worst of all by the fact that his arm was bent in a way that it was never meant to bend.

Chet Bramble was the son of a Georgia pig farmer. He had only one sibling, Bob, who had spent nearly an hour hung up in his mother's narrow birth canal. Rather than do a C-section, the country doctor yanked and pulled and twisted with a pair of forceps until little Bob was wrenched from his mother's womb. The end result was that Bob had a deformed head and was a little slow mentally. He was two years younger than Chet, but from the age of four on, he was nearly identical in size. Bob was his older brother's shadow for much of their youth. Chet loved him and fiercely defended him against any and all antagonists no matter their age or size, but as he became a teenager he quietly grew to resent him.

Chet's mother spent her days baking, doing chores, listening to Christian radio, and reading the Bible. His father, Jacob, or Jake, as his friends knew him, was a massive man with a puritan work ethic and absolutely no sense of humor. He drove both his boys hard, but drove Chet harder for the obvious reason that he wasn't half retarded. As soon as they could walk they were helping feed the pigs, and not long after that they were shoveling shit. So much shit that all these years later, the mere mention of it filled Chet's nostrils with the overpowering smell.

As far as Chet could tell, none of his DNA came from his mother's side. She was a frail little thing and her brothers, two lawyers and an insurance salesman, were pussies. Chet was big and strong like his dad, who had played football for the University of Georgia. There was, however, one big difference between father and son. While Jake was a stoic man who was slow to boil, Chet was hot-tempered and prone to flying off the handle with little or no warning. There was one exception—his brother Bob, and his endless simple questions. When it came to him, Chet had the patience of Job, but that was where it ended. The fights started early on and continued all the way through his senior year in high school.

It wasn't that Chet couldn't control his temper, it was that he chose not to. He'd learned at an early age that it felt good to pummel another person with his fists. His first real fight was in second grade, and like most fights at that age, it started on the bus. A couple of fifth-graders were picking on Bob, who was a kindergartener at the time. In addition to his odd-shaped head and his simplemindedness, Bob had a speech impediment that Trevor Smith and Nate Huckster simply couldn't resist imitating. The first day Chet sat in his seat and stewed, worried that if he did what he was thinking he'd end up in such big trouble that his father would whip him. That night he didn't sleep well. He lay in the bottom bunk, with his brother sleeping soundly a few feet above him, and plotted. He imagined all of the things he would do to Trevor and Nate if they dared make fun of his brother again. Chet decided there would be no warning. He instinctively knew that warnings wouldn't do a thing—that talking was useless, and that he needed to send a clear message to everyone who even thought about teasing Bob.

Trevor and Nate started in the next day from the moment they got on the bus. Chet was sitting next to his brother when the two goons grabbed the seat behind them and started in with their stuttering and teasing and laughing, and with each passing mile, Chet let his anger grow. Clenching and unclenching his fists, he passed the time by imagining what he would do to these two when they got off the bus.

It went down on the sidewalk in front of Benjamin Lincoln Elementary School. The two fifth-graders followed Chet and Bob as they filed toward the front door with all the other students and continued to heckle Bob, who, although he was a kindergartener, was as tall as the average fourth-grader. Chet was by far the biggest second-grader, and he was unnaturally strong thanks to his father's genetics and all of the heavy lifting he had to do around the farm. There was one other thing: Chet was quick, lightning quick, from chasing pigs. Without warning, Chet spun to his left, his GI Joe lunchbox clutched firmly in his right hand. He swung it with such force that he broke Nate Huckster's jaw, knocking him out cold. The fifth-grader slid to the sidewalk like a wet noodle.

Trevor Smith froze as he watched his friend go down. Nowhere in his imagination had he seen this coming. His own fight or flight reflex never had a chance to engage. The dirty little pig farmer was on him like a violent summer storm. A flurry of punches and then kicks were delivered, and Trevor Smith ended up curled on the sidewalk next to his friend begging for the beating to stop. It was a teacher who saved him, by literally yanking Chet off his feet.

The fallout was interesting, and it taught Chet a lesson he would never forget. Chet didn't care what they were going to do to him. The beating he'd delivered to those two jerks was worth it. He'd never been in trouble before, but he knew what happened to kids who fought in school. They were sent to the principal's office and usually given detention, which almost always involved cleaning erasers after school. That punishment would be light. He got the feeling he would get a little more than that. They'd probably paddle him, but he was tough enough to take it. There wasn't a thing they could do to him that could match the wrath of his father. That was the one thing that had him worried— his father. But then again his father had told him on more than one occasion to make sure no one picked on his brother. All Chet knew was that watching his defenseless brother get picked on made him sick to his stomach, and that he couldn't live with himself if he didn't do something about it. He was prepared to take whatever punishment they gave him. One other very important thing happened that day— Chet realized he enjoyed beating the crap out of other boys.

The principal was nowhere near as upset as Chet thought he would be. Apparently, there was something very novel about a second-grader beating the snot out of two fifth-graders. Chet learned by certain things that he heard in the following days that Trevor and Nate weren't much liked by the faculty. Evidently, they had been terrorizing the school for several years and the teachers couldn't wait for them to move on to the middle school across the street. The other thing he learned was that teachers in general don't take very kindly to kids picking on mentally challenged students. Where Chet had really miscalculated, though, was with his parents. His father barely said a word, while his mother lost her mind. She was obsessed with the fact that Nate Huckster was the son of the preacher at their church. In Chet's mind, this was all the more reason to give him a beating, since the son of a preacher should know better than to pick on a slow-minded kindergartener. However, that's not the way Emma saw it. This was an embarrassment to the family. The Hucksters were good people. Great-Grandma Huckster was a founding member of the United Daughters of the Confederacy, and Trevor Smith's grandfather owned the bank, which carried the note on their farm.

Chet rode home in the backseat of his mom's Ford wagon with Bob and listened to her scream at his father about a lot of things that he didn't understand. When they were finally home, his father took him out to the barn, where he fully expected he would be told to drop his pants and assume the position. It never happened. His father placed his giant hand on his shoulder and nudged him toward a hay bale. He made no attempt to enlighten him on the meaning of social pariah, uncouth dirt farmer, or any of the other things that he had heard his mother scream about in the car. He told Chet in no uncertain terms that he would deal with his mother, he was proud of him that he had stuck up for his brother, and yes, the son of a preacher should know better than to make fun of a gentle boy like Bob, and if he didn't know better, he deserved to have the snot knocked out of him. As far as the Smiths and the note on the farm were concerned, there was nothing to worry about. Trevor's father had been an all-conference running back in high school for one reason. Jake Bramble blocked for him and as starting right tackle, there wasn't a defender in the conference who could stop him. Trevor's dad was a good man, and when he found out his son was picking on little Bob, he would be delivering a second beating.

Chet couldn't understand any of it, but something had changed in him. He didn't tell his father, and he sure as hell didn't tell his mom. He had enjoyed beating those two boys more than anything he had ever done in his life. He replayed it over in his mind with pure glee, often smiling and laughing aloud to himself. As happens in rural communities, word spread pretty quickly that Jacob Bramble, the three-time all-conference tackle for the beloved Georgia Bulldogs, had a seven-year-old son who had beaten the snot out of two eleven-year-old boys. A period of calm followed where the other boys gave him due respect, not wanting to get smacked in the head with a GI Joe lunchbox by the psychotic pig farmer. The high school wrestling coach, however, stopped by to talk to his dad about channeling Chet's natural talents in the right direction.

Chet never knew this, but his dad had been worrying about his son long before the fight in front of the school. He had sensed a mean streak in him that was evident when he was around the animals. He would kick the pigs and spit on them when they didn't do what he wanted them to do, and there was the time he caught him dropping the cat from the rafters of the barn. Jake hoped it was a phase, but in the meantime, he saw wrestling as a way to channel his son's energy into something with discipline.

At first it worked. Chet devoted himself to wrestling with the zeal of a missionary. By the age of ten, he was Georgia state champ for his age and weight class. As he continued to excel in wrestling, he began playing full-contact football. He was an absolute beast. He played full-back and linebacker. Other teams were afraid to run against him, and when he carried the ball, he would often choose to run opposing defenders over rather than seek the open field. By the time high school rolled around, his body was transformed into a mass of solid muscle. He started for both varsity teams as a freshman, and as a junior he was all-state in two sports. The girls loved him, the boys feared him, and unfortunately, Bob was becoming a bigger and bigger embarrassment. As everyone advanced, Bob's brain seemed to be stuck somewhere between third and fourth grade. In Chet's junior year, they were playing their archrivals for the conference championship and one of the linemen on the other team started to make fun of Chet's brother, calling him a retard and every other cruel thing he could think of. Chet, who was already known as a dirty player, responded decisively. Several plays later the team ran a sweep. Just as the whistle blew, Chet caught the oaf standing around the pile and he buried his helmet in the side of the kid's knee, snapping it at a ninety-degree angle.

Chet had been extremely proud of himself. To this day, he could put a smile on his face when he remembered that big fat bastard lying on the ground crying like a little girl. The following year, in the same game, the fat bastard's little brother returned the favor. He performed a crackback block on a reverse and shattered Chet's knee. At the time, every team in the SEC was recruiting Chet. The following week every single offer was rescinded, and Chet's football career was over. His grades were never great, so going to college to do anything other than play football seemed like a waste of time. He spent six months in a cast and then another six months lying around growing increasingly bitter about life while he made little effort to rehab his knee.

His father could see what would become of his son if he were damned to the pig farm for the rest of his life, so he drove him to the army recruiting station. Jake Bramble already lived with a bitter woman who ignored the fact that they were steadily building an extremely profitable operation. She couldn't get past the public embarrassment that she was married to a pig farmer. He wasn't going to watch his son sit around and waste the rest of his life wondering what could have been.

So at eighteen Chet joined the army. Two years later he was a ranger, and three years after that he joined the baddest of the bad— Delta Force. There were some bumps along the way, most of them involving bar fights or reprimands from officers who didn't appreciate Chet's sarcastic sense of humor and chose to focus on his lack of respect for rank. The odds were good that eventually Chet's penchant for drinking and fighting and disrespecting officers would up and land his ass in big trouble.

Sure enough, it happened off-post one hot August night at a popular joint in Fayetteville, North Carolina. It was one of those places with dining on one side and a big dance hall on the other, where they would crank the country music and southern rock all night long. Scantily clad girls with tied-up T-shirts and short shorts served ice-cold beer out of galvanized tubs, and the booze flowed at the right prices. On weekends, the place was packed with army personnel, some in uniform but most in mufti. Chet and his Delta buddies wouldn't be caught dead wearing their uniforms off-post in a bar, so when a group of officers rolled in with their dates wearing their dress blues, Chet couldn't resist. It started simply enough. He threw some insults in their direction that were more or less drowned out by the loud music. The group of officers could smell the Delta boys from a mile away, with their long hair, beards, mustaches, and bulging muscles. Things took a decided turn for the worse when Chet tried to cut in on a young second lieutenant whose wife was the hottest chick in the joint by a mile.

The lieutenant, who was considerably smaller than Chet, took offense. Chet shoved him, and before anyone had a chance to calm things down, a full bird colonel with jump wings, a combat infantry badge, two purple hearts, and a chest full of ribbons was right in the thick of it. The rest of the Delta boys had the sense to back off, but Chet was too pissed drunk to realize he was about to cross a Rubicon that an enlisted man should never cross. The colonel informed Chet that his commanding officer was an old friend, and if he went back to his table right now, he would be willing to look the other way and forget that he ever saw him lay a hand on an officer. Chet nodded drunkenly and for a long moment seemed to consider the colonel's offer. Then he told the officer to fuck off. The colonel was sober, squared away, and a badass in his own right. He looked to the other Delta boys and advised them to get their buddy the hell out of here before he had him thrown in the stockade.

And that was when Chet unleashed a big left hook that glanced off the top of the colonel's head. Before anyone could react, the colonel delivered two lightning punches—the first to Chet's nuts and the second to his solar plexus. As Chet dropped to his knees, the colonel delivered the coup de grace with an open-handed chop to the back of the neck that knocked Chet out cold.

The next day Chet woke up on a concrete floor with his neck so sore he couldn't lift his head to take in his surroundings. It took him a moment to realize he was in the stockade at Fort Bragg. Then he heard voices. One of them was familiar. It was his CO. The events of the previous night came back to him in a fuzzy haze. Chet knew he was in some deep shit. He heard another voice and thought it sounded like that peacock colonel that he was going to pound the crap out of. Chet rolled over to get a look at them and realized he had thrown up on himself.

"Mike, it's your call," his CO said. "I got no problem if you want to court-martial his stupid ass."

The colonel was dressed in his green BDUs, his pants bloused into a shiny pair of jump boots and his hands clasped behind him as if he was standing at parade rest. "I'm tempted. How the fuck does someone this stupid get into Delta these days?" He cocked his head to the side to look at the Delta CO. "When I was in with you, they actually tested us to make sure we had a brain."

"Yeah, well, unfortunately we don't test them when they're drunk."

"Maybe you should start."

The CO turned to the door and said, "Stan, why would you want such an obvious retard?"

With great effort, Chet craned his neck to see who his commanding officer was talking to. A man in a gray suit was standing in the doorway. His hair was cut military short, but there was a casualness in the way he stood.

He regarded Chet for a long moment and then said, "I remember a few times where I wanted to take a swing at an officer. I think I did once actually. Not sure, though. I was pretty drunk, too."

The colonel who had kicked Chet's ass shook his head in disgust. "I don't want to waste my time dealing with this shithead . . . and God knows, Jim, your D boys don't need any more bad publicity."

The CO was quietly relieved. His old buddy was right. The best outcome here was to hit the eject button and let Hurley deal with this jackass. "Stan, he's all yours."

Stan Hurley stroked his mustache and nodded with a sense of anticipation. "Nice doing business with you, gentlemen."

"You're welcome." The two officers moved down the hallway, relieved to be rid of this problem.

"Get up," Hurley commanded.

"Who the fuck are you?" Chet mumbled.

Hurley grinned. This hayseed might have to learn things the hard way. "Who I am is none of your business. All you need to know is that I just saved you from spending the next five years of your life in Leavenworth. Now get your ass moving, Victor."

"My name isn't Victor."

"It is now. Let's go."

That was three years ago, and at first Chet wasn't sure about his new line of work. He was grateful to have avoided going to jail, but he wasn't too thrilled that he was no longer a member of the world's most elite commando team. Before he knew it, though, Chet could see he had found the perfect place and the ultimate mentor. No more saluting, no more rules, and the best part—he got to kill people.

Bramble looked above the monitors at the photos taped to the wall of the van. There were five of them. The first one was a simple headshot, black and white. It made Bramble hate Rapp even more. The man was ruggedly handsome. Where Bramble had to chase pussy, it seemed to fall into Rapp's lap. To add insult to the whole thing, the jerk seemed to always turn it down. "I hate you, you arrogant prick."

Bramble wondered where Hurley had gotten the photo. They weren't big on photos in this line of work—especially posed photos. The other four were all surveillance pics, one of them taken on this exact block in Paris, right in front of the safe house. Again, how it had been obtained, and why, gave Bramble a healthy dose of concern. Hurley or that twat Kennedy had ordered the surveillance on Rapp. *No,* he thought to himself, *she loves him too much. He's her little pet. She would never put him under surveillance.*

It had to be Hurley. He was a smart fucker. At times Bramble thought the tough SOB hated Rapp almost as much as he did. *He wants me to kill him,* Bramble thought. *He wants me to rid him of this problem and I'm going to be more than happy to oblige him.*

CHAPTER 18

ALEXANDRIA, VIRGINIA

IRENE Kennedy was sitting in the sunroom of her two-bedroom brownstone in Old Town. Her husband was out training for yet another marathon while she was midway through her second newspaper and her third cup of tea. Her marriage could be better, but it could just as easily be worse. There was no shouting or violence, but there was an unstated truce and an underlying knowledge that they did not love each other more today than they had the year before. Kennedy was wrapped up in her work, and he was wrapped up in himself, and she couldn't decide if she should stick with it or move on. Divorce was a messy, protracted battle, and besides, she wasn't the kind of person who quit something so important so easily.

There was a fair amount of self-recrimination over her lack of effort, but her job afforded her little time to come up for air, and, as she'd learned over the years, her husband was hardly the kind of person who would meet her halfway. He was basically a spoiled, selfish boy who refused to grow up. This was all lost on her when they were dating—when things were easy. He was turned on by the fact that she worked for the CIA, and she was turned on by the fact that he was a good-looking, smart man who made her laugh. He was a college professor who had a very flexible schedule, which worked well for her. When they were dating Kennedy didn't see any of the negatives. Even the first few years of marriage went well. Then the complaining started. Karl always seemed to be getting the raw end of some deal. It usually involved a simple discussion at a party, or a double date with one of the tenured members of his department. To Kennedy the conversations seemed normal—two adults agreeing to disagree. But then they'd get home and Karl would go on for hours about how rude the other person was. How insulting the person had been and that he could tolerate a lot of things but ill-mannered adults was not one of them. Kennedy never saw it. She worked in the ultimate defend-your-position job. Day in and day out she had to take tough stances and was often told by her superiors that she was wrong. With so much going on, there was no time to pout. Kennedy eventually began to see him as an incredibly insecure man who couldn't bear the thought of being upstaged, at least intellectually. She reasoned that this was why he was teaching philosophy to freshmen at American University. The job allowed him to play God to a bunch of kids who were just thrilled to be living away from their parents, and wouldn't dare challenge a learned professor.

As she saw this ugly side of him, she instinctively withdrew, and he instinctively saw her retreat as a betrayal, and that was how they ended up in their current state of marital detente. So on Sunday mornings he ran, and she got some much-needed downtime. It also happened to be the only day she wasn't expected to work, although if a crisis popped up it didn't matter what day or time it was, she had to head in. None of this bothered Kennedy. Her job was interesting, challenging, frustrating, and ultimately crucial to the security of the country. What Sundays offered, as long as the enemy was cooperating, was a certain degree of solitude. It gave her the necessary time to filter through the thousands of data points she'd been dealing with during the week—all of the various operations and needs of her people and the operations that were being mounted against her country.

She needed at least one day out of the week to step away from all of it and try to gain some perspective.

She was doing that on a subconscious level, while plowing through the Arts section of the *Times,* when the phone rang. Kennedy was irritated. It wasn't yet 9:00 a.m., which for a Sunday morning was early. Kennedy considered not answering it, and then thought that it might be her mother. She set down her tea and walked to the kitchen where the phone was hanging from the wall. She looked at the small readout of the caller ID and her eyes narrowed. It was an international call. Kennedy had already checked the message service twice since getting out of bed and had spent a good portion of the morning wondering if Rapp had crawled into a Parisian sewer and died, which although she liked him would not be the worst possible outcome for her employer.

Calling her house directly was a major breach of protocol, but then again Rapp had proven that he wasn't big on following her rules. Curiosity got the better of her and she reached for the handset. "Hello."

"Good morning."

There was no mistaking the voice on the other end. It was Rapp. Kennedy's face flushed with resentment over his reckless ways. "You know this isn't a secure line," she said, not able to completely mask the annoyance in her voice. There was a frustrating sigh on the other end and then . . .

"Listen carefully." His voice had a hard, *I don't give a shit* edge to it. "As far as I'm concerned, there is no such thing as a secure line on your end."

"What is that supposed to mean?"

"You're smart, figure it out."

"I'm in no mood for your games," she said in an attempt to assert control. "You're in some hot water. There are some people who think you've screwed this thing up in the worst possible way, and since you haven't bothered to check in, you've led them to speculate about how much you can be trusted."

"I'm glad you fucking desk jockeys have it all figured out from four thousand miles away. I can just hear your uncle second-guessing every move I made even though he hasn't a clue what went down."

"Listen . . . this thing wouldn't look any better from ten feet. It's a mess and it's your mess."

"You're damn right it is. The only problem is none of you have the foggiest idea what happened."

"It's hard to know what happened when your subordinate doesn't bother to pick up the phone and check in."

"Well . . . while you were sipping on your latte or tea or whatever the fuck it is that you drink, your subordinate was floating down a river with a bullet hole in his shoulder."

Kennedy stared wide-eyed at the wall for a moment. Two visuals crowded her thoughts. The first was a wounded Rapp submerged in the murky water of the Seine and the second was the massive cavern beneath the National Security Agency in Maryland that housed the Cray Supercomputers, which were more than likely recording and processing this call. Chastened by Rapp's information, she said, "I didn't know. I'm sorry. Listen, I can be in the office in twenty minutes. Can you call me there?"

Rapp laughed. "I don't think you understand the problem. I was set up."

"Set up?" Her face twisted into a frown.

"They were waiting for me. Your advance team missed them, and I missed them. They knew I was coming. I barely made it out of there alive."

Kennedy was thunderstruck. "I don't understand how that could have happened."

"I thought that's what you'd say. I'll make this real simple. You've been compromised. I don't know by whom, but either someone has penetrated our little group or we have a traitor among us, and since I'm the one way out on a limb getting shot at, you'll have to excuse me if I don't exactly trust any of you until you get it figured out."

Kennedy was pacing from one end of the kitchen to the other, frantically trying to figure out what in hell was going on. A dozen obvious questions popped into her mind, but they were on her damn home phone, and she couldn't risk asking what she needed to ask. She glanced at the clock on the microwave and wondered if she could catch the next flight to Paris. "I'll come to you. I'll bring you in."

"And how do I know I can trust you?"

Kennedy scrambled to come up with an answer. She thought of how she had recruited him, how she had been his only advocate from the very beginning. The only one who truly recognized his talent and potential. And then she put herself in his shoes. She'd been in the field many times, but never in a situation as stressful as the one he was in right now. The sense of isolation would be overwhelming. Dr. Lewis's admonition came back to her forcefully. They had created him, and if he turned on them . . . She shuddered at the thought. "You can trust me, and you know it."

"I'm not really in the mood to trust anyone at the moment."

"I've had your back every step of the way," she pleaded. "I went to the mat for you yesterday." She thought of the argument in Stansfield's office. "Just as you guessed, my uncle was very critical."

"That's a shock."

Kennedy started to say something and then held back. She really needed to talk to Stansfield and tell him what Rapp had told her. "Listen, we need to get off this line. I am going to come to you. Check the service in an hour and I will have more information for you."

"And what makes you so sure I want to be brought in? Knowing how your uncle operates I'll end up in solitary for a month hooked up to a car battery."

Kennedy cringed. He was right, of course. Taking a big risk, she said, "I want you to be careful. Check the service and . . . one other thing . . . he sent some guys over yesterday to look for you."

"Who?" Rapp said, the suspicion evident in his voice.

Kennedy hesitated and then said, "Victor, your old friend, was one of them. I argued against it."

The omission was greeted with silence. Kennedy imagined him on the other end of the line seething—his laserlike focus feeding off his hatred for Victor. "They're keeping an eye on the apartment. Don't go there," Kennedy offered. "I will be there as soon as I can to bring you in. All right? Check the service. Don't do anything stupid."

"I'll think about it." There was a long pause and then Rapp said, "There were five men who crashed the meeting. I took care of four of them. There was one left . . . the one who winged me. Do you understand what I'm saying?"

Kennedy's brow creased with wrinkles, as she tried to decipher what he was saying. "No."

"I stuck to protocol. I didn't do anything I wasn't authorized to do."

"Okay," Kennedy said, still trying to figure out what he was hinting at.

"I wasn't the only one who walked out of there. The fifth man is responsible for the other three. I went out the window."

"I'm still not sure I understand . . ."

"You'll figure it out. I have to go."

The line went dead and Kennedy slowly placed the handset back in its cradle. She replayed the entire conversation in her head, wondering if there was anything that the NSA or FBI could use against her. It was all pretty vague, but it might be enough to land her on someone's radar screen. She cursed Rapp for calling her at home and then thought about what he'd told her. That it had been a setup. She was moving across the room for the front hall closet without thinking. She needed to brief Stansfield immediately. She grabbed her coat and her car keys from the hook by the door. She hoped Stansfield would see things her way. If he didn't, she prayed Dr. Lewis was wrong. The last thing they needed was an enraged Rapp looking to settle a score.

CHAPTER 19

PARIS, FRANCE

THE black Renault sedan had tinted windows that made it impossible to see who was in the backseat. It was double-parked in front of the luxurious Hotel Balzac only a few blocks from the Arc de Triomphe. A policeman had already tried to move the car but was rebuffed by the driver, who sat securely behind the sedan's bulletproof windows. The driver was armed with a unique badge that sent the police officer on his way. He also wore a gun on his right hip. The other man in the front seat had the same badge and gun and also had access to an Uzi submachine gun, which was hidden under the dashboard. The vehicle was retrofitted with a thin skin of Kevlar between its frame and the metal exterior. The man in the backseat had traveled the world and had seen more than a few men gunned down in their cars, so he took this aspect of his personal security very seriously.

When Fournier was younger he had carried a gun. It was part of his job, and it didn't hurt that certain women were turned on by the cold steel he wore on his hip. He had killed precisely three men during his career—all of them execution style. His bosses ordered the hits, and he carried them out without question. The men were ne'er-do-wells and reprobates. In one case, the target was a traitor who was selling state secrets; in another, it was an agent who was fomenting problems in Algeria; and the third was a Syrian woman. He was never told why she was to be killed, and she was the one of the three that sometimes visited him in his dreams. She was a stunning woman in her midforties with a perfect oval face, raven black hair, and eyes to match. It had been in a Parisian hotel. She was eating breakfast dressed in a white robe. When Fournier entered the room she gave him a knowing nod, set her coffee cup down, shook out her long black hair, and looked up at him with unblinking eyes. When Fournier drew his silenced weapon she showed no fear and instead offered him a small smile. The other two men he'd shot in the head, but for some reason he couldn't put a bullet in the exquisite face before him, so he lowered his muzzle a few inches and placed three bullets in her left breast.

His gun-toting days were done. Fournier had access to virtually any gun he wanted, but in general, he found them to be a pain in the butt. They were bulky, and they made his suits look lopsided. Fournier spent enough on his suits that it wouldn't do to have them look off. He was a man of style. Besides, he was no longer on the front lines. He was the one giving the kill orders now. The guns and his protection could be left to his trusted bodyguards.

Pierre Mermet brushed a wisp of thin brown hair from his forehead, opened the file on his lap, and extracted the first set of photographs. "Mossad . . . Efram Bentov is his name. He arrived this morning along with at least two others. They passed through customs separately, took different forms of transportation into town, and all miraculously ended up at the Israeli Embassy."

Fournier frowned and took the photos. "Not very smart."

"I agree."

"Counting yesterday, that brings the total number of suspected Mossad agents to six."

"That we know of."

"And the three that flew in yesterday . . . they're still lying low at the hotel on Rivoli?" Fournier asked.

"That's right."

Fournier took the other photographs. "Any weapons?"

"Not that we know of, but we must assume."

Fournier nodded.

"Do you want them picked up for questioning?"

"Not yet. I want to see what they're up to first."

Mermet's mouth twisted into a pensive frown.

Fournier had seen the look many times. "You don't like my decision?"

"The three at the hotel have no diplomatic papers. We could force the issue. If they have guns in their room or on their persons we could hold them and question them indefinitely."

"We could do that," Fournier said in an easy voice, "and then my counterpart Big Ben Friedman would grab some of our people in Israel and do the exact same thing and where would that get us?"

"Given what happened at the hotel the other night, I think we have more leeway than we could normally expect."

"We do, but Ben Friedman is a bear I would prefer not to poke."

Mermet took the rebuke well. "It's just that we're spread thin. We have six men following the Russians, eight following the Brits, and ten on the Americans."

Fournier knew what Mermet was thinking. If this continued for any length of time, they would have to call in more men and ask for more money and that would mean more eyes in the government would be drawn to what they were up to. "I understand your worries. If nothing has happened by tomorrow, we'll reassess . . . maybe even nicely ask a few of these gents to leave so we don't have so many heads to keep an eye on."

"And there's undoubtedly a few we missed."

Fournier had thought of the same thing, but he had certain information that he wasn't willing to share. "One more day and then we will focus on the Jews, the Brits, and the Americans. Any more interesting news to share about our American friends?"

"Yes," Mermet said, almost forgetting that he had a new face to run by his boss. "The three who showed up yesterday . . . they're still cooped up in the van on Chaplain. Another man showed up this afternoon." Mermet found the photo and handed it to his boss.

Fournier's eyes widened with disbelief. "Oh, my God."

"What is it?"

"Who . . . who is it, you mean." He shook his head. "This is a man I have not seen in some time." Fournier looked out the window, thinking of one of his earliest assignments in Southeast Asia. "He is very dangerous."

"Who is he?"

"Stan Hurley. CIA, or I should say, was CIA. I had heard he'd retired a few years ago."

"He looks a little young to retire."

Fournier nodded. "Hurley is like a shark. They only know one thing. Men like that don't retire . . . they just simply die one day. I should have known better."

"I assume he was on the operations side of the business."

"Yes." Fournier shook his head as he thought of the time he'd watched Hurley slice a man's ears off in Vietnam. And then there were the stories he'd heard over the years involving the Soviets. "He was very good at his job. Drove the Russians nuts, or so I've been told."

"So what is he doing in our fair city?"

"That is a very good question. Did your men follow him?"

"No . . . we didn't know who he was and thought it was better to stay with the surveillance van."

Knowing how thin they were stretched, Fournier couldn't chastise Mermet. "Tell our people to check the customs database. Look for the name Stan Hurley and any other aliases we may have on file. The next time he shows up, I want him followed. I want to know every move he makes."

"I assume they should exercise a fair amount of caution."

"That is a very astute observation, Pierre. He is a man very comfortable with violence."

"An ally, though?"

The idea made Fournier smile. France's relationship with the United States was fraught with complications. "Traditionally yes, but we have no way of knowing who he is working for at the moment." The truth was Fournier trusted no one, but he knew that position would sound a bit too paranoid to a pleaser like Mermet. "We shouldn't assume he is still beholden to the CIA. Just find him and let me know as soon as you do." Fournier reached for the door handle, assuming the meeting was over.

"There are two more things. Your friend, the Spaniard."

Fournier let his hand fall to his knee. He was parked in front of the Balzac because he was going in to meet Max Vega. "Yes."

"Well . . . his friend has not left the country."

Fournier thought of Samir the idiot. He so disliked the man that he didn't bother to hide his irritation. "You're certain."

Mermet nodded. "He's upstairs in Vega's suite right now."

Fournier swore to himself. These fundamentalist morons were turning out to be more trouble than they were worth.

Mermet saw the frustration on his boss's face and offered, "I can have him forcibly deported if you'd like."

Fournier shook his head vehemently. "We don't need to draw any more attention to these fools than they've done on their own." He might have him killed, though, if the man continued to be such an irritant. "What's the last issue?"

"Your old friend, Commandant Neville?"

Fournier smiled as he remembered the passionate sex they'd had. "Yes."

"She had a forensics team on the roof of the hotel all morning."

"There is nothing for her to find. You took care of that problem."

"I removed the rope, but there is undoubtedly some evidence that was left behind."

Fournier shrugged. He supposed the problem was unavoidable. Sooner or later, Neville was going to figure out that all the ballistics didn't add up. The Libyans were holding up their part of the deal, but that would work for only so long. Neville would figure out that the bodyguards weren't in fact bodyguards. The only question was what type of evidence she could collect to prove her suspicions. The entire crime scene was a mess and he and Mermet had done just enough to make her job all the more confusing. Turning to his most trusted aide, he said, "I would not worry about her. She is not going to get very far in solving this case."

"Well, she's looking for you, and I've been told she's suddenly very interested in compiling a list of everyone who was at the crime scene the morning in question. Especially a certain sandy-brown-haired man who was with you." Mermet was speaking about himself. "What would you like me to do?"

"Lie low. Stay away from the office. I will handle her."

"All right."

Fournier reached for the door again and Mermet asked, "Anything else?"

With one foot on the pavement, Fournier turned back to Mermet and said, "Yes. Find me Mr. Stan Hurley. I would very much like to have a talk with him."

CHAPTER 20

N general, big cities the world over shared the same basic makeup.
They had centers for banking and finance, business districts,
retail meccas where you could buy almost anything, museums and
concert halls, above- and belowground rail systems, and roads that
traveled out from the central downtown to suburbs like arteries from
a heart. There were parks and neighborhoods that accommodated
the super rich, the destitute, and everything in between. The affluent
neighborhoods had fine restaurants, fine jewelers, art dealers, and
boutique stores that carried the most expensive clothes. The poor
neighborhoods had pawn shops, greasy restaurants that had to bribe
health inspectors to keep their doors open, gambling shops, houses of
prostitution, check-cashing hovels with bars on their windows, and of
course drug dealers.

Paris was no different really, other than the fact that Parisians
loved their art so much that they had more museums than most. While
Rapp was confident that he could handle himself in any neighborhood, no matter how rough, he thought it was best not to complicate
things. What he was looking for could be found in little pockets of

almost every quarter of Paris. He could jump on the Metro and go out to one of the slums in the outer ring, but a hardened criminal would ask too many questions, and might bring a few of his cohorts along, all of which would unnecessarily complicate things. Rapp didn't need a true thug. He just needed someone looking to make a little money. Paris was filled with lonely strung-out souls—men and women who had fallen to the addiction of heroin, or crank, or crack, or whatever else they were calling it these days.

Over the last year, Rapp had gotten to know many of the intimate details of the City of Love. Paris had been his base of operations, and other than working out and acting as if he was employed by an American software importer, he was left with time to explore and observe. In between assignments he would return to the apartment in Montparnasse and recharge by attempting to live life like a normal person, which was no easy thing when you were constantly looking over your shoulder. Rapp had been born with a great sense of awareness, but to survive in his line of work, he knew he had to take that awareness to another level. He needed to be keenly attuned to his environment at all times.

The easiest way for him to do this was to practice on his runs and stay very alert while eating most of his meals at nearby cafés. There was no better way to watch and observe people than sitting at a café with a cup of coffee in one hand and a book in the other, or depending on the time of day, maybe a glass of wine and a cigarette. He was always on the lookout for a face that he had seen one too many times—someone new to the neighborhood who might have more than a passing interest in his comings and goings. He spent a great deal of his time working out. He ran nearly every day, his routes always varied, but as things worked in Paris he usually ended up at the river where he didn't have to contend with traffic and stoplights.

Rapp often cut through the Latin Quarter, home to some of France's greatest institutions of higher learning, such as the Sorbonne and the Collège de France. The narrow streets of the quarter were lined with cafés and bookstores that catered to the literary elite of France—poets, writers, theorists, and philosophers who were treated with a respect that no other city could match. These demigods of Parisian culture had certain needs that the public in general accepted. In order to tap into their genius and break their earthly bonds, many of them needed the assistance of certain hallucinogenic drugs. Rapp wasn't interested in these people. They were too old and too wise for what he had in mind. The quarter was also populated by thousands of students, and a subset who wanted drugs for no other reason than to delay their passage into adulthood. Drugs had a powerful effect on certain people. They created dependence and were expensive. Over the years, this harsh paradox had driven countless souls to sell their bodies for sex and commit crimes as small as theft and as heinous as murder to feed their addiction. The longer the time between fixes, the more quickly logic and rational thought fell to the wayside.

Rapp was looking for just such a desperate soul as he emerged from the St. Michel Metro stop wearing a pair of black Persol sunglasses and a three-quarter-length black trench coat with the collar flipped up and his chin down.

"Why won't you tell me your plan?" Greta asked.

It was a bright afternoon and the sidewalk was heavy with a blend of Parisians and tourists. The North Americans were easily identified by their girth, their bulky clothes, their various packs, fanny, back, or otherwise, and cameras dangling from their wrists. The Asians traveled in tight packs, were smaller, and had nicer cameras that were slung around their necks. The Russians and other Eastern Europeans added another interesting mix. The women usually wore too much makeup, their hair was bleached and dried at the ends, with dark roots, and their men wore lots of jewelry and track suits, or at least track jackets and oversized sunglasses as if they were Elvis impersonators. The Brits, Germans, and other Europeans were a little more difficult to pick out, but Rapp could still tell the difference.

He placed a hand on Greta's waist. With her good looks and blond hair, she stood out like a beacon. "I told you I have a thing for brunettes."

"A weird sex fetish, no doubt."

"Something like that."

Greta stuck out her tongue and made a sour face.

"If you're going to make faces like that we could skip the wig and put you in a pair of pigtails."

She smacked him in the chest with the palm of her hand and tried to pull away.

Rapp held her tight. "I already explained, if you want to come with me tonight we need to put you in a wig."

"No one knows who I am."

They'd already been over all of this back at the hotel. "Probably not, although Stan most certainly knows you and he's about as alert as they come."

"I don't understand why you can't just go to him. He is a good man. He will hear you out."

"And then he will lock me up and put me through the wringer for a month."

"The wringer?" Greta asked with a confused frown.

"He'll take away my watch and all my clothes and put me in a very dark cold room and fuck with my mind for as long as it takes for him to make sure I'm telling the truth."

"I don't believe it. I've known him since I was a little girl."

"There's another side to Stan. A very dark side." He could tell she wasn't buying it. "Greta, you know what we do for a living."

"You're spies."

More or less, Rapp thought. "And spies kill people. We deceive and we lie and we conspire to get what we need and we put on all kinds of fake fronts to make sure that nice people like you don't see the nasty ugly man behind the mask."

She succeeded in pushing away this time. "You're telling me that's who you are?"

"No," Rapp moaned. "I'm telling you that's who Stan is . . . and maybe that's who I'll be someday, but I sure as hell don't plan on it."

"But you are a good liar?"

"Not like Stan Hurley, but when I'm on assignment I do what it takes to get the job done."

"And when it comes to me?"

Rapp placed both hands on her shoulders. "If I didn't care about you I wouldn't have bothered to call. I would have let you go to Brussels and you would have been a nervous wreck when I didn't show. Instead, I called you. You came to Paris and this morning I told you things that could get me killed and you still doubt me. Greta, you can't discuss any of this with your grandfather or anyone else. I like your grandfather. I know what he did during World War II and then after when the Russians started throwing their weight around. If he found out that I had involved you in this in any way, I have no doubt he would pick up the phone, call in a favor, and I would spend the rest of my life looking over my shoulder. Sooner or later someone would catch me snoozing and put a bullet in my head."

"My grandfather would never do that."

"Your grandfather is a very serious man, and he would consider it a betrayal that his granddaughter had fallen in love with someone like me. He would want to protect you and the best way to do that would be to have me eliminated."

"I don't believe it."

"I don't know what else to tell you." Rapp was starting to get frustrated. "You can go home any time you'd like, Greta. I'm not going to sit here and debate every move with you."

"You don't want me here?"

"I didn't say that. Don't put words in my mouth. I wanted to see you and I want your help, but this isn't a debate club. I'm actually good at what I do, despite what happened the other night." Rapp had explained all of it to her, the bodyguards who weren't bodyguards, what Tarek had done for a living before he became oil minister, and his opinion that it had all been an elaborate trap.

"I think the fact that you are still alive is proof that you are good at your job."

"Thank you, now will you stop questioning me and go buy the wig?"

She nodded and then wrapped her arms around his waist, burying her face in his chest. She squeezed tight but didn't speak.

Rapp kissed the top of her head and then said, "I'll meet you back at the hotel in a few hours."

Greta nodded. "Can't we just meet back here instead of the hotel?"

"There you go questioning me again. I told you I don't know how long this will take. It's better if we meet at the hotel." Her expression told him she was nervous. "Don't worry, honey, nothing is going to happen to me."

Greta got up on her toes and kissed him on the lips. "I love you."

Rapp took a deep breath and said, "I love you, too. Now go get your wig." He spun her around and sent her on her way with a playful pat on her backside. Every ten feet or so she looked over her shoulder to see if Rapp was still there. He held his ground, knowing there was a good chance she would try to follow him. When she was two blocks away, Rapp made his move. He started toward the river and then doubled back. The Quai de Montebello was crowded with tourists and Parisians alike. The looming Gothic cathedral of Notre Dame sat on its island in the middle of the river.

Tourists on this side of the waterway were blocking traffic as they snapped photos of the famous church. Rapp kept his chin down, and like the other Parisians on the sidewalk, he darted in and around the tourists without breaking stride. He had a destination in mind. A place he had passed many times. A place where he'd seen the hopped-up, jumpy amble of users who were desperate for a little something to take the edge off their comedown or a more powerful fix that could launch them back into nirvana. Rapp took a right on the Rue du Petit Pont. Two blocks later, he was standing in front of St. Severin's Catholic church. That was another thing about Paris. Unlike Berlin or London, the odds were overwhelming that almost every church you encountered would be Catholic. They were like the Italians and the Spaniards that way. The Protestant Reformation had never really taken root along the southern edge of Europe.

Very few people were taking photos of the church. St. Severin's was rich in history, and was a perfect example of Gothic architecture, but it simply couldn't compete with the grand scale of Notre Dame a short distance to the north. Rapp spotted three beggars. They were perfectly spaced, one directly in front of the church, and one on each corner. There was a chance they were working together but probably not. The more important thing was that all three had drug habits, as was evidenced by their dark, shallow eye sockets and fidgety behavior. Rapp chose one of the cafés across the street and picked a small sidewalk table with a good vantage point. When the waitress arrived, he ordered a coffee and sandwich in perfect French. When she returned with the coffee, he asked if there were any extra papers lying around, and a moment later she returned with three.

Rapp pretended to read the newspapers while he studied the various faces at the nearby cafés and tried to ignore the nagging pain in his left shoulder. By the time his sandwich arrived, he had two good candidates. One of the beggars in front of the church had scrounged up enough cash to make a purchase, and he made a beeline for Rapp's café and a young man sitting just four tables away. He located a second pusher across the street at another café when the second beggar had reached his quota. For the next hour, Rapp took his time and studied the men and women who stopped by to visit the dealers. The practiced maneuvers of quiet hands exchanging things under the table while the free hands gestured wildly to distract anyone from noticing the illicit trade—it was all part of the drug culture. The pusher across the street was too short and fat to work for Rapp's purposes, but the one nearby had the general look. Rapp watched a few more transactions take place, left some cash on the table, and picked up his coffee. He approached the man with a smile on his face and gestured toward the open chair.

The man was six feet tall with jet-black hair and a two-day-old growth of black stubble on his face. He was wearing sunglasses, a dark green canvas jacket, jeans, and a pair of brown boots. He motioned for Rapp to take a seat.

Rapp sat and placed his coffee on the table. "Do you speak English?" he asked softly.

"Yes," the man said easily.

"Good." Rapp exhaled nervously and looked around.

The man smiled. He could always charge foreigners a premium. "Is there something I can do for you?"

"I hope so." Rapp rubbed his palms on his jeans, continuing to fake nervousness.

The man began to mumble off a short list of drugs and prices.

Rapp shook his head emphatically. "I'm not a druggie."

This brought a smile to the man's face. Denial was all part of the trade. "Of course not. What can I do for you?"

"I have a proposal. A job that could earn you a lot of money."

"And what would this job involve?"

"It involves me giving you the key to an apartment and the combination to a safe."

The man took a drag from his cigarette and smiled. "What's in the safe?"

"Some cash."

"How much?"

"A lot."

The Frenchman tilted his head from side to side. "A lot is a relative thing. What might be a lot to you, might not be so much to me."

"At least twenty thousand . . . and some jewelry that's worth more than that."

He stabbed out his cigarette. "Why me?"

Rapp blinked his eyes nervously and said, "Because I'm an American and I don't fucking know anyone in Paris. At least not anyone who'd be willing to walk into this bitch's apartment and take what's mine."

"This money is yours?" he asked skeptically.

"Yeah . . . I earned it. We had an arrangement. She was supposed to pay me, but now she's fucking screwing me."

"What kind of deal?"

"That's not important." Rapp looked over each shoulder as if she'd walk up on them at any moment. "The bitch treats me like a slave. She's got my passport in the safe, and my money, and she won't give it to me."

"So why don't you just open it yourself and take what's yours?"

"She doesn't know that I know the combination and . . ." Rapp let his voice trail off as if he was too embarrassed to continue.

"And what?"

"She's friends with my parents. Good friends. If they found out I've been sleeping with her they would shit."

The Frenchman lit another cigarette, exhaling a cloud of smoke. "Let's back up for a second. Why me? How did you find me?"

"I'm not a druggie," Rapp said defensively. "I mean, I'm not hooked. I use them from time to time, but I'm not strung out. I have some friends at the university. Everybody knows this is a place where you can get hooked up. You and the fat guy across the street." Rapp jerked his head in the man's direction.

The Frenchman smiled broadly, revealing a pair of sharp canine teeth. "So why do you think I would want to help you steal from this woman?"

"You sell drugs. You already break the law and what you do day in and day out is a lot riskier than this. Here's the deal," Rapp said, pressing his case. "This bitch is rich. She isn't going to miss any of this. We're supposed to go to an art gallery exhibit tonight. We'll be gone for at least two hours. I can give you the key, the security code, and the code for the safe. I don't give a fuck what you take. I just want my cash and my passport."

"You say there's a lot of jewelry."

"Yeah."

"Jewelry is not easy to get rid of."

"When I say jewelry I mean diamonds . . . little packets of them." Rapp held his hands together. "I don't know how much they're worth, but it's got to be a lot."

The man nodded while he thought it over. "If I decide to do this I will take half the cash and all the jewels."

"Shit!" Rapp came half out of his chair. "Why does everyone want to fuck me?"

"I don't want to fuck you, I just want it to be worth my while."

Rapp took a couple of deep breaths and settled down. "Fifty-fifty . . . that's the only way I'll do it. You want half the cash then I get half the diamonds."

"I don't think so. I am taking all the risk."

"If I don't bring this to you, you get nothing. Now you get half of a lot, and all you have to do is walk in there while we're at the gallery tonight."

"And how do I know you're not setting me up?"

Rapp shook his head as if the idea was preposterous. "What . . . you think I work for the fucking police? They hire Americans now? If they wanted to bust you they'd roll up on you right now. I just want my money and my passport and some of those diamonds."

The man was quiet for a long moment as he looked off into the distance. "How do you know you can trust me?"

"Easy . . . everybody around here knows who you are. If you don't meet me tomorrow with my stuff, I'll turn you over to the cops. They'll know where to find you."

"Then you will be implicated."

"I'll play the dumb American and tell them you got me high and I blacked out. I woke up and my wallet was gone. I had the key and codes written down on a piece of paper in my wallet." Rapp stopped and waved his hands. "But listen, we don't need to go down that road. There's more than enough for us to split. No need to get greedy. You do it tonight, we meet up two days from now right here, and we're both happy men."

Luke Auclair was more than intrigued. He'd been studying business on and off at the Collège de France for five years. His grades were less than spectacular and he'd taken to selling narcotics to pay his burdensome bills. Why he never looked for an honest job was a question Auclair avoided asking himself. The truth was he was lazy, always had been lazy, and would likely be lazy until his dying day. If there were a way to avoid work, he would find it. This American was desperate. That much was obvious. He tried to calculate the worst-case scenario. Getting caught in the apartment, but then again he would have a key. He could claim the American invited him. After that, it was cash and diamonds. It sounded like maybe a lot of diamonds. His take could easily be over twenty thousand for a few hours of risk. He liked that kind of return. Auclair began to nod. "All right . . . but if I get there tonight and I don't think it looks right, I will walk."

"Fair enough."

"What should I call you?"

"Frank . . . Frank Harris." Rapp figured the guy would see the name on the passport, so he might as well tell him the truth. Rapp doubted this guy would even make it through the front door. If they stopped him and were nice, it would be a good indication that he could trust Kennedy and possibly Hurley. If they grabbed him, threw a bag over his head, and stuffed him in a trunk, he'd know he had bigger problems. "What should I call you?"

"You may call me Luke."

"Good." Rapp slid a piece of paper across the table. It had the name and address of a café written in black ink. "You know this place?"

Luke nodded.

"Good, I'll meet you there tonight at seven. It's only a few blocks from the apartment. I'll give you the key, the codes, and tell you where the safe is."

Auclair nodded. "And, again, if I think things don't look right I will walk."

"Got it." Rapp stuck out his hand and they both shook. Standing, he said, "I'll see you tonight."

CHAPTER 21

LANGLEY, VIRGINIA

THOMAS Stansfield was sitting behind his desk wearing khaki slacks and a blue oxford shirt. It was his Sunday uniform. He'd been to church with his wife and several of his children and grandchildren and was looking forward to heading back to the house on the Potomac for a nice egg bake and some time with his grandkids: Molly, Bert, and little Thomas. Molly was four, and in Stansfield's biased opinion, she already showed great potential. She was in fact the only person in the entire family who dared boss him around, which provided great entertainment for Stansfield's grown children. Stansfield himself was highly amused at the confidence displayed by this three-foot-tall towhead. Her little brother Bert didn't do much other than run around the house and run into things, and little Thomas was, well, little. He was only three months old and Stansfield didn't have much interest in them until they could verbalize their demands. His wife liked the infants, so they divided and conquered, and it was great fun.

His own kids were shocked by how hands-on he was, since he had been absent for much of their childhood. It had been a different time, of course. Dads were nowhere near as involved in the lives of their children as they were now. There had been some interesting debates about this at the family dinner table of late, and Stansfield for the most part let his kids voice their opinions and take their shots at him. They knew where he worked. Beyond that, they were smart enough to fill in the blanks and extrapolate. They'd been raised in multiple countries and again it was no secret who Dad worked for, but he never talked about it. It was a steadfast rule that he had not broken once during his entire career.

Stansfield was the kind of father who showed his disapproval by a few carefully selected words, and maybe a disappointed look. He never raised his voice, and after they reached the age of five or so, he never laid a hand on them. The truth was his wife had done an amazing job. It also didn't hurt that the genetics on the brain side were stacked in the favor of the kids. They'd all graduated from college, and three of the kids had postgraduate degrees. Not a single one of them had a drug or alcohol problem, and there had been just one divorce. All in all not so bad, and Stansfield liked to quietly remind them of this when they spouted off about the fact that he spent more time with his grandkids than he had with them. They had all turned out just fine in spite of him. He also liked to point out that the verdict on what type of parents they were was still out. Stansfield had a bad feeling that all of this hands-on parenting was going to come back and bite the next generation in the ass, but that was their problem and not his. His job, as he saw it, was to enjoy his grandchildren and spoil them rotten.

He looked at his gold Timex watch and noted the time. Kennedy was late, which was not normal, even more so because she was the person who had requested this emergency meeting. When Stansfield had walked out of church, he could tell by the look on his bodyguard's face that something had come up. He told his wife and the kids to head back to the house and that he would be back as soon as possible. He was used to these interruptions, and it normally wouldn't have bothered him, but he was hungry and looking forward to some downtime. He looked out the window at the tops of the colorful trees. It was a beautiful fall afternoon and Molly would be anxious to explore the woods with their lush bed of vibrant leaves. He was about to call Kennedy when there was a knock on the door.

As was his habit, he closed the file on his desk and concealed the secure cable that had been sent by his station chief in Thailand only an hour earlier. "Enter," he half yelled due to the soundproofing of the room. The door opened and Stansfield was surprised to see the number-two man at Langley. Paul Cooke was the deputy director of the Central Intelligence Agency. "Paul, I wasn't expecting you. Come in." Stansfield stood and motioned to the couch and chairs near the window.

"Sorry to interrupt," Cooke said as he closed the door behind him. He was also wearing a blue oxford shirt and a pair of khakis as well as a blue sport coat. "How have you been?"

Even though their offices were only a few doors down from each other, the two men did not talk much. Stansfield was not a chatty person, and his job required him to be guarded in all conversations. As the man who ran America's operatives and spies, he trusted very few people. The previous director had had great faith in Stansfield and left him to make his own decisions for the most part, and when he did get involved, he never consulted his deputy director. Cooke's job was to oversee the day-to-day operations of Langley and its ten-thousand-plus employees. Stansfield took care of his small but important fiefdom, and Marvin Land, the deputy director of Intelligence, had a similar arrangement. The place was now in a sort of limbo, with Stansfield and Land running their own crucial departments until the next director was appointed and confirmed. So far, Cooke had let that old arrangement stand.

Stansfield said, "Just fine."

"I thought you had a standing rule to stay out of here on Sundays?" Cooke asked.

Stansfield offered him a small smile. "You know how it is . . . just because it's Sunday doesn't mean our enemies take the day off."

"Very true," Cooke said as he sat in one of the gray armchairs.

Stansfield leaned back into the couch. "What can I help you with?"

Cooke clasped his hands in front of his chin and seemed to consider where he should start. After another moment and a sharp inhalation, he said, "This thing in Paris . . . it's causing quite a stir."

Stansfield nodded. He wasn't a big talker and wasn't about to expand on the obvious.

Several long moments passed before Cooke continued, saying, "I had a strange meeting yesterday." He looked out the window as if he was unsure of how to proceed.

Stansfield gave him nothing more than a slight nod that told him he was welcome to continue. If Cooke had a story to tell, he was going to have to do it on his own.

"Franklin Wilson asked me over to his house."

The often overwrought secretary of state had undergone some type of reformation since his wife's decline in health. As far as Stansfield understood it, Cooke and Wilson barely knew each other. Asking Cooke to meet him at his house was a little odd. "On a Saturday afternoon?"

"Yes, I know." Cooke played along as if he thought it was all a little bizarre himself. "He is very upset about this Paris thing."

"A lot of people are upset about what happened in Paris . . . none more so than the Libyans and the French. Why is our secretary of state so distressed?"

"He's upset because he thinks you're not being honest with him." Cooke studied Stansfield for a hint of nervousness, but the old granite bastard didn't give him so much as a twitch. "Does that concern you?"

"I learned a long time ago, Paul, that I can't control what people say or do in this town. Franklin Wilson is a very opinionated man, who has been acting a bit strange since he institutionalized his wife. If he has a reason to be upset with me, he can pick up the phone and tell me himself."

Cooke crossed his legs and then uncrossed them. He would have to tell Wilson exactly what Stansfield had said about his wife. Maybe even play it up a bit. If the man had a hard-on for Stansfield now, he was going to want to gang-rape him after he heard this. "It goes a little deeper than that," Cooke said. He cleared his throat and then added, "He thinks you were involved in what happened the other night."

"The other night meaning . . ."

"Paris."

Stansfield stared back at him without saying a word.

"You don't have anything you'd like to say?" Cooke asked.

"I've found it best not to respond to wild accusations."

"Well," Cooke said with a big exhalation, "I'm just trying to give you a little heads-up. The man has the president's ear, for God's sake, and for some reason he thinks you were involved in the assassination of the Libyan oil minister."

"And he came to this belief how?"

"He wouldn't say."

"Interesting."

"That's your response?" Cooke asked, making no attempt to hide his frustration. "That is a very serious accusation. You're not going to deny it?"

Stansfield studied Cooke for a long moment. He sensed something that he didn't like. Cooke was fishing, and he got the specific feeling that Wilson had put him up to it. With the director's office open down the hall, who knew what delusions of grandeur were floating through people's heads these days. Cooke did not have the analytical abilities to run Langley, but he could certainly see Wilson waving the job in front of his face to get him to do his bidding. "Paul, you should remind the secretary that we're all on the same team, and he should probably think twice before he starts throwing around wild accusations that could seriously harm this country and our foreign policy."

"So you had nothing to do with what happened the other night?"

Cooke might not have known it at the time, but Stansfield could see that a line had been drawn. Any Langley man who was dumb enough to be a messenger for the State Department was dangerous. Stansfield looked Cooke straight in the eyes and said, "I had nothing to do with it. Are you satisfied?"

Cooke accepted the answer even though he knew it was a lie. "Well." He slapped his knees and stood. "I'm heading over to Paris in the morning. See if I can help smooth things over."

"What exactly do you have to smooth over?"

"That might be the wrong choice of words. I want to reassure our allies that we had nothing to do with this." Cooke started for the door and when he reached it, he looked back to Stansfield and said, "You're more than welcome to join me if you'd like."

Stansfield took the invitation with a reasonable nod. "I'll think about it. I'd have to move a few things around, but it might be worth the trip. It's been a while since I paid a visit to our friends at the DGSE."

"Good." Cooke left the office, closing the door behind him, a satisfied grin on his face.

Stansfield sat motionless for a minute or so, running the various possibilities through his head. Any way he looked at it, he didn't like what he sensed. The old spy's strength was his ability to take facts, plug in a person's motivation, and predict what he was after. Cooke was up to something. Stansfield considered the possibility that he had underestimated the man. He very quickly concluded that there was a good possibility that he had. Frowning, he decided that he would have to move quickly to deal with the situation. He ran down a list of trusted operatives he could call on. There were no files for these men; all of them were retired yet still very useful. Stansfield decided on an asset and then asked himself if he should have a talk with Marvin Land. Stansfield and Land had a great deal of professional respect for each other, as they had fought side by side against the Soviets. He wondered if Cooke had already tried to play Land. That would be an interesting yet very stupid move.

CHAPTER 22

PARIS, FRANCE

IT was midafternoon on Sunday and the restaurant at the Hotel Balzac was crowded. The place was always swarming, as it was ideally located for tourists, diplomats, and high-society shoppers. There were a handful of hotels in Paris that catered to the ultra-rich, and this was one of them. The head maître d' was on Fournier's payroll, as were a few of the top waiters. For special occasions, Fournier was not opposed to putting his own people in the uniforms of restaurant employees so they could eavesdrop on certain influential diners. Not today, however. The head of the DGSE's Action Division had ordered his men to make sure the corner table and the surrounding area were swept for listening devices. One of his men was standing five feet from them, blocking them from the rest of the restaurant. He was trained to look for directional listening devices, and he would subtly shift his position by an inch or two every half minute to block any would-be listener from having a direct line of sight to his boss.

Fournier had a hefty expense account for this exact reason. He needed to rub shoulders with the right people, and with rare exceptions, those people had expensive tastes. Switzerland was known for banking, but Paris was where international businessmen came to get deals done. Fournier had no problem meeting Max Vega in public. In fact, it was good for him to legitimize their dealings. Industrial espionage was a big part of Fournier's job, and any intel he could get on foreign companies that were conducting business in France or competing against French companies abroad was a top priority.

Vega sat on the board of one of Spain's top telecommunications companies. He was considered a rising star in the burgeoning market of mobile phones. Vega was a bit of a contradiction. His mother was Spanish and his father a wealthy Saudi prince. His Spanish mother didn't take too kindly to her royal husband taking a second wife. She hung around for nearly a year, and then when he married wife number three, a seventeen-year-old Yemeni, her Spanish pride could take no more. She left him and returned to Madrid. She took her son Omar with her, and legally changed his name to Max Vega after her father, who had been against her marriage to the Saudi in the first place. Two years later, at the age of ten, Max was shipped off to a boarding school in Switzerland and then at eighteen to the London School of Economics. After that he blazed a trail through three investment houses and a mergers and acquisitions firm, and all the while he performed brilliantly and accrued a nice tidy sum for his talents.

Fournier only half listened to Vega talking on his mobile phone. His office had tried to ascertain the thirty-eight-year-old's net worth, but it had proven difficult. He was easily worth twenty million on his own, but Fournier's top financial analyst thought that he was receiving funds from his father, who had well-known radical leanings. Twenty million was a nice number, but Vega lived way beyond that. The theory was that while Vega was talented and relatively well off, it was his father who had bought his seat on Telefonica's board.

Fournier could only guess at what had driven Vega to reconnect with his Saudi father. Curiosity was undoubtedly a part of it, and he was sure the psychiatrists at DGSE, one a devotee of Carl Jung and the other of Sigmund Freud, could go on for hours telling him how it had something to do with his collective unconscious or his unfulfilled ego and his insecure id and some oral fixation he'd had as a child. All of it bored Fournier. He was less concerned with *how* people became who they were than simply *who* they were. He wasn't in the business of changing people. He was in the business of getting valuable information from them, and bending them to the use of the Republic.

These radical Islamists were all mentally unstable as far as Fournier was concerned. What he was still trying to figure out was where Vega came down on the religion side of this mess, and in general what he was after. He appeared to be the classic smooth European businessman, but Fournier had real fears that underneath his five-thousand-dollar Savile Row suit lurked a fundamentalist who might bite him in the ass. Fournier didn't like not knowing. He was the one who deceived, stacked the deck, and got things to work out in his favor. He couldn't shake the feeling that Vega was manipulating him. This deal that Vega had offered him was going to blow up in his face if he didn't get it under control quickly, and he didn't like that feeling one bit.

These were the thoughts that were circulating through Fournier's brain as he took a sip from his second glass of Syrah and looked into Vega's oily black eyes. It was easy to like Vega when you compared him to the two imbeciles, Rafique and Samir. It still irritated Fournier that Samir had fucked things up so badly. He had given the fools everything they asked for, and Tarek, that greedy idiot, had been the perfect bait. As far as the Directorate was concerned, Fournier would be killing two birds with one stone. He would get rid of Tarek, and he would also receive assurances from these radicals that they would keep their suicide bombers out of France. His superiors would understand his motives and appreciate his initiative. As for the cash on the side, Fournier had already moved it from one bank in Switzerland to another. It would be untraceable, and unlike other intelligence agencies the DGSE wasn't too hung up about its people padding their retirement accounts. It was considered the wise thing to do. As long as the Republic's best interests were kept at the forefront, it was a beneficial situation for all.

As far as this assassin was concerned, Fournier was fairly ambivalent. He'd seen the list of men that he'd killed, and not a one of them would be missed by those who were allied against terrorism. But while Fournier had no love for Islamists, his number-one job was to keep France secure from the reprisals of the zealots. That meant protecting France both at home and abroad. If Vega and his people wanted this killer dead, it was of no concern to France. But he wasn't dead. It had all failed, and in a spectacular fashion. Fournier had worked his contacts, found out that the Libyan oil minister was on the list, and helped them set the trap. At first Fournier had been hit with a wave of panic over the news that this assassin had killed not only Tarek but four of Samir's men as well. He immediately assumed the assassin was that good, but with another day came more perspective. Samir was an idiot. That much was undeniable, which meant that maybe this assassin wasn't quite so talented.

Fournier took a sip of wine and wondered for a moment where the assassin might be. The man had almost certainly fled France. Fournier was confident that his role in the hotel massacre would never see the light of day, but there were a few loose ends to tie up, and as soon as Vega got off his phone Fournier would jam his terms down the younger man's throat. And then he would restructure their deal.

Vega finally snapped his phone shut and laid it on the table. "I am sorry, but that was a very important call."

Fournier swirled the red wine around in his glass and then said, "Max, I have enjoyed working with you."

"And I with you as well." Vega smiled and held up his glass of Perrier.

The congenial expression melted from Fournier's face. "I have, however, not enjoyed working with your two associates."

Vega smiled as if that was a minor thing. "They are a little rough around the edges."

"That is an understatement." Fournier set his glass down and asked, "Are they up in your suite right now?"

Vega got the feeling that the Frenchman already knew the answer to his question, but Vega was not so ready to concede the point. "I'm not at liberty to say."

Fournier grunted. "Not at liberty. Don't jerk me around, Max. After what happened the other night, my hospitality is wearing thin. I made a simple request. I told you I wanted Samir out of my country immediately."

Vega nodded.

"If our relationship is going to work I need you to understand certain things. When I tell you that I want something to happen, and I want it to happen immediately, it needs to happen."

"I understand, but there are certain complications."

"The only complication that I can see is that Samir is still in France. The police are expanding their investigation. It is only a matter of time before they figure out there was a fifth man. Samir has become a liability. I cannot afford to have him walking around. He knows too much."

"I think you worry too much. Samir is a loyal man. Nothing will come of this."

"Samir is loyal to you and your organization. He has no loyalty to me . . . in fact he has threatened me." Fournier shook his head as if he could still barely believe it. He ran the Action Division for the DGSE, this little Arab puke threatened him in his own country, and now Vega was trying to play it off as if it was no big deal. The stupidity of it all pushed him to make a rash decision. "Max, I do not think you take me seriously enough. I am losing faith in you and your people . . ."

"But," Vega said, trying to interrupt him.

"But nothing," Fournier snapped. "Have any of my men threatened you?"

"No."

"They don't even speak to you. But you let this incompetent fool Samir threaten me. Don't mistake my civility for a bottomless wealth of hospitality. I have worked with you because it is in our mutual interest but I am now starting to think that dealing with you is no longer in the best interest of France."

"I disagree . . ."

"Don't interrupt me," Fournier said in an icy tone. "I like you, Max, but I am worried about your judgment. If you can't honor a simple request, then I can no longer deal with you, and make no mistake, this is France." Fournier tapped the linen tablecloth and leaned in to within a few inches of Vega. "If Samir is not out of this country by tomorrow morning, you will force my hand."

Vega felt the hair on the back of his neck stand up. He cleared his throat and pushed his chair back a few inches. "There has been a complication."

Fournier half laughed, expecting some lame excuse. "Please do tell."

"I have been informed that I am on the list."

"The list?" It took Fournier a moment to understand which list he was referring to. "You mean the same list Tarek was on?"

"Yes," Vega said with a solemn nod.

Fournier took in the new information and his mind immediately seized on a potential problem. "You are sure?"

"Yes."

"How?"

"My father passed along the information. He wants Samir and Rafique to keep a very close eye on me." Vega paused for a beat. "And he is sending more men to help protect me."

Fournier didn't bother to hide his displeasure. "And when were you going to inform me of this?"

"I only found out this afternoon."

"On your phone?" Fournier asked as he pointed at the black mobile phone on the table.

Vega nodded.

Fournier cringed. "I have told you before, you cannot trust those devices. We can intercept them. So can the Russians, the British, and the Americans."

"We have our codes," Vega said, shaking his head. "They can listen all they want. All they will ever hear is a man talking to his father about business."

Fournier didn't share his confidence. He knew the capabilities of his own organization, and they paled in comparison to what the Americans could do. This meeting had taken a decidedly bad turn. Fournier thought of his various options and was about to tell Vega it was time for him to leave France when a very unwelcome visitor appeared at the table.

CHAPTER 23

LANGLEY, VIRGINIA

STANSFIELD was still rolling Cooke's visit around in his mind when Kennedy finally showed up with the youthful-looking Dr. Lewis. He set the one problem aside and prepared to deal with another one. Kennedy had refused to tell the head of Stansfield's security detail why she needed to see him so urgently, and the deputy director of Operations was not surprised. CIA headquarters was just five minutes from their house, and it was common for him to be called in on a moment's notice for the simple reason that most of his conversations had to be held in a secure environment.

Kennedy plopped down in one chair and Lewis took the other. Stansfield returned to the couch and looked at Kennedy. "What's the problem?"

She had been thinking about how much she should tell Stansfield, and in the time it had taken to get dressed, pick up Lewis, and get to Langley, she had decided that it was best to keep nothing from him. "Rapp called me this morning."

"I assume you mean he called the service and left you a message." There was a touch of concern in his voice.

Kennedy nervously cleared her throat and said, "He called me at home."

He took the news stoically and said, "So he's alive."

"Yes."

"Did he have an explanation for missing his check-in?"

"Yes. He was shot."

If Stansfield was alarmed, he didn't show it. "How bad?"

"I'm not sure. He said he'd been hit in the shoulder. That was all."

"And this was on your home phone?"

His tone was devoid of judgment, but Kennedy knew it was there. She nodded reluctantly.

Stansfield was far from thrilled to hear this news. He sat motionless for a few moments and then said, "Your phones are clean as far as you know?"

"They were swept two weeks ago."

"Do you record your calls?" Stansfield asked this only as a precaution.

"No," she answered honestly, "I've never seen the need."

"How long did the call last?"

"Less than two minutes."

The answer seemed to take some of the tension out of Stansfield. "I need you to repeat everything that was said."

Kennedy relayed nearly verbatim what Rapp had said. The only thing she omitted was her warning Rapp about Victor's keeping an eye on the apartment.

"Have you talked to Ridley?" Stansfield asked, referring to Rob Ridley, the leader of the advance team.

"Yesterday. He assured me that Tarek was traveling without bodyguards."

"So the advance team missed them and Rapp missed them as well," Stansfield said. "I find it hard to believe both of them would miss something so obvious."

"I do as well."

"So . . . we have four dead men in the room that the Libyans are claiming were Tarek's bodyguards, but our best advance team and one of our best operatives somehow never saw them." He took off his glasses and set them in his lap. "That doesn't add up."

"No it doesn't. And this part about the fifth man . . . the one who shot Rapp."

"Yes."

"I didn't get it at first, but now it seems obvious. He's telling us that he had nothing to do with the deaths of the two hotel guests and the worker in the alley. He specifically said he stuck to protocol. That he went out the window and the fifth man was responsible for the other three."

Stansfield had understood what Rapp was trying to say the first time Kennedy repeated the conversation. His mind had already jumped to another detail. "I received a report from our station chief last night. He said the four dead bodyguards all had silenced MP5s."

Kennedy pursed her lips. "I'm not sure I follow."

"You've had protection details. Have you ever seen your details carry silenced weapons?"

Kennedy thought about the men who occasionally kept an eye on her when she was in a particularly nasty part of the world. "No . . . come to think of it."

"There's also a rumor that the Paris police are having a hard time finding anyone who saw these bodyguards with Tarek."

"You mean in the days preceding the attack?"

"Yes."

"This doesn't add up."

"No it doesn't," Stansfield said. "You said Mitch said it was a trap?"

"Yes."

Stansfield stood and walked over to his desk. He stopped and looked out the window at the rolling Virginia countryside. He began connecting the dots and after a half a minute he said, "I think he's probably right. Bodyguards don't carry silenced weapons." Stansfield turned around. "Bodyguards make sure they are visible so they can act as a deterrent and bodyguards don't fire their weapons aimlessly . . . at least not good ones."

"I'm not sure I follow the last part?" Lewis asked.

"Apparently over three hundred rounds were fired in that hotel room. Doesn't that seem a bit excessive to either of you?" Stansfield shook his head. "Put yourself in their shoes. You are tasked with protecting one of your country's most important ministers. Do you think you are going to simply rush into the room, guns blazing on full automatic? Tarek and the prostitute were shot more than a dozen times each. I took another look at Mitch's file yesterday. He's one or two shots to the head and that's it."

Lewis nodded. "That's how Hurley trained him. The caliber of the weapon and the distance to the target dictate the number of shots. Rapp likes to get close for the kill shot . . . that's what Hurley calls it."

Stansfield had heard it all before. Rapp was not the first person Hurley had trained. "Get close, keep it simple, one or two shots to the head, and then get clear."

"That's what he tells his trainees," Lewis said.

"So does either of you believe that Rapp went into that hotel room and shot Tarek a dozen-plus times and then pumped as many rounds into the prostitute?"

"Not unless he lost his mind," Lewis replied.

Kennedy frowned and said, "It's not his MO. He uses a nine-millimeter Beretta . . . 92F. Eighteen rounds in the grip plus one in the chamber. Two backup magazines and a small backup nine-millimeter. There's no way he'd waste that many rounds on two people."

"No," Stansfield said, "plus we have to assume he killed four of the bodyguards."

Kennedy looked at her boss and said, "The two hotel guests and the employee were all sprayed with bullets. Multiple shots to the chest and face, in one case." Kennedy shook her head. "I should have seen it sooner."

"And I should have, too." Stansfield put his hands on his hips and tried to focus on what was bothering him. He was missing something in the midst of this sea of facts—something that was right in front of him.

Kennedy knew him well enough to see what was going on, so she kept her mouth shut. Lewis wasn't much of a talker, so he simply observed.

Stansfield turned the problem around and looked at it from the other side. Rapp had said it was a trap. How would you lure someone like Rapp into a trap? You offered him up a nice fat target like Tarek. But how would they know Tarek was on the list, and why would they be so willing to sacrifice him? Both questions bothered Stansfield, but in vastly different ways. "Rapp thinks we have a leak."

"Yes."

"How many people have seen the list?"

"The complete list," Kennedy said. "As far as I know, you, Stan, myself, Rapp, and Ridley."

"But there could be more?"

"There can always be more. You taught me that."

Stansfield nodded. "True, but what about your list?"

"I destroyed my copy. I keep the list up here." Kennedy tapped her forehead.

Stansfield had done the same. "And Mitch?"

"I spent a weekend reviewing it with him and then the entire file was destroyed."

"You're sure?"

"Yes."

"But he could have written things down later," Lewis added.

"I don't think that's his style," Kennedy said. "He has a pretty good memory."

"And Ridley?"

"I have no way of knowing for certain, but he's pretty thorough."

"Where is he right now?"

"Amsterdam."

"I want a full debriefing, and I want you two to handle it. Head over there. It will be easier."

Kennedy nodded and asked, "What about Stan?"

"I'll deal with Stan."

With obvious trepidation, Kennedy asked, "How soon?"

"I think I might be Paris bound in the morning."

"Really?" Kennedy asked, her surprise obvious.

"Cooke asked me to go over with him. Help smooth some things over." Stansfield intentionally kept his suspicions about Cooke to himself.

"I'd like to head over as soon as possible," Kennedy said to her boss. "Hopefully this afternoon."

"Why?"

"Because I think I'm the only one he really trusts. I should be the one to bring him in."

"You don't think he trusts Stan?"

Kennedy looked to Lewis for help.

As was his habit, Lewis had his hands steepled under his chin. Glancing at Kennedy he said, "Tell Thomas what Mitch told you about Stan."

"He thinks if Stan brings him in he'll shove him in solitary for a month and slap him around."

Stansfield pondered that for a moment. Rapp was likely not far from the truth. Maybe it wouldn't be such a bad idea to send Kennedy over. He could have Hurley begin looking into how Tarek might have upset the Libyans.

"I'm concerned that we have a deeper problem here," Lewis said to Stansfield.

"Such as?"

"I'm putting a report together right now. I want to make sure I've drawn the right conclusions before I give my final recommendation, but in the meantime, I would argue very strongly that you keep Stan and Victor away from Rapp. Let Irene bring him in and she and I can handle the debriefing."

Stansfield considered that for a moment and then nodded.

"I'll need you to order Stan to stay away from Mitch. And there can be no doubt in Stan's mind that you want your orders followed to the letter."

"Does this have anything to do with Rapp's suspicion that we have a leak?" Stansfield asked.

"Possibly, but my bigger concern is that we need to avoid a confrontation right now, and I think we can all agree that Stan and Victor enjoy confrontation."

Stansfield came back to the couch and sat. "You're worried about Mitch?"

Since receiving the call from Kennedy, Lewis had been trying to figure out the best way to phrase his thoughts without alarming Stansfield to the extent that he might do something rash. He placed his hands in his lap and said, "Rapp is a unique individual . . . extremely effective. When you look at what he's done this past year, I think we would be foolish to question his loyalty. But . . . I think certain resentments have built up."

"With Stan?"

"Yes . . . and others. He has become our wonder boy. We have turned him loose to great effect, and up until now, he's given us amazing results. Stan doesn't appreciate what he's done and Victor seems to hate him for the sake of hating him. As you well know, Stan has control issues, and he doesn't like the fact that Irene and Mitch have been allowed to operate outside his direct authority. He was very quick to blame Mitch for what went wrong in Paris, and he did so without any evidence. Now it looks as if none of this can be laid at Mitch's feet. In fact, it's quite amazing that he managed to eliminate the target and get away."

Stansfield nodded. "Hearing this new information, I see your point."

"Rapp said something to Irene on the phone this morning that I think is very telling. I'm paraphrasing, but he said something to the effect of, 'I'm glad you desk jockeys have it all figured out. I can just hear your uncle second-guessing every move I made even though he has no idea what went down.' That is a statement filled with resentment."

"Toward Stan?"

"Yes and possibly others. I'm sure you remember how it was at certain points in your career. We have all been there . . . thousands of miles away, feeling isolated and abandoned by bosses who issue orders without the foggiest idea what the situation on the ground is actually like."

Stansfield could recall many such instances. "So I send Irene over to bring him in, I keep him away from Stan, and then we sit down and sort the rest of this out."

"Basically, but I do have to bring up a concern. I have a good handle on Rapp's psyche. He's far less complicated than you would think. He's very linear. He has it in his mind right now that someone in our group has betrayed him and almost got him killed. It is my estimate that he will not stop until he finds who that person is, and when he does, he will kill him."

Stansfield considered this for a moment and then asked, "Even if I order him to stand down?"

"He has a great deal of respect for you. If you can convince him that you are going to deal with this person, he might stand down, but he is going to want proof that the problem has been dealt with."

Stansfield nodded, turned to Kennedy, and said, "Bring him in. I'll call off Stan, and then we are all going to sit down, and I am going to put an end to all of this infighting. From now on when I give an order I expect it to be carried out and anyone who can't abide by that will no longer be a part of this team."

Lewis and Kennedy shared a quick look and then nodded.

"I mean it," Stansfield said, obviously tired of the squabbling, "and trust me, I'm well aware that I have a blind spot where Stan is concerned." The two men had a long history that stretched from Berlin to Budapest to Moscow and the Middle East and beyond. Stansfield shook his head in disgust over his mistakes. "This crap is going to end and it's going to end right now."

"Yes, sir." Kennedy stood and thanked him for his time. "Is it okay if we do Ridley's debriefing in Paris?"

"Fine. Just make sure the location is locked down and secure."

"I will. Thank you. We'll give you an update as soon as we're on the ground."

Stansfield watched them go. He wasn't sure they understood how precarious things had become. If they had a leak, it needed to be stopped before they were all hauled before a congressional committee and eventually to jail. They had the right of it about Rapp. That was for certain. Stansfield had always understood the risk of ordering a talented, highly motivated man to kill for his country. The cold, detached killers were easier to predict. Rapp, though, was far from dispassionate about his job. He couldn't kill these men fast enough. It was his hatred for terrorists that drove him to kill with such efficiency. How would he react if he was pulled in and shut down? Not well, was Stansfield's guess. How would he react if he found out someone at Langley was selling their secrets to their enemies? By definition, that individual would be a traitor, and Stansfield had little doubt what Rapp would want to do to such a person.

CHAPTER 24

PARIS, FRANCE

THE plates had been fairly easy to find. There was a big underground car park a few blocks from the Eiffel Tower. Rapp went to the third subfloor and found a sedan in a nice dark corner. He quickly unscrewed the front and rear plates and then headed for the fourth subfloor. The private vehicle plates started with a string of four numbers followed by two letters and then two numbers. It took him a few minutes to find a vehicle that had plates that matched the first two numbers. Most people didn't know their tag number, but as a precaution, it was better to get the first number or two right. People tended to ignore what looked familiar. He popped the plates off and then quickly installed the plates he'd taken from the first car. It was standard tradecraft.

The owner of the first car would soon notice that his plates had been lifted because there would be a blank space where he was accustomed to seeing a plate. He would then report them stolen. Paris was a big city with serious crime. Stolen license plates were not high on the list of things to track down, but nonetheless, Rapp wanted some separation in case luck turned against him. It might be months before the man or woman who owned the second car was pulled over for having stolen plates. He or she would then realize that the plates were stolen and report them as such. By then, Rapp and Greta would be long gone. Greta's silver A4 Audi was not the problem. It was the Swiss plates that drew too much attention. If they had to flee, they didn't need an innocent bystander giving her license tag to a police officer, and they certainly didn't want Hurley to see them.

Rapp arrived back at the hotel with his shoulder feeling marginally better and his mind satisfied that they were ready for tonight. Greta was waiting for him in the room and looking a bit nervous despite her effort to seem otherwise. She wanted to know what had taken so long, and he told her about the license plates and a few other seemingly meaningless tasks that he'd performed. Before she got on a roll he turned the tables and started asking her questions about her afternoon. While he listened, he emptied the contents of one of his shopping bags onto the bed. There was a sewing kit, a pair of jeans, a new jacket, and some other items. Rapp laid the jeans on the bed and retrieved his silenced Glock from the back of his waistband. Greta stopped talking at the sight of the gun. Rapp placed it over the left thigh of the jeans, grabbed a marker, and began to make an outline.

"Did you try on the wig?"

Greta ignored him. "What are you doing?"

"My shoulder holster is rigged for a lefty and my left hand isn't much use right now. I need to make a holster for my gun. Keeping it stuffed in the back of my pants isn't the best move."

"Why . . . because you might shoot yourself?"

"No, it's not very comfortable and not very easy to draw when you need it."

She nodded while she watched him take a pair of scissors to the new jeans.

When Rapp had his hunk of fabric he placed the new black denim jacket on the bed and opened it to reveal the inside front left side. He set the gun down and then laid the jean patch over it until he had the angle right. He pinned the fabric to the flannel liner and then got out a needle and thread.

"I didn't know you knew how to sew."

Rapp gave her a lopsided grin. "It's one of my many talents. Are you hungry?"

She shook her head. "Just tired."

Rapp plunged the needle through the denim and the flannel and then brought it back up before he pierced the denim on the outside of the jacket. "Why don't you try the wig on for me? We don't want any surprises tonight."

Greta wanted to ask him why he needed to bring a gun if there was no risk, but she knew it was a stupid question. His whole life was a risk, and she'd been trying to ignore that fact for as long as she'd known him. She grabbed her shopping bag and went into the bathroom, closing the door behind her. She took her ponytail and twisted it into a bun and then carefully placed the wig over her blond hair. After tugging the left side down and then the right, she patted the top and shook it out. It was fine, but she didn't like the fact that she was looking at a stranger.

Rapp heard the door open and looked up from his needle and thread. The black hair ran several inches past her shoulders. Her perfect face was framed by black bangs that stopped an inch above her eyebrows. Rapp didn't realize it, but his mouth was hanging open.

"What do you think?" Greta asked.

"I think I'm horny."

"Not funny."

"I'm not trying to be." Rapp set the jacket on the bed and stood. He walked over to Greta, stopping only a foot away. She looked at him for a second and then protectively folded her arms across her chest and looked across the room at the blank wall. Her body language was clear enough, but Rapp was not so easily deterred. He gently placed his right hand on her chin and turned her face toward his. "I'm sorry I got you involved in this. Maybe it would be better if you went back to Zurich.

I'll do what I need to do and when things have settled down I'll come see you."

"And if things don't settle down?"

Then I'll probably be dead, he thought, but he didn't dare say it. "They will. I'm good at my job, honey. Trust me when I tell you these guys have more to fear than I do."

She shook her head and her eyes began to fill with tears. "You were almost killed the other night. If that bullet had been just a few inches to the right you would have bled to death. As it was, you almost fell to your death. I just don't understand why you can't leave with me right now. Walk away from this insanity."

"This isn't the type of job you just quit. You're going to have to trust me on this, Greta, and if you can't then you should head back to Zurich."

"Is that what you want me to do?" The first tear began to roll down her left cheek.

Rapp didn't like to see her like this. He wiped the tear away with his thumb. "I want you to be safe and the safest place for you is definitely not with me, but there's another part of me . . ." Rapp's voice trailed off.

"What?"

"There's another part of me that can't bear the thought of never seeing you again."

More tears fell. "It doesn't have to be that way. All you have to do is . . ."

"Walk away." Rapp shook his head. "It's not going to happen, darling. I need to see this thing through, and then we can talk about it."

Greta reached up and grabbed his face with both hands. "I love you."

Rapp smiled. "I love you, too." He bent down and kissed her. His right hand left her chin and found the small of her back, pulling her in tight. Their kisses became deeper and more passionate. Rapp's breathing grew heavier and he slid his hand down to her perfect little ass.

Greta moaned. She knew what he wanted and she wanted it every bit as badly. She missed him and wanted nothing more than to lie in his arms and spend the rest of the weekend in bed. But she pushed herself back a few inches and asked, "What about your shoulder?"

Pulling her close, Rapp whispered in her ear, "We'll just have to be careful."

Greta started unbuttoning his shirt.

Rapp hooked his thumb under her sweater and slid it around her hip to the front of her jeans. He found the top button and with his thumb and forefinger he popped the button open. It was suddenly as if the starter had fired the gun. They began tearing each other's clothes off, stopping only to help the other with a particularly stubborn garment. Shirts, pants, sweater, socks, and shoes flew in every direction until Rapp was left in his white boxers and Greta in her sheer black bra and thong. Other than the bullet hole in Rapp's shoulder and his bruising, they were the picture of perfection. He was hard and chiseled, every muscle defined and ripped tight. She was lithe and shapely in all the right places and her skin was as soft as anything he'd ever felt.

Greta pushed him back onto the bed, where he sat looking up at her, his hands on her hips. Greta grabbed his face and said, "I'm not wearing the wig."

Rapp wasn't going to deny that the wig was a turn-on, but Greta was so beautiful she could have been bald and she still would have driven him nuts. "You don't have to wear the wig."

Greta smiled, pushed him onto his back, and climbed on top of him. She reached up and pulled the wig off with one hand while she undid her blond hair with the other. A gentle shake of the head and her hair fell to her shoulders. "Just sit back and relax. I'll take care of everything."

Rapp smiled, closed his eyes, and for the first time in days his mind was clear of thoughts of retribution and murder.

CHAPTER 25

PARIS, FRANCE

THE bodyguard did his best, but chivalry got the better of him—that and the fact that the woman called out his boss's name with such intimacy that he was disarmed. Francine Neville stepped around the fit DGSE sentry and offered her right cheek to Fournier. She knew that would put him in an impossible situation. Part of Fournier's carefully constructed image was that he was both a ladies' man and a gentleman. Neville knew she was still a desirable woman, and in front of this well-coiffed crowd, the spook would have no choice but to greet her with a kiss.

Fournier was startled, but managed to hide it by pretending to plant a kiss on Neville's right cheek and then the left. "Francine," he said enthusiastically, "how nice to see you."

"And you as well, Paul." She grabbed the back of a chair and asked loudly enough for a third of the restaurant to hear, "May I join you?"

In a voice barely above a whisper, Fournier said, "I would love for you to join us, but we are in the middle of a rather private matter."

Neville waved her hand in the air to dismiss any concerns and said, "Don't worry. I won't overstay my welcome." She pulled out the chair and sat. She then motioned to the last available chair for Simon to join her. "Paul, this is Martin Simon, one of my top people." Before Fournier could respond, Neville turned her delicate brown eyes on the foreigner sitting to his right. "Hello." She extended her hand across the table, palm down. "I'm Francine."

Vega smiled warmly and took her hand. "Very nice to meet you, Francine. I'm Max." He intentionally ignored the mousy-looking man who was with her.

"I hope I'm not interrupting anything important," Neville said.

"My dear, the business of the Directorate is always important," Fournier said, not bothering to hide his irritation. "But obviously the security of the Republic is not so important to you."

"Unfortunately, we don't all agree on the best way to keep the Republic safe." Not wanting to give Fournier a chance to reply, Neville turned to Max and said, "I detect a slight accent. Are you Spanish?"

He nodded.

"CESID?" Neville asked, wondering if he worked for Spain's main intelligence agency.

Vega laughed. "No, I am a simple businessman."

Neville returned her gaze to Fournier, not believing a word that came out of the Spaniard's mouth. Her smile vanished. "I thought you would like a quick briefing on the investigation."

Fournier glanced uncomfortably at his guest and then returned his attention to his old conquest. "Now is not such a good time. Maybe we could talk later. Why don't you call my office and set up an appointment."

"I've been trying to reach you all day. Your office hasn't been much help."

Fournier wondered how she had found him.

"No worries, though. This will only take a few minutes, and then I'll be on my way." She took great joy in seeing the pained expression on Fournier's face. "Yesterday you offered to help with the investigation and my superiors were thrilled. They asked me to see if you could help with a little problem."

"If it is within my power, I would love to be of assistance."

"Good. I am told you have a very cozy relationship with the Libyans." Neville smiled in a humble way. "Being local law enforcement, we have no such contacts, so I was wondering if you could ask them why these supposed bodyguards were never seen in public with the Libyan oil minister."

Fournier blinked several times before responding. "I'm not sure I understand your question."

"The four dead men who you referred to as Tarek's bodyguards . . . We can't find a single witness who saw them. Tarek checked into the hotel with his assistant, who told one of my officers that they were traveling without bodyguards."

"That seems a little strange," Fournier said.

"What seems strange? You telling me they were Tarek's bodyguards or Tarek's assistant telling my officer that they were traveling without protection?"

"Francine, my dear, I assumed they were Tarek's bodyguards, just as you did. I have no information that would say otherwise."

She nodded. "Well, the assistant is now at the Libyan Embassy. They won't let us interview him."

"I'll see if I can change their minds," Fournier offered in a helpful tone, even though he had no such intention.

"There's another interesting tidbit. We have been unable to locate five of the hotel guests."

"I'm not totally surprised. The place was crawling with cops and reporters. They probably left and checked into other hotels."

"No," Neville said, shaking her head. "Their bags are still in their rooms and you wouldn't believe the coincidence," she said in mock shock. "Four of those guests match the descriptions of the four dead bodyguards."

"Really?"

"Yes, and we found a room down the hall from Tarek's that was loaded with surveillance equipment."

"I thought that was the room where Tarek's bodyguards were keeping watch."

"That's what we thought, but according to Tarek's assistant he didn't have a security detail with him."

Fournier pursed his lips into a thoughtful expression and then in a helpful tone said, "This assistant was probably scared out of his mind when your officer interviewed him. Maybe he left out a rather important detail."

"And what about the hotel staff and guests we interviewed? Tarek left the hotel at least seven times and no one remembers seeing a security detail with him."

"Well," Fournier said, trying to come up with a logical explanation. "Maybe Tarek didn't want them with him in public. Maybe he preferred a low profile."

"The room with all of the surveillance equipment in it . . . the hotel computers had it blocked off. The computer said it was being renovated even though it was renovated only a year ago."

Fournier frowned. "That doesn't make any sense."

"No, it doesn't." Neville could see through the act. "Do you know what else doesn't make sense?"

Fournier got a bad feeling that he wasn't going to like the answer to this question. "No."

"My officers say that while you were in Tarek's suite with me, one of your men made a little visit to the roof."

"I had several men with me. I don't know where they were specifically. I instructed them to spread out and see what they could find out."

"I'm sure you did," Neville said, her tone changing from congenial to suspicious. "A rope was taken from the roof." She wasn't going to tell him how she knew. "Any idea what happened to it?"

"Surely you are not trying to say one of my men tampered with evidence." Fournier acted as if he was offended by the accusation.

Neville kept her eyes locked on him. "Paul, I know you better than most. I know you are an extremely deceptive man who is involved in all kinds of nasty things that, God forbid they ever came to light, might possibly destroy our country, so please don't act offended. Deny all you like, but we both know you are capable of transgressions far worse than interfering with my investigation."

Vega cleared his throat and grabbed his phone. "I have other business to attend to. If you'll excuse me."

Fournier placed his hand on Vega's wrist and kept his gaze on Neville. "Francine and I have a long history. I fell in love with her, but she broke my heart. One should never mix business and pleasure. I'm afraid our history is complicating matters."

Neville tossed her head back in fake laughter. "Actually, Max, I found out he was cheating on me, and I told him I never wanted to see him again. Lying comes very easy to Paul, so you have to be very careful in dealing with him."

"Come now, Francine," he said with a pouty grin.

"Don't worry, Paul, I got over you a long time ago, but I did learn some valuable lessons. For instance . . . that you are an incredibly selfish and deceptive man." She turned to Simon. "What would our profilers call that?"

"Narcissistic."

"Yes . . . thank you. That is the right word."

Fournier held his hands up in mock surrender. "I should have treated you better. It is one of my great regrets. Now if you'll excuse us, Max and I have some important business to attend to."

Neville turned to Simon. "We seem to have worn out our welcome."

"It appears so."

Neville stood and, looking at Fournier, said, "You will of course make your men available for me to interview?"

"Anything I can do to help," he said with a playful grin.

Neville took one step away from the table and then turned back. "I forgot to mention that we are looking for that fifth guest. He fits the general description of the other four men who were killed . . . the supposed bodyguards. You wouldn't happen to know where we could find him?" Neville asked with a provocative smile.

Fournier pushed his glass forward and stood. He walked around the table and put his hand on Neville's shoulder. With his mouth only a few inches from her ear he said, "Darling, I don't know what you are up to, but I would suggest you run back to your husband and children. This is a dangerous game you are playing, and if you are as smart as you think you are, you should know that I am not someone to be trifled with."

Neville jerked away from him, slapping his hand off her shoulder. "Do not touch me!" she snapped, loudly enough for most of the restaurant to hear. "This mess has your smell all over it, and don't think that just because you work for the Directorate you are above the law."

Fournier's bodyguard stepped in and grabbed Neville by the elbow.

She responded by pulling out her badge and shoving it in the man's face. "Take your hands off me." Wheeling back to Fournier, she said, "I have already spoken to the inspector general's office. We have a meeting in the morning where I am going to fully brief him on my investigation, and my fears that your department is somehow involved in this. I will also inform him that you threatened me."

"I did not threaten you, Francine." Fournier sighed as if the idea was preposterous.

Neville composed herself. "I'm on to you, Paul. You show up at the scene of the crime at practically the same time as I did, one of your men is seen going to the roof, and now we're missing a crucial piece of evidence. You float this idea that these four dead men were Tarek's bodyguards, but I can't find anyone who says he had bodyguards protecting him. This entire mess is beginning to smell like one of your dirty little operations."

"Francine, you should be very careful about throwing around such wild accusations."

"They might sound wild to the average person, but anyone who is familiar with your work will understand that this is right up your alley. In fact," Neville said, just realizing something, "I'd be willing to bet an entire year's salary that Tarek was on your payroll."

It was Simon who reached out and touched his boss this time. "Francine, we need to go." Simon, looking at the exchange from afar, realized that Neville had more than likely hit uncomfortably close to the truth. It would be a legal nightmare trying to get the DGSE to open the files they kept on Tarek.

"I am not afraid of you, Paul. I know how you like to do things in the shadows. You can't stand being exposed in the open like this. Mark my words, you will regret your decision to involve yourself in this mess." Neville turned and marched through the restaurant, Simon in tow.

When they reached the lobby, Simon said, "Well, that wasn't exactly what I expected."

"It wasn't what I expected either," Neville snapped.

"Boss, do you know what Tarek did before he became Libya's oil minister?"

Neville stopped in the middle of the lobby and faced Simon. She searched his face for a clue. "What?"

"The word is he worked for the Mukhabarat . . . Libyan Intelligence."

"Shit," Neville mumbled under her breath. She grabbed a clump of her black hair, shook her head, and in a voice filled with desperation, said, "This just keeps getting worse."

"We need to be careful."

She looked back toward the restaurant. "That's what he wants us to do. He wants us to be afraid of our shadows. Move slowly . . . that's why I made that scene in there. He can't stand the thought of his dirty little secrets being made public. If we want to get to the bottom of this, moving cautiously is the last thing we should do. We need to expose him and do it quickly."

Simon grimaced. "Francine, this is very dangerous. We have nothing that ties him to any of this."

"You think he just showed up before the bodies were cool because he was out for a walk? His man just wanders onto the roof while we're all focused on the room? I don't buy any of it."

"I know it doesn't look good, but none of this is solid enough to implicate him."

"Then we'll have to find something. The crime scene should be wrapped up by tonight. We will have plenty of manpower available, and I want to find out who that man was . . . Max."

"Francine," Simon said with caution, "he is more than likely a source for the Directorate. I'm telling you, this is dangerous."

"Yes, and we work for the National Police. The Directorate can play all of the games they want when they are abroad, but not here in Paris. We are the law." She could see that the always-rational Simon did not like this turn of events. Like many, he feared the reputation of the Directorate. Neville knew their only hope in getting to the bottom of what really happened was to ignore the fear and push forward. Any pause would give Fournier the time he needed to pressure the people who could relieve her from the case. "Just trust me . . . we need to move fast. Don't worry about Fournier. He put himself in the middle of this by showing up at the crime scene and sending his man up onto the roof. I want answers. I want you to start with this Max guy and then get me the name of Fournier's man who was on the roof. I want to question him myself."

Simon knew there was no dissuading her from this path, so he nodded. This was part of what made her so good at her job. If a case became personal, she was tenacious. Maybe he could talk some sense into her in a day or two. That was if they had that much time. Fournier and his type would not play fair. As they stepped into the late-afternoon light an ominous feeling clutched at him. Would Fournier and his faceless minions be so brash as to harm his boss? Simon shuddered at the possibility. He couldn't let that happen. As he opened the rear door of the sedan for Neville he took a quick look up and down the street. There were all sorts of men standing about—assistants, drivers, and bodyguards for the affluent who were inside the hotel. Undoubtedly one or more belonged to Paul Fournier. Simon made a mental note of each face. He'd been a police officer for sixteen years. He'd started out walking the narrow streets of the Marais Quarter. Early on, he learned he had a gift for faces. He hoped that gift hadn't left him.

Simon settled into the backseat next to his boss and paused for a second before saying, "I think it would be wise to give you and your family a little protection until this has blown over." He knew she wouldn't like it, but he said it anyway, mostly because it was the right thing to do. Neville didn't speak for a long moment, and when she did, it was what Simon expected.

"I'm not afraid of Paul Fournier."

Well, you should be, Simon thought to himself, but he didn't dare say it. "I never said you were. This is a very high-profile case that is going to attract a lot of attention. I think it would be a wise precaution."

"Nice try. This is about you being spooked by a spook from DGSE." Neville shook her head. "I'm not afraid of the man. He's a coward. He can't intimidate and use his dirty tricks in the bright light of day, and he sure as hell isn't going to harm a ranking detective of the Judicial Police."

He knew her well enough to know that at least for now it would make little sense to try to pursue the matter. He nodded his agreement, but silently he began exploring the various precautions he could put into place. As long as Neville never knew what he was up to, there would be no harm done, but if she found out, he cringed to think of how she would react. Simon looked out the window and decided he would simply need to be careful. To ignore the threat would be foolish.

CHAPTER 26

THEY made love and fell asleep in each other's arms, his one good one and her two. When Rapp woke up an hour and forty minutes later he stared unblinkingly at the ceiling. There was no fluttering or blurred vision, confusion over where he was or the time. He felt alive and sharp and relaxed all at the same time. Greta could do that to him. He didn't know how exactly, but he suspected it had something to do with her naked body pressed against his. They always slept with their bodies intertwined, as much skin on skin as possible. Her warmth and energy simultaneously comforted him and made him feel alive.

There was no denying she made him happy, happier than he'd been in a long time. So much so that, as he lay there, he actually thought about dropping everything and driving back to Zurich with her. He could scare the shit out of Kennedy and quite a few others. The phone call would be easy. Just dial the service and leave a message. Tell her that he was done. That he'd put his ass on the line, and they'd repaid him by betraying him. And then would come the part that would make everything very definitive. He would have to threaten her, by explain-

ing in detail what he would do to anyone who came looking for him
and that if that happened he would fly back to the States and leave a
trail of bodies. Maybe even add something about a packet of information that would be mailed to the FBI or the Department of Justice or
God forbid the media.

He frowned at that last part. He couldn't do it. It would make him
no better than all the egomaniacal, opportunistic politicians who were
constantly taking shots at the CIA. Kennedy and Stansfield were good
people, or at least they tried to do the right thing. Hurley, maybe not so
much. Whether Stansfield ordered it or not, Hurley would come after
him. The man was funny that way. If Rapp cut a corner or did things
his own way, Hurley would fly into a rage, but the man never bothered
to confront the fact that there wasn't a rule he himself hadn't broken.
Stansfield had told Rapp once that the problem he and Hurley had was
that they were too much alike. Rapp sure as hell hoped they weren't.
Hurley could be petty and sadistic and extremely unfair and Rapp had
told Stansfield so. The deputy director added a few more negative observations to Rapp's list and then said, "And ultimately very good at
what he does. He cuts through all the BS. He sees the purest path toward achieving his objective and he seizes it . . . just like you."

Rapp had replied, "But he's a prick."

Stansfield smiled in his easy way and said, "Yes, he is, and after
you've been at this for three decades you might be one, too."

Rapp desperately hoped not. Part of him respected Hurley for
his toughness and tenacity, but he couldn't imagine going through
life as such a sour bastard. Rapp wondered if he really could kill him.
There'd been plenty of times when he'd envisioned it, but never in a
definitive, professional way. His fantasies were more along the lines
of bashing his head into the floor over and over again until his brains
spilled out. Rapp realized there was a very real chance that taking Hurley out was exactly where this was headed. If he ran, and he might have
no choice, he'd have to kill Hurley or the man would hunt him for the
rest of his days.

Greta's head was resting on his chest and his right arm was wrapped around her. They'd met nearly a year ago in Zurich and it had been love, or at least lust, at first sight. Greta's family had a string of banks located in most of the major financial centers. Her grandfather and Thomas Stansfield had been allies in the fight against communism, and the family still helped Stansfield with some of the more delicate aspects of their operations. So far they had kept their relationship a secret. Greta knew what Rapp did, to an extent, but the wound in his shoulder was a harsh reminder that she had fallen in love with a man who was in a very dangerous line of work.

Rapp slid his hand down her side, her slender waist, and then her hip. He kissed the top of her head and took a deep breath. He wanted to remember this. Total peace; joy in his heart and a woman he passionately loved at his side. This was how normal people lived, but not him. His training had been thorough, and in ways Rapp hadn't expected. Hurley had talked to each of them about women. His policy was gruff and to the point. "You can hump all the women you want, but you can't fall in love and you sure as hell can't get married. If you fall in love or get married, I'll put you out to pasture or kill you." And that was just one of many reasons Rapp thought Hurley was a jackass.

It was tempting to spend the rest of his life naked and in bed with Greta, but he knew it was a romantic fantasy. If that was ever his hope there was a lot of work to be done first. There had probably been a time when he could have taken the road more frequently traveled, but that was gone. The truth was more than the simple fact that he was a trained killer. He was good at it, he enjoyed it, and he was not ready to walk away from it. Maybe he really would turn out like Hurley if he lived long enough. The thought depressed him.

As Rapp carefully slid his arm from under Greta, he promised himself that he would never let that happen. In the bathroom he closed the door and checked his reflection in the mirror. The black circles under his eyes were almost gone. It was amazing what the body could do with some food and a lot of sleep. The bandage on his shoulder was blood-free, but the bruising on his back looked pretty bad. Rapp flexed his fingers on his left hand and then moved his arm around in a small clockwise motion. The flex didn't hurt but rotating his shoulder hurt like hell. He tried a few more motions with varied success and then got in the shower. Not wanting to get his bandages wet, he cleaned from the waist down, toweled off, and contemplated shaving. He had two days of thick stubble. There were pros and cons to keeping it, but in the end the cons won out and he shaved. Any concealment it offered would be marginal, and on the other side of the ledger was a mountain of evidence about how police treated men who were dressed nicely and clean-shaven versus men who were not.

Greta was still asleep while he put on his dark jeans, a black T-shirt, and lace-up black combat boots. Unfortunately, she awoke at the sound of Rapp adjusting the Velcro straps on his bulletproof vest. She propped her head up with a second pillow and pulled the sheet up high around her neck.

"Why are you wearing that?"

"Just a precaution," Rapp said truthfully.

Greta wasn't buying it. "Mitch?"

"Greta?" Rapp said.

"I'm serious."

"And so am I, and that's why I'm putting it on."

She stared at him for a long moment, her blue eyes a bit more chilly than normal. "I thought you said this was going to be easy."

Rapp got the two bottom straps just the way he liked them and said, "I don't plan on getting in an accident every time I get behind the wheel, but I still wear a seat belt."

"Your point?"

"I don't plan on getting shot, but since it's already happened once this week you'll have to excuse me if I decide this is a good idea."

She frowned and lay there unflinching, but in the end she decided there wasn't much else she could add. She watched as Rapp carefully pulled on a black cotton dress shirt. He buttoned all but the top button so his white vest was concealed. He came over and sat on the edge of the bed. Cupping her cheek with his hand, he said, "You have two hours to get ready and be in position. If you don't want to come along that's fine. You can wait here or head home if you want."

She shook her head. "I'm coming with."

"Good. And can you be ready and in position in two hours?"

"No problem, but where are you going?"

"I have a few more things I need to pick up and I need to take a look around."

"You can't stay and eat with me?"

"I'd love to, but there's not enough time. Order some room service and when you're ready make sure you pack all of your stuff and put it in your trunk."

"I know," she repeated like a good student. "And take your backpack and make sure I don't check out because we might need to come back."

Rapp considered the tense, anxious expression on her face. He leaned in and kissed her on the forehead. "Don't worry so much. This is just going to be a little observation from a safe distance. Nothing will go wrong. I promise."

"Famous last words."

Rapp smiled. "You're such an optimist."

CHAPTER 27

WASHINGTON, D.C.

JIM Talmage chose the four-year-old metallic gray Toyota Camry because it was the most common make in the District and also the most common color. He had three dogs to choose from, and the choice was easy. The German shepherd would stand out too much and the white Scottish terrier only slightly less, so it would be his trusted mutt, Bert. Talmage had picked him up from a pound three years ago. Bert was only four months old at the time. The pound had no papers on him but a lot of opinions as to who his parents were. As Bert grew it became obvious to Talmage that he was a mix of border collie and Labrador. Of his three dogs, Bert was the smartest by a long shot. He had a black coat with a fist-sized patch of white at the chest, and the only reason he needed a leash was so as to not alarm one of the many fascists that walked the streets of the District looking to scream at anyone who didn't have his dog on a leash.

Bert sat near the trunk of the car while the sixty-one-year-old Talmage surveyed his equipment. He looked older today because he had put some powder in his hair giving it more of a gray look. All of his equipment was contained in four black cases that could easily be moved from one trunk to another. One case contained a variety of cameras, from big SLRs that could handle thick, long lenses to tiny cameras not much bigger than a man's thumb. Talmage chose the camera he would use, but didn't pick it up. Instead he opened a medium-sized square duffel bag with two zippers along the top. A piece of nylon fabric connected both zippers so they could be opened at the same time. Talmage pulled them back and the top of the duffel bag opened like a tongue. Neatly folded jackets were arranged inside along with a variety of hats. Talmage chose a houndstooth driving cap to start with and then he put on a trench coat that reversed from black to khaki. He chose the khaki side and moved on to another black case.

Inside were a variety of transmitters as big as a box of playing cards and as small as a ladybug. He considered his subject before deciding and then pulled on a thin pair of brown leather gloves and grabbed two options as well as a receiver. He didn't bother checking them, as he had done so back in his basement shop earlier in the day. The receiver was placed in the left pocket of the trench coat and the two transmitters in the right. Next he chose a medium-sized SLR. It was a Canon, the kind of camera carried by tourists who were serious about their photos, but not the kind of monster carried by a pro. He twisted a 135mm lens onto the end and hung the camera around his neck. He closed both cases and then his hand hovered over the third for a second. It was full of directional listening devices, and he wouldn't need any of them for the next hour. His hand stopped over the fourth case and he seemed hesitant to open it. He knew what was inside, he just wasn't sure he needed to be packing heat.

There had been a time in his career when he wouldn't have even considered not carrying, especially in the District. He had all the proper paperwork should the police stop him, but that wasn't why he carried. He carried because many of his subjects were under extreme pressure, the kind of pressure that could cause certain men to do stupid things if they discovered they were being followed. The other reason he carried in the District was the criminal element. D.C. had been in the top five in the nation for murders for more than a decade and running. It was the thugs that made him decide to punch in the code and pop the case. Inside were a Browning 1911 .45 caliber pistol, a Beretta 9mm pistol, and a customized Colt .45 caliber machine pistol with a collapsible butt stock and threads for a suppressor. Talmage grabbed the Browning. He was in a nice part of town, the part of town that the city's criminal element liked to visit to commit violent crimes.

The last things he grabbed were a copy of the *New York Times*, Bert's dog leash, and a plastic shopping bag. Talmage closed the trunk and activated his customized alarm with a key fob. Bert sat perfectly still while Talmage attached the leash. He even stopped slapping his tail against the pavement. The man and beast then started across the parking lot toward the trees, the walking and biking paths, and the dark brown Potomac River. Bert kept pace with his owner, never pulling on the leash or tripping him up by walking underfoot. When they made it to the first path, both dog and owner stopped. In unison they looked left and then right and then stepped off.

They continued to the next path and then onto the threadbare grass just beyond. Talmage surveyed the river. Twenty-five yards away a young couple in a kayak zigzagged their way upstream, laughing at their own inexperience. Out in the middle of the river a six-man crew slapped the water in unison as they flew back downstream. Closer to the far shore and a little to the north, two more kayaks were navigating the rocks. This time of year it wasn't too difficult, but come spring it would not be for the faint of heart. To his left a single scull worked its way against the current. Talmage looked down at his camera and flipped a couple of the dials before bringing the viewfinder up to his right eye. He swung casually to the left, zoomed in on the lone rower, and snapped three photos.

And then he and Bert started south on the walking path. As Talmage and his subject drew parallel Talmage kept his eyes front and center. Only an amateur would try to steal a look and risk exposing himself. For nine minutes, they walked the path, minding their own business and smiling back at the occasional dog owner who wanted to share their common association with a smile and a nod. They eventually reached their objective, a dumpy little place called Jack's Boathouse. The business model was fairly simple. Rowing, crewing, and sculling were popular on the East Coast, especially with those who went to certain upper-crust schools and even a few where drinking was more important than academics. A fair number of those graduates matriculated to D.C. after graduation, and rather than act like a gerbil on a wheel at their local health club, they came to the Potomac during the warmer months and got one of the best workouts known to man. Jack's catered to these people by renting various boats, sculls, and kayaks and also providing storage for those who didn't have the room at home for their equipment, or didn't want to bother lugging it back and forth.

Talmage had already learned two things about his subject: He owned his own single scull and he was too cheap to rent a spot for it, so he drove it back and forth, tying it to the roof of his eight-year-old sky blue Volvo station wagon. Talmage could now see the station wagon to his left parked among the various vehicles in Jack's packed parking lot. He checked upriver first to see the location of the subject. Talmage judged he was too far away to notice what he was about to do. And if he could see he'd be too out of breath and focused to notice what was going on nearly a mile downriver.

Talmage started talking to Bert, for no other reason than to buy some time. Surveillance was a tricky business, especially in this town. You never knew who else might be lurking about with eyes on your target. After a minute of looking crazy talking to his dog, Talmage thought he was clear. He started for the cars, not directly for the Volvo, but in its general direction. He casually nudged Bert where he wanted him to go, and when he had him in near-perfect position he gave a one-word command.

Bert stopped right on his mark and squatted down, his left rear leg tapping the ground as if he was priming a pump. A few seconds later,

Bert was finished with his business and Talmage slid him a treat and said, "Good boy."

Bert took the treat and wagged his tail while his owner got down on one knee and pulled out the shopping bag. With the bag turned inside out, Talmage scooped up the pile and tied the bag in a knot. He transferred the bag to his left hand and then before standing he reached out and steadied himself on the front bumper of the Volvo. Even a trained professional would have had a hard time seeing what he'd done. Talmage then walked over to the nearest garbage can and deposited Bert's droppings. They started back up the path to the north. Up ahead through the trees Talmage could see the man in the lone scull turning around. He was just a speck at this distance. Talmage knew it was him only because he'd catalogued every person on the river and the walking and biking paths as well. He was as certain as he could be that he was the only person surveilling the deputy director of the CIA. It wasn't something that he'd been thrilled about at first. If the Gestapo at Langley or the FBI busted him, he would likely spend several long months behind bars being denied his legal right to counsel.

As to why he was following Cooke, Talmage had no idea, but he trusted the man who had given him the job. Talmage owed Thomas Stansfield his life, and he'd decided a long time ago that he would probably never be able to repay him, but showing him a little gratitude was at least a good start.

CHAPTER 28

PARIS, FRANCE

His checklist complete, Rapp moved through the neighborhood with the collar of his jeans jacket pulled up high around his ears and his chin tucked down. The early evening air was damp and cool. A plain blue baseball cap covered his thick black hair and he was wearing a pair of black eyeglasses with clear lenses. With his hands shoved in his pockets, his eyes swept both sides of the street. He'd done some loose reconnaissance an hour earlier and had spotted two vans within a block of the apartment. He was fairly confident which one contained Victor and the other men. Rapp's only real worry at this point was whether his new drug-dealing friend would show up for their meeting. If he didn't, Rapp would either have to go knock on the door of the van or figure something else out. So far nothing obvious had presented itself, but he had time. His conversation with Kennedy had gone about as well as he could have hoped. She would take his concerns straight to Stansfield, and the old Cold Warrior would never disregard something this serious. If the Orion Team had been penetrated, Stansfield would have a major dilemma on his hands, and he would move at top speed to find out the identity of the traitor.

Rapp showed up at the café and took a quick look at the crowd. Night was on the city, and the dinner crowd was brisk. The temperature hovered near sixty degrees and there were only a few people sitting outside at the small green bistro tables. Rapp glanced inside. There was no sign of Luke, so he grabbed one of the small tables outside that gave him a good view of the intersection and placed his back to the building. He checked his watch. He was five minutes early. He wondered briefly if drug dealers were punctual and decided more than likely not. He picked up a paper, and when the waitress approached he ordered a glass of red wine. Rapp rested his left hand in his lap and made a fist. A muted stab of pain went from his fingertips all the way up his arm, into his shoulder, and then flared up his neck. Part of his training had covered the nasty hazards of his business, and how to stay alive should he fall on the receiving end of a gunshot or a variety of other attacks meant to kill him. The electric shock that ran up his left arm told him he had some nerve damage. It would more than likely heal, but only if he babied it. The pain pills were a mixed blessing. They allowed him to go about his business without having to deal with the distraction of pain, but they also gave him a false sense of confidence that could cause more damage. His best guess was that his arm was no better than 50 percent. He could use it if he had to do something like making a simple magazine change, but if he had to punch or grab with any sort of force or leverage the damage would be intense. The wound would reopen and the bleeding would begin anew.

That's why he'd decided to sew the new holster into the left side of the quilted jeans jacket. This way he could reach across his body with his right arm for an easy draw. Now more than ever, he understood why they'd trained him to shoot with both hands. He was a lefty with a natural eye, but it had taken a good deal of work to get his right hand up to snuff. At twenty-five feet he could place all one hundred rounds in the black shooting left-handed, and he could place all but a handful in the black when shooting with his right hand.

Rapp glanced down and unbuttoned one of the brass buttons on the jacket so he could have easier access to the pistol, just in case his new drug-dealing friend did something stupid. He had been trained to think ahead, to always cover the gamut of possibilities. He took a sip of wine and placed a pack of Gauloises cigarettes on the table. It was a nasty habit, and one that Rapp had reluctantly begun, but his job required long periods of sitting and watching while trying to act as if he wasn't watching. He had become the worthless man who hung out at cafés for long hours, drinking, smoking, working on crossword puzzles, and reading important books that barely held his attention. If you wanted to fit in, if you wanted to pass the time without looking like a private eye, a policeman, or an intelligence officer, it was better to adopt the appearance of yet another Bohemian artist who was trying to avoid work.

As the appointed hour came and went Rapp nursed his wine and lit a cigarette. He decided he would wait until thirty minutes past the hour, maybe ten minutes past that at the most, and then he would abandon his plan, meet up with Greta, and try to come up with something else. Five minutes later Luke approached from the west, a cigarette dangling from his lips. Rapp was pleased to reconfirm that they were roughly the same size and build. Luke hadn't shaved in a few days and his face was covered with thick black stubble. They moved differently, of course, but on second thought Rapp realized that would help. Victor and his crew would assume Rapp had adopted some kind of disguise and had changed his gait. Only Rapp, Ridley, Kennedy, and Hurley had access to the apartment. When Luke showed up they would jump to the most logical conclusion and Rapp would watch how they reacted.

He watched Luke stop at the nearest intersection. Even though the light had turned green he did not move. Rapp was wondering what he was up to when he saw Luke turn and greet another man. He was a big fellow, almost six and a half feet tall, with a big, knobby, bald head and arms that hung halfway to his knees. Rapp had learned to spot that on the lacrosse pitch. Rapp himself had long arms, but only a few inches longer than most. It was enough to give him a nice advantage in things like fights and stick handling. This mountain of a man, however, looked more like an ape, and his hunched shoulders made his arms appear even longer than they were.

Rapp had specifically told Luke to come alone, and he could tell by the smile on his face that he had knowingly decided not to honor Rapp's request.

With his cigarette dangling from his lips, Luke sauntered up to the table and sat on Rapp's right. The goon loitered for a moment and then grabbed a small chair and spun it around backward and sat with his arms folded over the back of his chair. He stared at Rapp as if he was contemplating eating him for dinner.

"Good evening," Luke said, "I'd like you to meet my friend Alfred."

The big man stuck out a scarred and puffy right paw. Rapp reluctantly offered his own hand. Alfred clamped down and began to crush Rapp's hand. Rapp squeezed just hard enough to prevent the man from breaking any bones. When he was done with his juvenile game Rapp turned his attention back to Luke. "I told you to come alone."

Luke shrugged. "I don't like traveling alone at night. Paris can be a very dangerous city." With a thin smile he added, "I find that Alfred has a way of deterring people who would like to harm me."

Rapp took a closer look at Alfred. His nose was broken in at least two places and there was a fair amount of scar tissue built up under each eye, as well as some cuts above each eyebrow and along his cleft chin. Rapp had to consider the bullet hole in his left shoulder. He was sure he could take him, but if things didn't go smoothly and quickly he would also probably open the wound and begin bleeding again. If it came to violence Rapp would need to be certain he landed a decisive blow right at the start. He decided to force the issue. He picked up his cigarettes and shoved them in his pocket. "It's too bad we won't be able to work with each other."

"And why is that?"

"I already told you."

Luke scoffed as if it had been a minor request. "My friend Alfred is very trustworthy. You need not worry about him."

"Your friend Alfred will stick out like a sore thumb . . . did you bother to think about that? He might as well have 'I'm a violent criminal' tattooed on his forehead. If anyone sees him in the building they will know he doesn't belong, and they will call the police. You, on the other hand, look enough like me that no one will bother you with a second look."

Luke signaled for the waitress and said, "It doesn't matter. I will be bringing Alfred along for protection." Turning his attention to the waitress, Luke ordered a glass of wine for himself and a beer for Alfred.

When the waitress was gone, Rapp said, "This isn't going to work. I'll have to find someone else." Rapp set down his wine and started to stand.

"Alfred," was all Luke had to say.

Rapp felt the pull in his shoulder as the big man grabbed him by the forearm and yanked him back into his chair. Rapp masked the pain coursing through his shoulder and looked at Luke with a cool expression.

"No need to rush off," Luke said. "Nothing has changed. I simply wanted someone I trusted to join me for this strange job that you have brought to me."

Rapp looked down at his arm, which Alfred still held tightly. He had already taken inventory of his surroundings. In a voice that shouldn't have left any doubt about his seriousness, Rapp said, "Luke, you have misjudged me. I am not someone you want to screw with. Tell your man to let go of my arm right now, or we are going to have a big problem."

Luke gave an amused giggle and the big man leaned forward, his pronounced underbite making him look like he had an IQ of sixty. "I'll let go of your arm when I'm fucking ready."

Rapp gave a quick nod, turned his attention back to Luke, and said, "I'm going to count to ten, and when I'm done your goon will have either let go of my arm, or I'm going to cause him a great deal of pain."

Alfred laughed loudly, and Luke said, "There is no reason to make threats."

"One . . . two . . ."

Luke was smiling. "You Americans are so dramatic. Stop your counting and hear me out."

"Three . . . four . . ." Rapp's eyes were locked on Luke, but he could hear the big man to his left laughing. Rapp decided to stop counting, and his right arm shot across his body. His fingers were folded under, his second row of knuckles forming a jagged edge of hard bones. Rapp's eyes zeroed in like bomber sights on Alfred's pronounced Adam's apple and guided the strike with precision, the rigid knuckles of his right hand connecting with the soft thyroid cartilage and the larynx behind it. There was a crunching noise followed by a heavy exhalation of air as it left Alfred's mouth.

The big man immediately released Rapp's arm. His hands shot to his own throat, his eyes bulging in shock. Alfred stood and began stumbling backward, knocking over a table.

Rapp ignored the pain in his shoulder and scowled at Luke. "Are you done fucking around? I came to you with a serious proposal and rather than doing as we agreed, you decided to bring along this half-wit, and then you try to strong-arm me." Rapp brought his fist up as if he might strike him.

Luke flinched and then tried to hide his concern over the fact that Rapp had so easily bested his man. Alfred had tipped over another table and chair and then managed to bounce into a streetlight, which he was now leaning against, clutching his throat and gasping for air.

"He'll be fine," Rapp said in an irritated tone. Trying to allay some of Luke's concern, he added, "I didn't hit him that hard." A moment passed while they both watched Alfred lean over and gulp for air.

"You could have killed him."

"That's right, but I didn't. Now are you done fucking around?"

Luke nodded, his eyes still a bit wide from the shocking turn of events.

"This was probably for the best," Rapp said, taking a sip of wine. "I'm easy to deal with as long as you don't try to fuck me." Placing his right elbow on the table, Rapp looked into Luke's still-shocked eyes and said, "This is serious business and it's best to know right now where we stand. You are not afraid to resort to violence and neither am I." Rapp opened his jacket just enough to give Luke a glimpse of the black grip of his pistol. "We made a deal, and I expect you to honor that deal. If you plan on screwing me, or don't think you are capable of honoring our arrangement, you should get up and leave right now." Rapp released the fold of his jacket. "I don't really care. I will find someone else if I have to." Rapp let a beat pass. "However, I'd prefer to get this done tonight. Everything is in place. The question is, are you going to be greedy or smart?"

Ignoring the question, Luke craned his neck around and studied Alfred. He seemed to find some relief in the fact that his friend was breathing more regularly. A couple passed on the sidewalk, and for a moment it looked as if they were going to stop and help Alfred, but once they got a good look at him they decided to hurry past. Luke shook his head and turned back to Rapp. In a voice full of suspicion he asked, "Who are you?"

For most people it would have been a fairly easy question to answer. You are who you are, after all, but for Rapp his life had become something far more complicated. There were times when even he wasn't sure who he was. He had five separate identities that he used on a regular basis and several more that were tucked away in a safe-deposit box in Switzerland. His existence had become a lie within a lie.

His own brother had not a clue what he was up to, nor did any of his friends. Over the last several years he had distanced himself from all of them. Not an entirely unusual thing after graduating from college, but his reasons were different.

The kid who had grown up in Virginia and played lacrosse for Syracuse University was gone. Replaced by a killer. There was no melancholy or regrets. He was on a path he had chosen. Rapp softened his hard stare and said to Luke, "I'm someone who could make you a lot of money tonight. All I need to know is are you in or are you out, and if you're in, I need you to play by my rules." Rapp sat back, fished out a fresh cigarette, and lit it. After he exhaled a cloud of smoke he asked, "So what's your answer?"

Luke did not answer right away. Rapp watched him. He knew what the other man was thinking and answered his own question for him. "Luke, if I worked for the police, why would I go through all of this when we could simply arrest you for selling drugs? This is exactly what I told you it is. You either want to make a boatload of money tonight, for very little work, or you don't, but I need an answer right now."

Luke regarded Rapp for a long moment before nodding. "I'm in, but I'm warning you, I have friends with the police and a very good attorney. If anything goes wrong you will be the one taking the blame. Not me."

"Nothing is going to go wrong, Luke. Trust me."

"Famous last words."

Rapp cocked his head, revealing a bit of surprise. "You're the second person who's said that to me today."

"Maybe God is trying to send you a message."

"I don't think so." Rapp took off his hat and handed it to Luke. "Here, wear this. If anyone sees you, they'll think it's me."

Rapp fished out the keys and a piece of paper with instructions and the codes for the security system and the safe. He went over everything with Luke and answered his questions as patiently as he could.

Alfred wandered back to the table at some point and Rapp showed just enough of the pistol to get him to back off. Luke told him he would meet up with him in a few hours. When Rapp was done he pointed to his watch and said, "You have one hour. Be on time. All right?"

Luke nodded and Rapp got up and left.

CHAPTER 29

THERE were days when his job truly sucked, but this was not one of them. Tonight Stan Hurley was a happy man. He had over ten grand in his pocket and a beautiful, classy woman at his side, who he happened to have fantastic intimate memories with. The food was off the charts and the sommelier had come through with two phenomenal bottles of Bordeaux. She'd aged a bit, but so had he, and on her it looked good. Her raven black hair was shorter now, just below her ears, and she'd added a few wrinkles around her eyes and mouth, but in a strange way it made her even sexier. That a woman could age so gracefully was something that turned Hurley on. Whether it was due to genetics or some daily regimen, he didn't care. The end result was all that interested him, and the end result was a gorgeous forty-four-year-old woman who had never tried to place any constraints on him. There were never any games with this one. No matter how long it had been since they had seen each other, they always picked up where they'd left off. Which was dinner, lots of laughs, and great sex.

Paulette was a refined metropolitan woman who oozed confidence. She was nearly ten years younger than the rough-and-tumble Hurley, but she had a wisdom about her that Hurley had found extremely un-usual for a reporter. She had pegged Hurley for a spook from almost the moment they'd met in Moscow nearly twenty years earlier. Pau-lette LeFevre had been a reporter back then and was stationed in Mos-cow, where Hurley was running around doing all kinds of bad things for the CIA. Now she had risen to the position of chief editor of *Le Monde,* the left-leaning French newspaper. While it was easy to clas-sify the political bent of the newspaper, LeFevre was more complex. She was too independent to march in step with any political party and she had a contrarian streak in her that, depending on her mood, made her either predictable or unpredictable. She had been raised an only child by two devout communists who had thoroughly indoctrinated her into the utopian ways of the Soviet form of governance. She was raised in a commune an hour outside of Lyon where she had grown up speaking both French and Russian. Her parents had taken her on multiple trips behind the Iron Curtain, and she had watched them lie to themselves and their friends about how much better life was under the benign, velvet glove of the Politburo. When she was eleven they were having a picnic in Gorky Park in Moscow with several families from the commune who were all extolling the virtues of centralized planning and shared sacrifice when Paulette's mother announced that she needed to use the bathroom. She then asked one of their compan-ions for the communal roll of toilet paper. The future reporter looked up at her mother and said, "If communism is so great, then why do we have to bring our own toilet paper everywhere we go?" It was one of Hurley's favorite stories. He'd spent drunken weekends arguing with entrenched communists and gotten nowhere, but somehow an eleven-year-old girl had managed to break the debate down to the most basic level. How could one form of government be superior to another when it couldn't even keep its public restrooms supplied with toilet paper?

Hurley smiled at her and thought back to their first meeting. It was at a party in Moscow hosted by the French Embassy. LeFevre, with shoulder-length shiny black hair, was dressed in a pair of form-fitting black pants, a white blouse, and a pair of black leather riding boots. From Hurley's vantage she looked to have the nicest ass he'd ever laid eyes on. She was an intoxicating combination of simple and stunning at the same time. Hurley couldn't resist her pull and began to make his way across the crowded room. Within an hour he had talked her into leaving the party. Unlike most foreigners, Hurley knew the local hot spots. One of the secrets of his success was that he understood the inherent economic need for a black market economy in the one-size-fits-all Eastern Bloc. Hurley specialized in getting to know the people who ran these underground markets. He'd done so in Budapest, Prague, and then Moscow. It was a world where American cash was king and the profit margins were enormous. Hurley helped these individuals set up new lines of distribution for goods, especially American ones, that were in high demand but extremely hard to come by. His wares ran the gamut from jeans, to music, to pharmaceuticals, to booze, to cars, and everything in between. The CIA was hesitant at first, but when Hurley explained that the venture would generate a profit and also enable them to find out which Communist Party officials were on the take, the powers that be back in Langley, Virginia, got out of his way.

LeFevre was amazed at the clubs he took her to. She did not think such places existed outside of Paris or New York—never in Moscow. After consuming large amounts of vodka they ended up back at Hurley's apartment. Neither was very inhibited where sex was concerned, so they were naked within minutes. The next morning the reporter in LeFevre kicked in, and she began to ask a lot of questions. Hurley didn't think his apartment was bugged, he knew it was bugged, and the people who bugged it knew that he knew. That was the way the game was played. After a few hand gestures he got her to understand that it wasn't safe to talk in the apartment, so they went for a walk, and it was the beginning of a beautiful relationship that to Hurley's great surprise ended up being about much more than just sex.

LeFevre was an intellectual dynamo with a tireless thirst for the truth and a mind that could quickly dissect the incongruities in an argument, movement, or philosophy. He remembered her saying on that walk, "If communism is so wonderful, then why must they force people to participate? If it is so wonderful, why do they control the press? Why do they have to spy on their own people?"

Hurley would have asked her to marry him right there on the spot, but he was already twice divorced and had come to the conclusion that marriage was not an institution he should participate in. His life was full of too many lies, too many late-night phone calls, too many sudden business trips where a long weekend turned into months away from his family, and worst of all too much death. LeFevre had somehow managed to make it work. She'd been married for eleven years and seemed to be happy, which sometimes irritated the heck out of Hurley.

He snagged a fresh cigarette and asked, "So how is your husband?"

Without bothering to look, LeFevre smacked him in the shoulder. "The last time I saw you, you promised you would put your jealous ways to bed."

"I said I wanted to take you to bed. I never said anything about putting my jealous ways to bed."

"You always want to take me to bed, so that is nothing new. As for my husband, he is fine."

"And he's home tonight . . . ?"

LeFevre folded her arms across her chest and leaned back. "Where he is, is none of your concern. I have told you before. We have an open relationship. He has his mistresses and I have you. As long as we are discreet there is not a problem."

Hurley did his best to look wounded, and she laughed him off. "Are there any other men that I need to know about?"

"I have lost track, there have been so many, but you are definitely in the top five."

Hurley felt his cell phone vibrate in the inside pocket of his suit coat. He snatched it out and looked at the caller ID. It came up as private. There was a good chance it was Stansfield. Hurley closed the phone and put it back in his pocket. He didn't need HQ ruining a promising evening. Looking back at LeFevre, he said, "I'm sorry, where were we?"

"You were about to tell me about all the women you have been sleeping with."

Hurley laughed. "There's only you, baby."

"I am not so naïve. I know you too well. You are a very thirsty man. It would be impossible for you to be so saintly in between our rendez-vous."

Hurley was about to reply when the phone began to vibrate again. He checked the small screen and again it came up as private. He grunted disapprovingly and silenced it again. These new phones would be the end of him. Hurley detested the notion of his bosses' being able to get hold of him whenever they wanted. He was used to going days, weeks, and sometimes even months without checking in with them. These phones were nothing more than a leash, and he had known it the first time they gave him one. He closed the phone, stuffed it back in his pocket, and forced a smile on his face. "I'm sorry, darling. I hate these things."

"You are a man of international intrigue," she said with a thin smile. "I would imagine the call might be important."

"Not as important as you." He reached out and grabbed her hand. "Whatever it is, it can wait until tomorrow." The phone began to vibrate for a third time. The smile melted off Hurley's face and his chin dropped in frustration.

"I don't want to see you this way," Paulette said. "Take your call. Get it out of the way. I will go to the washroom and when I get back you will be relaxed again."

Hurley nodded, knowing she was right. If the phone kept ringing he might kill someone. "Thank you." He pulled the phone out of his pocket and watched her slide out of the booth. Flipping it open, he pressed the green Send button and said, "This had better be good."

The metallic voice on the other end said, "Don't be a prima donna. I didn't send you over there to ignore my calls."

It was Stansfield. "And I've done just fine all these years without you snapping my leash every time the wind blows." Hurley listened to silence for a long five seconds. He hated these damn phones. The call had probably dropped. He was about to hang up when he heard an uncharacteristically angry Stansfield begin to speak.

"Things have changed," the old warrior snapped. "I'm on my way over in the morning. I want you to pull Victor and the boys immediately . . . stick them in a hotel and tell them I don't want them to move unless I say so. Have I made myself clear?"

"What the fuck are you talking about? I've got things under control. I don't need any help."

"And I don't need you second-guessing me. There are things you don't know. I will explain in the morning."

"But . . ."

"But nothing," Stansfield said. "Consider it an order to be followed precisely, as you should have done back in Beirut all those years ago. If there are any decisions that countermand my order between now and tomorrow morning you are done. Am I understood?"

Hurley looked around the restaurant. Covering the phone and his mouth with his free hand, he asked Stansfield, "Why don't you just tell me what the hell is going on?"

"Don't be stupid. We'll talk in person. Now carry out my order and give my best to Paulette."

"How did . . ." The line went dead and Hurley pulled the phone away from his ear to look at the screen. How in hell did Stansfield know he was with Paulette? He stared at the phone for a long moment. Every instinct he had was telling him not to make the next call. Rapp was no good. He had broken every rule in their dirty little book and if he wouldn't come in on his own, he needed to be dragged in. But Hurley had rarely if ever heard Stansfield more adamant. The individualist in him wanted to ignore his boss's order and leave the men right where they were for another twelve hours, but Stansfield had made his intentions clear. After another moment of indecision, Hurley said, "Screw it." He pressed the number 2 and held it down until the phone started to dial the number.

"Hello."

"You've been yanked. Head back to the hotel and sit tight until I give you further orders."

"What the fuck are you talking about?"

"Listen, dickhead. You think this is a debate club? If I wanted any shit out of you I'd come down there and squeeze your head. Pack everything up and get your ass back to the hotel, and do it now. Get some sleep, and I'll call you in the morning."

"But . . ."

"But nothing. Do what you're told. End of discussion." Hurley stabbed the red End button, flipped the phone shut, and dropped the small black device on the table. After two big gulps of wine he called the waiter over and told him he wanted a bourbon on the rocks. *Why in hell would Stansfield be flying over here?* he asked himself. *He'd bring way too much heat. He was the damn deputy director, for Christ's sake. This doesn't make any fucking sense.* The bourbon arrived before Paulette and Hurley took a big gulp. He was trying to sort through the different possibilities so he could put this thing out of his mind and focus on Paulette for the rest of the evening when a man approached the table. Hurley looked up, assuming he worked for the restaurant. He had a neatly trimmed mustache and was dressed in an expensive suit. As was his habit, Hurley sized up the fit of the man's jacket for any bulges that might mean a concealed gun.

"Stan. It's been a long time." The man spoke in English with a French accent.

Hurley studied the face of the vaguely familiar man. It must have been the mustache. He couldn't place him.

"I know," the man said with an easy smile. "It's been a long time and your reputation was far beyond mine back then."

"I've been to a lot of places over the years. You're going to have to do better than that."

Just then LeFevre returned from the washroom. "You two know each other? I should have guessed." She eased into the semicircular booth and inched her way around until she was nestled next to Hurley. She pointed to the other side of the booth and said, "By all means join us for a drink. I'm sure you two have a lot to catch up on."

Hurley said, "I don't have the foggiest fucking idea who this guy is."

"Oh," LeFevre said, surprised. "This is Paul Fournier. He runs the Special Action Division for the DGSE. The same spooky black bag stuff that you do. I would have thought you two would know each other."

Hurley instantly knew the name, and it helped the face fall into place. "Shit," he said to Fournier, "it sure as hell has been a long time. Vietnam more than twenty years ago. You were a virgin."

Fournier smiled. "We all have to start somewhere."

Hurley vividly remembered the brutal interrogation he'd conducted all those years ago. "You weren't squeamish like the rest of those pussies."

"That has never been a problem for me. The ends almost always justify the means."

Hurley held up his glass and gave him a salute.

"Sit," LeFevre commanded. After she flagged down a waiter, she asked for another glass and ordered another bottle of wine. "Paul," she said to Fournier, "I get the feeling that you have some things you'd like to discuss with my friend." She hooked her arm around Hurley's.

"Men like us can always find something useful to talk about."

"I'm sure that's true, but I know you well enough that I think it highly improbable that you just happened to wander into this particular restaurant tonight."

Fournier shrugged as if to say guilty as charged.

"I am very possessive of Stan. I do not get to see him often enough, so I am going to sit here and quietly listen to the two of you share state secrets. I give you both my word that none of what I hear will be published until I write my memoirs in thirty years. If you cannot abide by that, I suggest the two of you meet for breakfast tomorrow. Are we all in agreement?"

Fournier laughed. "Yes. We are in agreement. I would not want to ruin your evening. Although, Paulette, you do not have to go to America to find your lovers. There are plenty of men here in Paris who would jump at the chance to worship you. In fact I would place myself at the top of the list."

The congenial smile melted from Hurley's face. "Listen here, douche bag. I don't give a fuck where you work. One more comment like that and I'll rip your tongue out of your mouth and shove it up your ass."

Paulette squeezed his leg under the table and said, "Darling, there is no reason to get angry. Paul is merely trying to pay you a compliment. Aren't you, Paul?"

Fournier did not answer. He remained locked in a staring contest with Hurley. He knew Hurley was capable of extreme violence, but then again this was not the jungles of Southeast Asia. This was Paris. It was his city. "As my friends will tell you, I am exceedingly polite. My enemies, though, will sing you a different song." Fournier tilted his head to the side and asked, "Are you my friend, Stan, or are you my enemy?"

Hurley didn't blink. "I stopped taking applications for friends years ago. I'm full up."

"Surely you have room for one more . . . or at least a professional acquaintance."

"That depends."

"On what?"

"If you're going to drop your little bullshit charade and get down to business, or keep blowing smoke up my ass."

Fournier smiled. "Fair enough."

The waiter arrived with a fresh glass and new bottle. He poured a taste for Fournier, and after it was approved, he poured more into the glass, set the bottle down, and retreated. Fournier took a drink and placed the glass on the white tablecloth, holding the stem between the thumb and forefinger of his right hand. Looking across the table at Hurley, he asked, "So what brings you to my beautiful city?"

"Just a little sightseeing, and Paulette, of course."

Fournier laughed. "You'll have to excuse me for being so blunt, but I think it is you who are blowing smoke up my ass."

Hurley smiled in return, but inside he was boiling. Stansfield had pulled the plug on Victor, he'd announced he was flying over in the morning, and now this suit from DGSE had shown up. Individually, none of it was good; taken together, it was a mess, and now he had to dick around with this asshole for God only knew how long before he and Paulette could be alone. A night that had started out with such great promise appeared to be going to shit.

CHAPTER 30

THE alley was dark and narrow, six feet wide at one end and just four at the other. It was one of those antiquated paths that made sense before the invention of the internal combustion engine. Back in the day, a horse could have pulled a small cart down the alley to collect garbage and make deliveries. Today the garbagemen drove a three-wheeled scooter down the alley to collect the refuse.

Rapp had seen them do it and was fascinated by how they adapted. Growing up in the suburbs of D.C., all he'd ever seen were big lumbering garbage trucks with a massive steel maul in the back that swallowed and compacted the refuse as it rolled through the spacious neighborhoods. Paris was older and more cramped by American standards, but compared to many of Europe's other gems it was downright spacious. At night, the space was like a tunnel, but Rapp wasn't worried. This was a gentrified neighborhood, and if he happened to run into a criminal it would be the other man's unlucky night, not his.

He took one last look around and then disappeared into the darkness. He had been in the apartment before. It had been a breach of protocol, or at least not reporting it had been. In just one year's time in the field Rapp had grown tired of the tedious aspects of his job. He also had a healthy skepticism of the one-way street that ran between him and his handlers in Virginia. While they kept him in the dark on a great many things, he was supposed to report to Kennedy the minutiae of his relatively mundane life. When he was on the hunt things were different, of course, but here in Paris, where he cooled his heels between assignments, his life was as boring as the average Joe's.

Kennedy wanted weekly reports that contained, among other things, the particulars of any person Rapp came in contact with. Her fear was that another intelligence agency would target him for surveillance and possibly try to turn him or, worse, eliminate him. There was one other concern, but until recently, Rapp hadn't thought it was possible. Kennedy feared that a terrorist organization, possibly with the help of a friendly state security service, would somehow ensnare him, torture him, and then show the world that the hated Satan employed assassins. The video would then end with them slicing his throat and Rapp drowning in his own blood.

Rapp reached the back entrance, and he could just barely make out Greta in the faint glow of the streetlights. He reached out and touched her arm, asking, "Any trouble?"

"No. I parked right where you showed me, waited until the right time, and walked straight here."

"Good." Rapp extracted the key and slid it into the brass lock with a steady hand. He turned, pushed, and stepped into a small back landing that smelled of equal parts garbage and bleach. Greta followed on his heels and the spring-loaded door closed quietly behind them. Rapp paused and listened for any noises that would tell him someone was moving about on the floors above them.

The next door was metal with glass on the top half. It had been painted the same cream color so many times to cover up the scuff marks from furniture, luggage, grocers' carts, and garbage and whatever else people hauled in and out the service door that the paint was uneven and lumpy, especially at the bottom. Rapp nudged the door open and looked up the winding back staircase. There was another staircase at the front of the building and a small elevator as well. He was greeted with silence, so he motioned for Greta to follow and started up the carpeted stairs two at a time.

There was a simple reason he had decided to ignore Kennedy's orders. If they could keep secrets from him, he could keep secrets from them. Besides, something had told Rapp that this place might come in handy one day. He reached the second floor and moved quietly but quickly down the length of the hallway to the last door on the right. The key was out and Rapp slid it into the old lock without hesitation. His greatest fear at this point was a nosy neighbor. He knew the key would work, because he had tried it before. The deadbolt opened with a faint click and Rapp turned the handle and stepped into the apartment. Greta was close behind. Rapp softly shut the door and did not reach for the light switch. Instead he stood there and listened. He was almost certain the owners weren't home, but he wanted to know if anyone was moving about in the hallway.

Rapp had already filled Greta in on the owners of the apartment. It belonged to the McMahons, Bob and Teresa. Rapp had run into big Bob McMahon at Le Ponte Café five months before. A snobbish French waiter was doing his best to not understand McMahon's simple order. Rapp had seen it before. Because he was fluent in French, it wasn't a problem for him, but it was not uncommon for a bored waiter to pretend that he didn't understand a thing that an American patron was trying to say. At first Rapp found it a bit amusing himself, until he thought about the number of Americans who passed through Paris daily and who by staying a bit, sightseeing and eating, pumped millions of dollars into the Parisian economy.

The big American looked as if he was about to grab the waiter by the scruff of the neck and drag him over the counter, so Rapp stepped in and translated McMahon's order for him. The waiter snorted and marched off. McMahon turned to Rapp and asked, "What just happened?"

Rapp switched to English and said, "He understands English. He was just jerking you around. I told him to knock it off and get you what you wanted or I'd never tip him again."

McMahon laughed, thanked Rapp, and then asked him where he was from. Rapp told him Orlando. It was part of his legend that Kennedy had meticulously prepared. Orlando was vanilla. People visited, but were hard-pressed to actually know anyone who grew up in the city that Disney had built. The metropolitan area had grown from several hundred thousand people to over a million in just two decades and it was still expanding. Tourism and retirement communities were the anchors of the local economy, and they both attracted a lot of workers from out of state. It was also home to the University of Central Florida, the second-largest university in America behind Arizona State University, which according to Rapp's legend was his alma mater. The fast growth of the population and the transient nature of the workforce gave Rapp a near ideal cover.

The best way to protect a legend, though, was not to sit around and answer questions. You needed to turn the tables and be the one asking the questions. Rapp had found out Bob had helped build Target Corp into the successful company that it was today and that now he was retired with a boatload of stock options and a wife who wanted to live in Paris and travel across Europe. Bob wasn't so keen on the idea, but then again she'd raised the kids and held the family together while he was off expanding one of America's most successful retail chains.

Over the ensuing months Rapp would occasionally bump into McMahon and his wife, Teresa, or Tibby as she was known to her friends. More often than not Bob, bored out of his mind, would jump at the chance to, as he put it, talk to someone who was normal. They invited him over for dinner and Rapp was trying to figure out a way to get out of it when Bob pointed up and showed Rapp where their apartment was located. It was directly across the street from the front entrance to Rapp's apartment. Even back then Rapp realized that this place could come in handy. The rest was easy. He showed up for dinner with a bottle of wine and some flowers and while they were busy finishing the meal Rapp made an imprint of the key.

He and Greta walked through the dark apartment to the living room and the window that looked down onto Rapp's stoop. They stopped a few paces from the window and Rapp said, "We don't want to get too close."

"I know, you told me. Even though the lights are off, they might be able to see us."

Rapp angled to the left so he could see down the length of the diagonal street where the surveillance van was parked.

"How do you know these people won't just show up at their apartment?"

Rapp kept his eyes on the van. "Because the only thing Tibby loves more than this apartment is the fact that her first grandchild was born last week. They flew home for two weeks. Bob hopes longer."

"How much longer?"

"Forever, I think."

Greta moved behind him and looked around his shoulder. "What are you looking at?"

"That van, halfway down the block."

"The black one?"

"Yep."

"You think there are men in it?"

"Pretty sure." Rapp's eyes were scanning the roofline across the street.

"So what do we do?"

"You're going to go stand on the other side of the window so you have a good view of anyone approaching from the east, and we're going to wait for the show to start."

CHAPTER 31

BRAMBLE was about to shove his fist through twenty-five grand worth of electronics. Why the hell was Hurley pulling him? They were on the same page. He was as gung ho to catch the little fucker as Bramble was. Rapp was an arrogant, reckless little prick and Bramble had asked for point and Hurley had given it to him. He'd been waiting for more than a year for his chance and he sure as hell wasn't going to fold up shop and go sit in some hotel bar and wait for orders.

What could have changed Hurley's mind? Bramble wondered. He started sorting through possibilities, and pretty quickly realized that it wasn't what, but who. It had to be someone high up on the food chain. In fact there was only one man Bramble could think of who issued Hurley orders. It was Thomas Stansfield, but the last Bramble had heard, Stansfield was on board with yanking Rapp's leash.

That meant Stansfield had been given some information that they weren't privy to, or someone had intervened on Rapp's behalf. Bramble rapped his scarred knuckles on the small metal shelf that created the base of the surveillance console and sifted through the possibilities.

His mind stuck on one person. She was a royal pain in the ass and Bramble couldn't understand for the life of him why she had anything to do with their unit. He'd heard she was smart, but he had yet to see any proof of it. All she did was get in their way and thwart Hurley at nearly every turn. She was the one who had found Rapp, recruited him, and forced him onto the team. Bramble couldn't understand it, and in a moment of frustration he'd asked Hurley why he put up with the stupid cunt.

Hurley's reaction had been swift and decisive. He stepped toward Bramble without a hint of violence and kicked him so hard in the groin that Bramble collapsed into the fetal position and stayed there for five full minutes. After that, he never brought Irene Kennedy up to Hurley again. She continued to meddle in their training, selection, and deployments, though, and Bramble watched with increasing irritation as she seemed to have her way with every major decision. The only reason was that she worked at Langley and had Stansfield's ear. After they were all placed on the sidelines and Rapp was given free rein to start taking out targets, Bramble was on the verge of quitting. He'd rather freelance, or move out to Hollywood and start tagging a little ass while pretending to protect some teenage superstar from imagined killers. He'd heard there was a lot of money to be made, but he also suspected he'd end up killing someone. It was one thing to smoke some turd in a Third World shithole. That was like going on safari. Do it in the United States, though, and he was likely to end up behind bars.

Fortunately, Hurley had talked him out of it. He assured him that Rapp would stumble, and more than likely, he'd stumble in a spectacular fashion, and when that happened they would move in and clean up the mess. And by clean up the mess, Bramble took Hurley to mean that he would be allowed to kill the little shit and end this dumb-ass experiment.

Bramble had heard the arguments between Hurley, Kennedy, and that faggot shrink Lewis. Kennedy had created this problem, and

Lewis and God himself Thomas Stansfield had abetted her. The shrink was worthless. If any of them needed to talk about their feelings they were in the wrong line of work. Kennedy was nothing more than a glorified desk jockey with a hold over Hurley that he couldn't understand. And Bramble had spent far too much time trying to figure it out. The only thing he could come up with was that Kennedy had caught Hurley doing something so embarrassing that he had no choice but to back down every time there was a confrontation. Ultimately, though, it was Stansfield who was the problem. He was a damn relic from way back when. Rumor was he'd been OSS during World War II and had parachuted into France and then Norway, and Bramble could give a shit. So the guy knew how to cross-country ski, operate a ham radio, and live off pine needles and tree bark—big deal. The fossil needed to be put out to pasture and let guys like Hurley run the show.

None of it made any sense to Bramble, not then and especially not now. Based on what had happened over the past thirty-six-plus hours, Hurley's order to stand down seemed downright stupid.

"Was that Stan?"

Bramble slowly turned his head to look at Steve McGuirk. "Shut up. I'm thinking."

McGuirk smiled and asked, "Does that hurt?"

"Does what hurt?" Bramble asked.

"Thinking."

Bramble was in no mood for McGuirk's smartass attitude. He sprang from his chair and smashed the smaller man against the back of the driver's carriage. "Did I somehow give you the impression that I was in the mood to listen to your bullshit today? Because I'm not."

McGuirk was wiry and strong, but in such close quarters he was no match for Victor's size. He wedged his right arm up under the bigger Bramble's and pushed back just enough so he could breathe. "You need to lighten up, Victor."

"I don't think so. I think I'm done taking your shit. I think I'm going to tell Stan to cut your ass loose. What do you think of that? Or maybe I'll just break your fucking neck right now." Bramble felt something hard press against his back.

Todd Borneman, the third man in the van, held his silenced pistol against Bramble's lower spine. "Take your hands off, Steve, or I'm going to lodge a hollow-tipped bullet in your spine, and you can spend the rest of your life wearing a diaper."

Bramble slowly backed off, holding his hands up in the air. Borneman was former Delta, the kind of guy who measured his words very carefully. If he said he'd shoot him, Bramble wasn't about to doubt him.

McGuirk sat up straight and said, "You're a real prick, Victor. We're on a fucking stakeout, for Christ's sake. Take a joke."

Bramble looked at McGuirk and then Borneman, who still had his gun out. "Sorry . . . I'm frustrated. Put that thing away," he said to Borneman.

Borneman pointed the gun at the floor, but kept it out. "Who was that on the phone?"

Bramble considered lying but decided it would do little good. "It was Stan."

"What did he want?"

"Nothing."

McGuirk shook his head and said, "So you were pissed off about nothing. You're so full of shit."

Victor wished Borneman would put his gun away so he could slug the shit out of McGuirk. "He wants us to hang out here for another hour or two and then head back to the hotel and wait for orders."

"And what could be so bad about that?" Borneman asked.

"This is our only lead. That little prick is going to show up eventually, and we need to be here. Not sitting on our asses back at the hotel."

Borneman cocked his head an inch to the right and asked, "Why do you hate him so much?"

"Who . . . Rapp?"

"Who else would he be asking about, you mental midget?" McGuirk snapped. This time he was ready, sitting on the edge of his seat, ready to move if Victor came after him a second time.

Bramble stifled his anger and ignored McGuirk. Looking at Borneman he said, "It's a long story. There's a lot of stuff you two don't know about. Stuff Stan hasn't shared with you."

"This wouldn't have anything to do with him breaking your arm . . . would it?" Borneman hadn't been there that day, but he'd heard the story. Victor was a real prick, especially to the new recruits. Hurley had come up with the idea to insert Victor among the recruits so he could gain their confidence and then trip them up. Supposedly Rapp had seen right through it, and when given the chance he removed Victor from the equation. As far as Borneman could see, Rapp had only done what everyone else had dreamed of doing.

"He should have been washed out because of that. Even Stan says so."

"Did Stan say that before or after Rapp saved his life?" McGuirk asked.

"Don't believe every rumor you hear. Stan was doing just fine on his own. If anything he saved Rapp's life."

"That's bullshit," Borneman said. "I was part of the extraction team. Stan was too fucked up to walk. Rapp saved his ass and all you two can do is bitch about him."

"And I'm telling you," Victor said, leaning forward, no longer caring that Borneman had a gun in his hand, "there's a lot of shit you don't know. I have orders to kill him if he so much as looks like he's going to run."

"And why haven't we been given those orders?" McGuirk asked.

"Because you're on the bottom of the totem pole."

"Does Irene know about this order?" Borneman asked.

"How the fuck would I know? Stan doesn't read me in on every aspect of every order."

"This is going to be interesting."

"What?"

"Kennedy's on her way over." Borneman checked his watch. "She's due to land within the hour."

Just the mention of her name soured Bramble's already foul mood. That must be why Hurley was pulling the plug. If Bramble could only figure out a way to kill both Kennedy and Rapp. He was at the beginning of exploring that fantasy when the surveillance console began to beep. Bramble spun around in his chair, his heart already picking up the pace. His eyes flashed to the blinking light on the panel. The motion sensor in the front hallway of the apartment had been tripped.

Bramble's eyes darted from one monitor to the next.

"What is it?" McGuirk asked.

"While you two ladies were asking a thousand questions and distracting me, someone walked up the front steps, climbed one flight of stairs, and is now poking around the apartment."

"How do you know it wasn't the back door?" McGuirk asked.

"I don't, so why don't you get over here and find out how he got in."

McGuirk stood in front of the far side of the console and began typing in commands and winding dials. A few seconds later they had footage of a man walking up the front steps of the building and into the entryway.

"That's him," Bramble announced.

"Are you sure?" Borneman asked.

"I'd put a million bucks on it." Bramble's eyes danced over the other monitors. McGuirk and Borneman traded an *oh fuck* expression.

"Damn!" Bramble grabbed a radio and an earpiece. "You two shit-heads stay right here and don't move a fucking muscle unless I tell you to do so. Am I clear?"

Both men nodded, McGuirk a little more enthusiastically than Borneman.

"Good, and if I call for the van be ready to move!" Victor suddenly had the beginnings of a plan forming. He clipped the radio to his hip and ran a wire up the inside of his brown leather jacket. After wrapping the coil around the back of his ear, he wedged the little flesh-colored earpiece into position. Bramble turned up the volume and did a quick radio check. The last thing he did was tell them to give him constant updates on what was going on inside the apartment, and then he was out the back door of the van like a shot.

CHAPTER 32

GEORGETOWN, WASHINGTON, D.C.

Two suits from diplomatic security were posted at the front door of the five-story brownstone. Their black Suburban was parked directly in front of the house between two orange cones meant to keep the space available 24/7 for the men and women who babysat the secretary of state. Security here in the United States wasn't a big deal. The biggest threat on a weekly basis was the Georgetown students who wandered past late at night smashed out of their minds. Always loud and short on common sense, they sometimes thought it was a good idea to stop in front of Secretary Wilson's house and try to bait the security personnel. The men and women on the detail were professionals, but every once in a while they had to strong-arm someone on their way.

Cooke paid the two men more than a passing glance as he drove past looking for a parking place. If he became the director of the CIA he'd have his own security detail. As the deputy director he was on his own. Thomas Stansfield, who was his subordinate, had a security team, and while Cooke had never said a word to anybody, it irritated him that he didn't have one, too. He outranked Stansfield, after all. Cooke had heard the reasons. The detail had been in place long before he'd become deputy director. It had something to do with the number of threats that Stansfield received and the consensus that he knew more state secrets than any other person in Washington and that it wouldn't do to have him kidnapped and interrogated.

Having a security team in Washington was a real status symbol. Only the most important players received around-the-clock protection. The president and vice president, of course, the secretary of state, secretary of defense, director of the FBI, and Thomas Stansfield. From time to time other cabinet-level people would receive protection, but only if they'd received a specific threat. Cooke hated it that Stansfield was part of that rarefied club. He decided that the moment he became director he would yank Stansfield's detail. And then with Wilson's help, he'd force Stansfield to retire and put one of his own people in charge of Operations. Someone whom he could control. Someone who understood loyalty.

On his third pass Cooke gave up on finding a spot and decided he would wedge his Volvo into the short driveway that led to the heavy lacquered black garage door of Wilson's house. He wasn't blocking the street, but the back end of his wagon made the sidewalk nearly impassable. It wasn't the ideal spot, but Cooke was in a hurry. He needed to have this meeting with Wilson, head back to the office to check on a few things, and then pack for France. They had an early flight. Cooke looked through his windshield at the two bodyguards on the front stoop. They both had brown hair, but one of them had more of it. Both men had casually opened their suit coats and placed their hands on their sidearms. Cooke knew he should have called ahead, but he wanted to surprise Wilson.

Cooke got out of the car. He was wearing gray sweatpants and a gray hooded sweatshirt that had Harvard Crew stenciled in crimson across the front. He put his right hand on the shiny red hull of the scull he had strapped to the hood of his car, looked up at the bodyguards, and said, "Guys, Deputy Director Cooke here. I need to have a brief word with the secretary. Is it okay if I leave my car here?"

The men exchanged a brief look and one of them said, "I'm sorry . . . who did you say you were?"

"Deputy Director Cooke."

It was obvious by the way the two men looked at each other that they had no idea who they were talking to. "I'm sorry, which agency, sir?"

You've got to be kidding me, Cooke thought. "CIA," he said with an impatient face. "Please tell the secretary it's rather urgent."

The one with more hair disappeared into the house while the other one stayed at his post. He looked down at the visitor and asked, "Do you have any identification on you, sir?"

Cooke shook his head and thought, *How is it that these simpletons have no idea who I am?* "Sorry, I don't carry my wallet with me when I'm rowing." Cooke patted his scull like a proud father. "And leaving it in the car isn't very bright, is it?"

The man didn't respond. He just stared at Cooke with a suspicious glare and wondered what kind of person drove around D.C. without any identification. A deputy director at the CIA should have more common sense. A few moments later his partner popped his head out of the door and the two exchanged a few words. The one who was losing the follicle battle motioned for Cooke to approach. Cooke swung around the back of his car and started up the steps. There were five of them, made out of the same brick as the house, and then a landing, a left turn, and five more steps. The front stoop was big enough for the three of them to stand comfortably, or at least so Cooke thought, until Mr. Male Pattern Baldness ordered him to raise his hands so he could frisk him.

"You're kidding me," Cooke said, irritated by the request. "I run the CIA. The secretary and I talk all the time."

The bodyguard remained unfazed by the information. "If you run the CIA, where is your security detail?"

Now Cooke was really bothered. Who the hell did this rent-a-suit think he was, asking him questions? Staring the man down, Cooke lied. "I gave them the day off."

The man considered the response for a moment. It didn't make a lot of sense. The CIA was a serious place, with serious threats. Why would any sane man give his security detail the day off? "No disrespect, sir, but I don't know you, you don't have an appointment, and you don't have any identification. My job is to protect the secretary, period. If I were to let a complete stranger into this house I wouldn't be very good at my job, would I?"

Myriad retorts flashed across his mind, most of them involving Cooke putting the man in his place and insulting his intellect, but in the end he decided that making a scene on the secretary's front stoop was unwise, so he raised his arms and allowed the guy to run his hands up and down his body.

When they were done checking everything but the deepest recesses of his groin, Cooke was escorted into the house. The second bodyguard told him they were to wait in the foyer. The two men stood on the black and white checked marble floor in silence for a few minutes until the secretary came down the long staircase. He was dressed in a pair of charcoal gray, wool dress pants, with a white button-down shirt, and he'd traded in the yellow cardigan from yesterday for a red one.

"Paul . . . two days in a row. Something must be very urgent."

"Sorry, Franklin, but I'm off to Paris in the morning and I thought it would be a good idea if we discussed a few things."

Wilson stopped on the far side of the foyer and eyed his visitor. He looked as if he might have been napping. "Paris . . . does this have anything to do with what we discussed the other day?"

"Yes." Cooke gave the bodyguard a sideways glance and Wilson took the hint.

"Why don't we go downstairs?"

"I think that would be a good idea." Cooke crossed the foyer.

The two men proceeded down the long hallway to the kitchen. Wilson opened the door to the basement, flipped a light switch, and then motioned for Cooke to go ahead. The secretary followed and closed the door behind him.

Cooke watched the older man go through the same routine he'd been through the day before. He went behind the bar, opened a panel, and pressed several buttons. A few seconds later the sound of a string quartet drifted down from the ceiling speakers. After that Wilson grabbed two lowballs, tossed in a few ice cubes, and filled them with scotch. Cooke was about to protest. He had work to do, and the middle of a Sunday was no time to start drinking, but Franklin Wilson was not the type of man to be rebuffed. It was better to take the drink and baby it.

Wilson came out from behind the bar with a glass in each hand and gestured toward the two leather club chairs on each side of the fireplace. Apparently there would be no billiards today. "If I'd known you were stopping by, I would have had a fire going." Wilson handed Cooke his scotch on the rocks and after both men were seated he asked, "So what's on your mind?"

"As I said, I'm headed to Paris in the morning."

"Yes, what's that all about?"

"A couple of things. I want to see my people at our embassy and get a sense of their morale." Cooke looked at his drink and added, "I also have a meeting with some of my contacts at the DGSE."

"French Intelligence?" Wilson asked with an arched brow.

Cooke nodded. "As you can imagine, they're not very happy about the current situation."

"Have they told you who they think was behind the attack?"

"No," Cooke answered with a shake of his head, "but there are certain things in my business that we're loath to discuss over the phone."

"Of course." Wilson took a gulp from his drink and sighed as it warmed his throat. "Do you have a sense, though, that they might have some leads?"

"Apparently it's turned into a spook convention in Paris and everyone is a suspect."

"And Stansfield?"

"He's flying over with me."

Wilson stared at his visitor for a moment. "Your idea or his?"

"Mine. I thought it would be a good idea to get him out of his element. I have some surveillance teams set up to follow him. If he does anything unusual or meets with anyone of interest we'll know."

"Sounds like a good idea. What else?"

Cooke took a tiny sip and said, "Hurley showed up."

Wilson edged forward in his seat. "Interesting. Where is he?"

"Paris . . . DGSE has him under surveillance."

"You're good," Wilson said with an admiring tone. "Has he done anything stupid?"

"Not yet, but knowing his history, there's a good chance he'll give the French a reason to arrest him before the week is over."

Wilson smiled. "I hope you're right. What else?"

Cooke nodded and then took his time. He took another small sip, set his glass down on a cork coaster sitting atop a small wood side table, and leaned forward, placed his elbows on his knees, and folded his hands. "I'm not sure how to put this, so I'm just going to come out and say it. Is there something between you and Stansfield you haven't told me about?"

Wilson gauged that Cooke was in possession of some information that had caused him to ask the question. Being an attorney by trade, he did what all good attorneys do: Rather than answer the question he asked one. "What do you mean?"

"I mean some problem . . . some bad blood between the two of you?"

Wilson shook his head, gazed into his drink for a moment, and then said, "Other than the fact that I don't trust the man, and that I think he should be tried and thrown in jail, no . . . there's nothing I can think of."

"Nothing specific?"

"Paul," Wilson said, his tone turning testy, "if you have some information, come out and say it. There isn't anything that I can specifically think of that has transpired between Thomas Stansfield and me. He is my subordinate and has always been. When I was a senator, and I sat on the Intelligence Committee, we had our brawls, but so did every other senator. It was our job to push him, and in light of his uncooperative nature, there were a lot of heated moments."

"Trust me, I know."

"And now that I'm secretary of state, and one of the president's closest advisors, he is, well, so far beneath me, he would hardly warrant a thought if it wasn't for the fact that I fear he is ruining our relationship with one of our closest allies."

Cooke nodded as if he only half bought Wilson's explanation. "You might spend very little time thinking about him, but it doesn't go both ways."

"What do you mean?"

Cooke hemmed and hawed for a moment and then just said it. "I don't think the man likes you."

Wilson smiled as if he was proud of the information. "There are a lot of people in this town who are jealous of me. I don't doubt for a moment that Thomas Stansfield is one of them."

Cooke decided to push him a little. "Thomas Stansfield isn't some amateur, and you're not the first cabinet member to go after him. He's outlasted more directors and presidents and Senate oversight committees than we could begin to count."

Wilson shifted in his leather chair and straightened his back a few degrees. "Your point?"

"You'd be a fool to underestimate him."

"I never underestimate my enemies and I have a strategy that will prevail."

"What's that?"

"I'm going to win because I will refuse to play Stansfield's games. I don't operate in the shadows. I work in the harsh light of day where the truth can flourish. These others who have gone after him were foolish enough to think they could beat him at his own game. I'm not so naïve."

"Fine," Cooke said, even though he was thinking the exact opposite. The only way to take on Thomas Stansfield was to plot so carefully, walk so softly, that he never saw you coming until you shoved the knife in his back. "Well, either you have him scared or you did something to really piss him off, because I've never seen him like this."

"Like what?"

"I stopped by his office this morning to ask him about Paris."

"And?"

"He denied any involvement, of course . . . not that I expected anything different."

"So it was an unremarkable meeting?"

"I would say yes . . . at least until your name came up, and then he became uncharacteristically heated."

Wilson liked this. He'd never seen so much as a crack in Stansfield's sphinxlike demeanor. "What did he say?"

Cooke cleared his throat and started with his first lie. "He said that you should worry about managing all the dilettantes at the State Department and leave the espionage game up to us."

Wilson didn't flinch. "What else did he say?"

"Do you want the sanitized version or the unvarnished?"

"Unvarnished."

Cooke had tried to figure out the best way to deliver this next part. With the right embellishment of Stansfield's own words and a few lies, he would cut close to Wilson's heart. "He said that you've turned into a bitter, angry man."

Wilson laughed a little, thought about the comment, and then asked, "Why would I be bitter? I've had an amazing life. I'm one of the most powerful men in this country. What could I possibly be bitter about?"

Cooke tried his best to look uncomfortable. He stared at his own shoes for a moment and then he stared at Wilson's. When he thought the proper amount of embarrassment had been conveyed, he said, "Your wife." The words seemed to hang in the air for an eternity. Cooke could see that he was on the right track. Just the mention of the wife had put Wilson on edge.

"What about my wife?"

"Well . . ." Cooke shook his head. "I don't like repeating this, but as I said, it's so out of character that I thought you must have done something to really piss Stansfield off."

Wilson's patience had hit a wall. "What did he say?"

Cooke cleared his throat. "He said you tossed her in an institution the second she became a political liability. That if you truly loved her, as you tell everyone, you would have kept her at home." Cooke did his best to look embarrassed and added, "I'm sorry, Franklin."

Wilson's stately demeanor crumbled. His complexion turned ruddy, his jaw clenched, his nostrils flared, and he looked at the wall to his right. In a wounded voice tinged with anger he proclaimed, "How dare he."

Cooke was pleased with himself but did a good job concealing it. "This was a private conversation, Franklin, between the deputy director of Langley and the deputy director of Operations. If word were to get out that I shared this information with you, there would be some very upset people at Langley. Even so, I felt you needed to know. I myself was shocked that he would make such an insensitive comment. I had no idea he disliked you so much."

"Trust me . . . the feeling is mutual, and I get your point. I won't be saying anything to Stansfield that would put you in a compromising position. That's not how we're going to win this battle."

"I'm sorry," Cooke said again, shaking his head for dramatic effect, "but I felt that I had to bring this to you. If anyone had said anything like that about me and my wife I'd want to know."

Wilson nodded but didn't say anything, he just stared off into space looking wounded.

Cooke stood. "There's a dark side to him, Franklin. He's a very dangerous man." When Wilson didn't respond Cooke said, "I'll keep you informed about what I find out in Paris." Cooke still didn't get a response, so he started for the door. Letting Wilson stew over his words could only serve his purpose. As he reached the stairs, though, Wilson called out.

"Paul, don't worry . . . I'm not going to shoot the messenger. I appreciate your honesty."

Cooke nodded. "Don't worry, Franklin. He's going to get what he deserves and you and I are going to be the ones to finally take him down."

Wilson seemed to not hear anything that Cooke had said. "This is the part of this town that I truly despise. Where is the honor in going after a man's wife?"

"There is none."

"No, there isn't, but I'm not going to let this distract us from our objective. Thomas Stansfield is a dangerous man and he needs to be dealt with before he brings the Agency crashing down around you. I appreciate your friendship, Paul, but I need to know that you are committed to seeing this through."

"I am, sir. Thomas Stansfield has poisoned the CIA and the only way to right the ship is to get rid of him. Once he's out of the way I can go about instituting the changes that will ensure the Agency follows the policies of the executive branch and the laws of this country."

CHAPTER 33

PARIS, FRANCE

RAPP smiled. Luke was playing his role to perfection. He had his hands stuffed in both pockets of his jacket and every five steps or so he scanned the block to see if there were any signs of danger. It was not the way Rapp would have acted, but then again he'd told Kennedy that he'd been shot. It wasn't a stretch for the men in the van to think that he was a little more jumpy than normal.

Rapp had a pretty good idea what was going on inside the van, and he wouldn't deny that he was taking a certain amount of delight knowing that they were probably falling all over each other trying to figure out what to do. As to who was in the van, he didn't have a clue, and until right now he hadn't really considered the question. There were only a handful of people who had watched him closely enough to be able to tell the difference between him and an impostor. Even so, the street was dark and Luke had the same general build. In these situations they would see what they wanted, and that was Rapp returning to the safe house for something that he needed.

Of all the possible assets, Rob Ridley was probably the one who had the most practical knowledge of how Rapp operated. Kennedy and

Hurley knew his movements well enough, but neither of them would be pulling surveillance duty. Hurley was too impatient. He needed to be moving, or at least have the option to move, especially after his abduction in Beirut. The man would never admit it, but there were some psychological scars that he still hadn't dealt with. The most likely option would be Ridley, who specialized in surveillance and advance work. He and his people had done the advance work on the Tarek hit and then vacated the city the day before Rapp had killed the oil minister. Rapp didn't know where they were headed, but Hurley would have had a day and a half to turn them around and get them back into position. It was possible, but Rapp had a feeling it was someone else.

It would all come down to the call he'd made to Kennedy and whether she was able to convince Stansfield that he'd been set up. If she had failed, Rapp had little doubt who was in the van. Hurley would be calling the shots and he would have his pet dog, that asshole Victor, on duty. Rapp had spent very little time at the farm over the past year, and the year before that they had gone to great lengths to keep his identity a secret from the other visitors. Over that time he'd seen a little over a dozen faces. Men who had returned from operations overseas and guys who were trying to make the team. One of those faces was already gone, killed in Beirut. Rapp didn't like to think about that day. It was too stark a reminder that his life could go the same way in the blink of an eye.

Kennedy had said she was coming to Paris. How that would play out was obvious. Hurley would be pissed, and he'd tell her to go back to Langley and sit behind her desk and do it in very insensitive, colorful language. The only way she could make any headway was with Stansfield calling the shots. That's what it came down to. He was the only man who could rein in Hurley.

Rapp stood behind Greta's shoulder and watched Luke inch closer to the front steps of the apartment. He took a step back and moved to the other side of the window. The van was easy to spot. It was a black Mercedes-Benz Sprinter van. Boxy and tall, it offered the men inside room to move around and they were fairly common in most big cities, as workers used them to navigate the narrow, congested streets. What made this one stand out was the roof rack. The rack had a ladder and several tubes that looked like they could contain anything from rolled-up wallpaper to flooring. In truth they were part of a customized surveillance system that concealed cameras, antennas, and directional microphones.

His money was on Victor, but beyond that he had no idea who would be on duty. More than likely they had pulled assets from stations across Europe, although most of those men would be attached to embassies with official covers, and exposing them to someone like Victor would be a big gamble. Rapp put himself in Hurley's shoes and decided he'd never do it. Hurley would grab some of his ex–Special Forces assets, guys who didn't have squeamish stomachs and knew how to keep their mouths shut.

"Greta," Rapp asked as he kept his eyes on the van, "what do you see?"

"The man in the hat. Nothing else."

Rapp stepped back two steps and crossed over to Greta's side of the window. Luke was roughly thirty feet from the front door. Rapp scanned the area beyond to see if there was any movement. There was none, so he went back to the other side of the window to keep an eye on the van. He thought he saw the van rock slightly but it was hard to tell from this distance.

"He's going up the steps," Greta announced.

Rapp didn't bother looking. He was too focused on the van.

"He's inside."

In that moment, it occurred to Rapp that they might be waiting in the apartment. His eyes darted from the van to the second floor across the street. He counted three windows in from the corner. The shades were drawn on both the third and fourth windows. There was no way of telling if anyone was in there. Rapp grew a little tense. If they grabbed him, and interrogated him, they might come to the conclusion that Rapp was nearby watching them. "Greta, remember what I said to you. If I tell you I want you to head to your car, I don't want you to argue with me."

She took her eyes off the building. "But I don't understand why you wouldn't come with me."

"We're not going to argue about this," Rapp said in a firm tone. "I need to know you're going to do exactly what I want you to do when I ask you. Your safety is my first priority. If you're not willing to do what I ask you to do, then you might as well leave right now."

Greta shook her head and frowned. Taking orders was not her strong suit.

Rapp turned his eyes back to the van. Kennedy had told him they had the safe house under surveillance. The guys were either asleep in the van or they had men inside the apartment. If that was the case, Rapp expected to see some lights come on any second. Luke would be in for one hell of a surprise and likely a two- or three-day debriefing where he would literally have the shit scared out of him. Rapp didn't feel good about it, but Luke would survive. His story would check out because Rapp planned on calling Kennedy and telling her what he'd done. They would be pissed that he had exposed a safe house by giving the keys and codes to a drug dealer. Rapp's defense would remain consistent. Someone on their end had betrayed him. He'd been set up, and until he knew who he could trust they would have to excuse his paranoia.

Rapp checked his watch. Luke had gone through the front door nearly forty seconds ago. He looked down the length of the street at the Mercedes van and he finally saw some movement. The van rocked and then a moment later someone was moving up the sidewalk in a hurry. He was crouched down and running. Rapp caught glimpses of the man as he passed in between cars, and then as he drew closer he got a more consistent view.

It was Victor. Even in the poor light of the hazy street lamps he was easy to make out. He was half man, half gorilla, lumbering down the street as if he might run through a brick wall if he needed to. Rapp didn't like Hurley, but he respected the salty bastard. Victor was another matter. Rapp loathed him, couldn't understand why he hadn't been drummed out, and spent a fair amount of time analyzing all the different ways he'd kill him if he was ever given the chance.

Rapp watched him hug the building as he got closer to the front door. The building across the street was a near mirror image of this one. There was a garden level on the main floor and each unit had its own entrance and a small patio that was four feet beneath the sidewalk and fenced off by a black wrought-iron fence and gate. The first floor was elevated above the sidewalk by eight feet, so the front steps were fairly steep and led to a pair of double doors. Victor positioned himself exactly where Rapp expected. He sank into the shadows beside the front stoop. Rapp squinted but it did no good. Victor was dressed in black. He was a shadow among shadows.

Rapp checked the lights in the apartment. They were still off. He looked at his watch. Luke had been in the apartment for close to two minutes. Rapp had timed it in his head. If he did exactly as Rapp ordered, he could be in and out in less than five minutes. Something told Rapp, though, that Luke might take a little extra time to see what else he could take.

"Who is that man?" Greta asked.

"The one I warned you about . . . Victor."

Things settled into a slow pattern as Rapp continued to check the van, Victor's position, and the apartment windows. For four minutes and twenty-seven seconds nothing happened, and then suddenly the moment was upon them. The front door of the apartment building opened and Luke stepped into the night air. He hustled down the steps and turned to the right just as Rapp had instructed. Victor suddenly materialized from the shadows and fell in behind Luke, just four steps behind him. His right hand came up and Rapp immediately recognized the length of black steel in his hand as a pistol with a suppressor attached to the end.

Rapp shook his head and under his breath mumbled, "What a prick."

What happened next was completely unexpected. There was a muzzle flash followed by Luke's entire body being propelled forward for one more step. Then he crashed to the sidewalk face-first.

Greta gasped and covered her mouth.

Rapp blinked just once and reached for his gun. In that split second he realized he had just witnessed what was supposed to be his own murder, and a second after that he realized he had caused the death of a completely innocent man. The realization filled him with embarrassment and rage and the absolute conviction that he would kill Victor.

CHAPTER 34

BRAMBLE had already scoped out the spot. That was the way his brain worked. He was a hunter, a natural-born killer, and a badass to boot, which was why Rapp didn't stand a chance. Rapp was a college puke who hesitated. A pussy who'd been indoctrinated into the world of political correctness. His brain was filled with too much crap. Stuff that got in the way of millions of years of predatory evolution. It was his loss and Bramble's gain. Rapp was probably the kind of guy who puked after he killed someone. Bramble had once watched a fellow Ranger do that after a mission. He'd never lost so much respect for someone so quickly.

The alcove next to the front steps was the perfect spot. Bramble's heart was racing and he knew it wasn't from the short run up the block. It was the anticipation of the kill. The adrenaline that was coursing through his veins. It was an amateur reaction and he chided himself for it. He forced himself to take deep, steady breaths. There was nothing to be tense about. His position was ideal. He was completely concealed by darkness and he was in a textbook spot to ambush Rapp when he came back out. His heart began to slow and then he realized he had a problem.

Two actually. What would he do with McGuirk and Borneman? They were about to watch him kill Rapp, and while he could easily explain to them that Hurley had given him the kill order, the problems would pop up later, when they got back to the States. They would all be debriefed and Kennedy would lose her mind when she found out that he'd killed her baby. Even Hurley might take it badly. He despised Rapp, but he wouldn't take kindly to one of his men initiating a kill order on his own, especially after having been told to stand down. Bramble was scrambling to come up with an out when McGuirk's voice came over his earpiece.

"He's going for the safe."

Of course he is, Bramble thought, and then he remembered an order Hurley had given him. He panicked and asked, "Did you guys empty the safe?"

"Why would we do that?" McGuirk replied.

"Because I told you to," Bramble snapped.

"The hell you did. Todd, did Victor tell us to clean out the safe?"

Bramble listened to the one-sided conversation and then McGuirk told him he must be sniffing glue. "You never told us to empty the safe."

Bramble swore to himself, looked back down the street at the van, and asked, "What's he doing?"

"He's got the safe open, and it looks like he's emptying it."

Hurley was going to freak. It was the first thing he'd told him to do. "Clean out the safe and don't get any stupid ideas. Kennedy and I have an exact accounting of what's inside," he'd said.

"He's closing the safe," McGuirk announced. "It looks like he's stuffing a bag down the front of his pants."

"Shit," Bramble mumbled. "What else?"

"Looks like he's headed for the door. Yep, he's in the front hallway and headed straight for the door. What do you want us to do?"

"Sit tight." He was too focused on solving his problem. This was an opportunity he couldn't pass up, and if he did he'd kick himself in the ass for the rest of his life.

"Repeat that last order."

Bramble recognized Borneman's voice. He was going to be the problem. McGuirk he could deal with. "I said sit still. We don't want to spook him. Just be ready to pull the van up and keep giving me updates."

Bramble listened to McGuirk give him the play-by-play of Rapp's exit. His chief tactical concern at this point was whether he was going to come out the same way he went in. A few seconds later Bramble got the confirmation he was looking for. He stood in the shadows, a huge smile spreading across his face. "You're all mine, asshole."

He heard the door open and he began to edge forward, his right arm extended, ready to fire. McGuirk kept giving him updates and Bramble could see Rapp coming down the steps in his mind's eye. As soon as he heard that Rapp had taken a right turn, Bramble left his spot. He knew the monitors in the van didn't exactly offer a crystal-clear picture of what was happening on the street and he was going to use that to his advantage. He stepped into the hazy glow of the street-lights and fell in behind his prey.

Rapp was standing right in front of him, only a few yards away and moving quickly. Bramble matched his pace, extended his gun, sighted in on the back of Rapp's head, said, "Gun," and squeezed the trigger. It was the most beautiful thing he'd ever seen. The bullet entered the back of his head and exited his face with a spray of red mist. Rapp took one more step and then collapsed face-first on the pavement.

"Get that van up here. Chop, chop!" Gloating, Bramble stood over the body and said, "Ding dong, the witch is dead." Behind him he heard the engine rev and the van race up the street. A second later it skidded to a stop on the other side of several parked cars and the side door sprang open.

Borneman jumped out, and the first thing Bramble noticed was that he had a gun in his hand. He ignored the gun and pointed at the corpse. "Grab his feet. We need to pack him up and get out of here before the cops show up."

"You killed him," Borneman yelled.

"That's what this was all about. Sorry I couldn't let you in on it, but Stan wanted it that way." Bramble bent over and grabbed the back of the jacket with his left hand. "Come on, grab his feet. We need to get the hell out of here."

Borneman hesitated for a second and then slid his gun into the back of his waistband. He grabbed both ankles while Bramble picked up the front end with one arm, as if picking up a suitcase. The corpse sagged between them. Bramble led the way between two parked cars and heaved the head and torso into the van.

Bramble looked at McGuirk, who was behind the wheel, and ordered, "Grab him by the hands and pull him all the way in." While McGuirk jumped out of the driver's seat and started tugging on the corpse, Borneman swung the legs into the back of the van. The motion left him leaning forward into the open cargo door. Bramble took advantage of the opportunity. He stepped back, swung his pistol up, placed it a few inches from the back of Borneman's skull, and pulled the trigger.

Borneman's upper body fell into the van. Bramble looked at a wide-eyed McGuirk and said, "God, I'm good." And then he shot him in the face. The velocity of the bullet caused McGuirk to stand up for a second, but it wasn't enough to knock him over. He hung in the air motionless for a second and then he fell face-first on top of the first corpse.

Bramble was grinning from ear to ear. He'd get a medal for this one. Rapp had gone haywire and killed both McGuirk and Borneman, but he'd stepped in and killed the little shit. And then to really show how big a superstar he was, he'd managed to contain the fallout by stuffing all three bodies into the van before the locals showed up. This was the CIA, not the FBI. His job was to destroy evidence, not to preserve it. There would be no crime scene investigators and detectives.

Hurley would take him at his word and be grateful that he'd cleaned up the mess.

Borneman's legs were still hanging out of the van. Bramble was about to grab them when a voice called out to his left. He slowly turned his head and saw two men in suits coming toward him. They were fifty to fifty-five feet away and their guns were drawn. Bramble knew they were close to fifty feet away because he'd fired over twenty thousand pistol rounds at that distance. He was willing to bet these two hadn't fired a fraction of that amount.

Bramble's French wasn't great, but he got the sense they were asking him to put his hands up. He obliged by putting his left hand up a little ahead of his right and then as he began to raise his right hand he casually swung his gun into position and fired two quick shots. The relative still of the night air was shattered by one of the men firing his gun. Since the weapon wasn't suppressed, it cracked like a thunderbolt. Bramble heard the snap of the bullet as it whistled harmlessly past his head.

Both men were down, and Bramble did what he often did in the aftermath of a near-death experience. He began to laugh. Not a giggle or a chuckle, but a belly-splitting roar of a release of tension and an absolute euphoric embrace of victory. He was the king of the hill, the last man standing, a man among children. Five bullets and five bodies. "Shit," Bramble said, "they should write a song about me."

Bramble heard a moan and turned to see that one of the men fifty feet away was moving. "Damn it." He liked the idea of five bullets for five men. It sounded like an Eastwood movie. Six bullets for five men had no ring to it. No flow. Bramble was pretty sure he'd hit the first guy in the face. He'd rushed the second shot a bit. It was always possible that the guy had a mortal wound and was simply in his final death throes. He started walking toward him and remembered that he had his knife on him. If he needed to he could save the bullet and slit the guy's throat. It would still be five bullets for five men—kind of.

Bramble was right about the first shot. He'd caught the guy square in the middle of the face, right between his nose and upper lip. "Now that's a hell of a shot."

The second man was clutching at his chest. His pistol was five feet away, but it might as well have been a mile. There was a little blood at the corner of his mouth and he was looking up at Bramble with pleading eyes. Bramble smiled at the man, raised his gun, and was about to pull the trigger, when for the second time in as many minutes a bullet zipped past his head.

CHAPTER 35

THEY stood in silence for what seemed like an eternity, but was in reality only a prolonged moment. The van pulled around and Rapp saw a man get out. He was one of Hurley's ex–Special Forces guys, and by the look on his face he was none too happy about what had just transpired. It looked as if he was yelling at Victor, and Rapp could tell by his body language that he was on high alert. Victor said something that appeared to calm the man down, and then the two of them grabbed Luke's body and carried it to the van. They both disappeared for a moment, and then Victor stepped back into sight. Rapp saw him raise his right arm, smile, and then there was a quick flash followed a few seconds later by another.

Greta asked, "What just happened?"

Rapp shook his head. "I think he just shot the two men."

"Who?"

"The two men he was with."

"Why?"

"That's a good question. I think I'm going to go find out." Rapp already had his gun in his right hand. "Greta, remember the plan. Go out the back door, get in your car, but don't start it. Wait for five minutes and not a second longer. If I'm not there, leave. I will either call you at the hotel, or meet up with you by tomorrow morning."

"But—"

Rapp cut her off. "Don't! You promised me. No more questions. I can take care of myself."

Greta bit her lower lip and nodded. She looked out the window, and Rapp could tell by the expression on her face that something was going on.

Rapp turned to see what she was looking at. Two men were coming up the sidewalk with their pistols drawn. Rapp knew what would happen next. Victor was not the kind of guy who would surrender. "Come on." He grabbed Greta by the arm and pulled her toward the door. "Go straight to the car. Don't stop for anything, and if you don't hear from me by tomorrow morning, I want you to tell your grandfather what you saw. Tell him it was Victor." He got the sense she was in a bit of shock so he added, "Now tell me what you're supposed to tell your grandfather."

"It was Victor. Victor killed everyone."

"Good." Rapp opened the door and they stepped into the hallway. She had tears in her eyes. "There's no time for that, honey. Don't worry, I can kill that fucker and still get to the car in five minutes and I don't even need my good hand." Rapp kissed her on the forehead. "I'll see you in five minutes." Rapp pushed her on her way. "Get going."

He then turned and raced down the stairs. There were ten steps and then a landing and then ten more steps. Rapp burst through the first set of doors, and beyond the glass of the second doors he saw Victor with his damn gun pointed at what he assumed was a man on the ground. And he had that stupid grin on his face again. Rapp wondered what kind of nut job took such perverse joy in killing another person. Rapp knew he didn't have time to strategize or get cute with this, so he burst through the second set of doors, raised his pistol, and fired. The silenced round whistled through the air and Rapp heard it slam into the building across the street.

"Victor, you asshole," Rapp yelled as he bounded down the steps and squeezed off another round. This one hit the side window of the car in front of Victor. "You killed the wrong guy, you stupid prick." Rapp hit the sidewalk and cut to his right. He had surprise on his side, but he needed to get Victor away from the men or man whom he was about to execute. Victor had dashed out of sight but even so Rapp squeezed off two more rounds. One of them hit the building and the other skipped off the trunk of the car Victor was hiding behind. Rapp moved down the sidewalk, putting more distance between himself and Victor and keeping his mouth shut. It worked. A gun popped up above the trunk and Victor fired three shots in the direction of the front door of the apartment building. Rapp swung around the back end of a big four-door Mercedes sedan and lay down under the trunk.

With his gun stretched out in front of him, he searched for movement under the cars across the street and to his left. Rapp saw part of a leg next to a rear wheel. He sighted in on it, fired two shots, and was rewarded with a howl and a string of expletives. Rapp rolled out from under the trunk, ignored the pain in his shoulder, and sprang to his feet. He looked over the trunk of the Mercedes and then darted across the street, moving one more car to his right. It was the basic rule of a gunfight: Fire and move.

Rapp found refuge between a small two-door Peugeot and an even smaller Ford Fiesta. This next part was the biggest gamble. He was about to place himself in a shooting alley with Victor, and he had no idea what kind of weapon the guy was carrying. Waiting was not to his benefit, though, so he shaded his right eye around the rear bumper of the Peugeot. Victor was moving as fast as his crippled leg would carry him toward the van. He was already two-thirds of the way there and a good eighty feet from Rapp.

Rapp broke from his cover and gave chase. After about ten steps he passed the two men on the ground, and he could see Victor was going to beat him to the van by a good distance, so he raised his gun and started firing one steady round after another. Victor's running crouch made him a poor target. Rapp expended his last round and was in the midst of changing magazines when Victor dove into the open side door of the van.

Rapp swore to himself as he seated a fresh magazine and released the slide. He pressed forward and then skidded to a stop when the black barrel of a submachine gun popped out of the side door of the van. The night erupted with the loud blasts of over twenty bullets fired on full automatic. Rapp dove for cover behind a parked car and made himself as small as possible. Several more bursts were fired and then Rapp heard the sound of an engine revving and wheels squealing on the pavement. Rapp reacted quickly and moved into the street. He sighted in on the back left door of the van and started unloading rounds as fast as he could fire them. A body fell from the side door of the van and a second after that he was empty. The van turned right and disappeared. Rapp eyed the body, but didn't bother to investigate. It was one of Hurley's SF guys.

Rapp turned and ran back to the two men on the sidewalk. They were both in suits. The one on the right was shot in the face and obviously dead, but the one on the left was alive and gasping for air. A few feet away his FN pistol lay on the ground. Rapp grabbed it and stuffed it in his pocket. Then he knelt next to the man and started searching for his wound. He heard it before he saw it. A chest wound makes a strange sucking noise that once heard, is never forgotten. The man was wearing a black dress shirt and a dark gray suit. Rapp grabbed his shirt and ripped it open. The wound was right there on the right side of his chest. He might live, but not without some immediate medical attention.

Rapp remembered the small medical kit that he carried. The pull to flee was strong, but he knew if he didn't help this guy, there was a good chance he'd die. Grumbling and fighting the urge to run, he pulled the pack from the small of his back, set it on the ground next to the man, and went to work. He had only one packet of Quickclot. He ripped open the top and held the open packet right above the entry wound. He sprinkled half the powder around and down the hole and used his fingers to push as much of it into the wound as possible. Rapp then rolled him onto his stomach and yanked his jacket and shirt up around his shoulders. He put the rest of the powder in the exit wound and grabbed a square adhesive bandage with a plastic backing. He placed it over the hole, flipped him onto his back, and bandaged the entry wound. Rapp listened for a moment and was relieved when the sucking noise subsided.

Sirens were suddenly wailing in the distance. Rapp got close to the man's face and looked into his eyes. He saw genuine fear. In French, Rapp told the man, "You're going to be all right. Do you understand me?"

The man looked into Rapp's eyes and gave him an anemic nod while weakly trying to grab his arm.

"Don't give up. They're going to be here any minute." Rapp looked at the ground and saw his bloody fingerprints on the remnants of the medical supplies. He frantically collected the backings and spent packages and stuffed them into his pack. A leather ID case that had fallen from the man's jacket caught Rapp's eye. He grabbed it and flipped it open. He didn't recognize the seal but he sure as hell had heard of the Direction Générale de la Securité Exterieure. The DGSE was France's version of the CIA. "Victor," Rapp muttered, "what in the hell have you done?"

The agent clutched at Rapp's arm and said, "Don't leave."

Rapp stuffed the ID case in his jacket. The sirens were growing louder. "You're going to be fine," Rapp said, even though he wasn't sure he believed it. "Don't give up. They'll be here any minute, and remember . . . the asshole who did this to you . . . his name is Victor."

Rapp looked up, and there, standing thirty feet away, were two men. The one on the right was short and stocky with thick black hair and a beard. The man on the left was tall and skinny with sandy blond hair. They were staring right at him. Rapp could hardly shoot them, so he did the only thing that seemed normal. He yelled at them. "Get over here! Hurry up! I need your help."

The tall man hung back, but the stocky man rushed forward.

"Get down here," Rapp said, "and put pressure on this bandage. Hold his hand and keep talking to him." The man knelt and did as Rapp instructed. The tall man was still standing a good five paces away. Rapp screamed this time. "Get over here! Take that scarf off and put it under his head. Lay your jacket over his stomach." Rapp stood. "Hurry up! I'm going to run and get help."

And with that Rapp was sprinting down the street, hoping that the two men were not good at remembering faces. Just before the next intersection he crossed the street and kept moving at a full clip. The sirens were growing louder, but they were still far enough away, so he kept running full speed. He'd grabbed the gun because he could use the extra firepower, but he knew he might have to dump it sooner than he'd like. The same was true with the ID case, but he had to clean it first. He couldn't leave his fingerprints on it.

Greta's car was three blocks away, and up ahead there looked to be a crowd of people gathering. They had probably come outside to see what the commotion was. Rapp stopped running. There was no quicker way to attract attention than running in street clothes at night when gunshots had been fired. The sirens were much closer now. At the next intersection a police car came skidding around the corner. Rapp's training kicked in. He stopped and stared directly at the two policemen in the front seat. That's what innocent people did. Guilty people looked away, hid their faces, and even ran.

He spotted Greta's Audi and had no idea if his five minutes were up or not. Some internal clock told him they were, but he also knew Greta would sit there for an hour. She'd disregard everything he'd told her and hold on to hope. He traveled the last block at a brisk pace and tried the passenger door, but it was locked. Greta practically jumped out of the front seat. She unlocked the door and Rapp climbed in.

"Let's go," Rapp said, breathing heavily. "Drive the speed limit and act normal."

As they were pulling out, another police car and an ambulance raced past them, going in the other direction. Rapp thought of the DGSE agent and prayed that he would make it. Two more police cars raced past them.

Greta kept her eyes on the road until they'd passed, and then she looked over at Rapp. "You're bleeding."

Rapp looked down at his hands. They were covered in blood. Both literally and figuratively. "It's not mine."

"Did you . . . did you kill someone?"

He shook his head. "I don't think so."

"Then where did the blood come from?"

"A man I tried to save." Rapp stared straight ahead. "We can talk about this later. Right now I need to think."

"Where should I drive?"

"Just keep heading east. We'll find a new hotel. Sit tight for the night and figure out what to do next." He sank down in his seat. Kennedy had warned him to stay away from the apartment. She'd tried to save him, but someone else had ordered his death. *What a bunch of ungrateful bastards,* Rapp thought. *They have no idea who they're fucking with.*

CHAPTER 36

THE eastern horizon was orange with the premorning light. Kennedy stood on the concrete tarmac and watched the private jet bank and settle in on its final approach, the sun glistening off its skin. She was in a dark brown pantsuit and cream-colored shirt. The morning air was a bit chilly, but it didn't faze her. She was too preoccupied with what had transpired the previous evening. It had been an unmitigated disaster that could mushroom into something serious enough to set the CIA back decades. There would be hearings on Capitol Hill and then trials in federal courthouses. Good people would lose their jobs and more than likely a few more people would die.

As Kennedy watched the plane touch down her mind was swimming with details, innuendos, and God only knew how many deceptions. Stansfield would want answers, and unfortunately she was running short on them. She had been in the country only a few hours when Hurley had called her with the news that the safe house had been compromised, and worse, that there had been casualties. He then said the words that she still found impossible to believe.

"It was your boy. He ambushed them."

Kennedy replied by saying, "I thought your men had been pulled?"

"They were, and that was when your broken toy struck. I warned you this would happen." In typical Hurley fashion he hung up on her before she could ask more questions.

Kennedy had no idea who was dead, or how many, and after an hour of trying to find answers, she gave up and drove to the safe house.

The police had cordoned the entire block. At each end of the street curious neighbors and reporters pressed against the barricades. It was easy to tell the reporters from the locals as they carried Dictaphones or steno pads and some of them had cameramen attached at the hip. Unlike the locals, they were shouting questions at the police. Kennedy stayed away from the press and began canvassing the locals. Her French was flawless, so no one gave her a second glance. The stories varied from person to person, but a common theme emerged; at least two people were dead and another had been rushed to the hospital. The bombshell came later when she overheard two police officers talking. The man who had been taken to the hospital was DGSE. If this was true, Kennedy instantly understood the dire implications. It was highly unlikely that a Directorate agent had accidentally stumbled upon a gunfight in this little Parisian enclave. Kennedy could think of only two reasons for the DGSE to be on this block. They'd either discovered the safe house or followed Hurley's men. Either road led back to the CIA.

Kennedy returned to the Embassy, called Stansfield on a secure line, and told him everything she knew. He listened patiently, then told her he was moving up his travel plans. Stansfield immediately understood if he couldn't put a lid on this, and do it quickly, it would irreparably damage U.S.-French relations. Kennedy then sought out Hurley and the sparks started to fly. Over the ensuing hours it seemed that he lost it every thirty minutes. Hurley was stuck at the Embassy, knowing if he left, it was highly likely that his new friend Paul Fournier would

snatch him off the street and conduct a thorough, not very gentle interrogation. After his sixth or seventh tirade, Kennedy had reached her
limit. She told Hurley, "I've listened to you for the past two hours, and
I haven't said a thing. But let me give you a little advice. You're putting
a lot of faith in a man who has some serious flaws. Chet Bramble is
no saint. He's a narcissist and a proven liar, and I don't believe anything he says, so here's the deal. If you're right . . . then I'm done. I'll
resign and you'll never have to deal with me again. But if you're wrong,
you're done. Your ranting and your raving and all your other bullshit,
it's over. You resign, you walk away from all of this, and you admit to
me and everyone else who was involved in this that it was your fault for
not supervising your stupid goon." Kennedy didn't stick around for his
answer.

She left the basement office of the Embassy and moved to the
rooms that were reserved for CIA operatives in search of a bed. She
found one, but she didn't sleep. The best she could do was close her eyes
and ask herself the same questions over and over. In the end she knew
there was only one way she would get any answers that would satisfy
her. She needed to sit down with Rapp and hear his side of the story.

The next morning, after having slept only a few hours, she was
standing on the flat tarmac hoping Stansfield would for once put Hurley in his place. Three black Range Rovers were idling bumper to bumper. The Gulfstream IV taxied to a stop 150 feet from the trucks. The
stairs were lowered and a customs agent walked out to meet the plane.
The head of Stansfield's security detail presented him with the proper
paperwork. The man looked at the forms and then the passports and
applied the appropriate stamps. Two secured diplomatic pouches were
presented and the man gave them a consenting nod. Kennedy kept
looking over her shoulder to see if some of their friends from the DGSE
had shown up.

Stansfield finally appeared with another security officer behind
him. He was in a suit and tie and a gray trench coat. The boot at the

rear of the plane was opened and four small roller bags and some black cases were offloaded by the crewmember. A fourth man exited the plane and Kennedy tried to figure out why he looked familiar. Stansfield spoke to him briefly and then he walked over to Kennedy.

Kennedy opened the rear door of the middle SUV. "Good morning, sir."

Stansfield nodded, climbed in, and closed the door. Kennedy climbed in the other side and the head of Stansfield's detail got in the front seat. The other bodyguard got in the first vehicle and the fourth man got in the last vehicle with the luggage. The convoy started to roll toward the gate.

The deputy director of Operations leaned over and peered through the front windshield. "Any new fallout?"

"It's hard to say. A lot of people have been asleep and are going to wake up to some rather ugly news. The Directorate will be understandably upset."

"I'd say so . . . And Stan?"

Kennedy decided to leave out all the melodrama of their late-night argument and keep it to the facts. "He's safe, but not by much. He was with Paulette. A few minutes after he left she had her door kicked in."

Stansfield nodded. "Have these vehicles been swept?"

Kennedy shrugged. "The Embassy claims they're checked on a routine basis."

Stansfield frowned and pulled out a pad of paper and a pen. They'd have to do this the old-fashioned way. He placed a lighter in the center cup holder in case he needed to act quickly and destroy the notes. "Where is Rob?"

Kennedy knew he was asking about Rob Ridley, one of their top field operatives. "He's in the city."

"I need to speak with him this morning. How does the Embassy look?" Stansfield asked, and then started writing.

"The Directorate has the front and rear entrances covered."

"We'll have to figure something out. I want Rob to personally sweep everything, and I have a little job for him." Stansfield slid the pad over and showed her what he'd written. "Mitch?"

Kennedy shook her head. "Nothing so far."

Stansfield scribbled, "Message Service?"

"I've been checking." Again she shook her head.

"Victor?" Stansfield wrote.

Kennedy shrugged. She didn't believe a word that came out of his mouth, but he was going to hear it from Hurley, so she reasoned she might as well give him the latest. She was about to speak, and then she reached for the pen and paper. She began printing in neat block letters. "Claims Mitch sent a decoy into the safe house and then ambushed them. Killed McGuirk, Borneman, and two DGSE agents."

Stansfield was reading as she wrote. "Oh, my God."

Kennedy kept scratching. "V in the process of destroying surveillance van, and the other incriminating evidence. Claims he had to flee for his life and Borneman's body was left at the scene."

The deputy director of Operations kept his composure despite the fact the situation had just become drastically worse. He grabbed the pad from Kennedy. Held the pen for a moment and then wrote, "Do you believe him?"

Kennedy shook her head vigorously.

"Are they looking for him?" Stansfield asked.

"Not that we know of."

The deputy director scratched out another question. "Have they ID'd Borneman?"

"We have no idea. The police are handling the investigation and the Directorate isn't exactly known for their cooperation."

"Unless it's to their advantage." Stansfield put the pen to paper again, "What was DGSE doing there?"

"Not sure, but if I had to guess I'd say they followed V and his people there."

"Why do you say that? They could have known about it beforehand."

"Stan and Paulette had dinner last night." Kennedy grabbed the pen. "Paul Fournier showed up unannounced and joined them for a bottle of wine."

"You think they had Stan under surveillance?"

"Yes. I was followed all the way from the airport to the Embassy when I arrived last night."

"And this morning?"

"There was a car. It's probably behind us right now."

Stansfield nodded.

"Does Deputy Director Cooke have any idea what's going on?"

"No."

"Did you let him know you were leaving?"

"No, I ordered another jet. His will be waiting for him when he gets to the airport in another six hours."

"And when he asks where you are?"

"I have Waldvogel flying over with him. He's going to tell him I was forced to make other travel arrangements."

"And if he digs?"

"The Brits wanted to meet with me about something."

"And if he checks with the Brits?"

"He'll find out that I had breakfast at the British Embassy this morning." Kennedy's eyes narrowed, revealing tiny wrinkles.

"He could probably verify that if he wanted to."

"And he can go right ahead."

"We're having breakfast at the British Embassy?"

"That's right."

"May I ask why?"

"You'll find out when we get there."

They rode in silence for a while and then Stansfield wrote, "You need to convince Mitch to talk to me."

"I can't even get him to talk to me."

Stansfield tapped the pen on what he'd already written.

"I know. I've been trying to figure something out, but he doesn't exactly trust us at the moment."

"He's going to have to start, Irene, or I'm going to be left with no other choice."

She took him to mean that he would issue a kill order. She'd seen it done before. A dossier would be put together, a price would be determined, and then the usual suspects would be contacted. Certain assets within Langley would also be used, but this type of stuff was usually handled with outside contractors. Rapp was good. He could probably last for a year or two, longer if he was willing to undergo plastic surgery, and there was a better than fifty-fifty chance that he would eliminate the first man or two who were sent to deal with him. She was suddenly reminded of what Dr. Lewis had said to her only a few days earlier. *If there comes a time where you need to neutralize him, you'd better not screw up. Because if he survives, he'll kill every last one of us.*

The thought sent shivers up Kennedy's spine. What if she'd already lost control of Rapp? What if Victor was telling the truth? She refused to believe it. She knew better than anyone. He wasn't just another one of Hurley's heartless killers. She needed time and she needed to convince Stansfield. Lewis could help with the latter. Looking at her mentor, Kennedy said, "I need you to talk to our good doctor this morning. He has some observations you need to hear."

"In regard to what?"

"Who." Kennedy grabbed the pad and pen and wrote down Victor's name.

"Fine," Stansfield said. He knew what was going on here. His two chief lieutenants were both going to champion their men. He should have never let it get this far. There was too much bad blood between Rapp and Bramble. He should have cut one of them loose a long time ago, and despite the current evidence against Rapp, it was Bramble whom he would have dumped. He was Stan's man, though, and what

Stan wanted he almost always got. Unfortunately, what Stan wanted right now was a dead Mitch Rapp.

Stansfield stretched his legs and leaned against the door's armrest. He couldn't allow his personal bias to interfere. Rapp was far more likable. Bramble was an obtuse brute, but he had his purposes. If Rapp didn't come in and tell him exactly what he'd been up to, Stansfield would be left with only one choice. He would have to order the execution of perhaps his best operative.

CHAPTER 37

THE crane moved the heavy magnet into position and then the cable was played out and the rusty steel disk dropped until it was a few feet from the van. The magnet was turned on and the rear tires of the van levitated off the ground until the roof was pinned against the steel disk. The power was increased and slowly the front end, weighted down by the engine, began to inch upward. When the roof was firmly immobilized to the underside of the magnet, the big diesel engine on the crane revved and belched black smoke and then the thick steel cable moaned until it had the van twenty feet off the ground and swinging toward the industrial-sized compactor.

Bramble watched as the van was not so gently placed inside the three-sided metal box. The magnet disengaged, leaving the van in place, and moved clear. Steel jaws swung into place above the van and the crushing began, top to bottom first for a few feet and then the sides. It went back and forth like that for several minutes. When the van was finally smashed into a four-by-four-foot cube, Bramble noticed a red liquid leaking from the base. It was expected. There were two bodies inside, after all. There should have been three, but Borneman had been lost along the way.

The man next to Bramble held out his hand and said something in his gruff native Serbian tongue. Bramble didn't understand a word of any of the Slavic languages, but he didn't need to. They had an agreement and the man wanted to be paid. Bramble had already counted the money, twenty-five hundred dollars in advance and twenty-five hundred when they were done, and the guy was going to throw in a piece-of-shit two-door Renault that he would drive back to Paris.

Bramble had wiped the prints from his gun and left it in the van to be crushed with all the other evidence, the bodies, the surveillance equipment, and most important, the recording of him shooting the man he thought was Rapp. It had all appeared to be going perfectly. Rapp was dead, and he'd dealt with Borneman and McGuirk. All of that he could have explained to Hurley. They were pulling out when Rapp ambushed them. He killed Borneman and McGuirk and then Bramble jumped in and put a bullet in the back of Rapp's head, end of story. But then those two *Frenchies* showed up. Bramble still had no idea who they were. More than likely cops, or maybe French Intelligence, either way it wasn't good. Bramble was still proud of the shot. He bet there weren't more than a dozen men on the planet that could have hit that first guy square in the face, as he had. They'd been stupid in how they came after him, no cover, and they were standing too close together. In Bramble's mind they had gotten what they deserved.

Bramble handed the man the rest of the cash, and the dirty mutt gave him the keys to the Renault. In his broken French, Bramble did his best to convey the fact that he'd be back in two days, and if what was left of the van wasn't melted down he'd be sticking some people in the compactor. He'd never come back, of course, but Bramble only knew of one way to conduct business—threaten.

Limping, Bramble walked across the yard toward his subcompact piece of shit. He folded himself into the driver's seat, inserted the key, and gunned the little four-cylinder engine. The car was a stick shift and under normal circumstances Bramble wouldn't have given it a second thought, but he had a bullet hole in his right calf and a bullet lodged in the brawny triceps muscle of his right arm. Driving one-handed was not possible, so he engaged the clutch, bit down hard, and jammed the stubborn stick shift into first gear. The bald front tires spun on the gravel and then bit, and the car lurched forward, Bramble acutely feeling every bump and pitch.

He had a few bruised ribs as well, courtesy of that pussy Rapp lodging four slugs in the back of his bulletproof vest. If the dumbass had used a .45 caliber like Bramble he may have succeeded in killing him, but his little 9mm slugs couldn't do the job. Bramble shifted the dusty car into second gear and popped the clutch a bit too early. The jolt made him wonder if one or more of his ribs weren't broken. It was all good, he decided. The more beat up he was the more believable his story.

After fleeing for his life, Bramble had stopped five blocks later and closed the van's side door. He flipped over the man he'd thought was Rapp and shook his head at his own stupidity. A canvas bag was peeking out of his waistband. Bramble grabbed it and looked inside. The cash and diamonds might come in handy. Rapp's fake passports were worthless. Bramble wasn't thrilled about losing Borneman, but it was all going to be laid at Rapp's feet, so he guessed it didn't matter. His immediate problem at that point was to get clear of the area. His wounds were not life-threatening, but Rapp was. Bramble needed to get his story straight and do it fast and then get hold of Hurley. As he put distance between himself and his handiwork, he began to refine his lie. By the time he was out of the city proper he felt that he had things about as good as he was going to get them. He dialed Hurley's cell phone five times but got no answer. The last time he left a cryptic message with enough innuendo that Hurley would get the gist of what had gone down.

He didn't know the exact location of the scrap yard, but Hurley had mentioned it in the premission briefing. He apparently knew the ugly mutt of a Serb from something he'd done in Yugoslavia back

when Yugoslavia was a country. Hurley had helped the man emigrate
to France, where he became very involved in organized crime. Hurley
said for the right amount of money the Serb could be trusted. It was
past ten in the evening when Hurley finally called back. Over an unsecure line it was impossible to give all the details of what had happened,
but Hurley still got the gist. Bramble explained that the van was a piece
of crap and that he needed to scrap it. Hurley took the hint and told
him where to go and after that he told him to check the message service
for instructions.

Bramble went straight to the scrap yard. It was just over an hour
from Paris. The rear of the van was riddled with bullet holes and he
had no idea if the police had a description of it, so he made the cautious decision to get off the road as soon as possible. There were only
two problems: The scrap yard was closed and there were two bodies in
the back. The second part didn't bother Bramble so much. He'd been
around bodies and they weren't bad, at least until they started to smell.
The problem was being caught with them if the police showed up.

Bramble had backed the van in near the gate so the bullet holes
would be concealed and then covered the bodies with a tarp in case
a cop decided to take a look. He wiped down his .45 caliber Colt and
placed it in McGuirk's lifeless hand so it would have his prints on it.
Bramble stuffed the weapon under the dead man's body and then took
McGuirk's sissy 9mm Beretta 92F. He hated the Italian piece of garbage but it was better than nothing. The same gun Rapp used.

Next he dug out the magnet from the LED box under the surveillance console and ran it in circles around the surveillance videotapes.
It was standard practice in situations like this: Destroy all evidence
that could tie you to the crime. It just so happened that it also suited his
needs. It wouldn't do to have footage of him sneaking up on the man he
thought was Rapp and shooting him in the back of the head.

With that done, Bramble dug out the first-aid kit and tended to
his wounds. The calf was easy to deal with, the triceps, less so. And
as far as the ribs went, the only thing he could do was try to relax and

not move. Bramble reclined the driver's seat, ignored the pain, and thought about Rapp: how he would react, what kind of story he would try to tell, and who he would try to tell it to. Every way he looked at it, he figured Rapp was screwed. He was the one who had failed to check in after he'd fucked up the original job. He was the one who had sent a decoy into the apartment so he could ambush them. Hurley was going to be all over this. Kennedy could piss and moan all she wanted, but her little golden boy was going to be hunted down.

Bramble fell asleep with those happy thoughts, only to be awakened by a dirty man missing at least half of his teeth knocking on his window. Bramble sat up too quickly and immediately regretted it. His ribs screamed with pain and the rising sun was shining directly in his eyes. He rolled down the window halfway and tried to make sense of what the man was saying. His French was somehow worse than Bramble's, which was no easy thing. Eventually, he got the gist that this was Hurley's formidable Mafioso friend.

Bramble pulled the van into the yard and the gate was closed behind him. He looked around the yard and realized immediately that he was at the right place. Once they fired up the equipment the van would be cubed and stacked amongst all the other trashed vehicles. The negotiation, however, proved to be more difficult. The Serbian wanted to look in the van, and Bramble most definitely didn't want him looking in the van. There was sensitive surveillance equipment in there, two bodies, and some guns and a rifle that Bramble wanted destroyed.

In the end Bramble knew he'd been played, but he didn't really care. The money wasn't his, and it wasn't even his responsibility. He paid for the demolition and all of the evidence inside with Rapp's money. He took a certain amount of pleasure in the irony of the whole thing, but he didn't have time to enjoy it. He needed to get his head screwed on and he needed some medical attention. Getting his story straight was the first priority. The CIA could be very thorough, and even though he had destroyed pretty much all the evidence, they would put his story through the wringer and that would involve both human and mechanical lie detectors trying to trip him up. By the time he got to that juncture, and it would begin almost immediately, he would have to believe his own BS.

A few miles down the road, Bramble found a pay phone, parked, and climbed out of the car as if he were an eighty-year-old man. He grunted and moaned and then stiffly walked over and plugged some money into the slot. When he got a dial tone he punched in a long string of numbers and his personal code. Hurley's voice played back a specific coded message. Bramble listened intently and breathed a sigh of relief when he realized they wanted to bring him in. And "in" specifically meant the U.S. Embassy in Paris where a real doctor would treat him. Bramble dialed the second message service and again punched in a long string of numbers and a different code. There was no code or hidden meaning in this message, just a straightforward order. Bramble looked at his watch. Depending on what happened at the Embassy, he might be able to make it work, but that would be up to Hurley.

Bramble shuffled back to the car. He would have to get patched up and convince Hurley to put him back on the street so he could hunt down Rapp and finish the job. Rapp had surprised him last night, but that was stupid luck. Bramble wouldn't let it happen again. The next time he saw Rapp, he'd finish the job, and if he got lucky, maybe he could take Kennedy out at the same time.

CHAPTER 38

NEVILLE was dressed for the cameras: black pumps, dark gray tights, black skirt, and a cerulean silk blouse. She'd called it a day after her confrontation with Fournier. The encounter had left her in such a foul mood that she had told Martin Simon she didn't want to be disturbed for the rest of the day. She'd gone home to an empty apartment and remembered that her husband had taken the kids to see his parents. The bare apartment only served to worsen her mood until she realized that with a two-and-a-half-year-old son and a nine-month-old daughter, she needed to take advantage of a little solitude. She drew a bath, lit some candles, turned on some jazz music, got in the tub, and began to plot the destruction of Paul Fournier.

Neville had been a police officer for sixteen years, and she'd developed a very good ear for lies. Fournier was one of the best liars she'd ever met. He demonstrated none of the telltale signs. He could lie without blinking if it served the moment and he could do it while frowning or smiling, or with a completely passive face. The only thing that was safe to assume was that when his mouth was moving, he was lying. As accurate as she knew her assessment to be, she needed more than a hunch to get her bosses to move. She was going to have to present some evidence. By the end of the long bath she had done a 180. What she needed to show was that the DGSE had no place in a police investigation. And then with Simon's help she needed to share their opinion that someone from the Directorate had manipulated evidence. If she could get her bosses to believe Fournier and his minions were interfering with her investigation, it could start a turf battle and people might push back.

It was the kind of juicy governmental tidbit that the press would fall all over. The Directorate had no business playing their games inside the borders of France. Their mission was abroad. Inside France it was the National Police. The National Assembly and the Senate were filled with politicians who would be furious at the mere perception that the Directorate was up to its old games. That was where Neville knew she had to take this. Fournier was like a vampire. He could only operate in darkness. Expose him and sic the politicians and press on him and he would crumble.

Neville arrived at her office early to help prepare for her meeting and the first press conference that was scheduled to discuss the massacre at the hotel early Saturday morning. She found her deputy, Martin Simon, sitting at his desk looking as if he hadn't been home in two days, which turned out to be the case.

"What do you mean you stayed here last night? What could have possibly happened in the investigation?"

Simon smoothed his red hair and said, "There were two murders last night, and one of the deceased is an agent with the Directorate, or I should say was."

Neville was incredulous. "Why didn't you call me?"

"Because you told me you didn't want to be bothered. You said you needed to be left alone so you could figure out how you were going to handle your ex-boyfriend."

Neville lifted her hand as if she might slap Simon. "I told you . . . do not call him my boyfriend. If you do it again, I'm going to hurt you."

"Don't be so sensitive. I didn't get much sleep last night, so I can't remember which of your ex-boyfriends I can still refer to as your exes and which ones I must call by their first names. It's all very confusing."

"What else do you have?"

"A second DGSE agent in the hospital. He's in critical condition. And a deceased unidentified Caucasian." Simon opened the file on his desk and showed her the crime scene photos.

Neville gave them a quick glance. "So this guy shoots these two DGSE agents and the wounded agent shoots back and kills him."

"If only it were that simple. This guy," Simon said as he pointed at the corpse in the street, "was shot in the back of the head at point-blank range . . . less than a foot away. Gunpowder residue was all over his head, but his hands were clean and his gun was not fired."

"So he didn't shoot the two DGSE agents."

"That's the assumption so far."

"Have you talked to the wounded man?"

Simon gave her a bitter laugh. "What do you think?"

Neville thought about it for a second. "They won't let you anywhere near him."

"You got that right."

"I'm so sick of this bullshit. Was Fournier there last night?"

"He was there briefly to issue some orders and then he disappeared."

Neville folded her arms across her chest and studied the crime scene photos. She tapped the photo of the man in the street. "No wallet . . . no ID. Nothing."

"No, but I just left the morgue an hour ago and our people found something very interesting. They think his dental work looks American, but the big break came when they inspected the body. They were using the UV black light to check for gunshot residue, and they found faint traces of a tattoo that the man had had removed." Simon found the photo and showed her.

Neville read the words aloud. "Rangers Lead. What does that mean?"

"Rangers are U.S. Army Special Forces. 'Rangers Lead' is their motto."

"Ballistics?"

"That's where things get really interesting. We found shell casings from four different weapons, only one of which was recovered at the scene. It belonged to the deceased DGSE agent, and he only fired one shot. The rough count on shell casings is sixty-two."

"Sixty-two," Neville repeated, not really believing the number.

"And we found five different types of blood at the scene."

"Three bodies and five different types of blood."

"So we can assume at least five people were involved, and my guess is more than that."

"And the DGSE isn't telling us a thing."

"That's right."

Neville shook her head in disgust. "Anything else?"

Simon glanced down at the file. "There is one other slightly odd piece of information. The first two witnesses on the scene were Americans. I've already checked them out. One of them is a network TV correspondent and the other one is his cameraman. When they showed up, there was a man delivering first aid to the wounded DGSE agent. He yelled at the two Americans to help and then he ran off to get help."

"And he never came back?"

"That's right."

"Was he French?"

"They think so."

"Have the Americans given us a description of the man?"

"Yes, but it's pretty generic."

Neville shrugged and said, "Could be nothing."

"Or it could be the key to everything."

"The key is to get in and talk to that DGSE agent before Fournier has him shipped off to Polynesia."

"Good luck with that."

The thought of having to butt heads with Fournier again was enough to make her decide she would assign the case to someone else. They had their hands full. She looked at Simon and said, "We need to get upstairs for the meeting with Mutz."

Simon pictured Michael Mutz, the newly appointed prefecture of police. He had a high, sloping forehead, a hook nose, and an ample body that was soft in all the wrong places. "And why would I want to go see Mutz with you?"

"Want has nothing to do with it. I'm ordering you."

Simon rose and followed her to the stairs. The top cop's office was only two floors up. Simon followed in silence, and was thinking how nice it would be to get through this meeting without having to speak. Mutz was a political creature who cared more for the pomp and circumstance of the office than the sometimes dirty nature of police work. When they reached the outer office Simon got his first hint that this wasn't going to be an easy meeting. The prefect's secretary gave them a nervous look and told them to head in. Neville was so focused she missed it.

It was a large corner office, fitting both the title and the ego of the man who occupied the space. There were four floor-to-ceiling windows, two on each of the outer walls, and twelve-foot bookcases filled with dusty tomes, antiques, and dozens of photographs of Prefect Mutz and the rich, famous, and notorious. Simon picked up on two clues the moment he walked into the office. The first was the absence of coffee and pastries. Mutz loved both and he'd never been in the office without both items being offered. The second clue was more obvious.

Not only was Prefect Mutz waiting for them, but his boss, Director General Jacques Gisquet, and his boss's boss, Minister of the Interior Pierre Blot, were waiting for them. Neville saw this as a sign that they were taking her accusations seriously. Simon saw the potential for something very different, but before he could stop his boss, she started in.

"Minister Blot, good to see you. Director Gisquet, thank you for coming. Prefect Mutz, thank you for taking the time to hear me out."

Simon didn't say a word. He watched as Neville charged in, unaware that the mood in the room was anything but welcoming. She began to present her case, explaining to her three superiors the strange behavior of Paul Fournier and his uncooperative nature. She was building toward the tampered evidence when Director General Gisquet waved her off.

"Commandant Neville, I'm afraid I'm going to have to stop you. Minister Blot received a rather serious call last night from the prime minister."

"The prime minister," Neville said, not understanding what this could have to do with Paul Fournier interfering with her investigation.

"Yes, the prime minister. He received a very serious complaint from the minister of defense that you have been harassing one of his top people."

"Harassing," Neville said in disbelief.

"Yes."

"Who?"

Blot said, "Paul Fournier."

"You can't be serious?"

"Unfortunately, I am. Fournier claims that the two of you dated briefly a number of years ago and that when he broke it off, you became despondent and threatened suicide."

"Suicide," Neville repeated, her mouth agape. "I caught him cheating on me. I was the one who broke up with him, and I was happy to do it. The man is a selfish prick, but that's beside the point."

"He alleges that you have been stalking him for several years."

"I haven't seen him in five years."

Blot cleared his throat. "He has sworn testimonies from three women who claim you intimidated and harassed them because they were dating Fournier."

Neville was on the verge of losing it, but fortunately Simon asked, "May we see the file?"

All three men looked at Simon with disappointment. There was a long period of silence, and then Blot said, "I saw the file last night, but I was not allowed to take it with me. It looked genuine. Very damning."

"And why do you think you weren't given a copy?" Neville asked. "Because it's all made up. It's fake. Fournier is the very man who has been interfering in our investigation. You don't find it a little strange that the night before I'm going to bring you a formal complaint, a file magically appears that says I'm the problem?" Neville looked at each man and asked, "You don't smell anything rotten here?"

Director General Gisquet answered her question. "I don't like any of this. I don't trust Fournier, I don't believe that this file magically appeared, but there isn't a lot we can do right now."

"You can demand that he bring the file and his accusers down here right now. File a formal complaint."

Blot cleared his throat. "The DGSE would prefer to keep this under wraps. They have no desire to adversely affect your career. All they are asking is that you be reassigned from your current case and you stay away from Deputy Director Fournier."

"And why do you think they want me assigned away from the hotel massacre? I'll tell you why. Because I caught Fournier and his people tampering with evidence. I'm telling all three of you, the DGSE was involved in what happened the other night. I don't know how deeply or in what way, but they were involved."

Blot twisted his wedding ring and asked, "Were you at the Hotel Balzac yesterday afternoon?"

Neville had a bad feeling that the little confrontation had been twisted and blown out of proportion to serve Fournier's purpose. "Yes, I was there."

"Deputy Director Fournier has sworn statements from five individuals that you accosted him."

"Accosted him! I asked him why he was interfering in my investigation."

"The file says you yelled at him and made a scene. To make matters worse, he was conducting a meeting with a foreign intelligence asset."

Neville was thunderstruck. "Am I the only person who sees what's going on here? The Libyan oil minister is assassinated in our beautiful city the other night, the prostitute lying next to him is killed, two hotel guests are killed, a hotel employee is killed, and so are the minister's four bodyguards. There's only one problem. The minister was traveling without security. We can't find a single person who saw him arrive or leave the hotel with a security detail, yet these four men magically appear in the middle of the night, and with silenced weapons." Neville zeroed in on the minister of the interior. "You travel with security. When was the last time your men carried silenced weapons?"

Blot let out a heavy sigh. "These are all interesting points and I'm sure they'll be sorted out by someone, but it won't be you, Commandant Neville. We are removing you from the investigation. Prefect Mutz will be reassigning you this morning. If you handle this with grace, I can promise you that none of this will go on your record and there will be no formal investigation. Your career will continue to progress based on the merits of your work."

Neville was speechless for a long moment, and then Prefect Mutz spoke up. "Francine, this is for the best. I'll give you an extra week. Take the kids and go visit your parents. When you come back all of this will be over."

Two things were ringing in her mind. The first was that it wouldn't be over in a week and the second was that Fournier must be really nervous to pull a move like this. That knowledge gave her the strength to speak to her bosses in a way she would never have dreamed of before today. "So this is how we do things now. A sneaky little agency like the DGSE, which has no business doing anything inside the borders of this country, can pull in some favors with well-connected politicians, make some wild, completely unfounded accusations, and the mighty National Police of France surrender."

Prefect Mutz gave her a stern look. "Francine, you're out of line."

"No, she isn't," Director General Gisquet growled. "This entire thing stinks. Paul Fournier is a snake and he's playing us. I don't like it one bit . . . but . . ."

"But what?" Neville asked, hoping that there was still a chance.

Gisquet looked her in the eye and said, "For the moment, we have to play this game, but I promise you, Francine, this is not going to hurt you. We need to follow through with this request because it came from some very serious people and then in a few weeks when things cool down, we will take a good look at the facts."

"In a few weeks," Neville said, her impatience showing through. "You mean after Fournier and his goons have destroyed all the evidence and eliminated any witnesses who could help us solve the case."

"I'm sorry, Francine, but it's the best we can do right now."

"I'm sorry, too." Neville looked at each of her bosses, stopping with Minister of the Interior Blot. "I'm sorry that you men don't have the balls to stand up against an agency that has no jurisdiction in Paris. Why bother with laws? I'm sure the people of Paris will appreciate the fact that their police department is afraid of an asshole like Paul Fournier." Neville turned and started for the door. At the last second she turned and said, "Are the two of you aware that two DGSE agents were shot last night? One of them is dead. The other one is in the hospital, but Mr. Fournier will not allow the police to question him." She could tell by the startled look on their faces that this was the first they'd heard of this. "Over sixty shots were fired. In addition to the DGSE agents we have an unidentified American with a Rangers tattoo. The media are going to be all over this and I sure hope for your sake they don't find out that you were complicit in covering up whatever the hell it is that Paul Fournier is up to."

Simon couldn't follow her out the door fast enough. Halfway down the first flight of stairs he said, "Well, I'm glad I came along for that. I think it's really going to help my career. Thank you for bringing me with you."

"Sorry," Neville tried to say with some sincerity despite the anger that was flowing through her veins.

Simon followed in silence for a while and then said, "You know, they might be doing you a favor . . . if what you said up there is true."

"How so?"

"They just removed you from the front lines of a battle that looks like it's going to end badly. The press will devour anyone involved in this."

"The press?"

"Yes, the people who write for newspapers and magazines. They do news shows on this thing called television. As a group they're often referred to as the press."

Neville was so used to his smartass personality that she ignored him. "The press conference." She checked her watch. "It's supposed to start in twenty minutes."

"I think it's probably going to be canceled."

"Maybe." Neville stopped at their floor and looked down the stair-well. "I bet they're all gathered right now. Waiting for it to start."

"I'm sure Mutz is going to have it canceled, or your replacement will get up and read a brief statement."

"What about me?"

"They'll probably say you had to take a leave of absence. Your cramps are really bad this month. You know, something nice and mi-sogynistic."

"Stop being such a smartass for a second. I think I should make a statement."

"I don't think you could come up with a worse idea."

"It's the perfect idea." Neville turned for her office. "I need to gather my stuff."

"I think you should, because they'll probably fire you and throw you out of the building."

"They can't fire me for telling the truth, Martin."

"Sure they can. People do it all the time. Especially the police."

Neville had her mind made up. She grabbed her jacket and purse and on the way out closed and locked her office door. "You can come along if you want," she told Simon, "but I won't blame you if you stay up here and hide under your desk."

"I wouldn't miss this for the world. The opportunity to see one of the brightest minds in law enforcement destroy her career in front of an entire nation. It'll be pure Schadenfreude."

CHAPTER 39

RAPP'S feet glided along the pavement, beating out a steady five-and-a-half-minute-a-mile pace. His shoulder throbbed, but he did his best to ignore it, and when he couldn't ignore it he told himself he deserved worse. A man was dead. Luke Auclair, an innocent man who had been minding his own business, living his own life, until Rapp had sought him out and included him in his great miscalculation.

It had been a rough night. They'd traveled to the outskirts of Paris, where they'd stopped for gas and Rapp scrubbed the dried blood of the DGSE agent from his hands. He still had no idea if the man had made it. Maybe one life could be saved from the debacle. After that, they drove north a bit and checked into one of the big chain hotels by Charles de Gaulle Airport. The place was run-down, one of those five-hundred-room behemoths for business travelers who were willing to sacrifice service and cleanliness to be near the airport. The place was in dire need of remodeling, but Rapp barely noticed. He wasn't in shock, but rather a bit jumbled from an evening of unexpected events.

He and Greta sat in near silence as they ate a late dinner, and then they went up to the room. She was good enough to not ask too many questions. She could tell he was trying to sort through some very heavy questions. Around midnight, with them both tossing and turning, he started to talk. The part about Luke weighed the heaviest on him. He was an innocent, a noncombatant, and the first rule of his job was to never harm noncombatants.

"But you didn't know they would act the way they did," Greta said. "You were testing them."

"It doesn't matter. I should have never involved him."

Greta was quiet for a moment and then said, "But if you hadn't it would have been you down on the street."

"No," Rapp said with self-loathing, "I knew better than to go into that apartment, and even if I had, I would have gone out the back door and my gun would have been ready and I would have been on guard. No one could have snuck up on me like that."

They talked for a while longer and then Rapp kissed her on the forehead, told her he loved her, and said, "Let's try to get some sleep."

He held her with his good arm, and was grateful when he heard her breathing settle into a sleep pattern a short while later. Rapp continued to stare at the ceiling, replaying the events that he had watched from Bob and Tibby McMahon's apartment as if it were a box seat at the theater. He dozed off a few times, but not for long. Sleep was rarely a struggle for him, and the more elusive it became, the more restless he grew. He ran through every conceivable scenario to determine who could have betrayed him. He pictured each face and then considered the possibility that they'd all conspired to have him killed. Had they decided to kill him based on bad information, or some information he wasn't aware of? He slid his arm out from under Greta and decided he had to trust Kennedy. She had warned him to stay away from the safe house. She knew Victor was there, but did she know he'd been ordered to kill Rapp?

He finally fell asleep for a few hours and then woke just before 7:00 a.m. More restless than ever, he got out of bed and dug out his running shoes and some sweats.

Greta woke sleepily and asked, "Where are you going?"

"For a run. I need to work a few things out." Rapp could tell she wasn't pleased at the idea of his leaving, but she didn't say anything. "Don't worry, I'll be back in an hour and then we can have some breakfast and make some decisions."

"What kind of decisions?"

"I'm not sure." Rapp had been struggling with that question all night, but he felt that a good run would give him the clarity to see the best path forward.

He asked the front desk if there was a decent place to run and was directed to a park a kilometer from the hotel. Running at an easy pace, he found the park with little difficulty and then pushed himself. In hindsight, it was all brutally clear. His cavalier attitude had gotten a harmless man killed. Now, an inner voice he did not recognize told him Luke was nothing more than a piece-of-shit drug dealer. That the world would be a better place without him. That he needed to suck it up and push on. The last part was right, but the first two weren't. Rapp fought the instinct to rationalize his mistakes and his stupidity. This was a lesson that needed to be imprinted on his brain and never forgotten. Rapp knew if he failed on that front he would be on the express track to become Stan Hurley II, and he would sooner jump off a bridge than allow that to happen.

As he circled the park, pushing himself harder and harder, the clarity he sought began to emerge from the chaos. Kennedy was the one person he could trust and the one person he wouldn't harm. Victor was as good as dead. Rapp didn't care where he saw him next, but he hoped it was face-to-face. He wanted to look him in the eye when he pulled the trigger. It occurred to Rapp that it was unlikely that Victor would make such a bold move all on his own. He wasn't smart enough, and that meant Hurley was the one calling the shots. The big question mark was Stansfield. Of the three people who directly managed him, he knew Stansfield the least.

In large part that was due to the man's job. As deputy director of Operations he had more than a thousand people working under him. He received hundreds of calls and cables every day from his station chiefs at various outposts around the globe. There were deputies down the hall and all over the building who wouldn't move without his guidance, and Rapp was just one cog in a very big intricate wheel, although he was a very important cog. Rapp got the impression Stansfield was heavily involved in the decision to turn him loose and it only made sense that he would be equally involved in the decision to terminate him.

All of Stansfield's authority, however, could be ignored by the most stubborn man he'd ever known. Hurley was the problem, and yes, Rapp was biased when it came to him, but that bias was based entirely on how the man had behaved since he'd met him two years ago. He was everything that he accused Rapp of being and then some. The man was egomaniacal, reckless, disrespectful, dictatorial, and petty. Rapp concluded that Hurley was more than capable of issuing the kill order without Stansfield's knowledge. But why have Victor kill the other two guys on the team? What were they guilty of?

Rapp knew his running pace almost to the second, and after three miles, he nudged it to an even five-minute mile. Two miles later his shoulder was stinging and his lungs were burning and a thought struck him like a lightning bolt. Rapp's legs stopped pumping and he slowed to a stop. His chest was heaving, his lungs working extra hard to pull in oxygen. He stood as upright as possible and looked off in the distance at three cooling towers for a nuclear power plant. He kept running the idea over and over in his head, and the more he did so, the more it became the only thing that made sense. Victor thought he had killed him, and then he turned his gun on his unsuspecting fellow team members. Why would a man do such a thing? There were only two possible reasons. Either they'd done something seriously wrong, and had been targeted for elimination, or they were killed because of what they'd seen.

It was as if a bad picture had suddenly come into focus. If the other two guys had done something wrong there were much better, and quieter, ways to get rid of them. Rapp was suddenly convinced that they'd been killed because they saw Victor shoot a man they thought was Rapp in the back of the head. Victor and Hurley had made it brutally obvious that they didn't approve of him. Were they willing to frame him to get rid of him? Victor was incapable of accepting blame, which meant he would have to blame the other deaths on someone else, and that someone else was going to be Rapp.

Rapp turned and started running back in the direction of the hotel. He needed to get hold of Kennedy, and in order to do that he'd have to be mobile and, if at all possible, keep Hurley out of the loop.

CHAPTER 40

KENNEDY accompanied Stansfield into the Embassy while everyone else stayed with the vehicles. Rollie Smith was waiting for them and escorted them through security with only a word. Kennedy had heard a great many stories about Smith over the years. He had a substantial mustache that he kept perfectly trimmed and waxed. He had started growing it in his early twenties to help diminish his overbite, and over the years it became his signature trait, that and his bow ties. Smith prided himself on being the consummate British gentleman. He was a lifelong member of Britain's Secret Intelligence Service, more commonly known as MI6. His father had been a midlevel diplomat for Britain's Foreign Office, and the young Smith and his two sisters had spent almost their entire youth living on the Continent. Their father's longest posting was in France, but he'd also spent time in Belgium, Austria, and Germany.

Smith was eighteen and living in Belgium when Hitler rolled into Poland and kicked off World War II. The following spring the Nazis did their famous end run around the Maginot Line and the family was recalled to London. The father recognized that young Roland was going to join the war effort with or without his permission, so he pulled a few strings and got Rollie placed with MI6. Four years later he met an American who had spent the greater portion of the last year of the war behind Nazi lines.

Over the following decades, as the Cold War heated up, Thomas Stansfield and Rollie Smith shared a common passion—they both wanted to destroy the Soviet Union. Sometimes they were stationed in the same cities, their embassies often only blocks from each other. Other times they were continents away, but the distance never mattered. They remained the closest of friends and confidants.

The two men greeted each other with solid handshakes and warm smiles. They were stoically and unapologetically from a generation in which men did not hug men.

Smith turned his charm on Kennedy. "What a nice surprise to see you, Dr. Kennedy."

Kennedy smiled. "And you as well, Sir Roland." For some reason, Kennedy couldn't help but think of George MacDonald Fraser's hilarious character Flashman whenever she encountered Smith.

Smith was either in a hurry or more than likely shared the same fear that was common with intelligence officers the world over. Talking in transient, unsecure places was never a good idea, unless you wanted to be heard. As was the case with the U.S. Embassy in Paris, MI6's secure offices were located in the second subbasement. They took the stairs, and when they got to a heavy steel door with a camera above it, Smith punched a code into a cipher lock and they entered. He greeted a man behind a desk but didn't bother with introductions. They continued down a long hall with ugly cream-colored walls and linoleum floors. Unlike the rest of the Embassy, this area had missed the big remodeling.

Smith opened a door on the right and motioned for Kennedy and Stansfield to enter. Kennedy felt immediately familiar with the type of room. The floor was rubber and the walls and ceiling were covered in gray acoustic foam. This was where the MI6 gang would hold their most delicate meetings. The table had four chairs on each side and a chair at each end. At the far end a very small man dressed in black was seated and smiling at her. She smiled back and guessed his age to be somewhere close to ninety.

Kennedy noticed the white tab at the front of the man's collar. She approached him, extended her hand, and introduced herself.

The man continued to smile and in French said, "Very nice to meet you, Ms. Kennedy. I am Monsignor Peter de Fleury."

Stansfield asked, "I'm not going to have to kiss the back of your hand now, am I?"

"Yes," the old priest said, "and my bony white butt while you're at it."

Kennedy was caught completely off-guard. Her boss never joked.

Stansfield and Smith were now laughing like schoolboys.

"Your Eminence," Stansfield said, "it is such an honor to be in your holy presence."

De Fleury smiled and said, "I should have you excommunicated."

"You probably should, and then I'll just join the Church of England like Rollie here."

"And you will burn in hell with Rollie and all the other pagans."

Now all three of them were laughing, and they continued their ribbing for another few minutes until they finally settled down. De Fleury looked at Kennedy and said, "I'm sorry you have to put up with such childish behavior, but you should have seen these two at the end of World War II." The monsignor turned his cloudy eyes on Smith and Stansfield and said, "Remember the time I had to save you from that whorehouse when the—"

"Hey, hey," Stansfield shouted, "don't start telling lies, or I'll be forced to hand my secret files over to the Vatican. You'll be stripped of that new fancy title and live out your final years in shame."

"Go ahead," de Fleury replied. "It would be the most exciting thing those old peacocks have read in years."

There was another round of laughter and more stories. Kennedy had never seen her boss like this, and it made her view him in a different light. With his relative youthfulness and sharp mind it was easy to forget that he had served in World War II. When the men had finally settled down and were done teasing each other things took on a more serious tone.

Smith turned to Stansfield and said, "I wish things were different right now. I would love nothing more than to spend an evening with the two of you telling lies about each other, but I'm afraid in light of what happened last night that is not going to happen on this trip. The DGSE will be harassing you, no doubt."

Stansfield was unfazed. "Once you've run a station in Moscow, the DGSE isn't so intimidating."

"True," Rollie said in a reflective tone, "but this new man they have running their Special Action Division is not someone to take lightly."

"So I've heard."

"Peter will fill you in on something very important in a moment, but first I, too, have something rather important to share."

This was not a surprise to Stansfield. He had taken a call from Rollie at home on Saturday. A few coded words were dropped into the conversation and when Stansfield arrived at the office he found a secure cable from his London station chief waiting for him. It was a request for a face-to-face meeting. The topic to be discussed was the murder of the Libyan oil minister. "I appreciate you reaching out, Rollie."

"That's how you and I do things. We look out for each other." Smith drummed his fingers on the table for a moment and then said, "The Libyan oil minister, Tarek al-Magariha . . . he was on our payroll."

Stansfield didn't seem surprised. "I thought that's what this might be about."

"There's a slight wrinkle, however. He was also on the DGSE's payroll."

This time Stansfield was surprised. "Who had him first?"

"They did."

"And then you turned him."

"Not me personally, but yes, my people did."

Stansfield took a moment to measure what he had learned and then he asked the most obvious question. "Did the Directorate know?"

Smith shrugged. "Probably."

"Probably is the best you can do?"

"We have nothing definitive, but Tarek's handler said he was growing increasingly nervous. He wanted us to bring him in. He thought the Directorate had become suspicious and then he was sent abroad for this most recent trip without any security. He told his handler that they were going to kill him."

"They?"

"I've been told he was more afraid of his Islamic associates than of the Directorate."

Kennedy's heart was beating a little fast as she thought of Rapp's words. That it was a setup. That they had been waiting for him. "Did you say they sent him abroad without any security?"

"Yes."

"I thought the papers said four of his bodyguards were killed."

Smith turned his attention from Kennedy to Stansfield and gave him a hard stare.

Stansfield cleared his throat and said, "Rollie knows, Irene."

"Rollie knows what?"

"He knows about Mitch. He knows he was there the other night."

Kennedy didn't move a muscle, but she felt blood rushing to her face. Before she could respond Stansfield gave an explanation of sorts.

"We have no better ally than Rollie and MI6. They have access to areas that we don't and vice versa. I trust Rollie more than a good number of people in our building."

Kennedy nodded. "I am in no position to judge, sir. You don't owe me an explanation. You just caught me off-guard."

"There is a tendency," Smith said, "in this business to hoard information. We all know why. We don't want certain people to get their hands on that information, but as you're going to learn this morning, when you trust certain people, they can help fill in gaping holes that you would be incapable of filling on your own." Smith turned to de Fleury and said, "Right, Peter?"

"That is very true."

Keeping his eyes on Kennedy, Smith said, "Monsignor de Fleury was very active in the French Resistance during the war. He was so successful that after the war he was awarded the Legion of Honor by General Charles de Gaulle in a private ceremony. Over the ensuing decades he has helped French Intelligence and both our services when he can."

"Don't listen to him," de Fleury said, "I have grown old and worthless, but there was a time when I did my part."

"And you are still doing your part as they will soon find out." Smith prodded him. "Tell them what you were witness to Saturday night."

De Fleury smiled at Kennedy and said, "My church is Sacré-Coeur Basilica . . . you have heard of it?"

"Of course."

"It is a very busy place. Lots of tourists. Lots of people coming and going. It also happens to be the perfect place to hold certain meetings for the Directorate. Such a meeting took place on Saturday night." De Fleury reached inside his coat, fumbled for a moment, and retrieved several sheets of white paper folded once the long way. He placed the papers in front of Kennedy. "I took notes. My mind isn't as sharp as it once was. A man named Paul Fournier who works for the Directorate set up the meeting. The other men were wicked. Or at least two of them were. I've been around evil before and these two men were evil. They were killers. They were Muslims and they were very rude. They complained about meeting at the church."

Kennedy nodded.

"The third man was polite. He was dark-skinned, but his French was much better than that of the other two. His name was Max. They started talking about the murders at the hotel. Fournier said to one of the angry men . . . I can't remember his name but it is in my notes.

He said, 'You came here to kill one man and now I have nine bodies to deal with.' Fournier said, 'I gave you this assassin on a silver platter and you fucked it up so badly I spent the entire day cleaning up your mess.'"

"You were there while they talked about this?" Kennedy asked.

"No." De Fleury smiled. "They were in the crypt. I was above them, in the church. There is a vent that carries their voice as clear as day to one of the confessionals."

Kennedy nodded and said, "Please continue."

"Things became very heated, with the terrorists blaming Fournier for setting them up and Fournier blaming them for ruining their best chance to kill this assassin. Fournier blamed this Samir, that was his name, for killing three innocent civilians as he was leaving the hotel."

Kennedy and Stansfield shared a quick look and then turned their attention back to de Fleury.

"They threatened Fournier, and he threatened to drown them in the ocean. That was when they said that Libya might begin to divert some of its oil and that maybe they would start setting off bombs in France again. Fournier laughed at them and told them he'd hand the files he had on them over to the assassin and he would hunt them all down. They threatened to inform his bosses. Fournier told them his bosses knew all about their arrangement. It went round and round like that until the one named Max stepped in. Then they talked about the assassin some more and the crime scene." De Fleury's eyes became unfocused, and he looked at the far wall for a moment. "After that . . . I can't really remember what they said." His eyes focused again and he looked at Kennedy, saying, "It's all in my report. I checked it several times. It's all there." He nodded. "It's just not all up here anymore." De Fleury tapped his head with a near translucent finger.

Kennedy didn't realize it, but her mouth was hanging open in disbelief. She blinked several times and then looked down at the papers in her hands and quickly shuffled through them. There were eight handwritten pages, all in beautiful flowing cursive. They felt like the greatest gift she'd ever received. Everything Rapp had said was true. "Thank you, Monsignor."

"And that," Rollie Smith said in a jovial voice, "is why we share information."

CHAPTER 41

PAUL Fournier was reclining on his office couch with a cold compress on his forehead, his top shirt button undone, his tie loosened, and his shoes and jacket off. He rarely had headaches, but this morning was an exception, so he'd just taken three Extra Strength Tylenol and told his number two, Pierre Mermet, that he was not to be disturbed. Fournier had worked through the night trying to manage the damage that had been done. One dead agent and another in critical condition was not good. His bosses were going to be extremely upset. If a DGSE agent was killed abroad, no one batted an eye. If one was gunned down on a Sunday night in Paris, however, it was a big embarrassment for a lot of people.

The press was going to be asking a lot of questions, and Fournier did not like talking to reporters, at least en masse. They were too unruly, too hard to manipulate when they were in a feeding frenzy. One on one was his preferred method. He found them incredibly easy to manipulate. So many of them were insecure and in constant need of validation. He'd slept with more than a few of the female reporters in Paris and had stayed on good terms with them.

Fournier played out every conceivable development. The key would be to keep the police confused, and his play with the minister of defense would go a long way in slowing the police down. Having Neville removed from the case would send a message to all of the other investigators that they needed to be careful where they stepped. The case would take on the aura of a place where careers went to die. He was amazed at Neville and her naïve ways. He had hoped she would be smarter, but in the end she had asked for it.

At least in that regard, Fournier was pleased with himself. The bigger issue would be the CIA. He had surveillance photos of Hurley and his goons entering the country and driving to the very street where the shootings had taken place. Fournier's orders to have his men follow them were completely within the charter of the Directorate. They were not monitoring French citizens, they were keeping an eye on foreign intelligence assets who had entered the country a little more than twelve hours after the massacre at the hotel.

The delicate part for Fournier would be withholding that information, so he could use it as leverage with the CIA. Turning the photo of the dead American agent over to the police would be a waste. If he could keep it private he could force the CIA to make some concessions and a fairly sizable cash transfer as well. They would be left with no choice, once presented with the photos of Hurley and his men. The conclusion was obvious. The DGSE men were not shot by some local criminals. They were too good for that. It was Hurley's trained assassins who had been involved in the shootout. Fournier had other questions as well. Why were Hurley's men on that particular street? Who were they looking for? Was it possible that it was the American assassin? Fournier had been working very hard for the past year to learn the man's real identity. The closest he had come was a list of targets. His source either didn't know the assassin's identity or was playing him for better terms. His two men being shot would change all of that.

Fournier and his source shared the same pragmatic opinion: that it was not good for either America or France to have a killer poking the volatile nests of terrorists who ringed the Mediterranean. Fournier had deftly managed the moods and fanatical beliefs of the various groups, with one goal in mind—to keep the carnage out of France. His superiors, all the way up to the president, had given either silent approval or verbal commitments to the plan. As to the tidy sum he had collected along the way, no one in government would begrudge him for that. Even some in the press would understand, but none of them would ever find out. Fournier was convinced he'd covered his tracks. There was no way anyone would be able to find his money.

Fournier was thinking of his next move when his assistant burst through the door without knocking.

"You're going to want to see this." Mermet went straight for the TV and a few seconds later the TV showed a room full of reporters asking questions.

Fournier removed the cold compress from his head and turned his attention to the TV. The screen was filled with the charming face of Francine Neville. Questions were being shouted in the background and Neville was nodding.

"Yes, that is correct," she said. "I have been removed from the case that I was assigned to barely forty-eight hours ago."

"You're talking about the murders at the Hotel Balzac."

"That's correct. Shortly after my investigators arrived at the crime scene, several DGSE employees showed up. One of them was Paul Fournier, who runs the Special Action Division for the Directorate. You're going to want to make sure you write that name down . . . Paul Fournier. I thought it was strange that he was there, but he told me that the death of the Libyan oil minister was very much the business of the Directorate. He and several of his men had access to the crime scene for a little over an hour. The next day we discovered that certain key pieces of evidence were missing from the crime scene. We had reason to believe that it was one of Fournier's men who took the evidence. I informed Mr. Fournier that I wanted to talk to this man, as well as several other people associated with the case." She paused. "Thus far Mr. Fournier has proven to be very uncooperative.

"Yesterday I informed my boss, Prefect Mutz, that I needed to meet with him this morning to discuss the fact that the Directorate was interfering with a police investigation. When I arrived in his office a short while ago, Director General of Police Jacques Gisquet and Minister of the Interior Pierre Blot were in attendance. I took this as a positive sign that they were taking my accusations seriously. I soon found out that they were there for an entirely different reason. Minister of the Interior Blot had received a call last night from the minister of defense, who said he was in possession of a very detailed file that claimed I have been stalking and sexually harassing Paul Fournier for several years." She paused again and looked around the room, giving the reporters a chance to catch up. "Full disclosure . . . Mr. Fournier and I dated briefly four years ago and we parted amicably. In the years since then I have married and have two beautiful children. I have not seen nor have I spoken to Mr. Fournier during this time. Somehow, though, this file contains statements from three women who claim I was threatened by their relationship with Fournier and that I stalked them.

"When I asked to see this file, I was told by Minister Blot that he had not seen the file, but he and the minister of defense had decided it would be best for the short term if I was removed from the case. In all my years with the police I have never been removed from a case. I have not received so much as a tiny mark against me. I am routinely ranked among the top commandants by my peers and I am often given very high-profile cases. I demanded to see the file and was told that was not going to happen. That the best thing for my career would be to simply step aside and let someone else handle the investigation. I was not given a choice in the matter, so I am stepping aside, but I am not going to do so quietly. I'm going to file an official complaint, and I want to see this fabricated file that Mr. Fournier used to con the minister of defense. And I'm also asking all of you to look into the Directorate's involvement in this case. Their charter is to operate outside France, not to manipulate and interfere with police investigations here in Paris."

A reporter shouted, "Can you confirm that two Directorate agents were involved in a gunfight in Montparnasse last night?"

Neville paused for an instant and then said, "Yes, I can. One of the agents was killed, and the other one I'm told is in critical but stable condition at a local hospital."

The room erupted with questions coming from dozens of reporters. After about ten seconds Neville held up her hands and quieted the group. "I suggest you track down Mr. Fournier and ask him your questions. He is probably sitting in his office at the Directorate's headquarters at 141 Boulevard Mortier plotting his next deception."

Fournier was now up sitting on the edge of the couch. His eyes were locked on the TV as Neville stepped from behind the podium and left the room. He could hear his phone ringing from across the office but he made no effort to see who was calling. His mind was racing to find a way to limit the damage done by the stupid bitch. If she'd only just taken her banishment with grace he could have spared her the public embarrassment he'd now have to put her through. He quickly decided he could weather this minor storm. It would come down to he said she said, and he could provide fake evidence from now until the end of time. Neville had made a drastic miscalculation.

A woman with a flustered expression poked her head in the outer door and said, "Sir, the minister of defense is on line one and the director is on line two. They both want to speak with you immediately. They seem very upset."

Fournier looked at Mermet, who merely shrugged. Fournier turned to his secretary and said, "I'll speak to the minister first. Tell the director I'll call him back as soon as I can." Fournier rose from the couch and felt his headache begin stabbing at his temples. He picked up the handset on his desk, punched line one, and started to lie.

CHAPTER 42

THE interrogation room was used most often for debriefing assets, but occasionally it had been used for rougher stuff. The walls were painted off white and the floors were plain concrete. A six-by-four-foot metal table was anchored in the center of the room. Hurley sat on one side and Victor on the other. As much as Stansfield was inclined to authorize the screws being put to Victor, he thought there was a better way to proceed, so he calmly looked through the one-way glass and watched Stan Hurley walk Victor through the events of the last fourteen hours.

Kennedy approached the glass and said, "Sir, I think you need to hear what Thomas has to say."

Stansfield looked at Kennedy and nodded. Dr. Lewis joined them at the glass and asked, "Have you been reading all of my reports?"

"Most of them."

With a thorough man like Stansfield, that meant that either his reports had ceased to be important or that he was swamped with other work. Lewis took this in stride. "Have you read my most recent reports on Victor?"

"No." Stansfield watched Victor's face and listened to his voice as it was played over the ceiling speakers.

"Bramble, or Victor as most of the men call him, has become increasingly difficult to deal with."

"Most of the people in this outfit are difficult to deal with," Stansfield said without a hint of humor. "But continue."

"He is not well liked."

"I assume you mean by Mitch."

"Yes, and pretty much by everyone else."

"That's not true," Stansfield interjected. "Stan and Victor get along fine."

"That's because Victor is his trained dog," Kennedy said.

"And Stan would say the same thing about you and Mitch."

"Victor and Mitch are very different people." Looking at Lewis she said, "Explain."

Lewis nodded and turned his focus on Stansfield. "In my last report I outlined several serious concerns about Victor. I have noticed an extensive contempt and abuse of the rights of others. He is deceitful and lies to his colleagues with ease, especially if it will lead to his own personal gain. He is extremely irritable and aggressive and is prone to fighting even at the least hint of a slight. He has a reckless disregard for the safety of others, often manifesting itself in practical jokes that only he finds humorous. He shows almost no remorse when he hurts one of the recruits . . . in fact I think he takes a perverse joy in inflicting pain on others."

Stansfield drummed his fingers on the ledge in front of the glass for a second. "You just described a good portion of the men I've worked with over the years," he lamented.

Lewis cleared his throat. "On the surface it may sound like that, and you undoubtedly have worked with many tough men who share one or two of these qualities, Stan being chief among them, but I can assure you, there are seven traits that outline antisocial personality disorder and Victor has all seven."

Stansfield looked away from the interrogation and regarded the doctor. "How many does Stan have?"

"Three . . . maybe four."

"And me?" Stansfield asked with a straight face.

"Only one," Lewis said, and then with a slight smile he said, "but then again I would need more time to properly observe you . . . but I wouldn't worry. As a general rule you need to have at least four of the traits to be classified with the disease."

"And Mitch, how many does he have?"

"Just one or two."

"This assessment of yours . . . how serious is it?"

"Very."

"And you're confident that if I brought in someone else for a second opinion that person would reach the same conclusions."

"Very confident."

"Can this problem be resolved with treatment?"

Lewis waffled for a second and then shook his head. "It would take a great deal of time and effort and the patient would have to be willing."

Looking through the glass Stansfield asked, "And do you think Victor would be willing to undergo treatment?"

"No."

Stansfield stared through the glass and said, "Stan's not going to like this."

"No he isn't, but he's blind to the realities of the problem. This is far bigger than Stan and who he likes or dislikes. I put all of this in my report. People like Victor are extremely volatile. They usually end up in jail, or financially ruined, or both."

Stansfield stepped back from the glass. "We don't recruit Boy Scouts to this work. You two both know that. The Boy Scouts are all over at the FBI. We need guys who are willing to bend the rules . . . do certain things that your average mentally stable individual would never consider."

Lewis nodded and said, "And you hired me to keep an eye on

things . . . to make sure we have guys who know not to cross certain lines, and I'm telling you Victor will cross any line as long as it helps him get what he wants."

"You know I called Stan last night and I told him to pull Victor and his team?"

Lewis nodded.

"Victor claims they were in the process of packing up when Rapp sent in the decoy."

"I'm aware."

"Do you believe him?"

Lewis measured his response. "I'm not sure I believe anything Victor says."

"Anything else?"

"It's one thing to have him down at the farm brutalizing recruits . . . but turning him loose in Paris . . ." Lewis shook his head. "That was a bad idea."

"And why didn't you bring this to my attention sooner?"

"I did put much of this in my most recent report."

Stansfield turned his cold, gray, calculating eyes on the doctor. "I receive a lot of reports. Why didn't you come to me?"

Lewis sighed and said, "I wasn't there when he was recruited, but over the past year, I've grown increasingly concerned. And then there's Stan to consider."

"What about him?"

"The two of you are very loyal to each other."

"We have a history, Tom, but I know how Stan ticks."

"Permission to be brutally honest, sir?"

Stansfield knew this was the Green Beret coming out in the doctor, and he also knew that if he was asking for permission it was to say something that would be highly critical of Stansfield. He had never been afraid of the truth so he said, "Permission granted."

"You have a blind spot where Stan is concerned. I have tried repeatedly to bring certain things to your attention and so has Irene, but you brush us off. I understand that the man has a storied career, and he undoubtedly has his uses, but putting him in charge of the recruiting and training of these men, I fear, was a huge mistake. And Victor is exhibit A. The man should have washed out years ago."

Looking back through the one-way glass, Stansfield asked, "So what do you recommend I do about this problem?"

"Send Victor packing and do it as quickly as possible."

"And if he doesn't want to quit?"

The blue-eyed shrink and former Green Beret hesitated for a second and then said, "You should have him eliminated."

This was far more serious than Stansfield had expected. He knew Lewis as a thoughtful man who was very thorough about his recommendations. This was the first time in three years that he had suggested such a thing. Stansfield had no illusions about who he was. He'd killed men before and he'd ordered men killed. It was part of his job description. "I'll take all of this under advisement." Stansfield left the mirror and then stopped and looked back at Lewis. "And what would you have me do with Stan?"

Lewis had some very strong opinions on the subject, but he was not so presumptuous as to think that he should offer them to Stansfield. "You know him better than any of us, sir. I think you are more than capable of making that decision on your own."

The faintest of smiles creased Stansfield's mouth. "You're a smart man, Tom. I appreciate your honesty."

CHAPTER 43

JIM Talmage had his equipment set up in the observation room where he could monitor Bramble via cameras and sensors that were attached to various parts of the subject's body to measure blood pressure, pulse, skin conductivity, and respiration. Talmage knew he could fool a polygraph 100 percent of the time and he knew Hurley could as well, because they'd practiced on each other. Having operated in Indian country for much of their careers, it was a job requirement should they be dragged in by another intelligence agency or, worse, a terrorist organization. Being able to trick the polygraph could often mean the difference between life and death.

Stansfield appeared at Talmage's side. "How's it going?"

Talmage shook his head. "Not good."

"He's lying?"

"I'm not sure . . . that's the problem."

"Is he being evasive?" Stansfield asked.

"Yeah, but it's more than that. I think he knows just enough to beat the machine, and it's not helping that Stan's doing a shitty job."

"How so?"

"I've seen him press a lot harder than this. I can usually predict his next question. You need to get the guy thinking about one thing, get him leaning in a certain direction, and then slap him in the face with an accusation, try to trip him up and see how he's going to react."

"And he's not doing that."

"Nope. He's letting this guy tell his story. Every once in a while he'll go back and review something . . . ask him for clarification."

Stansfield was no novice when it came to polygraphs. He'd been given more of them than he could count and he'd ordered thousands. There were a lot of different techniques. Talmage had just described a technique they called giving the subject enough rope to hang himself. "That doesn't sound unusual."

Talmage shook his head and frowned. "Some people do it that way, but I can't even count how many of these I've done with Stan. This isn't his style. He's like a street fighter. Nothing's off-limits. Once he starts, he attacks and keeps attacking until he's got the guy so flustered he wouldn't dare lie to him."

Stansfield considered the situation and then asked, "Should I pull him?"

Now Talmage got really uncomfortable. "That's up to you, boss, but if there's any criticism it better come from you. I don't feel like getting my head bitten off."

"Got it." Stansfield didn't show it, but he was extremely unhappy that he'd let Hurley create an environment in which everyone was afraid to express an opinion. He turned to Kennedy and Lewis and said, "Why don't you two go check your voicemail? I need to have a word with Stan." He patted Talmage on the shoulder and said, "Tell him to take a break."

Talmage leaned forward and pressed the Transmit button on the microphone. "Guys, let's take a break. Victor, can we bring you anything?"

Victor asked for a black coffee.

Talmage looked through the glass at the big oaf. He should know better. "You know we can't give you coffee."

"Fine," the voice came over the speakers, "I'll take water."

Hurley got up and left the interrogation room. A moment later he joined Stansfield and Talmage. He looked at Talmage and said, "I think it's going pretty well. How do the readouts look?"

"Like shit."

Before Hurley could respond, Stansfield said, "Would you mind telling me what you're doing?"

"What are you talking about? I'm trying to get the truth out of him."

"I don't think you are," Stansfield said, without any extra emotion.

Hurley's face twisted into a pissed-off scowl. "Listen, this ain't my first rodeo. I don't stick my nose in what goes on in the rarefied air of the seventh floor at Langley. Just let me do my job like I let you do yours."

"Let?" A touch of anger crept into Stansfield's voice. "You seem to be confused about something, Stanley. I'm your boss. I'm your superior. I'm the one who gives orders. I don't just let you do your job, my job is to manage you. You don't let me do anything. You're my subordinate. Do you understand that?"

"I don't understand what the fucking problem is. I've been warning you for two years that Rapp was going to blow up in our faces and lo and behold it happens, and now everyone's pissed at me. I don't need this shit. Victor is telling the truth. It's obvious, and the rest of you better wake up and figure it out."

"We don't know if Victor is telling the truth, because you're going so easy on him, Jim can't get any readings that are worth a crap."

"What the fuck would you know about interrogating someone?"

Stansfield stared right through him, didn't speak for at least ten seconds, and then said, "Here's what you're going to do, Stan. You're going to go upstairs and get some fresh air, have a smoke, and then you're going to come to one of two conclusions. Either you're right, we're all wrong, and you have all the answers, or you're going to figure out that you've become an insufferable ass whom no one can work with."

Hurley lifted his chin and said, "You know I don't need this crap."

"You're wrong again. We're all sick of taking *your* crap. We're all sick of your attitude, so remember, I'm your boss. If you go upstairs and fifteen or thirty minutes from now, you still think we're all idiots and you're the only smart guy, then I want you to walk out the front gate of this Embassy and never come back. I don't care where you go as long as you stay the hell out of Virginia. But if you can somehow get it through your thick head that you don't have all the answers, and decide that you're going to stop biting people's heads off, then come back down here and we'll get serious about this interrogation."

Hurley had known Stansfield for nearly thirty years. He had never seen his friend this upset, and it bothered him. He took a step back and uttered a word that rarely left his lips. "I'm sorry. I think my nerves are a little shot."

Stansfield nodded. "Go upstairs. Clear your head and then make your mind up."

Hurley left the room sullen and dejected, and for once Stansfield didn't care. He looked through the glass at Chet Bramble and thought about the man's dossier. Stansfield had read it years ago, but he still had it memorized. Much of what Lewis had deduced was already in that file. Bramble had major issues with authority and rules. It was what had eventually gotten him bounced from the army. Stansfield was of the opinion that highly moral, well-balanced individuals would never do what his team did for a living, so he was willing to look the other way with regard to certain personality faults. Now he feared he had let his standards slide too far, or he'd at least given Hurley too much latitude. Either way, the blame lay squarely on his shoulders.

Lewis and Kennedy were good people. They had sound judgment and were in control of their emotions. Bramble most certainly wasn't. He was a brawler like Hurley. They were the type of men who could be trusted to handle very dirty jobs. The results weren't always pretty, but they got the job done. Rapp, on the other hand, was measured and precise. All of his kills until now had been minimalist in the best way. Stansfield was still in the process of comparing the two men when Kennedy came bursting into the room. "Sir," Kennedy said, "you need to listen to this." Kennedy grabbed the handset of a secure phone and began punching in a long string of numbers. "I just received a message on my service." She handed him the phone. "It's Mitch."

Stansfield grabbed the handset and listened. "We need to meet. I finally figured out I can trust you. Don't believe anything Victor says. I sent someone in my place last night. I wanted to see how he would be treated. I had no idea how bad the reception would be. I thought at worst he'd be roughed up. Unprovoked, Victor popped him and then did the same to the guys he was working with. Two locals showed up and he popped them, too. My guess is he's blaming me for all of this. His word against mine . . . well, there's only one problem. I have a witness. Someone your boss knows and trusts. I want to come in, but I don't want to see anyone other than you. Leave me a mobile number where I can reach you and have the boss ready to hear me out. And this is my only offer. If I see Stan or Victor anywhere, I'm done, and if anyone tries to find me, a lot of people are going to get hurt."

Stansfield handed her the phone. "Where is Ridley?"

"He's in the city." She checked her watch. "He and his team are prepping the vehicle and hotel for Cooke's arrival."

"Was he here last night?"

"Yes."

Stansfield thought about Rapp's message. "That must be who he's talking about."

"The witness."

Stansfield nodded and turned his attention back to Victor, who was leaning back in his chair drinking from a water bottle. "Call your service and leave him a number. Use your handler code. Get this set up as soon as possible, and then call Ridley and find out what he knows."

Kennedy had started punching numbers into the bulky secure phone.

Stansfield considered the overall situation and then added, "And tell Rapp I'm coming with you."

Kennedy punched in two more numbers before she realized what Stansfield had said. "Are you sure that's a good idea?"

Stansfield did not want to believe that Stan Hurley had betrayed him, but it was a possibility he had to face. At a bare minimum it sounded as if someone had given Fournier the list of targets. It was possible that it could have been electronically intercepted, but to the best of Stansfield's knowledge the list had never been sent via secure cable, Internet, or phone, or in any other known form. It had been compiled by Stansfield, Kennedy, and Hurley. The list was then destroyed. Stansfield had a photographic memory, as did Kennedy. Hurley did not, and there had been a few times earlier in their careers when Stansfield had had to chide Hurley for writing down stuff that should never be written down.

Stansfield studied Victor through the glass. He seemed relaxed, even confident, either that he was in the right, or that he was going to get away with what he'd done. As Lewis had pointed out, Victor was a man who would do whatever served him best. Rapp, on the other hand, had given them nothing but hard work and results.

The deputy director of Operations looked over his shoulder and said, "Yes, I think it's a good idea. I think it's the best idea I've had in a long time."

Kennedy left the number for Rapp and then called Ridley on his mobile phone. When she had him on the line she said, "Hold on, Thomas wants to talk to you."

Stansfield took the receiver. "Rob, you were in town last night?"

"Yep. Got in about four in the afternoon."

"Did you happen to run into a mutual friend?"

"I'm not sure what you mean."

"Were you with one of our colleagues last night . . . did you witness anything?"

There was a prolonged pause and then Ridley said, "I'm not following, sir."

"Never mind," Stansfield said. "You have everything in place for our guest?"

"Almost done. Maybe another thirty minutes."

"Good. Call me when he shows up." Stansfield hung up the phone and turned to Kennedy. "It's not Ridley."

"Then who in the world could it be?"

"I don't know, but let's not worry about it. We have bigger issues to deal with. Have the document people put together a diplomatic passport for Mitch. I don't want any glitches if we get stopped by the Directorate. And how are we for vehicles?"

"I assume the Range Rovers are too high-profile?"

He nodded. "No bodyguards. Just you and me. Let's use something from the motor pool that will blend in. We'll send the Rovers out first. Dr. Lewis can take a nice scenic drive around Paris with the DGSE trailing him."

"Good idea," Kennedy said. "I'd better get upstairs, my cell phone doesn't work down here."

"I'll go with you." Stansfield then said to Talmage, "I'm going to initiate a lockdown on this floor. No one enters or leaves without my knowledge."

"Understood."

Hurley came bursting into the room with his small clamshell phone in his hand. "My phone doesn't work down here," he said, slightly out of breath.

"I know. Irene just said the same thing."

"Well," he started with a shake of his head, "I completely forgot that I had ordered two assets to relieve Victor and his team last night. Remember Bernstein and Jones?"

"The reporter and the cameraman," Stansfield answered.

"Yeah, they're the ones."

Stansfield gave a disapproving frown. "They don't seem like the right choice."

"It's a longer story than we have time for right now, but I asked them to work their contacts with the police. Beyond that, Victor and his crew had been working all day without a break, so I sent them over to sit in the van and relieve the guys for a few hours."

Stansfield didn't think this was the brightest idea, but he got the sense that there was something more important that Hurley was trying to get to.

"I was down here all night and all morning and when I went upstairs, my phone started beeping like crazy. Bernstein had left me four messages so I called him back. He said that when they showed up last night two men had been shot. Turns out it was the two Directorate boys. One dead and one alive. He tells me there was a guy who was administering first aid to the wounded agent. I asked him to describe the guy. He said the guy was midtwenties, thick black hair, fit, and he's pretty sure he was French."

"Why?" Kennedy asked.

"He said he spoke French like a native. Started barking orders at Bernstein and Jones. Told them to sit with the agent while he went and got help."

"And?" Stansfield asked.

"He never came back. Bernstein, who's been in almost as many war zones as I have, said this mystery man used Quickclot on the wound and field bandages to stop the bleeding."

"You think it was Mitch?" Kennedy asked.

Hurley couldn't speak for a moment. He looked at the floor, shaking his head ever so slightly. "I don't know what the fuck is going on. It sounds like it could be him, but why the fuck would he shoot a DGSE agent and then patch him up?"

Kennedy and Stansfield shared a quick look, and then Stansfield said, "Because he didn't shoot the agents. Someone else did?"

All eyes turned to the man sitting in the interrogation room. There was a lengthy silence and then Stansfield said, "Stan and I need a moment alone. Irene, I'll meet you upstairs. Jim and Tom, stay close. This isn't going to take long." Once they were all gone Stansfield said, "I need an honest answer from you."

Hurley nodded.

"I need a verbal commitment. You need to look me in the eye and swear that you are going to answer this question honestly."

Hurley hated being penned in like this. "Fine," he said, looking his old friend in the eye. "I won't bullshit you. Ask away, and I'll tell you the truth."

"Remember when we made out the list of targets?"

"Yeah."

"And we memorized them, and then I shredded the list and put it in my burn bag?"

"Yeah."

Stansfield could already tell by the way Hurley was fidgeting that he'd done something wrong. To strangers or adversaries he was a world-class con artist and liar, but when it came to his closest friends he was lousy. "When you got back down to the farm, did you by chance re-create that list?"

"How do you mean?" He took a half step back and folded his arms across his chest.

"By writing the names down again?"

Hurley sighed. "Listen, I don't have your little computer brain. My strengths lie in other areas."

"How many lists did you make?"

"One . . . but it was more of a file really. I needed to keep track of these guys. Figure out where they were weakest, what they were up to, where they'd be next week and the week after that."

Stansfield was both relieved and irritated. "And knowing you, this file was kept in an unlocked drawer as opposed to a locked safe?"

"Listen, nobody gets within a mile of that farm without me knowing. The place is as secure as Fort Knox."

"How do you think Fournier got his hands on our list?"

"I have no idea."

"I certainly didn't tell him and I doubt Irene did." Stansfield turned and looked through the glass. "What about him? He had access."

"So did Rapp."

"Do you honestly believe that Mitch handed that list over so he could walk into a trap and get shot? That's preposterous."

"I don't know," Hurley said, his frustration apparent. "I can't figure this out."

"That's because you don't want to face the truth."

"And what truth would that be?"

"That you're not only wrong about Rapp, but you're wrong about him, too."

Hurley studied Victor, trying to discern some truth that he would never get standing on this side of the glass. He rubbed the stubble on his square jaw and said, "Bernstein and Jones are on their way in. I'm going to show them a picture of Rapp and if they ID him, Victor is going to have a really hard time explaining why Rapp would shoot the agents and then try to save one of them."

"And risk exposing himself in the process."

"Fuck," Hurley growled. He didn't like where this was headed.

"I told Jim I wanted this floor locked down," Stansfield said. "Victor is to be treated as a potential hostile until I say otherwise. I don't trust anyone in that room with him other than you. Do you know what I mean?"

"Yeah. You don't want him breaking some desk jockey's neck."

"Exactly. He's your creation. Do you think you can still handle him?"

Hurley nodded. "If it turns out he's been lying about all of this, I'll snap his fucking neck."

CHAPTER 44

RAPP hated meets like this. Even when he had the significant resources of the CIA behind him, there was always the unknown, the possibility that someone might go back on his word and kill you. He'd finally gotten to a place where he could trust Kennedy and now Stansfield had been thrown in the mix. Rapp said no when she first told him the deputy director was coming along. Stansfield had bodyguards, and God only knew how many assets the French would have on him. Kennedy told him they had contingencies to deal with all of that. Rapp still didn't like it and was about to call the whole thing off when Greta talked him down.

"I have known him since I was a little child. He is one of my grandfather's closest friends. If there is anyone I can trust it is him."

They were moving from pay phone to pay phone in Greta's car, running Kennedy through some hoops to make sure they weren't being tailed or driving into an entourage of vehicles filled with heavily armed men. Rapp had Kennedy give him the description of the car they were driving, and twice in thirty minutes Kennedy had passed within thirty feet of where he was standing. He couldn't see the backseat, and obviously had no idea if someone was in the trunk, but it was undeniable that Thomas Stansfield was in the front passenger seat.

After an hour of running them around town, he was ready. He'd purchased two very expensive mobile phones and was saving them. The second-to-last waypoint was someplace he and Kennedy had visited together. It was the final resting place of the Irish playwright Samuel Beckett, the unjustly accused French Army officer Alfred Dreyfus, and many other notables. Kennedy had read several books about the miscarriage of justice that had been heaped upon Dreyfus and the national scandal that eventually followed. Rapp had known nothing about the Dreyfus Affair, as it became known, but the previous winter they had stood in front of his grave for nearly thirty minutes while Kennedy explained the tragedy and the national crisis that had resulted from the false conviction and imprisonment of Dreyfus.

Rapp called her cell from a pay phone and said, "We're getting close. Remember the French Army officer we visited ten months ago?"

"The Jewish one?"

"That's right. Head there and await my next call." Rapp placed the phone back in the cradle and walked back to the car. He climbed behind the wheel and said to Greta, "It's not too late to back out."

She didn't bother looking at him. She simply said, "Shut up. I told you to stop saying that. Thomas Stansfield would never harm me."

"He's not the one I worry about. It's Hurley and the guy we saw last night. I don't want you anywhere near them."

"I have a hard time believing Stan is as bad as you say. He has always been kind to me."

"Well, he must like blondes, because he's been nothing but a prick to me." Rapp drove for a few minutes, maneuvering through the narrow streets. He parked the vehicle a block from the meeting place, and he and Greta got out. He kissed her and said, "You have your gun?"

"Yes."

"Don't be afraid to use it."

"You worry too much." She kissed him back and then headed off.

Rapp watched her walk away and then found his pay phone. He'd timed how long it would take Kennedy to get from the cemetery to the final meeting place. Rapp placed the call and stayed on the phone with her, telling her each turn he wanted her to make. He saw her turn onto Boulevard Raspail, two blocks away from his position. Rapp told her to park the car and get out. From his concealed position he saw Kennedy and Stansfield get out of the car. "There's an alley about a hundred feet ahead on your right. Take it and stop at the fourth door on your left." Rapp hung up the pay phone and fished out his first cell phone. He checked his watch and then headed around the block in the opposite direction. Thirty seconds later he punched Kennedy's number into the cell phone. She answered on the second ring.

"We're at the door."

"Good. I disabled the lock. Here's what I want you to do." Rapp walked her through the next move, which was pretty easy.

"All right," Kennedy said after following his instructions, "I'm on the second floor. What next?"

"Head all the way down the hallway. Last door on your right, it's unlocked." Rapp entered the alley from the opposite end and continued to the back door. He checked one last time to make sure no one was following him and then went into the building. Quietly he began to climb the stairs two at a time.

"I'm in front of the door. I assume you want us to enter."

"I said the door was unlocked. Knock twice and enter, and if either of you is carrying you'd better not have them out, or I'll blow your heads off." Rapp stopped halfway up the second run of stairs and edged his head up above the last tread. He got a glimpse of Kennedy and Stansfield. Neither was holding a gun. They walked into the apartment with Stansfield leading the way.

"Head into the living room and take a left," Rapp said. "Go to the window, put the phone on speaker, and tell me what you see."

A few seconds passed and Kennedy said, "You know what I see."

Rapp moved quickly down the hallway. "You're both standing where I was standing last night." Rapp reached the door and moved past to check the front stairwell. It was clear. "I didn't trust Stan, so I found someone who fit my general description and I sent him to the apartment to retrieve something . . . I wanted to see how rough Stan would be with him. I watched that asshole Victor leave the van and hide on the right side of the stoop, and when a completely innocent man left the apartment he came up behind him and shot him in the back of the head. He thought he was killing me." Rapp slowly turned the knob and slid through Bob and Tibby McMahon's apartment door without making a noise. He silently closed and locked the door. He moved quietly down the hall with his silenced gun ready, and turned the corner. Kennedy and Stansfield were standing exactly where he'd expected them to be. Rapp pressed the End button on the cell phone, slid it into his pocket, and said, "What I want to know is, who gave him the kill order?"

Kennedy jumped and dropped her phone. Stansfield, always the cool customer, didn't so much as flinch. They both turned to face the killer they'd helped create. Stansfield looked at the gun in Rapp's hand and said, "I don't suppose I can talk you into lowering that thing?"

"Not until you've done some explaining."

"What would you like to know?"

"Who authorized the kill?" Rapp asked.

"Neither of us did, and I don't think Stan did."

"So you expect me to believe Victor acted on his own."

"That's a possibility, but we have also recently discovered that someone has either been leaking or providing information to the DGSE."

"What kind of information?" Rapp asked.

"The target list. Who we were going to go after and in what order."

Rapp considered that for a moment. "So they knew Tarek was next on my list?"

"Possibly."

"That would explain a lot."

Stansfield could have provided much more information, but Rapp needed to answer a few questions first. "Victor claims you ambushed him and his men last night. Killed McGuirk and Borneman, and he barely escaped with his life. He said he didn't know anything about the DGSE agents. That you must have shot them after he fled."

Rapp shook his head. "Victor's not very smart. He's ballsy, he's reckless, but he's not very smart."

"How so?" Kennedy asked.

Rapp stepped forward. "Turn around." Rapp stood behind them. Down on the opposite sidewalk the crime scene markings were still fresh. "Across the street, down the block about two hundred feet, by that red BMW. That's where the van was parked last night. If I were to ambush them, wouldn't it have been down there?"

"Not if you used a decoy like Victor says." Stansfield pointed at the front stoop. "You got them to leave their position and then jumped them."

Rapp shook his head. "Victor got out of the van on his own. Ran down the sidewalk and took up position right down there." Rapp pointed out the location with the tip of his silencer. "Luke came out of the building, went down the steps, took a right turn, and Victor fell in behind him. The gun came up about a foot from Luke's head, and Victor pulled the trigger. Luke went down immediately and Victor looked like he might start dancing. Then the van pulled up about five seconds later. One of Stan's SF guys got out . . . I can't remember his name, but he looked like he was arguing with Victor for a second, and then he grabbed Luke's legs while Victor picked the body up by the neck of the jacket. Victor swung the torso into the open door and then stepped back while the other guy wrestled with the legs. Victor placed the gun against the back of his head and pulled the trigger."

"You were still standing up here?" Kennedy asked.

"Yep, and then I saw another muzzle flash. I assume Victor shot the other guy they were with. He thought he had gotten away with it.

He thought I was dead and he could blame me for killing the other two guys."

"And why would he want to do that?" Stansfield asked, already knowing the motive.

"I don't know. Because you ordered him to do it or Stan did."

"What if he did it because he was not authorized to kill you? He needed to make it look like you were out of control. You had killed McGuirk and Borneman, that way he was justified in killing you."

"Or Stan had ordered all of it."

Stansfield felt as if he was finally getting a handle on this. "What happened after that?"

"Two guys showed up right over there. They had guns out. I couldn't hear what they were saying, but it looked like they were shouting for Victor to drop his gun. Victor started to raise his hand and then turned and shot both men. One of them got a shot off, but missed. Both of them were down, and then I saw Victor start walking toward them. That was when I ran downstairs."

"And did what?" Kennedy asked.

"I didn't know who these two guys were yet, but I figured they were law enforcement. We have some pretty strict rules about shooting those guys, so I was going to stop him. I came through the front door and I saw Victor lining up to finish them off and I started shooting. I stayed on this side of the street and moved to the right so I could try to get him to break off and head back to the van. I found a spot under a car over here and that was when I shot him in the calf. After that I crossed the street, laid down some suppressive fire, and then when I jumped out Victor was running back toward the van. I fired some shots at him but he was able to jump in the open side door. I gave pursuit and then he opened fire with a rather loud submachine gun."

"And then drove off," Stansfield said. "What happened next?" Stansfield was hoping that he was going to hear what he thought he already knew.

"I went back and checked on the two guys. It turns out they were

DGSE. One of them was shot in the face and dead, but the other guy was alive and in trouble, so I got my med kit out and patched him up as best I could and then I cleared the area."

In Stansfield's mind the scales had just tipped in Rapp's favor. He breathed an inward sigh of relief and was about to ask a question, but Kennedy beat him to it.

"You said Victor was stupid. How so?"

"I think the man is stupid in general. But it's worse than that. He's dangerous. I think the guy is nuts, and what I can't believe is that you didn't wash him out a long time ago. I'm a step above a rookie, and I could see he was a train wreck from a mile away. How in hell did you miss it?"

"That's a conversation for another day," Kennedy said. "What was your point about him being stupid?"

"You guys will have no problem getting your hands on the police report. The ballistics will back up everything I just said. Victor uses a .45 caliber, I use a 9 millimeter, and the Directorate guys were carrying FNP .357 Sigs. His story won't hold up. They recovered the body of one of our guys, and you're going to find out he was shot with a .45 at near point-blank range. You're also going to find out that both of the DGSE agents were shot with a .45 . . . Victor's .45. And if you bother asking whoever patched Victor up, they're going to tell you Victor was shot by a 9 millimeter. My 9 millimeter. He thought I was dead, and he made a huge mistake."

It certainly did seem that way. Stansfield considered all of this. Rapp was right, they could get their hands on the police report and the information would back up one version or the other, but that might take a few days, and Stansfield wanted to put this thing to rest sooner than that. "You said you had a witness. Someone we could trust. Are we going to get a chance to talk to this person?"

"Nobody followed you guys?"

"No," Stansfield answered.

"You're not carrying any beacons or transmitters?" Rapp asked the question only halfheartedly. He didn't have the skill or the technology to check their answer. He nudged past Kennedy and looked up and down the street one last time to make sure there weren't any goons lurking about. There were none. He moved away from the window toward the middle of the apartment and called out. "It's clear. You can come out now." Rapp watched the door to one of the bedrooms open. Greta stepped into the hallway and Rapp turned to see the expression on Stansfield's face. It appeared to be a mix of relief and shock.

"Greta," Stansfield said in sheer disbelief. His mouth asked, "How in the world did you get involved in this?" while his brain was wondering how he would explain this to his dear friend Herr Ohlmeyer.

"Hello, Thomas," Greta said, stopping at Rapp's side. "Everything he said is true. I stood at that very window last night and watched this Victor man who works for you gun down five people. He is an animal. A sick dog."

Kennedy was completely thrown. She was supposed to know every detail of Rapp's life, yet she hadn't the foggiest idea who this pretty blonde was. Turning to Stansfield, she asked, "Who is this woman?"

"She is my good friend Herr Carl Ohlmeyer's granddaughter." Stansfield turned his eyes back to Rapp and Greta. It was not lost on him that Greta had reached out and was holding Rapp's arm. They were a couple. More than that, they were in love. One of his best friends, one of the most powerful, civilized men he knew, was going to have to be told that his precious granddaughter was dating one of the most dangerous men on the planet. A man Stansfield had helped create. A man Stansfield had brought into the Ohlmeyer home. The news was not going to be well received.

CHAPTER 45

THEY rode back to the Embassy in the black Mercedes sedan
that Kennedy had been driving. There was a brief, heated
exchange over who would drive, but Rapp had won out when Stansfield
intervened. He was trained to drive very aggressively if need be. Rapp
wasn't crazy about taking Greta back to the Embassy, but Stansfield
would have it no other way. The man was unusually shaken by the
revelation of their relationship. Rapp and Greta had both argued that
Greta could easily drive back to Switzerland and no one would be the
wiser.

Stansfield was vehement. "I'm going to have a lot of explaining to
do to your grandfather. He is not going to be happy. He would never
forgive me if something happened to you, and I would never forgive
myself. The safest place for you is at the Embassy. When things have
settled down I will take you back to Zurich personally."

They stopped at Greta's car, grabbed their bags, and were on their
way. A few minutes out from the Embassy Kennedy called the watch
desk, gave them their ETA, and told them to have the gate open. Paris
wasn't Moscow, but considering how often Paul Fournier's name had

been popping up, it was worth taking a few extra precautions. They rolled through the big gate without incident and proceeded into the Embassy's underground parking garage.

After Rapp and Greta had grabbed their bags from the trunk, Stansfield said, "Irene, would you please take Greta to see Gene? Tell him I said to make her comfortable. She might be staying the night." Gene was the CIA station chief.

As they entered the small underground lobby off the parking garage, Greta stopped and asked Mitch, "When am I going to see you again?"

Rapp glanced at Stansfield and said, "We have some work to do. I'm sure I'll see you tonight if not sooner."

Greta got on her toes and kissed him on the cheek. "Be careful." And then, turning to Stansfield, she said, "If anything happens to him, I am going to be very upset."

Stansfield gave her a disinterested nod. "Mr. Rapp is quite capable of taking care of himself."

The men watched as the ladies entered the elevator. Kennedy had Rapp's bag. When the doors closed Stansfield said, "Follow me."

"Where are we going?"

"Downstairs." When they were both in the stairwell, Stansfield asked, "How long have you been seeing her?"

Rapp followed two steps behind. "Almost a year."

"Do you love her?"

"That's kind of personal, boss."

Stansfield stopped in the middle of the next landing and turned to face Rapp. "There are literally billions of women on the planet, and you chose to fall in love with her."

"I never said I was in love with her."

"Well, she's most certainly in love with you. That much is obvious."

"Sir, I'd like to keep my personal life personal."

"If only it were that easy," Stansfield grumbled, and started down the next flight. "You have no idea the problems you have caused me."

Rapp followed in silence, not wishing to explore his personal life any further. The stairs emptied into a small vestibule with a single elevator and a secure door. Stansfield pressed a button next to the door and turned his head toward the camera. There was an electronic buzz and Stansfield grabbed the door and opened it. A long hallway was in front of them. Stansfield went straight for the second door on the right. Three men were inside. Two of them were Dr. Lewis and Rob Ridley, whom Rapp knew fairly well. The third one he'd never met before.

Stansfield asked, "How is it going?"

The man whom Rapp didn't know looked up from his equipment and said, "Much better. Stan's got him on the ropes. Victor's starting to slip up a bit, but he's sticking to his story."

"How are the readouts?" Stansfield asked, pointing at the polygraph machine.

"He's keeping his responses within the parameters, but my personal BS detector says he's lying through his teeth."

Rapp looked through the big viewing window and saw Victor and Hurley. His entire body tightened into a knot of energy. The first thought to cross his mind was how much he wanted to kill Victor. The second was that he wouldn't mind taking Hurley out at the same time.

They were both smoking. Victor was in a pair of jeans and a white T-shirt. The cotton fabric was stretched tightly over his massive arms. Leaning back in the chair, he was trying to look as casual as possible.

"I know we have to play this game, Stan. I can tell you don't like it any more than I do. We both know Rapp is a piece of shit. Let's get this over with so we can go hunt him down and put the bastard out of his misery."

Every eye in the observation room looked at Rapp. Mitch turned to Stansfield and said, "I think we both know who needs to be put out of his misery."

"In due time."

Lewis approached Rapp's side. "I know this isn't easy to hear, but you need to—"

"Shut up, Doc," Rapp said, without taking his eyes off Victor. "No offense, but I don't want to listen to any of your bullshit right now."

Hurley stabbed out his cigarette. "You know what I think . . . I think you're full of shit. I think you're lying through your fucking teeth. I told you to pull the plug last night. Head back to the hotel and get some sack time, and you disregarded my order."

"I didn't disregard anything. We were getting ready to leave when he sent in his decoy. McGuirk and Borneman went to cover the front door and that was when Rapp jumped them."

"And where was this decoy?"

"I don't know. I never saw him again."

"You're full of shit." Hurley leaned back and shook his head. "So full of shit."

Victor smiled. "I know you're just trying to do your job, but this is a waste of time. Let's wrap this up and go kill the little shit. I know you hate him just as much as I do."

"Just because I don't like him doesn't mean I want to kill him. There are a lot of people I don't like."

"Do a lot of those people gun down two of your operatives and compromise a safe house? Do they blow a mission in the middle of Paris and turn it into an international fucking embarrassment? Nine fucking bodies!" Victor banged his knuckles on the table and then pointed at Hurley and said, "And don't forget the two DGSE guys he plugged."

Hurley bobbed his head as if he was agreeing with him and then said, "About those two DGSE agents . . . I heard an interesting story. I have two witnesses who came on the scene shortly after you'd left Borneman's body on the street in your rush to save your own ass."

"I already told you Borneman fell out of the van. There was nothing I could do about it."

Hurley ignored him. "These two witnesses positively ID'd Rapp."

"There you have it. They put him at the scene."

"Take a guess what he was doing when they came upon him?"

"I don't know . . . running away?"

"No . . . that would be you. You were the one running away."

Victor leaned over the table. "You would have done the exact same fucking thing."

"You have no idea what I'd do, so shut your fucking mouth before I break your jaw. Now get back on point. What do you think Rapp was doing when these two guys walked up on him?"

Victor leaned back and folded his arms defiantly. "I don't know."

"He was giving first aid to one of the agents. One guy was hit in the face and the second was hit in the chest. These two witnesses I've worked with for almost two decades say Rapp was patching up the guy with the chest wound."

Victor shrugged as if it meant nothing.

"Tell me why in hell Rapp would shoot a guy and then try to save him."

"I don't know. He's a total nut job, and when we can catch him we can ask him all of these questions. But this," Victor said, throwing his hands out, "is all a bunch of bullshit and you know it."

One of the phones in the observation room rang and Ridley answered it. He listened for a half minute and then said, "Nice work. Stick with it. I'll call you as soon as we're mobile." Ridley set the phone back in the cradle and looked up at Stansfield with a big grin on his face. "Waldvogel got it done. We're wired for sound and we have a beacon. Guess who picked Cooke up at the airport?"

Stansfield was too fixated on Victor to change gears so quickly. "I have no idea."

"Paul Fournier."

"His name seems to be popping up a lot these days."

"Waldvogel says they're stopping for lunch and then they have a meeting. Fournier said, and I quote, 'They are very excited to meet you, but they expect the rest of the list, and they want to know the name of the assassin.'"

"What did Cooke say?"

"He said he didn't fly all the way to Paris just to have lunch."

Stansfield turned away from Ridley and looked through the glass. Tapping Talmage on the shoulder, he said, "Tell Stan to take a break. I need to talk with him."

Rapp walked over to Stansfield, and in a voice that only he could hear, said, "Give me five minutes with him. I'm the last guy he expects to see."

Stansfield was in the midst of considering it when Hurley came into the room looking as if he wanted to punch someone. He froze in midstride when he saw Rapp standing next to his boss. "What in hell is he doing here?"

"Easy," Stansfield warned. "His story checks out. He's not the problem," Stansfield said, nodding at Rapp. "*He* is." Stansfield pointed through the glass at Victor, who was looking rather smug, considering the situation he'd landed himself in. "Come here," Stansfield ordered Hurley. The two of them huddled in the corner, where Stansfield relayed everything he'd learned in the past few hours.

"Greta?" Hurley asked in shock at one point.

Stansfield quieted him down and finished. The two of them came out of the corner. Stansfield looked at Dr. Lewis and said, "Tom, Mitch would like to go in there and ask Victor a few questions. I'm running short on time. It appears our deputy director is in the midst of committing treason, and before I do anything about it, I'd like a little more proof."

"Can you keep your cool?" Lewis asked Rapp.

Rapp frowned. "I don't think keeping my cool is going to get us anywhere at this point. I watched that fucker kill four people last night. Not one of them was a terrorist. Two of them you knew pretty well. He's a piece of shit . . . a sick dog, and you guys should have put him out of his misery a long time ago. Now isn't the time to get weak in the knees." The last person Rapp expected to support him was Hurley.

"He's right. Victor thinks he has us outsmarted. The best way to knock him off his game is to send Rapp in."

"If Mitch walks into that room," Lewis said, "there's going to be violence."

Rapp drew his silenced Glock and said, "You're damn right there is."

Lewis looked pleadingly at Stansfield. "This isn't the way to do this. What if he kills him before we get the answers we need?"

"I promise I won't kill him, Doc. At least not before we get the answers we need." Rapp didn't want to wait around for permission, so he started for the door.

Hurley caught him in the hallway. He grabbed Rapp by the arm.

Rapp spun around with pure anger on his face. "Keep your fucking hands off me."

Hurley held up his hands and said, "This isn't easy for me, but I wanted to say I was wrong and I'm sorry."

Rapp took the apology with a nod and said, "Fine, now if you want to help me, make sure you don't let anyone into that interrogation room until I'm done with him. I don't care what you hear, you keep that door closed. Can you do that?"

"Yeah. I can do that."

CHAPTER 46

BRAMBLE thought the morning was going well. He could tell Hurley didn't have his heart in it. Stan hated Rapp every bit as much as he did and then some. The last round of questioning was a little more intense, but he supposed he had to put on a show for the people on the other side of the glass. That bitch Kennedy was probably henpecking him. The good news was she wasn't going to be around much longer. With Rapp's big fuckup there was going to be some housecleaning, and Kennedy would be the first one to receive the ax.

Stansfield, that fossil, was on his way out as well and Hurley wasn't getting any younger. In another ten years Bramble would be running the show and then he could really start to line his pockets. This job was a license to steal. Bramble pushed his chair back and angled it toward the big observation window. He could feel Kennedy on the other side of the glass, the little killjoy, ragging on Stan and anyone else who didn't think her little boy wonder was the second coming.

Bramble heard the door open and without turning to look he said, "Stan, let's stop wasting each other's time. The longer we dick around in here, the harder it's going to be to catch that little prick."

"Little prick?" Rapp said.

Bramble jumped up, knocking his chair over. "What the fuck are you doing here?" He saw the gun in Rapp's hand and said, "Put that thing down right now."

"Pick up that chair and sit down."

"Fuck you. I don't take orders from you. How did you get in here?"

"I'm not going to tell you again. Pick up the chair and sit down."

Bramble's mouth was just beginning to form his favorite word when a bullet struck him in his good knee. It must have shattered his kneecap, because his leg completely folded and he crashed to the floor. Bramble reached for his leg and started screaming.

Rapp stood over him and pointed the gun at his face. "Shut up, Victor. Everyone knows what happened last night. There were eyewitnesses who saw what you did. You're a fucking dirt bag."

"I didn't do anything. It was you."

Rapp pointed the gun at Bramble's left foot and fired another shot. He waited a few seconds for Bramble's screaming to subside and then said, "This is how it's going to work. I'm going to keep putting bullets in you until you tell us what we already know."

"If you already know it, then why are you asking me?"

"You're not very smart, are you? We need corroboration. You've been passing along information to the wrong people. You told them about Tarek. You described my methods. You helped set me up."

"Fuck you!"

"Wrong answer." Rapp pumped a round into Victor's right foot. There was more howling and more threats and Rapp ignored them all. When Victor finally ran out of steam Rapp said, "Stansfield gave me the green light to kill you. The only way you can save your ass is to tell us who you were working with."

"I don't know what the fuck you're talking about."

"So you want another bullet. I'm going to let you pick this time. Right hand or left hand?"

Victor covered his heart with both hands.

"You want me to kill you?" Rapp asked.

"Fuck you."

"You really need to work on some different comebacks." Rapp looked Victor over and said, "How about your elbows. That has to hurt like hell. Lots of bones and nerves. Which one . . . left or right?"

Victor squirmed on the floor, trying to push himself farther away, but the blood coming from his feet made the floor slick. "Don't shoot me again. I didn't do anything wrong."

"You've done a lot of wrong shit, Victor, and if you want to live you'd better start telling the truth. Now, who were you passing information to?"

"Stan."

Rapp shook his head. "That's pathetic, Victor. Stan knows everything. It has to be somebody else. Somebody outside the group. I need a name. Come on, let's go."

"I don't know what you're talking about."

"I'm going to count to five this time and then I shoot." Rapp started counting.

"I don't know what you're talking about."

"Four . . . five." Rapp chose the left elbow and squeezed.

Victor recoiled in pain and screamed for nearly half a minute. Rapp waited patiently and then asked, "Who was it, Victor? Who's your guy?"

Victor was mumbling now. Rapp thought he caught a name but he couldn't make it out. He bent down and jammed the suppressor into Victor's groin. "I didn't catch that name. You're going to have to say it a little louder."

Victor was writhing in pain. Snot was pouring out of his nose. He mumbled some more.

Rapp shoved the gun down hard. "I'm going to count to five again. Remember how that worked last time? One . . . two . . . three . . . four."

"Paul Cooke!" Victor yelled.

Rapp stood, looked at the glass, and nodded. He looked back down at Victor and said, "If it was up to me, Victor, I'd put a bullet in your head right now." Rapp turned for the door.

Victor started laughing. Slow and soft at first and then faster and loud.

Rapp stopped and turned back to face the man. "What's so funny, Victor?"

He got his laughter under control and said, "I knew you didn't have the balls for this line of work."

Rapp looked him over, considered his options, and then raised his gun. He fired two shots into Victor's groin and said, "Well, I guess that makes two of us."

Rapp knocked three times on the door and a moment later Hurley opened it. "How'd it go?"

"He fingered Cooke, so I guess we have one more rat to deal with."

"You got that right." Hurley looked beyond Rapp and saw all of the blood. "What the fuck did you do to him?"

"I gave him a bunch of chances to tell the truth. It just took him a while to figure out it was in his best interest to stop lying to me."

"What am I going to do with him?"

Rapp shrugged his shoulders. "I promised Doc that I wouldn't kill him, so it's up to you." He walked past Hurley and down the hall to the observation room. The door opened before he got there and Dr. Lewis stepped into the hallway.

With an anxious look on his face, he asked Rapp, "How are you feeling?"

Rapp stopped, considered the question for a second, and said, "Fucking great, Doc. Never better. How about you?"

CHAPTER 47

FOURNIER had arranged a private room at Les Enfants Terribles. He knew the manager well and could trust him for discretion. Fournier's morning had been horrible. He'd been forced to defend himself to virtually every bureaucrat and politician all the way up and down the line. The director general of the National Police wanted his head, and the feminists wanted his balls, and all he wanted was for this nonsense to go away. What were one woman's feelings when he was wrestling with the national security of the Republic?

Fortunately, Cooke had no idea about the morning's press conference. He stepped off the private jet with a bounce in his step, looking forward to concluding their business arrangement. Fournier liked Cooke for the simple reason that he was a mirror image of himself. He was intelligent and pragmatic. He never got caught up in the emotional component of things, which was the kiss of death in their business. There was no place for compassion or feelings. It was a brutal business and only the best and the brightest could survive.

It was partly why he had such respect for Stansfield and Hurley. They had been such a good team over the years. Stansfield's brains and Hurley's heartless, crush-the-enemy-at-any-cost attitude had been a very potent combination. But they were both getting old, and the fact that they'd let someone like Cooke slip under their radar was proof that it was time for them to go. Fournier worried about that. Would he know when to go himself? He had spent a lot of time thinking about it and planning for it. That's why he had all of his money neatly stashed away. When the time came he would simply vanish if he had to.

"So what can you tell me about these people?" Cooke asked.

Fournier took a sip of wine and said, "They pay handsomely for information. That's the most important thing."

"Have they ever threatened you?"

Fournier smiled. "They have a few uncivilized types, but Max keeps them in line. You'll like Max. He's a good man. He's not one of these radicals who's always threatening to blow things up."

Cooke laughed. "Well, as long as Max can keep them in line, this should go well."

Fournier looked at his watch, drained his wine, and said, "We should go. I like to keep them waiting, but not too long."

"What time were we supposed to meet with them?"

"One."

Cooke checked his own watch and frowned. It was 1:38. Both men stood. Fournier pulled back the curtain of their private room and made for the front door. Several patrons tried to get Fournier's attention and many more were staring and whispering. Fournier ignored them all. When they reached the front door, Fournier's security officer and Mermet were waiting. Mermet looked to be on the verge of an anxiety attack.

Fournier pulled him aside and asked, "More bad news?"

"Yes. The president's office called. They want to see the file."

Fournier inhaled through his nose. "That bitch has really caused me some trouble." He fished out a cigarette and said, "Tell them I am tied up debriefing a high-level intelligence asset and that we will get them the file tonight."

Mermet nodded and they started across the street. Fournier offered Cooke a cigarette but he declined, telling his friend that he still rowed and it wasn't good for his lungs. Fournier pretended not to hear a word he said.

The Hotel Balzac was directly across the street. They continued up the carpeted steps and stopped under the circular portico. Fournier turned to Mermet and said, "Wait down here. This should take thirty minutes or so." The truth was that Fournier didn't want too many eyes and ears around what was about to happen. A sizable amount of cash was going to change hands, and depending on how the meeting went, Fournier might be tempted to get into his car and drive straight for Switzerland when it was over.

He and Cooke proceeded across the lobby to the elevator bank. There were more stares and one person who tried to approach him, but Fournier kept his eyes front and center and pushed through. Fortunately, the middle elevator was available. He pressed the top button and in less than a minute they were on the top floor of the six-floor hotel. At the far end of the hall Max's bodyguard was standing post outside the hotel's nicest suite.

"Hello, Omar," Fournier called out. "Sorry we're late."

Omar didn't smile. He stepped forward and in very choppy French said, "Open your jackets."

"Must we always do this, Omar? This is my country, after all."

"Rules," was all he said.

After he was done making sure they weren't carrying guns, Omar pulled out a key and opened the door. Fournier entered first, with Cooke just a step back. They moved into the large main room, where Max was casually reclined on one of the three sofas.

"Max," Fournier said enthusiastically. "Good to see you."

"Yes," Max said with a wink and a nod toward the TV. "I see you have had a very rough day."

Fournier dismissed the comment with a scoff. "In this business, Max, I have weathered far worse."

"Yes, I'm sure you have." Max turned to Cooke and extended his hand. "I have been looking forward to meeting you for some time."

"And me as well," Cooke replied.

"Please sit. Is there anything I can get either of you?"

"No, thank you," Fournier answered for both of them. "We just finished lunch and we're on kind of a tight schedule." He sat on one of the big sofas and Cooke sat down next to him.

"I see." Max took the insult in stride and sat across from them. "So you would like to get down to business."

"That would be great. As you know, thanks to your friend Samir over there, I have some other problems I'm trying to deal with."

Cooke hadn't noticed the man with the bandage on his face until now. He smiled at him but received no warmth in return.

Fournier asked, "Where is Rafique?"

"You'll be pleased to know he is getting the plane ready. As soon as we are done with our business we will be departing the country."

"I am very happy to hear that. Thank you."

"So," Max said, looking at Cooke, "you have something for me."

"Yes, I do, but I would like to see the money first."

"Of course." Max looked over his shoulder. "Samir, bring the money."

"I assume mine will be wired as per my usual instructions," Fournier said.

"Of course. My personal secretary will handle everything as soon as I make the call."

"Good."

Samir came back with a large briefcase and set it on the table between the two sofas. He popped the clasps and showed Cooke the money.

"One million dollars, and another million in a Swiss bank account," Max said. "Now I need the information you promised."

Cooke smiled and retrieved a folded envelope from his jacket pocket. "His name is Mitch Rapp. I have a photo in there. Known addresses. He has a mother who is terminally ill, but he has a brother who could be used as leverage."

CHAPTER 48

RAPP and Hurley were parked four blocks away from the Hotel Balzac. Hurley was behind the wheel and Rapp in the front passenger seat. Rapp had seen Kennedy and Hurley argue more times than he could count, but he'd never seen anyone raise his voice with Stansfield, let alone argue with him as openly as Kennedy and Hurley had done. And to make the entire matter stranger, Hurley and Kennedy were for once in agreement. Stansfield was intent on coming with them to the Hotel Balzac, but Hurley had threatened to resign if his boss set foot outside the Embassy compound. There was a chance this could be nothing more than a simple surveillance mission, but it could also be something far more dangerous and complicated. Stansfield couldn't be anywhere near it. It was bad enough that the damn deputy director of Central Intelligence was off screwing his country, they didn't need to add to the list the deputy director of Operations getting arrested. Stanfield finally relented and gave Rapp and Hurley permission to go out without him.

They were both dressed in suits and ties and Rapp was carrying a new passport and credit card as well as the ID and gun he'd taken from the wounded DGSE agent.

Rapp had also put in blue contact lenses and added a goatee to try to match the general appearance of the DGSE agent. If anyone looked closely, he'd discover that Rapp was not the man in the photo, but if he needed to use it he wasn't planning on anyone looking closely.

Ridley and his people were three blocks away on the other side of the hotel in a surveillance van. Rapp and Hurley were getting a live feed from the devices they'd planted on Cooke. The plan was to record everything that was said, allow Cooke to incriminate himself, and then quietly grab him when he was dropped off at his own hotel.

Cooke and Fournier took a long lunch, so Rapp and Hurley were in position by the time they arrived at the Hotel Balzac. They'd heard the conversation outside the restaurant and now they were listening to the introductions inside the room. Rapp was taking everything in stride until he heard his name. He and Hurley looked at each other at the exact same time while they heard Cooke saying, "He attended the University of Syracuse and was recruited by Irene Kennedy. She happens to be a very close confidante of Thomas Stansfield and is someone else you could consider for leverage."

"Motherfucker!" Hurley yelled.

Rapp was already beyond that. He was imagining each person in the room. Cooke was a traitor, Fournier was a backstabbing snake, and based on the information and names provided by Monsignor de Fleury, Kennedy had identified the other two. Samir Fadi was a midlevel lieutenant from Islamic Jihad, and he was more than likely the prick who had shot Rapp in the shoulder. The second man was far more high-profile. Max Vega was a wealthy Spanish businessman with a radical Saudi father. Over the past several years he had become a key player in funding the various radical Muslim groups. Rapp had known about him because he was the next name on the list of authorized targets.

The decision was easy for Rapp. He grabbed the door handle and said, "Stan, you can shoot me if you want, but I'm going in there. I'm as good as dead if I don't kill every last one of those fuckers right now."

Hurley didn't move or say anything for what seemed like an eternity, and then he put the car into drive and said, "There's a side entrance for the employees and deliveries on Rue Lord Byron."

"I know where it is."

"There's a staircase almost immediately on your left. They're on the top floor. I suggest you leave the money. It'll make it look dirtier."

"Good idea."

Twenty seconds later they passed the front entrance. Five seconds after that Hurley stopped in front of the service entrance.

Rapp opened the door and said, "Thanks, Stan. I really appreciate this."

"No worries. Just don't get killed and don't leave any fingerprints."

"I never do."

"And just so you know, I never liked Thomas's plan. Our job is to kill these assholes, not try to turn them."

"You'll get no argument from me."

"I'll be waiting right down the street for you." Hurley pointed through the windshield. "You've got five minutes. You'd better get your ass moving."

Rapp slammed the door and ran around the trunk and onto the sidewalk. The employee entrance was a small garage door. It was unlocked. Rapp grabbed his DGSE badge and entered. A busboy barely gave him a passing glance. Rapp smiled, flipped open the badge, and said, "Police."

The staircase was right where Hurley said it would be. Rapp took the stairs two at a time as fast as he could. By the time he reached the top floor his heart was pumping, but he knew he would recover within seconds. He stopped just inside the fire door and took a couple of deep breaths. Then he used his hip on the crash bar so he wouldn't leave any fingerprints and pushed through. There at the opposite end of the hall

was Omar. All six and a half feet of him. He had to be close to three
hundred pounds.

Rapp walked straight for him at a brisk pace. He called out a few
soft apologies in French, and just as he had hoped, Omar started coming toward him. Rapp thought it was unlikely that he was armed, but
he had to assume he was. When they were thirty feet away Rapp said,
"I work for Director Fournier." He pulled the ID case out of his breast
pocket and said, "I need to speak with him."

Omar stopped in the middle of the hall, waiting to inspect the ID.

Rapp had to time it just right. Too close and Omar might get his
hands on him. Too far away and Omar might hit the floor so hard furniture would topple over. He had the ID in his left hand and extended
his arm all the way so it looked as if he was trying to help Omar. His
right hand slid between the folds of his suit coat and gripped the FNP.
Rapp drew the gun, kept his arm in tight, and pivoted his wrist so the
tip of the silencer was pointed directly at Omar's heart. Normally Rapp
would use only one bullet, but with a guy Omar's size you never knew,
so he squeezed three times and then lunged forward.

Omar's reaction was normal. Both hands clutched at his chest, and
then he started to stumble. Rapp closed the ID case and did his best
to help Omar gently to the floor. He went down on his knees first, and
then it was just a matter of tipping him backward. Rapp laid his head
on the ground and searched for the keys. He'd stayed at the Balzac and
knew they still used the old-fashioned kind. Big bulky things. Rapp
found it in the outside left pocket of his suit coat. Rapp pulled on a pair
of latex gloves, grabbed the key, and quickly moved down the hallway.
Moving Omar wasn't an option, so he had to work fast.

Rapp kept the gun out and silently slid the key into the lock. He
turned it, left it in the lock, and pushed the door open. Cooke and
Fournier were sitting almost directly in front of him and a little to the
right. Rapp held a finger up to his mouth, giving them the universal
sign to be quiet. It was just enough to freeze them as Rapp moved into
the room, finding the other two men on the couch to the left. The tall

one was about to open his mouth when Rapp shot him in the forehead. While he swung the pistol to the other man on the couch he moved his left hand inside his jacket and found the grip of his silenced Glock. Rapp fired the FNP a second time and hit the second man in the forehead.

As much as Rapp wanted to say something to Cooke and Fournier, he knew Ridley and others were listening, so he kept his mouth shut, swung the Glock around, and shot both men in the chest. He gave four to Fournier and three to Cooke. The first rounds were in the heart, and he spread the others around to make it look as if it was the work of someone with less skill. Moving to Samir, Rapp placed the Glock in his hand and fired two shots into the sofa across the way. He let the gun fall to the floor at Samir's feet and then grabbed the papers and envelope that were in Max's lap.

Rapp looked at the photos of himself and the biographical information. He folded them up and stuffed them in his right breast pocket. He grabbed a handkerchief from his back pocket and quickly wiped down the FNP pistol, then placed it in Fournier's hand, aimed the weapon at Max, and sent two rounds into his torso. He pumped three more into Samir and left the gun in Fournier's grip. The police would be intrigued when they discovered that both weapons had been used during the shooting of the two Directorate agents. Judging from Fournier's reputation, not a lot of people in Paris were going to be sad to hear this news. Rapp moved on to Cooke and ran his hands over the inside of his jacket to see if he had a duplicate copy of the information he'd given Max. He found another envelope and stuffed it in his pocket.

Rapp stepped back and did a quick 360 to see if he'd missed anything, then headed for the door. He grabbed the key and let the door close behind him. He ran to Omar's body, put the key back, and rushed for the staircase. He went down the same way he'd gone up, two at a time, except that he wasn't as tired this time. He took the latex gloves off just before he came upon two employees who were smoking by the back door. Rapp ignored them and pushed through into the bright afternoon sunlight. He turned left and walked at a brisk pace, but nothing that would bring any extra notice. He was just a busy guy trying to get back to his office after lunch.

A block later he looked around, but there was no Hurley. Rapp didn't wait. He continued up Rue Lord Byron and contemplated why Hurley had decided to screw him. He must have had second thoughts about how Stansfield would react. There was a good chance they'd put a price on his head, but there wasn't anything he could do about it now. He'd have to get to the closest Metro stop and get as far away as a train could take him.

His thoughts turned to Greta. Stansfield would take care of her, and he would also do his best to make sure that Rapp never saw her again. Her grandfather was their clandestine banker. He allowed them to move operational funds without tipping off the wrong people. His function within their group was crucial. The man would be livid when he found out his granddaughter had been placed in harm's way by one of Stansfield's assassins, but Rapp knew he would have to risk seeing her just one more time. He would never forgive himself if he didn't.

The black Mercedes raced up alongside him. Hurley stuck his head out the open window and asked, "You need a ride?"

Rapp stopped and shook his head. "Where the hell were you?"

"Some damn traffic cop made me move. I had to drive around the block."

Rapp climbed in and Hurley gunned the engine. Rapp's adrenaline hangover kicked in and he rolled down his window for some fresh air.

"How'd it go?" Hurley asked.

"Pretty good." Rapp reached in and grabbed the two envelopes. He opened the second one he hadn't checked and found Hurley's ugly mug staring back at him. "Look at this. He was going to sell your ass out, too."

Hurley looked over. "What an asshole. I was the kicker."

They took the next block in silence and then Rapp asked, "How much trouble am I in?"

"I'm not sure. I've been trying to figure it out, but I think it might be a good idea for you to lie low for a while."

"Yeah . . . you're probably right."

"Where do you want me to drop you off?"

"There's a Metro stop two blocks up. That should work."

Hurley nodded and said, "I haven't been very fair to you. I apologize for that." Hurley pulled the car into an open space. "Check in with me in a few weeks. I'll see if I can smooth things over."

Rapp handed Hurley his dossier. "I appreciate it."

"Take care of yourself."

"You, too." Rapp got out of the car and then looked back in at Hurley and said, "Four dead assholes. Not a bad afternoon."

"I'd say it was a pretty good one."

"Good luck."

"You too, kid."

Rapp closed the door and watched Hurley drive away. In a strange way he felt like his own man for the first time in two years. No one to answer to, and no place to be for the foreseeable future. He'd get on a train and then a plane and disappear for a few months. See what it was like to try to live a normal life. Rapp moved with the other people down the stairs into the Metro. By the time he reached the platform he knew it was all wishful thinking. He'd be back if they'd have him. He wasn't like other people and he never would be. They had changed him forever.